TIM SHOEMAKER

THE DEEP END

A HIGH WATER NOVEL

T0282100

FOCUS
ON
THE FAMILY.

A Focus on the Family Resource
Published by Tyndale House Publishers

A Focus on the Family book published by Tyndale House Publishers, Carol Stream, Illinois 60188

Focus on the Family and its accompanying logos and designs are federally registered trademarks, and *HighWater* is a trademark, of Focus on the Family, 8605 Explorer Drive, Colorado Springs, CO 80920.

Tyndale and Tyndale's quill logo are registered trademarks of Tyndale House Ministries.

Unless otherwise indicated, all Scripture quotations are from the *Holy Bible, New International Version,*® *NIV.*® Copyright © 1973, 1978, 1984 by Biblica, Inc.® Used by permission of Zondervan. All rights reserved worldwide. *(www.zondervan.com) NIV* and *New International Version* are trademarks registered in the United States Patent and Trademark Office by Biblica, Inc.®

Cover illustration and design by Michael Harrigan.

The author is represented by the Cyle Young Hartline Literary Agency.

The characters and events in this story are fictional. Any resemblance to actual persons or events is coincidental.

For Library of Congress Cataloging-in-Publication Data for this title,
visit http://www.loc.gov/help/contact-general.html.

For manufacturing information regarding this product, please call 1-855-277-9400.

For information about special discounts for bulk purchases, please contact Tyndale House Publishers at csresponse@tyndale.com or call 1-855-277-9400.

ISBN 978-1-64607-110-4

Printed in the United States of America

29	28	27	26	25	24	23
7	6	5	4	3	2	1

I believe a story is stronger when I picture my target audience as I write.
And when I write for those I love, the story grows even more powerful.
So . . .
Lily, Caleb, Norah, Claire, James, Miles, Daniel,
Grace, Sierra, Ethan, and Gabriel . . .
This one is for you.

"You'll never go off the deep end if you're clinging
to the One who keeps you from falling."

Every person has a push point. Something
that—if given enough pressure—has the
power to send them someplace dark. Deadly.
Someplace they never want to go.
Off the deep end.

—

CHAPTER 1

Friday, August 5, 5:30 p.m.

IT STARTS TODAY. YOUR WORLD WILL CHANGE.

The words were painted on a cardboard circle the size of a medium pizza. All caps. The letters were thick—in a dark red that had wept and run before it dried. Paint, or something else?

Creepy. Parker Buckman felt his stomach slowly twist. He turned the corrugated cardboard over. The other side was blank. "So, this was it? No other explanation?" he asked.

"Not a thing." Harley Lotitto nodded toward the entrance of the Rockport Dive Company. "I found it taped to the glass door when I opened this morning."

It could be nothing. But to Parker, way too many *nothings* had turned into really big *somethings* in the past. He read the sign again. "*It* starts. As in a motor? What about your motorcycle?"

Kemosabe. Harley's 1999 Harley-Davidson XL Sportster. The

1

bike Harley had rebuilt as a father/son project just months before his dad's death. The bike he wasn't even old enough to legally ride yet. But he was getting close. Parker eyed his friend. "Is Kemosabe in the repair shop?"

Harley snickered. "You think a mechanic might be leaving me a progress update? No, the bike is locked up tight in the Hangar where it belongs."

The Hangar was Harley's name for the shed behind the dive shop where he stored Kemosabe—and everything else he wanted to keep away from his Uncle Ray.

"And the bike is running just fine."

No surprise there. Harley started it up nearly every day just to be sure. Kemosabe was the one thing that tied him to his dad's memory more than anything else. "So, what are you going to do about this?" Parker tapped the cardboard sign.

"Nothing. This stupid sign doesn't change a thing," Harley said. "I've been looking forward to tonight all week."

Parker scanned the inside of the Rockport Dive Company for the owner, but it looked like Harley was manning the shop alone again. "What did your uncle say when you showed the sign to him?"

"'Be sure you get every bit of tape off that glass.'"

Parker laughed. That sounded about right. "Seriously, he wasn't concerned at all?"

"All he cares about," Harley said, "is getting the boat so we can take dive charters."

"Tell me he's not still trying to get you to sell Kemosabe."

Harley cut him a look. "He's obsessed with the idea. Like I'm his personal GoFundMe page. 'Sell the bike. Invest in the boat. I'll cut you in on the profits.' Like that will ever happen."

"Selling Kemosabe—or your uncle sharing the profits?"

"Both."

Parker didn't doubt that. He focused on the sign again. The letters looked like something from an old horror movie poster. "Any other weird things happen today at the shop?"

Harley shook his head. "We actually had a great day for a change. Some geezer came in here with his lady friend and bought a complete rig for both of them. Wet suits. BCD vests. Tanks. Regulators. Everything. Paid in cash. I got $3,500 sitting in the register right now."

"Bet that made your uncle happy."

"He was all grins. Went out to get a drink to celebrate."

"So maybe he'll stop riding you so hard."

"I wish." Harley boosted himself up on the counter. "He's getting worse. It's like I can't do a single thing right." He glanced at the front door, as if he wanted to make sure his uncle wasn't right outside. "Sometimes, when he's grousing at me, I want to hit him. So. Hard." He held up one hand with his thumb nearly touching his forefinger. "Like, I'm this close."

It was something Parker hadn't heard Harley say before. And he'd never seen his friend look so on edge, either. "You hit your uncle, and your world will definitely change," Parker said. "Next time you get the urge to smack him—call me. We'll take the *Boy's Bomb* out in the harbor or something."

"My dad and uncle never got along," Harley said. "Fought all the time, the way my dad told it. Sounds like my dad beat the tar out of him whenever they did." Harley's eyes narrowed slightly, like he was picturing it. "Maybe if I'm lucky I'll get out of here before he comes back. I'm locking the door the minute it hits six o'clock."

"I'll give you a hand cleaning up," Parker said. He had helped

Harley close up the dive shop plenty of times before. He knew the routine.

Harley nodded. "I just want to get away from him."

The front door opened—but Parker's back was to it. Harley didn't look at all happy to see whoever it was. Parker instantly felt the need to be busy so it wouldn't look like he was keeping Harley from his work. He straightened a Rockport Dive Company T-shirt on the rack.

"Gatorade . . . so *not* nice to see you." There was only one person who still called Parker that: Bryce Scorza. Rockport High's star quarterback. Harley's ex-best friend. Arrogant, pompous—

"This guy bothering you, Lotitto?" Scorza wore his football jersey with the big number eight on it, like the shirt was the master key to everything. He also had a stupid habit of carrying around a regulation football almost everywhere he went. "I'll just throw him out if you want."

Parker held his ground even as Scorza stepped into his personal space. Scorza gave Parker a quick jab in the gut with the tip of the football. "Just messing with you, Gatorade. Don't pee your pants."

"Whew," Parker said, wiping his forehead with the back of his hand in an exaggerated way. "Glad you cleared that one up for me. That was *close*."

Scorza's eyes narrowed, like he wasn't expecting Parker to push back even a little. And Parker had surprised himself a bit too. Mocking Scorza wasn't exactly the Christian thing to do, but . . .

"What do you want, barf bag?" Harley asked. He still hadn't left his perch on the counter.

For the second time in the last minute a hint of surprise registered on Scorza's face. "Barf bag. That's new."

It was the first time Parker had heard Harley use that expression when referring to Scorza too.

"What are you doing in the shop?" Harley asked. There was nothing friendly in Harley's tone. Parker had never heard him talk to a customer like that. "You don't dive."

"But maybe I like your uncle's catchy designs." Scorza held up one of Rockport Dive Company's *Don't Drink and Dive* T-shirts that Uncle Ray designed—and Harley hated. "I was thinking I'd buy one."

"Well, it's nice to hear you're thinking for a change." Harley still hadn't left the counter. "I'm closing soon, so pick one out fast. Fourteen ninety-five—plus tax."

Scorza grabbed a shirt. Balled it up and stuffed it in the pocket of his cargo shorts. Pulled out a twenty—along with a key ring with a Jeep logo fob. He dropped the keys on the counter with the cash. "Keep the change. Oh, and did you hear my dad got me a Wrangler?"

Everybody had heard—even Parker. It was gorgeous. Harley didn't say a word.

"I'll have my license in seven months. Dad wanted me to practice with the car I'd actually be driving later."

Harley faked a yawn—and his acting was horrible. "Congratulations."

"My dad is going to work on it with me," Scorza said. "We'll fix it up even better than it is now. Bigger tires. Add some chrome."

Parker was pretty sure Scorza wasn't stupid enough to get physical with Harley. But that didn't stop him from giving Harley a verbal gut-jab. "Just spending time with my dad . . . kind of looking forward to that," Scorza said. "Maybe you'll want to drop by sometime. You know . . . since you don't have a dad around anymore."

Harley boosted himself off the counter. He looked like he wanted to rip Scorza's head off. Parker hustled to get between the two, sure he was going to have to break up a fight. And he might have had to if the bell on the shop door hadn't jangled at that moment.

Angelica "Jelly" Malnatti and Ella Houston tumbled in—Jelly wearing a Rockport T-shirt and jeans, Ella wearing one of her loose gypsy dresses. The dress hung just below Ella's knees, almost down to the tops of her cowgirl boots. The girls stopped dead when they saw Mr. Football Jersey.

And suddenly Scorza seemed to forget all about Harley. He tucked the football under one arm and hustled to the door to meet them. "Black Beauty and Everglades Girl. It always amazes me how my fans show up wherever I go."

"You're delusional," Ella said. "You got no fans in this store."

Jelly walked right up to him. "Everglades Girl. Yeah . . . I'm strong like a gator." She jabbed the football loose. "And I strike like a snake."

Scorza chased down the football and scooped it up, laughing as if in disbelief.

Jelly held the door open for him. "Looks like you have some *real* fans waiting for you outside."

Sure enough, a handful of other guys in Rockport High football jerseys stood out front, peering through the display window. Scorza trotted out the door, grinning like he'd just made some brilliant play. He held out the ball to Jelly as he passed, then tucked it in tight before she could react. "I'll be ready for you next time, Everglades!"

"Doubt it." Jelly closed the door behind him and leaned against it. "Much better," she said.

"So," Parker said, doing his best to hold a straight face, "were you two really following him?"

"Watch it," Jelly said. "Or this Everglades Girl will teach you a lesson too." She nodded toward Ella. "We both will."

Harley grinned like he'd already forgotten about Scorza's comments.

"We want to see that note you found on your door," Jelly said.

Parker held the cardboard circle out to them.

Jelly gave Parker an incredulous look. "Wait. You've been touching the thing . . . without gloves? How can the police check it for prints now? This was *evidence*."

"Evidence of *what*?" Harley asked.

Parker thought that was a fair question.

Harley slipped back behind the counter where the register sat and swept his hand in an arc that covered half the narrow store. Racks of neoprene wet suits. A row of scuba tanks. Regulator kits displayed on the wall above. A case of dive knives. A pretty impressive inventory of masks. Fins and snorkels and all other sorts of dive gear. Racks of Rockport Dive Company's *Don't Drink and Dive* T-shirts in every size and color. "Does anything look out of place?" Everything was neat and in order. Harley was good about that.

"Out of place?" Ella smiled. "Well, actually, the guy working the shop seems kind of strange. But nothing new there."

"So, you're saying my Uncle Ray is weird?"

El gave the shop a quick scan—obviously fearing the guy was within earshot. "I was talking about you, and you know it, Harley Davidson Lotitto."

Harley grinned. Ella Houston could trash-talk him all day, but Harley never seemed to mind the teasing. Parker was pretty sure he was just happy to have her attention.

Jelly stepped closer to inspect the sign—still in Parker's hand. "This could be written in *blood*."

Exactly what Parker had thought.

"I can't believe you waited all day to text us about this." She ducked to look at the blank underside of the sign. "And nothing else out of the ordinary has happened today?"

Harley shook his head. "Just another Friday."

Ella glanced out the window as if she thought whoever left the sign might be watching the place. "Make any new enemies?"

"You mean," Harley said, "since Steadman disappeared?"

Nobody had seen or heard from the man after he'd tried to kill them in the quarry back in June. Parker silently thanked God for that.

"What about Scorza?" Ella nodded, like she was answering her own question.

"You said *new* enemies," Harley smiled.

"Well, *excuse* me, Mr. Lotitto," Ella said. "I should have been clearer. You were friends until early this summer. But now you're at each other's throats. So, could the sign be from him?"

Harley thought for a moment. "He gave me some trouble at football camp. But I gave worse back. He knows what will happen if he messes with me." He picked up the twenty-dollar bill Scorza had dropped on the counter—and stopped. Underneath sat Scorza's keys. Harley held them up, a wicked grin on his face. "Well, lookee what Mr. My-Dad-and-I-are-gonna-work-on-my-Jeep-together left behind."

Parker caught the girls up to speed on the conversation they'd missed.

Ella turned to the door. "Want me to see if he's still out there?"

"No," Harley said. "Definitely not." He tossed the keys into a box under the counter. "He probably won't even remember he left them here. I'll find something special to do with these."

Jelly still looked absorbed with the cardboard sign. "I don't like this. No strange customers today? Besides Scorza?"

Harley hesitated. To Parker, it didn't look like he was trying to remember the day so much as he wasn't sure how much to say.

"So, there *was* someone." El gave Jelly a nod.

"Actually, there were two."

El stepped up to the counter. Jelly joined her. "Two?"

"They came together. Asked a lot of questions—but nothing about diving. And they didn't look at any gear—or T-shirts. So, it was like . . . why are they coming in here, you know?" Harley shrugged. "At first, I didn't think anything of it, but now . . . I'm not so sure."

"Harley"—Jelly looked more than a little exasperated—"what if the only reason they came in was because of the sign—did you ever think of that?"

Harley shrugged. "I hate to say it, but I think you're right."

"Girls are always right." El thumped his head with her knuckle. "Remember that. Can you describe them?"

Harley looked like he wasn't sure where to start.

"Picture them. Their faces. The clothes they were wearing." Jelly said. "Could you identify them in a lineup?"

Ella reached forward and massaged his temples. "Think, Harley. Anything you remember about them that was, you know, weird or something?"

"Yes, and yes," Harley said.

"Well, come *on*," El said. "You've got to get the details down while they're still fresh."

"I don't have to write anything down." He closed his eyes like he was replaying the footage of the two strangers walking into the shop. "I'll never forget them 'til the day I die."

El and Jelly looked at each other—like someone had just offered them a free pizza.

"Hey, let's forget about it, okay?" Harley shook his head like he didn't want to think about it anymore. "Whatever the sign was about, it's over now. Nothing happened. I'll lock the door in ten, and then we're all off to Rockport House of Pizza. Somebody was just trying to spook me."

"Harley Davidson Lotitto," El said. "We are not forgetting about *any* of this."

"Nothing happened, okay? Whatever was supposed to start today obviously never got off the launchpad. Let's drop it." Harley shot Parker a partner-in-crime look.

Wait a sec. Parker forced himself not to smile.

Jelly locked arms with Ella. "We are not going anywhere. We're not closing the store. We're not going out for pizza. Not until you tell us more."

Parker sensed Harley was going to draw this out until closing. Even longer if he could.

"Let's get back to the two strange customers." El stared at him. "What did your uncle say about them?"

Harley shrugged. "He left before they came in—and hasn't been back since."

"But you *will* tell him." Jelly wasn't asking.

"I really don't see the poi—"

"The *point*, my dear football friend who has obviously taken too many hits to the head to think clearly," El said, "is that you could be in some kind of danger here. Did you think about that? 'It starts today.' *What* starts today . . . that's the question. 'Your world will change.' This is personal, Harley. Somebody is targeting you."

Harley shook his head. "It could have been meant for my Uncle Ray."

"Maybe," El said, "but anybody with an ounce of observation knows you open the store—so you'd be the one to see the note first . . . not your uncle."

Could Harley really be a target?

"What if this *is* Steadman?" Jelly looked dead serious. "What if he's back—out to even the score? I'm telling you, I don't like this."

Steadman was a long shot, right? Even the falling out with Bryce Scorza seemed like ancient history. Why would the guy do something now and not two months ago?

"Actually," Harley looked from Jelly to El again, "the more I hear you two, the more I'm feeling it. Not Steadman . . . but . . ."

Relief swept over El's face. "Okay, then. At least you're talking sense now."

"Tell us about the two strangers." Jelly whipped out her phone, swiped to a recording app, and held it close to Harley. "Talk to us. Tell us everything that comes to mind about them."

Harley closed his eyes. "They seemed all keyed up about something. Antsy. Like they were on a mission."

Jelly and El exchanged knowing looks. "Good, Harley. That's it. You said they were strange. How so?"

"When they came in, they stayed super close to each other, you know? Like they were attached. Most people spread out when they get in the store. Not these two. In fact, I'm pretty sure they were locked at the elbows—like arm in arm or something."

Jelly nodded. "So they were definitely together. Husband and wife, maybe?"

Harley shook his head. "Well, they were both girls. Seemed really young, too . . . like they were really afraid to let go of each other. Super insecure."

"Weird," El said.

Harley nodded. "That's what I thought."

"Did they say anything suspicious?" Jelly leaned in. "Something that made you think—even for a fraction of a second—that they were the ones who left the sign on your door?"

"Sometimes they were talking so fast I couldn't catch everything they said. I don't see how they could be the ones who left the note, but they definitely knew about it."

"Sheesh, Harley!" Jelly shook her head. "And it's taken you this long to tell us that little detail? Tell us what time they got here—and what they looked like. Then we're calling Officer Greenwood." She checked the screen on her phone as if to make sure it was recording okay.

Harley's eyes darted to Parker's for just an instant. "Well, I'm not sure I want to go into all kinds of physical details about how they looked—okay? I'm trying to be a decent guy here."

Jelly gave an exasperated groan. "Were they pretty? Ugly?"

"Were they pretty ugly?" Harley screwed his face into a look of total confusion. "I just told you, I'm trying to be—"

"I'm being serious, Harley. And you should do the same."

"Okay." Harley held up both hands. "Okay. I had a feeling when they walked in that they would give me trouble somehow."

Jelly nodded, like she was coaxing him on.

"My first impression? The two of them were just weird. Strange. Borderline freaky."

"How so? Explain."

Harley shrugged her question off. "Just a sense I got."

El looked frustrated. "You've got to give us more details. What time were they here? Let's start with that."

"About"—Harley checked the clock on the wall below the vintage neon Dacor sign—"ten minutes ago. They overlapped with Scorza for a few minutes."

Jelly stared in disbelief. "That was about when *we* got here. We probably walked right past them. Which way did they head when they left the store? What were they wearing?"

"The shorter one wore a pair of jeans. T-shirt. The taller one wore a dress." Harley grinned. "And cowgirl boots."

Jelly's eyes narrowed. "*You* . . . are a jerk." She nodded at El. "Time to teach mister funny-guy a lesson." She balled her fist and stepped around the counter.

El scooted around the display case from the other end—trapping Harley in the middle.

"This"—Jelly slugged him in the arm—"is for calling us *weird.*"

El punched his other arm. "And strange."

Harley laughed so hard he could hardly breathe.

Jelly hit him again. "And what's this about us talking so much?"

"And talking over each other?" El let him have it.

Harley tucked in, forearms over his face like a boxer taking a beating. "Parks—you gonna help me out or what?"

"Oh," El said. "Look who is *super-insecure* now."

Harley peeked out from between his forearms. "Parks?"

Parker took a step back. "Get in the middle of *that*? No thanks."

"*That* was the right answer." Jelly glared at him, but there was no hiding the smile in her eyes. "If I find out you knew what he was doing the whole time, you're next. Was the sign on the door for real—or was that part of the joke too?"

"I can answer that," Harley said. "If you two would stop beating me long enough to let me talk."

"You don't deserve it," Jelly said. "Right, Ella?"

The wall phone rang. Harley held up both hands in mock surrender. "The note was legit. Now stop long enough for me to grab this call."

Jelly and Ella both gave him some space but still didn't look like they'd finished with him yet.

Harley took a couple of deep breaths and picked up the receiver on the fourth ring, still grinning. "Rockport Dive Company." He listened for a moment, and his eyes changed. Got wider. The smile melted, fear growing over his face. "The shed right *here*—behind the dive shop?

"No!" Harley shouted. He dropped the phone, zig-zagged past El like she was an opponent on the field, and raced for the back room.

"Parks—help me! The Hangar is on fire!"

CHAPTER 2

PARKER RAN AFTER HARLEY through the back room and past the tank-filling station. His friend flew out the back door. Parker grabbed the five-gallon pail in the corner—dumping the broom and dustpan from inside on the fly.

Dark smoke tumbled upward from the eaves and a missing windowpane of Harley's shed. Too much smoke. The fire inside obviously had serious traction. Running the sixty feet to bucket water from Rockport Harbor seemed pointless. They'd need a firehose.

"Kemosabe!" Harley's eyes were absolutely wild. He dug for the key around his neck and jammed it into the shed padlock. "C'mon—c'mon!"

Parker felt the door. Still cool to the touch.

Smoke ghosted through the seams of the shed doors even as Harley whipped off the lock. The lock dropped to the ground, and together they swung the doors open. Black smoke roiled out—as if it was terrified of what it had seen inside. The entire shed was choked with smoke.

"I can't see." Harley flipped on the twelve-thousand-lumen shop light—which helped about as much as shining bright lights into a fogbank.

Before Parker could stop him—or hold him back—Harley disappeared inside.

"Harley!" Should he run in after him? "Harley!"

Jelly was on her phone, motioning frantically to whoever was on the line. El was already at the back of the neighboring store, wrestling a garden hose off a wall rack.

"Harley!" Hands out in front of him, Parker filled his lungs with air and took one step into the shed—then another. The smoke didn't seem as thick. He could barely make out Harley straddling the motorcycle now, rocking it off its stand.

Harley stepped it backwards even as Parker scooted to the front of the bike. No flames. Parker grabbed the handlebars and helped push Kemosabe out of the shed and down the short ramp.

The motorcycle roared to life, and Harley steered it wide of the shed and drove it onto Bradley Wharf. He parked it on the far side of a six-foot-high wall of lobster traps stacked near the famed Motif Number 1 fishing shack.

Coughing, Parker whipped off his T-shirt and used it to clear smoke from the opening of the shed.

El hit him with a shot of water.

Parker waved her off. "Stop—I'm not on fire." In fact, nothing was on fire. He would have seen the flames by now, right? Even now as the smoke drifted out of the shed and clung to the rafters, it was clear there was no fire at all.

"Smoke bombs?" Jelly was beside him. She ventured into the

hazy shed and bent over to inspect a smoking blob on the wood floor decking. Two others were dying out nearby.

If they were smoke bombs, they were not like anything Parker had ever seen before. For the massive amount of smoke they churned out, they were more like smoke machines, not smoke bombs.

"So . . . there's no fire?" El held the nozzle in a two-handed grip like it was a pistol, looking almost disappointed she couldn't hose somebody down.

Harley ran into view, covered with soot and still a little wild-eyed. "Everyone here okay?"

"We're good," Parker said. "Kemosabe?"

He nodded. "Needs a bath—but seems fine. I have to check him closer when the shed is safe." He peeled off his T-shirt and used it to beat at the smoldering smoke bomb.

"Harley," El said. "It's over."

He didn't let up. He was a madman, coughing and swinging at any spot where smoke rose now. The keys on the leather cord around his neck lurched and bucked against his chest.

"Hey . . . Smokey the Bear," El gave him a shot of water from the hose. "We got this. Go make sure Kemosabe is okay."

Harley dropped his T-shirt and glanced around the inside of the shed as if noticing for the first time that there really was no fire. "Kemosabe." He shot Parker a desperate look and disappeared around the corner of the shed.

Their original plans for the night were gone now. **IT STARTS TODAY. YOUR WORLD WILL CHANGE.** The words of the mystery sign streaked through Parker's mind. Something had started, all right. But he had the creepy feeling that the real changes hadn't even begun.

CHAPTER 3

Friday, August 5, 6:09 p.m.

HARLEY TOUCHED THE BIKE—tracing its strong lines with his fingertips as he inspected the frame. He laid his hand flat on the front tire. It felt cool. *Thank God.* For an instant he caught himself. *Thank God?* Now he was beginning to sound like Parker—even in his own head. But if God was to thank for his bike not tasting the fire, Harley would thank Him all day. He leaned in close and gave Kemosabe another quick scan. Even the wires looked perfect. No cracking on the rubber sheathing at all.

"He looks okay, right?" Parks pulled on his T-shirt and knelt on the other side of the motorcycle, examining it closely.

"I think so."

"Thank God," Parks said.

"Beat you to the punch on that one."

Parker gave him a funny look, but Harley wasn't about to explain.

18

Ella hurried over with Harley's T-shirt and tossed it to him. "Is Kemosabe okay?"

Harley nodded. "He looks perfect." He straddled Kemosabe and started the engine. He just needed to hear it again. Needed to absolutely assure himself that everything was okay.

There was never a better sound than the music coming out of those straight pipes. He revved the 1200cc motor over and over, just soaking in the strength. The power. The vibrations coursed through him—like they'd hitched a ride in his bloodstream—until his whole body pulsed in rhythm with the bike.

Honestly, Harley would bet there were healing elements deep in the cylinders of Kemosabe. The rumbling calmed him.

"Harley, look." El's face was full of concern. She pointed at the surface of the wraparound gas tank. "I think I see . . . a speck of dust!"

He smiled. "Don't worry. It won't be there long." He'd wipe the whole thing down and make sure the smoke cleared from inside the Hangar before rolling Kemosabe back.

"You'd better get yourself cleaned up too." El tapped her own cheeks and pointed back at his face.

Harley checked himself in the bike's side mirror. He definitely was a mess. His face was a couple shades darker—except where the tears had washed trails down his cheeks. Had he actually cried—or did she think he did? "Lousy smoke in my eyes." He made an exaggerated show of blinking a couple times and scrubbed his cheeks with the back of his hand.

Ella leaned in close. "You're not quite the tough guy you pretend to be, Mr. Lotitto." Her eyes smiled in that way they did so often since things had worked out for her and her Grams to stay in Rockport.

"Lucky you didn't lose the bike." Uncle Ray's voice rose over the rumble of the Harley.

Harley whirled to face him. Of all the people to walk up at this moment. The guy was in incredible shape—especially for all the beer he consumed. Harley nearly looked him in the eyes these days. He liked to think he'd grow a couple inches taller than Uncle Ray, but he wasn't so sure he'd be that lucky. They were built so similar in every other way, what were the chances Harley would grow taller? They had the same family genes. His uncle even walked like Harley did.

"Saw the smoke. Hustled over." Uncle Ray nodded from the direction of the T-wharf. "I was afraid maybe the dive shop was on fire—like the Blast Chamber took a real hit."

That was his name for the air tank fill station. And of course he'd be more worried about the shop than Harley's shed.

"I'm gone ten minutes and you practically burn the place down."

Actually, he'd been gone for more than an hour.

Uncle Ray squatted behind the bike. Closed one eye like he was sighting down the barrel of a rifle. "This bike is even sweeter than I remembered. I say we sell it. Like yesterday. My offer to let you invest in the boat for the dive charters is still open."

Uncle Ray owned the dive shop—but not the shed or anything inside it. And he was never going to get his mitts on Kemosabe. Harley had always been careful not to open the shed when Uncle Ray was around. And this was exactly why. Good ol' Uncle Ray was predictable. He was good for coming up with ways to use what belonged to Harley to make a fast buck for himself. He'd done enough of that already.

A Rockport, Massachusetts Fire Department truck swung onto

the back road running to Bradley Wharf. A police car rode the truck's bumper.

Parker motioned toward the flashing lights. "They'll want to hear what happened." Like he was trying to give Harley an excuse to get away from Uncle Ray.

Normally he'd have jumped at the chance, but he did *not* like the idea of leaving Uncle Ray alone with Kemosabe.

"You go," Harley said. "I'll be right there."

Parker hesitated for a moment, then gave a quick nod and hustled toward the shed. Ella stayed. Like she had no idea what she was supposed to do.

"I think fate is trying to tell you something, boy," Uncle Ray said. "It's showing you how fast things change. You think you can keep this bike forever? Fate says wake up. You keep this thing locked away in the shed like it's in a museum. Fate is telling you to do something with it."

Harley spun on the seat to look over the harbor. He couldn't stand to see his uncle's face. Since when did Uncle Ray ever care about what was best for him? "I told you—it's not for sale." And it never would be.

Ray stepped to the front of the bike and totally wrecked the view. "Don't talk out of the side of your head to me, boy." He looked at him long and hard. "I give you a chance to do something solid for your future, and this is how you treat me?"

Harley revved the bike. It didn't take much to drown out Uncle Ray's voice. Uncle Ray was a champion at taking the air out of him. The guy was a nail in his tire. More like a railroad spike. Ella walked to the side of Kemosabe. Like she'd decided she needed to stay. But her smile was definitely long gone.

"You're living in the past, boy," Uncle Ray said. "You're stupid that way—just like your dad."

Harley cut the motor. Swung a leg over Kemosabe to plant himself right in front of Uncle Ray. He was going to pick his uncle up and toss him right into the harbor.

Suddenly Ella was right there. Between them. "Harley! Look at me."

He took her by the arms to move her to the side. She clung to him instead.

"You're boneheaded, boy," Uncle Ray said. "Brainless imbecile. You don't know squat about how life works—just like your dad."

Ella gripped him tighter. "Harley—look at m—"

"My dad knew so much more about life than you!"

"Yet I'm alive," Uncle Ray put an exaggerated look of bewilderment on his face. "And he's not. Some expert on life he turned out to be."

"Ahhhhh!" Some primal cry growled up from deep inside Harley. He wouldn't just toss his uncle in the bay, he'd tackle him. Drive him off the edge of the granite pier and drag him to the bottom. See how long he'd last.

Ella leaned in hard against Harley, making it impossible to push past her without knocking her down. Her mouth was close to his ear. "Don't do it, don't do it. Listen to me, Harley. Please. He's not worth it. Hear me? He's the imbecile here. Don't take the bait. *Please,* Harley."

Her voice worked like a straitjacket, holding him in place until the rage slunk away to its hiding place. She loosened her grip. "You got this, Harley."

He had nothing. He felt the tears burning his eyes. Cheeks. Was he shaking?

"Hey," Uncle Ray said. "I'm just trying to help."

More like help himself. He was an expert at that. A world champion. Harley took in a deep breath. Let it out.

"I'll give you this much, kid," Uncle Ray said. "You got a gift . . . a real knack for making enemies. Because whatever happened to that shed was no accident. I say someone was out to destroy your precious motorcycle."

Uncle Ray was a selfish pig. An egocentric idiot. But at this moment he was actually making some rare sense. Not that he'd admit it to him. Bryce Scorza's shadowy face materialized in his head. Hadn't he been trying to hurt Harley with all his talk of the Wrangler and his dad? What better way to crush him than to destroy Kemosabe?

"I don't have any enemies." None that would dare mess with him, right?

"I'm not buying that," Uncle Ray said. "And I don't think you are either. But when you do figure it out, you stay away from him. Got it?"

Says the guy who was all about payback and retaliation.

"You get in a fight and word gets around. That's bad for business. Hurt somebody bad enough, and we're going to get sued—or you'll end up in juvey."

Harley glared at him. *Like you want to help.* He wished for the millionth time his dad was still alive. That he'd pull up on his Harley-Davidson Dyna Wide Glide and get him out of Uncle Ray's reach.

"We'll talk about this again." Uncle Ray shrugged and glanced toward the dive shop. "Tell me you locked up before you ran out to play junior firefighter."

The store. Sheesh. He'd left the front door unlocked. "Going to do that now."

Uncle Ray swore. "The store's been empty—and unlocked—all this time? Where's your head, boy?"

Harley grabbed Kemosabe's key from the ignition. Ella stepped out of the way as he passed. Parker was already talking to one of the firemen—and a cop. Officer Greenwood? For a moment Parker looked his way.

Parks—I need you to keep an eye on things. Harley pointed at his own eyes, then back at Kemosabe behind him.

Parks's eyes narrowed for a moment and he flashed Harley a thumbs-up. Immediately Parker led Greenwood and the fireman toward the bike.

Harley nodded. Parks definitely got it. That was one advantage of diving with someone—like he'd been doing with Parks ever since the encounter in the quarry. You learned to communicate pretty stinkin' good without needing words.

"You got lucky this time, boy."

Uncle Ray just couldn't resist the chance to grind his knuckle into Harley.

"Whoever did this just showed he can get at your bike if he wants to. How you going to deal with that?"

Harley didn't answer, but hustled for the back door of Rockport Dive Company. Scorza's face was in his head again. Taunting him. Did he have something to do with this?

Of course he did. It made sense. Harley was going to find out for sure.

And then he was going to make him pay.

CHAPTER 4

PARKER ALMOST WISHED THE SHED had really been on fire. Then he could have talked himself into believing it was nothing more than an accident. One of those dumb things that happen when someone gets careless.

But the broken window was no accident. And the smoke bombs? They were nothing like the amateur type that Parker had seen before. The fire chief recognized them right away as commercial grade smoke bombs—the kind you can't even buy without a pyrotechnic license. Not legally anyways. "They give a full three minutes of dense, black smoke. No wonder you thought it was a real fire."

Yeah, there was nothing random about what had happened to the shed. And the need for the pyrotechnic license pretty well ruled out that this was some impulsive prank. Whoever did this had a plan.

Parker kept Kemosabe in his line of vision—but stayed close enough to the first responders to overhear anything they might say to shed light on who might have done this. Uncle Ray did a slow walk around the bike. He took out his phone and appeared to be taking pictures. Was he going to try to make some kind of insurance claim out of it? Leave it to him to find a way to profit from someone else's pain.

Suddenly Jelly was there, standing beside Parker. Ella stood close.

"Steadman," Jelly said. "I'd bet money on that."

Parker wasn't so sure. "Payback?"

Jelly nodded.

"Then why not burn the shed down—and destroy Kemosabe? Why just put a scare into everyone?"

"Think about it," Jelly said. "Maybe he wants to draw this out. Put us on edge. Get us nice and scared before he settles the score for real."

It just didn't fit. "Why target Harley? Why not me?"

"Maybe you're next," Jelly said. "Look, Steadman was a Navy SEAL, right? He'd know where to get smoke bombs like this. I think he wants us to know it was him."

And tip everyone off that he was in town—when there was a warrant for his arrest? "Maybe. But he'd be taking a real risk coming back here, right?"

Jelly gave him the side eye. "That guy lives for risk."

Whatever Ella was thinking, she kept her thoughts to herself. But she had her hand curled around the Navajo cross hanging from her neck.

The only smoke left clung to the rafters of the shed now. It huddled there like it wanted to see what was going to happen next. A handful of firemen stood around the front of the engine, talking like they were disappointed the whole thing was a false alarm.

Uncle Ray stepped up beside the two girls. Hands on his hips like he was in charge. "Stupid." The guy looked peeved. "If Harley sold dive gear as easy as he makes enemies, I wouldn't need to do dive charters."

There was a part of Parker that wanted to push back on that. Harley wasn't stupid. And if he made enemies, it was only because he was trying to do the right things. Sometimes that's all it took.

Uncle Ray spit. "Whoever did this wanted Harley to know he can get at him anytime he has the urge. You want to be a good friend?" He scanned the three of them. "Tell that boy to sell the bike before whoever did this strikes again. Next time they may put a smoke grenade through the front window of the shop."

"I'm glad to hear you're concerned about Harley," Jelly said. Would Uncle Ray pick up the sarcasm in her voice? If he did, he sure wasn't showing it. "But he wouldn't listen even if all three of us begged him to sell Kemosabe."

Not that they would.

"Well, he sure ain't listening to me." Uncle Ray ventured inside the shed. He looked around and then walked back out toward the firemen. Kept his hands on his hips the whole time like they were fused to his belt.

"How Harley could be related to that man is a complete mystery." Ella stepped into the shed and started taking down the framed watercolor scenes of Rockport—now covered in soot. "I'm going to need your help bringing these home. We'll get them all cleaned up so Harley doesn't have to worry about it."

The road signs and license plates Harley had all over the shed would need scrubbing too. But Parker would need a screwdriver to get those down. Ella handed him watercolors, and Parker started a stack outside. He drew a face on the glass with his finger. The soot came off easily. That was something, anyway.

Jelly was busy doing a Google search. "No escapes by one-armed convicts from the Miami Correctional Facility. So we can rule Clayton Kingman out."

Kingman? The one who came way too close to killing Parker in the Everglades? If he broke out of jail and was crazy enough to track them down, he'd do a lot worse than a few smoke bombs. And why would he target Harley? Parker was the one he'd focus his revenge on. Actually, Jelly too.

"Thankfully nobody got hurt," Parker said. "No permanent damage done. Now we help him get this cleaned up. It's over now." But even as he said the words, Parker wasn't sure he believed them. *God? This is the end, right?*

"Over?" Jelly rolled up the sheet Harley had used to cover Kemosabe and swung one end in circles over her head. Wisps of trapped smoke twisted out the doors and rose heavenward like Parker's silent prayers.

"Somebody went to an awful lot of trouble for this to only be a one-and-done, over-and-out type of thing." Ella relayed another couple of framed watercolors to Parker. "And the mystery caller . . . the Good Samaritan who saw the smoke. How did they even know to call the dive shop?

"Yeah, why not call 911?" Jelly asked. "And why didn't they give their name or anything?"

"Maybe they did give their name—but Harley had already dropped the phone, racing to get outside," Parker said.

"I've never seen Harley's face look the way it looked at that instant," Ella said. "It was like he'd seen a ghost."

And he still looked pretty haunted. Harley appeared at the back door of the dive shop—half in, half out. He gave the area a quick scan, then locked eyes with Parker. "My Uncle Ray," he mouthed the words. "Is he gone?"

Parker shook his head and pointed. Uncle Ray stood on the granite block edge overlooking the North Basin of Rockport Harbor, talking to Officer Greenwood.

That's when he saw Bryce Scorza. Sitting on the north tip of the T-wharf, just staring at them. "Look who came to watch."

Parker made no effort to hide the fact that he saw Scorza. Clearly the guy wasn't trying to hide that he was there. Scorza waved. Not a simple raise of a hand, but an exaggerated, sweeping arm thing, high over his head. As if he was stranded and waving down the Coast Guard. "What is that guy's problem?"

Harley stepped out the back door of the shop and walked over . . . zombie-like. Maybe the reality of what he'd almost lost was beginning to register.

"I'm in deep weeds." Harley placed both palms on the side of the shed like some cop had ordered him into a spread-eagle position. He dropped his head. Shook it. "Deep. Weeds."

The bike and everything in the shed would be fine. They'd need cleaning, but that was about it. What was Parker missing? "Harley . . . it's going to be okay, man."

He shook his head. "He's going to kill me."

Who was going to kill him? It was way more likely Harley would kill the person who broke the window and planted the smoke bombs.

"Let's grab Officer Greenwood," El said. "We have to show him the sign from the window this morning, right?"

The sign. The smoke bombs. Maybe they were related. Maybe not. "Let's hold off a sec." Right now it was the spooked look on Harley's face that had him really concerned. Tendrils of smoke spiraled and teased their way upward from the shed doorway in a slow, almost hypnotic dance. There was something in-your-face about them. Mocking. Like they knew exactly who dropped the smoke bombs—but enjoyed flaunting that little fact too much to reveal a thing.

Harley looked like he was going to puke. "I'm in trouble. I'm dead."

Parker focused his attention back on Harley. All of them did. "What's going on?"

Harley looked like he was in shock. "When I went inside—to lock up? The register was open and the cash was gone—and there was a boatload of it before the call about the shed. While we were saving Kemosabe . . . somebody robbed the store."

"What?" But this changed everything, right?

Jelly snatched the cap off Parker's head and slapped it on her own head. "The sign. The smoke. The robbery. Still think we should hold off on talking to Officer Greenwood, Sherlock?"

No. He didn't. Now the only question was if this was a random burglary, or was this personal? Had some enemy just declared war on Harley or Uncle Ray?

He wanted to believe it was random. With all his heart. Because that would mean this was over. But deep down he knew better. If this was personal, it wasn't finished. This wasn't the end of it. An image of the mysterious sign flashed in his mind. **IT STARTS TODAY.**

CHAPTER 5

Friday, August 5, 11:15 p.m.

ELLA SAT ON THE EDGE OF HER BED, elbow propped on the window-sill of her second-story bedroom. Salty night air breezed in for a visit like a close friend. That combined with the scent rising from the Rockport Candle Company jar on the windowsill made for an almost intoxicating combination. If only life were that perfect.

Her Grams's old necklace had become part of Ella now. She only took it off to shower . . . or think. She looped the rough turquoise and silver bead chain once around her index finger. The oversize cross pendant dangled there, reflecting the candle's light. Navajo symbols decorated the face of the sterling silver cross, with a turquoise center stone polished smooth from years of rubbing. She had Grams to thank for that smoothness. She tapped one arm of the cross over and over until the chain twisted tight. Then she backed off and let the necklace unwind itself.

The cross spun slowly, glinting in the light. The ornate front spiraled past, then the plain back with *Deliver Us From Evil* engraved deep in the sterling. She tapped one arm of the cross, accelerating the spin. The words were harder to read now, but she thought there was something about the frantic *Deliver Us, Deliver Us, Deliver Us* flashing by that matched her soul.

If each turn would send up a prayer, she'd keep the thing twirling until midnight. But she was pretty sure prayer didn't work that way.

Jelly. Harley. Parker. Even Grams. They'd all come so far in the last two months. As it turned out, Harley was a really decent guy—a fact that was increasingly obvious the longer he'd kept his distance from Bryce Scorza. Was it being away from his jerk of an ex-friend that made the big difference? Or the fact that Harley had spent so much time with Parker lately—and even Parker's dad? Probably all of the above.

Harley was convinced Scorza was behind the smoke bombs— and the robbery. Ella wasn't so sure about that. Sure, Scorza's world had taken some ugly turns since the full scope of his dad's involvement with Mr. Steadman had come to light. Lucius Scorza had nothing to do with Devin Catsakis's death—or the attempted murder of Harley and Parker. But he'd not been honest with the police and had helped Steadman mastermind his scheme to practically steal Grams's home away. That made for some really bad press for the bank.

As a result, Scorza's dad was no longer employed at the bank in town—or any other bank. Even though he'd lost his job and his reputation, somehow the guy still landed on his feet. He'd managed to quickly sell their home before they lost it, and they were now renting a place in Gloucester—although Scorza claimed they'd be back living in Rockport soon. But Scorza could bike into Rockport easily. Had he been involved in this? The guy was a snake, but would he really rob the store? He was lazy . . . a moocher. Expecting others to do the work for him like it was a huge honor for them or something. He was the "I'm going to get a full ride scholarship someday" kind of guy. Would he do something that could completely mess that up?

When Scorza's dad got canned, the quarterback blamed Harley and Parker. Which was rich. Scorza didn't seem to consider his dad's total lack of integrity might have been a factor in him getting the axe. So, had Scorza just been waiting for a couple months so he wouldn't be suspected? Harley's ex-friend knew how much Kemosabe meant to Harley. The smoke bombs were a bold move—especially in the daylight. Scorza was more of a strike-from-the-shadows kind of guy. But what better way to hurt Harley than through his bike? Scorza would absolutely have known that.

The hall door opened and Jelly padded into the bedroom. Her dad had moved to Rockport, but until the fixer-upper he'd recently purchased was fully rehabbed, Jelly was going to be staying with her and Grams. Which suited Ella just fine.

"Hey." Jelly sat cross-legged on her bed on the other side of the room. "You've been quiet. Who do you think did this?"

The question Ella had been trying to avoid talking about. It was about fighting her own superstitions more than anything. She grasped the cross and stopped it from spinning. "I'm thinking the smoke bombs weren't just a diversionary tactic so someone could rob the dive shop."

Jelly nodded. "Same. Why?"

"The sign." It was obvious. "The smoke bombs made perfect decoys all by themselves. The sign wasn't needed—unless . . ."

"Unless this was really about sending a message."

"Exactly." Ella wasn't sure how much more to say. "It's the key—but the boys can't get that through their thick skulls."

"Do you think the letters were written in blood?"

Now Jelly was getting close to the real issue. "I imagine the police will find out soon enough. But it was supposed to look like blood—and that's enough."

"So," Jelly said, "what does the blood say to you?"

Ella was trying not to let her superstitions—or Grams's—cloud her thoughts on this. But how could they not? Blood meant this was no idle threat. "Something evil is at work here . . . or someone capable of great evil. And . . ." Should she say more?

"And *what*?"

She looked around the room. And instantly she knew why. Some little part of her wondered if they were really alone. "Sometimes there are things that are best not said aloud."

Jelly looked like she was trying to read Ella's eyes. "Like saying it out loud will make it come true somehow—or like some unseen presence is listening?"

Okay . . . obviously Jelly got it. "Both."

Jelly grabbed her phone. Pulled up a playlist and turned up the volume. She tiptoed over to Ella and leaned in close to her ear. "Tell me. Whisper it."

Like this was a spy movie or something. But maybe it would work. The truth was, she didn't want to be the only one with the thoughts she was thinking. She needed someone to tell her she was ridiculous. "Somebody—or some *being*—has targeted Harley for their unholy scheme. And they have taken a blood oath. That means they will see this through to the very end."

Did Jelly just shiver? She hugged herself and sat back down on her bed—which pretty well answered Ella's question.

Ella drew her legs up and hugged her knees. "Sometimes I wish I was a little more like Parker—as weird as that sounds. Believing God is truly in control. Sees all. Knows all."

"Sovereign." Jelly eyed her for a moment. "And you don't think He is?"

Ella shrugged. "I think He's got a lot on His plate. He can't see everything—and there's lots of bad things going on." She stopped . . . waiting for Jelly to respond. But Jelly just sat there staring at the candle. Ella leaned close to Jelly's ear. "Grams says that sometimes angels disguise themselves as humans to do good things. And if angels could do that, why not demons?"

That got Jelly's attention. "Disguise themselves as humans—to do evil?"

Ella nodded. "Or maybe possess them—and get them to do their bidding."

"Thanks for robbing me of any chance of sleeping tonight." Jelly laughed, but it sounded forced. "You remind me of Wilson . . . Parker's friend—well, I guess he was my friend too—from down in Everglades City. He's half Miccosukee—and takes superstition to a whole new level. You'd like meeting him."

"Parker has told me stories," Ella said. "Believe me . . . I've got no desire to meet the guy." But they were getting offtrack. Right now, they had to focus on what was in front of them. Somebody—or something—was trying to mess up Harley. If that was true, how could they sit by and let that happen without a fight?

"I talked to Harley after he'd closed up the shop," Ella said. "He seemed dead set determined to pay Scorza a visit. You know how bad that could be?"

"Monumentally bad." Jelly sat there for a moment. "Sometimes the boys can be so . . . reckless. And I can be kind of . . . *overprotective*. I'm trying to do better at that."

Ella got that. Just like she was trying not to let her superstitions be so much of a factor—at least when it came to the boys. "So maybe we keep an eye on the boys—but not so close that they can accuse us of being overprotective."

Jelly was quiet for a moment. "And we won't jump in and actually do something they'd notice until we're absolutely sure there's no other way."

Sometimes girls just had to step in when the guys didn't have the good sense to use the brains God gave them. "Agreed."

They fell into a comfortable quiet. Sometimes they were kind of in sync that way. Neither of them had to say a thing—they just drifted into their own thoughts for a bit. Ella held up the cross necklace again and tapped the arm over and over, spinning the beaded necklace tighter and tighter. She grabbed it before it had a chance to unwind.

What would happen to Harley in all this? How was he going to react to everything that had happened today? Even if he didn't do a thing wrong by trying to get even with Scorza, Harley's relationship with his Uncle Ray was absolutely volatile. Yes, Harley was a powder keg, but so was his uncle.

According to Harley, Uncle Ray went totally off the rails when he heard about the robbery. They'd had over thirty-five hundred dollars in the cash register—and every bit of it was gone. Harley was going to have to pay him back. Every dollar. And his uncle wasn't going to wait around to take it out of his wages. There was the trust set up for Harley—funded by his dad's life insurance policy after he died. A not-to-be-opened-until-after-he-was-twenty-five kind of thing. Ella had no idea how much was in it, but Uncle Ray seemed to think there had to be some kind of clause that allowed for it to be tapped in an emergency. In fact, Harley believed his uncle was getting this all checked out with an attorney. If he didn't get the money? Harley's sweet Uncle Ray had threatened to turn Harley back over to the state.

Ella let go of the cross. Wound as tight as it was, the sterling silver pendant immediately picked up speed until it became a blur in the candlelight.

Would Harley's uncle really kick him out? Ella didn't think so. He got a fat check from the state every month to "care" for Harley, right? But it definitely wasn't enough to make Uncle Ray care about *him*, not in any ways she'd noticed, anyway. Would he actually put Harley in the state system? The guy was always griping about needing more cash, so why would he turn away that kind of free money?

Harley was a huge help to his uncle—even if the jerk wouldn't admit it. But what if Harley paid Scorza a visit, like he'd apparently been itching to do, and it got ugly? And what if Uncle Ray then thought Harley was more trouble than he was worth?

The real question that was gnawing at her? Where would Harley go if he became some kind of ward of the state of Massachusetts? Would he have to leave Rockport? Even worse, if Harley did something bad to Scorza—and Uncle Ray got wind of it? He'd turn his nephew in to the police himself, wouldn't he? He'd have him institutionalized in some kind of detention center for juveniles— which was really a prison. As Harley's legal guardian, he'd still probably get checks from the state.

Ella stopped herself, realizing her thoughts were running away from her. The revolving cross necklace slowed as the beads twisted tight—and finally came to a complete stop for a moment.

It quivered there in the candlelight, and then slowly started turning the other way. *Deliver us from evil.* And at that moment she felt that somehow things *were* spinning backward. They'd had weeks of freedom since the incident at the quarry. Good things. No real fears. Were things reversing on them now? Dragging them back into the kind of mess they'd fought so hard to be free from?

A tap on her bedroom door tore her from her dark thoughts.

Grams poked her head inside. "Girls . . . I thought you two were going to bed early." Her eyes flicked down to the cross turning in the candlelight. "Still thinking about the robbery?"

Ella shrugged. She didn't want to worry Grams. "My imagination is just skipping ahead, thinking about where this may all lead. But I'm fine. Really."

"Me too, Grams," Jelly said. She'd been calling her Grams for weeks now.

Grams hesitated. "I'll leave you two to your thoughts. But don't you worry too much about those friends of yours. They're a good bunch. I absolutely think God smiles on young Parker."

He probably wouldn't be alive if God didn't. "It's Harley I'm worried about."

"He's no fool." Grams touched two fingers to her lips, then pointed at each of the girls. "If you two feel like talking, I'll welcome the company. Sleep has been playing hide-and-seek with me tonight. I'll check back in a little bit." She backed out the door.

He's no fool. Well yeah, of course. Grams was probably right. But he was impulsive. Reckless. And could be totally granite-headed. Before leaving the group and coming home tonight, she'd tried talking Harley out of going anywhere near Scorza. He'd been quiet, mostly.

"Promise me, Harley."

"I can't do that, Ella." He looked like saying the words hurt him as much as hearing them crushed her.

"You have a choice."

He shook his head. "He's got me in a corner. The smoke bombs were a threat—and a test. If I don't do something, Scorza will strike again—and he'll do something worse. I believe he totally wants to destroy something I had with my dad. Something his dad will never give him. If I don't shut him down hard, he'll be back. I know how he operates."

"You can't be sure it was him."

"Who else would it be?"

She honestly couldn't think of another person. "What will you do?"

He couldn't hold her gaze. Harley looked down. Shrugged. But he obviously had something in mind. "Tell me."

He raised his head, just a bit. Looked up at her through hair that hung over his eyebrows. "Scare him good, so he won't ever mess with me again."

No good would come of it. Ella had been sure of that. She'd tried stalling Harley. "Give it a couple days—will you do that? I won't ask you to promise not to see Scorza at all, but wait until Monday." She'd hoped his thinking would be clearer by then. That maybe Parker would be able to calm him down a bit over the weekend. "Would you at least promise me that? Monday."

Harley didn't make any promises. But he didn't flat out say no, either. Still, it had been massively unsettling to see him so determined to go in a disastrous direction like that.

She pushed the image out of her head. Focused on the here. The now. The breeze coming through her window.

The necklace was whirling in the candlelight now. Too fast to even read the prayer engraved on the back. And she felt it. Deep in her soul. They *were* going back . . . and there was no way to stop this.

"Dear God," she whispered. "Deliver us from evil."

CHAPTER 6

Friday, August 5, 11:50 p.m.

RAY LOTITTO HAD TO HAND IT TO HIMSELF. He'd made a plan—and executed it perfectly. Even if something had gone south, he'd had a backup scheme. And another if that one failed.

He was a survivor that way. Figure out what was best for himself—then chart a course to get there. Once he had the map, it was all about grabbing the helm and throwing himself into it—full throttle. He wasn't just the captain of his own ship; he'd learned to steer other people's ships at the same time.

That's how he got the sweet dive shop location on Bearskin Neck—for lower than the asking rent. When the owners dumped his offer, he had switched to another tactic. Sure, there'd been others willing to pay higher rent than he could, but he'd hired a professional to convince them to back away. He'd put their ships on *his* course. And it had been money well invested.

Ray laced his fingers behind his head and stared at the dark ceiling.

There were "users" and "losers" in this world. Ray knew how to manipulate people and situations to get what he wanted. He was a first-class user. His brother, on the other hand, was a loser. Didn't have a clue how to leverage others to get ahead. Then the dummy got himself killed and stuck Ray with the kid? As far as Ray was concerned, the kid was a stowaway—and nobody sails for free.

Ray needed the boat. Needed it. He'd make more money on a dive charter in one afternoon than he would slaving away a week in the shop. He'd finally found a way to make the kid useful—or at least his money. He might even sell the shop once the charters booked up. He'd kick back and live the good life.

People thought he was in the dive shop business. Honestly? His main job was looking out for number one. The dive shop was just the ship that sailed him where he wanted to go. That was something his dearly departed brother never understood. Maybe if he'd been a little more dedicated to looking out for himself, he wouldn't have gotten himself killed in that accident.

And then Harley wouldn't be such a rope around Ray's propeller. That kid was a constant reminder of Ray's fair-haired brother. The guy who named Ray as the legal guardian of his boy—but arranged for one hundred percent of the life insurance windfall to go into a trust for the kid. Not a penny for Ray's trouble.

It wasn't right. Sure, Ray got money from the state for taking care of the kid, but that was chump change compared to the funds tied up in the motorcycle—and the trust.

But all that was going to change. Ray's first attempts to convince the kid to sell the motorcycle and go in with him on the boat had fallen flat. Which is why he'd had to find another source. He didn't like the fact that he'd had to borrow from a guy like Quinn Lochran. But where else could he get the money fast enough to buy the boat? It was a calculated risk. Either a fourteen-day loan at ridiculous interest—or miss the chance to get the perfect dive charter boat at a killer price. He'd get all the money back anyway once he convinced the kid to sell the bike.

And if the kid still wasn't ready to sell, he'd step up his plans again. He'd given the kid plenty of chances, and he wasn't fooling around anymore. It was time for the kid to grow up. Harley *owed* him that bike. Tonight had been his final warning. If young Harley didn't let go of the bike fast, Ray would kick his plans into high gear. With Harley's approval or not, the bike would sell super fast. Long before the August 14 loan payback deadline. There was time . . . just not much. Five days already gone, nine to go.

So tomorrow he'd give the kid one final chance. In or out. Do or die. He chuckled at his own choice of words. Because if it was "no," the kid was going to croak when Plan B went into effect. And that would be Sunday night. Not a day later.

Even if the kid couldn't let go of his precious motorcycle, tonight's little scheme had gained Ray some great intel. He was pretty sure it gave him the key to making sure Sunday night's maneuvers ended victoriously. One way or another he'd land on his feet. He always did. And the $3,500 was proof of that. Ray had doubled his money with his little scheme. He had the cash he'd cleaned from the register while Harley was outside trying to save the motorcycle—and the stupid kid would have to pay him back another $3,500 to cover what he'd believed was stolen. Add that to the money he'd get from selling the kid's motorcycle, and he'd be golden.

But he had to keep everything moving. And he'd have to get

Harley's $3,500 from the trust fund. Surely the lawyer would find a way to pry a little moolah out of the kid's inheritance in this case. The kid owed it to him, for Pete's sake.

"You're a clever little devil, Ray Lotitto," he whispered. The kid would come to his senses now and sell the bike. He was sure of it.

And if he didn't? Ray smiled. The truth was he kind of hoped the kid dug in his heels and wouldn't agree to selling. Because Ray already had the last phase of Plan B all worked out . . . and it was a beauty.

CHAPTER 7

THE GARDEN OF EDEN. That was the thought that popped into Angelica's head Saturday morning as she took a side trek down Bearskin Neck and back, past the shops bordering Rockport Harbor on one side and Old Harbor and Sandy Bay on the other. Rockport was her Garden of Eden. Obviously, nothing could rival the original, but Rockport was all she needed. Especially the way the town hugged the rugged Massachusetts coastline. To her, this was the most gorgeous place on Earth. Dad had only been in town a week or so, but she was pretty sure he was beginning to see it that way too. It was a fresh start, anyway . . . something her dad needed more than he'd probably admit.

Parker was already outside the coffee shop. He waved and jogged down the block to meet her. "No Ella this morning?"

"Just trying to give her and Grams some space." She loved that she could still stay there while Dad was working on the place for the two of them, but she didn't want to wear out her welcome. "How's my dad this morning?"

"Worked a late one," Parker said, "so he's going to love the coffee that you'll bring back for him."

So weird. Dad was staying with Uncle Vaughn until he could get the house livable, so Parker often knew more about her dad's schedule than she did. But all that mattered was that Dad was here in Rockport, and they were a little family again. With Maria already off at college, it was just Dad and her now—and she was totally okay with that.

Parker opened the door to BayView Brew Coffee and Donut Shop, and Angelica stood on the threshold for a delicious moment before going in. Closed her eyes. Raised her face and drew in the fresh scents of coffee and donuts. Making coffee for her dad all those months after her mom walked out turned into a new tradition of joining her dad with a cup herself.

Now coffee was part of her little daily routine. A little coffee—with lots of cream and sugar—gave her day a predictable start—no matter how out of the ordinary the night before had been. And going out for coffee this morning seemed like a good idea after last night's events at the dive shop.

"Harley is in hot water with his uncle." Parker led her inside.

"You really think his uncle would bust into Harley's trust from his dad?"

"He's going to try." Parker shrugged. "Harley is afraid Uncle Ray will pressure the lawyer to see it his way."

"Nice guy."

"Right." Parker nodded toward the counter. "Grab your coffee. I'll wait."

Angelica marched to the front counter, eyes on the glass shelves of donuts mounted on the wall behind the counter. Unfortunately, the cash in her pocket wasn't going to stretch that far.

"Somebody's up and at 'em early." Victoria Lopez smoothed her apron and breezed over to Angelica's end of the counter. She was fortyish and single. Easy smile. Contagious laugh. Comfortable in her own skin.

"Hey, Pez."

"Getting coffee for your dad this morning—or just yourself?"

Angelica held up two fingers, and Pez went to work without asking more than that. It was amazing how she seemed to know everybody, including her dad in the week since he'd arrived. Angelica rose up on tiptoe to slide onto the mushroom-style stools lining the counter. Pez moved with such grace, it masked how fast she worked. Every movement smooth. Efficient. Like she worked to the strains of some orchestra playing a waltz in her head.

Angelica's mind drifted back to the original Eden. And even as great as the place had been, it wasn't perfect. There was an enemy who didn't want Adam and Eve to live happily ever after. The serpent was there to disrupt things—and the creepy reptile executed the plan well. Eve took the bait. Adam took his bite too. And it was *adios*, paradise.

Were the smoke bombs at Harley's last night nothing more than a well-planned robbery of an undermanned store? Or was there a reptilian influence behind it—targeting Harley?

"One small latte for Miss Angelica." Pez smiled. "And an extra-large coffee for that alligator-hunting dad of yours—with extra cream and *lots* of sugar."

Baby coffee. That's what Dad called it. "Yes, he loves his sweets," Angelica said.

"Nothing wrong with a man who loves his air salty and his coffee sweet. But how come he's got you making the coffee run instead of coming here himself?"

"He worked a long shift—and got in late. Thought I'd pick this up and surprise him."

Pez took a pair of tongs and reached for an apple-cider cinnamon donut. "In that case, bring this to that sweet dad of yours too." She slipped the ring of happiness into one of those waxy bags made to keep the donuts extra fresh.

"Oooh, you definitely know what he likes."

Pez patted Angelica's hand. "Well, you remind him you got it from somebody *really* sweet." She held up the bag and gave it a gentle shake. "You tell him to stop by and say hi, would you?"

Angelica definitely would. What she'd really like is if her dad asked Pez out. Her mom had walked out, what, over two years ago now? She'd gotten tired of the Everglades, the wife and mom routine, or maybe of being a decent human being. She went looking for her own Garden of Eden. Whether she found it or not, Angelica had no idea. All she knew was that Mom had sent the divorce papers six months before they'd moved up here. *Traitor.*

Dad let the envelope sit unopened on their bed for days. It wasn't like it was in the way or anything. He slept on the couch anyway. Had done so ever since Mom walked out. Like maybe he expected her to show up some night, and he'd be right there to welcome her back. Dad had worked extra shifts while the papers sat cooling on the bed.

It was a full two weeks before Dad opened the envelope. He asked Angelica if deep down she wanted him to sign—or hold out in case Mom changed her mind and finally agreed to try again.

"Sign them, Dad. And don't use a pencil." She'd handed him

a Sharpie permanent marker. "Make your signature as big and strong as you are. And when the transfer comes in, don't bother sending her our new address in Rockport."

"If she asks, I *have* to let her know where we've moved. You know that." But Dad uncapped the marker and signed with flair.

And that was that. If Dad grieved, he was careful to hide it around her. He seemed way more concerned that she was doing all right than he was about himself. Dad got in the habit of texting Angelica three or four times a day—just to make sure she was okay.

She always assured him she was fine—even when she wasn't. But since she'd been here, in Rockport—with Parker and his parents, Ella and Grams, and even with Harley—she'd been doing the best ever. Her home in the Everglades was forever wrecked. *Thanks, Mom!* But here, it had truly been a new start. She had no idea how a woman like Pez could tell right away that Dad was a really good guy, but Mom—who'd been married to him for eighteen years—never figured that out. As far as Angelica knew, Dad never sent the new address—which could only mean Mom never asked.

Which meant there was no chance Mom would show up in Rockport out of the blue. But still, Angelica found herself watching for her at the weirdest times.

Like now.

Parker walked her outside. "Harley is absolutely positive it was Scorza. The smoke bombs, anyway."

"That doesn't make sense. The smoke bombs and the robbery are totally connected. You can't separate them. So he did both—or he didn't do either one. And Scorza doesn't have what it takes to pull off a robbery like that, if you ask me."

"Brains or nerve?"

She gave that a moment's thought. "He's smart, but he's a

weasel. He might get someone else to do it, but he wouldn't risk it himself."

Parker nodded. "Agreed. I think somebody wanted to rob the store, and they set up the smoke bombs as a decoy. Plain and simple."

Parker was naive. He was forgetting all about the sign written in blood—or whatever it was. This was more than a robbery. There was something darker going on here. "So you think this was completely about the robbery . . . and there was nothing personal aimed at Harley or his uncle in all this?"

"Exactly." He slowed as he passed the mouth of Bearskin Neck, like maybe he wanted to go check on Harley. "Don't you see it that way?"

It was amazing to her how the boys just weren't connecting the dots on this. They weren't seeing the whole picture—and that's what made all the difference. Which confirmed exactly what she and Ella had talked about. They'd have to watch the boys. Make sure they weren't getting in over their heads. "So, whoever robbed the place just picked the Rockport Dive Company out of all the shops on Bearskin Neck? Why not pick a shop that has a lot more business—which means more money in the register? Why not Roy Moore's?"

Parker looked at her like he thought she was being ridiculous. "Roy Moore's has a couple of guys working there all the time. Even if the robber did create a distraction to get one of them out of the store, there'd still be one left inside. And the men working there . . . well, they can handle themselves, you know?"

"So . . . you're saying they can't be robbed?"

"No, I'm saying nobody would dare. Anyone who tried would find himself stuffed in a lobster tank before he got away with the money."

Angelica just wasn't ready to buy into the whole "this was a random robbery" angle. "The way you see it, the dive shop was picked for no other reason than it looked like an easy target—even though they just happened to do it on the same day that some jokester planted a threatening sign on the door. And nobody is out to nail Harley or Ray?"

"Bingo."

Angelica resisted the urge to roll her eyes. But it made no sense to continue arguing the point now. "I hope you're right." Part of her wished they'd taken a little detour to check out the front door of the dive shop—just to make sure there wasn't another warning sign today. "You think Harley will go after Scorza?"

"I'm definitely trying to talk him off that ledge, but it's not going to be easy." He gave kind of a half smile. "It looks like I've got my work cut out for me."

And Angelica did too. She'd need to keep her ear to the ground without them getting suspicious. The boys wouldn't love knowing Angelica felt they needed her protection. And if she was going to keep them out of danger, she'd have to stop Harley from going after Scorza. If she didn't, it was only a matter of time before Parker did something stupid himself.

Angelica stepped up her pace. She wanted to get the coffee to her dad while it was still hot. But still, when Parker sidetracked onto the T-wharf she went along with him. He stood at the end for a moment, looking out over Rockport Harbor. This is where it all started . . . the day she'd come to her Garden of Eden. But Parker wasn't looking at the harbor. His gaze seemed to be fixed on Harley's shed.

"So, you're going to talk Harley out of doing something stupid, right?" Angelica had to word this carefully. "If he even talks to Scorza—you do know it will get ugly fast, right?"

Parker nodded. "I'm on it."

She hoped so. "How do you know he's not headed there right now—before the shop opens?"

"His uncle is driving him to see that boat as we speak," Parker said. "Trying to convince him to sell the bike."

Like seeing the boat would change his mind? "Good luck on that, Uncle Ray."

"Totally. When the shop opens at ten, I'll drop in and hang out with him." Parker held up one hand like he was taking some kind of Boy Scout pledge. "I won't let him out of my sight."

Maybe a day in the dive shop would cool Harley down enough to start using his head. Angelica left Parker on the T-wharf. She had to get this coffee to her dad. As she walked, she couldn't stop thinking about what had happened the night before. How the attack on the shed had nearly ripped Harley apart. What would he have done if the bike had actually been damaged?

Angelica wanted it to be a random robbery. Done by somebody who didn't know Harley. She wanted to believe the warning sign on the door was all about making whoever was in the shop jumpy so they'd rush out of the store when they got the call about the smoking shed. As if it was all just a diversion set up by some lowlife who wanted to empty the cash register. Maybe the guy went from town to town with the same routine. Pick a shop that looked like an easy mark. Toss the smoke bombs in a shed or car out back. Make a call to the shop.

She'd have slept a lot easier last night if she believed that all of this was just part of a well-planned scheme like that. An elaborate decoy—and that none of it was personal. She wanted that to be the truth. She really did. Then this was already over. The smoke bomb bandit was long gone—planning another heist in some other town.

But that's not what she believed.

Deep down she was convinced that this *was* personal. There was a snake in Eden—with a dark agenda. And if she was right, she had the worst feeling that this wasn't the end of it. Angelica wasn't going to take that lying down. She wasn't about to let somebody mess up her little paradise—or her friends who lived there. She would fight that snake . . . once she figured out who it was.

CHAPTER 8

TAKING THE WINDING ROAD FROM ROCKPORT to Gloucester would have been a dream if Harley were riding on his bike—or on the back of his dad's bike like he used to do, close enough to smell his father's leather jacket. Feeling the cool sea breeze. The heat radiating off the motor. Lost in the heavy bass orchestra of the straight pipes.

But riding with Uncle Ray in the second-hand-smoke-choked cab of his Silverado? Even with the windows down, it was not a great way to start the day.

"I got something to say to you, Harley. Man to man." Uncle Ray crossed the bridge over Blynman Canal on the far end of the Gloucester waterfront. "And I'd like you to listen."

Like he had a choice.

"For a week you've made things pretty clear that you aren't interested in selling your cycle."

Got that right.

"But one thing has changed—and another is about to. So I'm going to give you one last chance."

Harley didn't need to rethink anything. Honestly, if Uncle Ray thought—

"Last night, if things had been just a little different, you could have lost your motorcycle," Uncle Ray said. "You know it, and I know it. Am I right?"

Harley wasn't going to give him the satisfaction of nodding.

"I say someone wanted to send you a message. And you know what that message was?"

Harley just couldn't wait to hear it. "What?"

His uncle gave him the "Laser Ray" stare. "Somebody wants you to know that they can take that bike from you anytime they want. And that somebody wants to make you squirm. What happened in that shed wasn't just a diversion for a robbery. We don't normally have that kind of dough in the register. They got lucky and picked a good day."

Pretty much what Harley was thinking.

"I think the robbery was the diversion—meant to keep the cops focused there instead of on what happened in the shed. That robbery was all about making you know just how easy it is to outmaneuver you. They got you running to the shed. Then they got you running back to the store. You were easy. Mr. Day-late-and-a-dollar-short Harley."

Harley wanted to pull the cigarette dangling from his uncle's lips and shove it up his nose.

"You got an enemy, boy."

"Scorza."

"Maybe. Maybe not. The question is, what are you going to do about it?"

Harley was way ahead of his uncle. He'd pay Scorza a visit. He'd probably be there right now if not for Uncle Ray's little field trip—and Ella practically begging him to wait until Monday. "Have a little talk with him."

"Stupid move." Uncle Ray pulled into the Cape Ann Marina on the south side of Gloucester. "You stay away from him, hear? You rough him up, and we get trouble. I got a business—and since you work there, anything you do will impact that business. Capisce?"

Of course Harley understood. He'd already gone over this, hadn't he?

"There will be a time to deal with that joker. But not now. It's too obvious." Uncle Ray pulled into a handicap parking space and pushed the gearshift into Park. "Look, I'm going to give it to you straight. You know why I'm alive today—and your dad isn't?"

Definitely not because Uncle Ray was a better man. "Cruel twist of fate?"

"Uncle Ray's Rules . . . *number three*."

Harley groaned inside. He should have all the rules on a list. That way Uncle Ray could just point at one of them rather than Harley having to hear them over and over.

"Be the survivor." Uncle Ray took a squinty-eyed drag on the cigarette. Blew it out with a slow nod like he'd just revealed some great cosmic truth. "It's a choice, boy. I watch out for myself—because I learned a long time ago that nobody else will. Your daddy didn't have the mental muscle to be a survivor."

Right now, Harley really just wanted to jump out of the cab, yank open his uncle's door, and serve him a double-decker knuckle sandwich.

"I was fifteen. Just like you. I was out in the park. Your dad was there—with a bunch of his stupid friends. They used to play this half-brained game called 'piggy-pile.' Someone shouts a name, and suddenly everyone chases that kid until they tackle him. And then they pile on. I hated the game."

Why was he telling him this?

Uncle Ray's jaw muscles flexed and released. Flexed and released. "I wasn't the fastest kid in the group. Always a little stocky. My growth spurt hit kind of late. Suddenly I hear 'Let's get Fatso!' You know who said it? Can you guess?"

"No idea."

Uncle Ray took a long pull on the cigarette. "I think you do." His eyes got that squinty look like he was daring the smoke to make his eyes water. "My big brother. Your dad."

Great.

"'Let's turn Fatso into *Flat*so!'" Those were your dad's exact words." He stared at Harley for a moment like he wanted to be sure the words sunk in.

"I ran as fast as my stubby legs could carry me, but those boys took me down at the base of a big rock. There was broken glass everywhere. Someone had probably tossed their empty longnecks against the rock to hear them shatter. I landed on my back—right on the broken glass. Before I could roll onto my stomach and get my arms under me so I could breathe, they were already piling on. I was pinned there—I mean it was like I was staked to the ground—except for my right arm."

He took another drag and blew the smoke out his open window.

"I didn't have enough air in my lungs to say *I. Can't. Breathe.* I beat the guy on top of me with that free hand—but he wasn't moving. I couldn't get any power in my swing. And they kept coming. Right there in that park, I was pretty sure I was going to die." He stared out the windshield like he was reliving the whole thing.

"But you made it."

Uncle Ray locked eyes with Harley. "No thanks to your dad."

"So did they just get off you?"

"Oh, no." His uncle smirked. "No, no, no. There was nobody looking out for poor little Fatso. I needed a rock. Something harder than my fist to get them off me. So I swept the ground with that free hand, frantic like, because I'm thinking I'm not going to last much longer. And I found the neck of one of those busted beer bottles. I gripped that thing knowing I might only get one shot at this—and I'd better get it right." He flicked his Marlboro out the window.

"Did you actually . . . ?" Harley made a stabbing motion like he was holding the broken bottle himself.

"Yeah. I stabbed at everyone within reach. Gave the bottle a little twist each time I connected. Drew blood every time. I was proud of that."

"Sheesh."

"Three of them went in for stiches. I was proud of that too. But they peeled off me quicker than you'd pull off a burning T-shirt. Blood everywhere. And I learned something that you need to hear."

So now Uncle Ray was going to teach him life lessons?

Uncle Ray leaned closer. "You want to be a survivor? Then don't be waiting for somebody to rescue you. You get out in front. You make something happen. The worst moment of my life became my best day ever. You think those boys called me Fatso— or Flatso—after that?"

"Probably not."

"Ray-zer. That's what they called me. Rayzer. Word got around, too. Mess with me, and you're going to get cut. From then on things were different. I did what was best for me. And if life knocked the legs out from under me, I did whatever it took to get back on my feet. To look out for this guy." He drummed his chest with his thumb. "Do you see what I'm trying to tell you?"

Yeah, he got it. "Don't let Scorza get away with this. Give him a good scare."

Uncle Ray looked at him long and hard. "Wrong. Forget about Scorza—or whoever is out to get you. Look, those boys wanted to hurt me. But I didn't let them win. I hurt them back—worse. If they bruised me, I was going to make them bleed."

Which sounded a whole lot like number twelve—or maybe it was thirteen—on the list of Uncle Ray's Rules.

"You gotta go over the top," Uncle Ray said. "I mean way beyond what they'd expect. But you have to be smart and do something that won't come back to bite you."

Which still sounded pretty much like Harley should deck Scorza good.

"Look," Uncle Ray said, "whoever turned that shed into a smokehouse thinks they got you pinned and scared. And maybe they decide they want to scare you some more. What will they do this time? Take a tire iron to your bike?"

Harley pictured Scorza beating dents into Kemosabe. "I'd kill him."

Uncle Ray shook his head. "So you'd let them pin you again, is that it? You have to mess up their plans. Make sure they can never trap you on your back like that again. They think they can get at you by getting at your bike, right?"

It sure seemed that way.

"So do something. Sell the bike. Somebody is using your own bike as a weapon against you. That bike is your weak spot—and they know it. Don't let them do that. Take the weapon away from them. You can't afford a weak spot. Don't allow it. They can't hurt you through your motorcycle if you sell it first. They won't see that coming."

They wouldn't see that coming because it would never happen.

"Invest in the boat, Harley. Make some big bucks, and in a couple years you can buy a new motorcycle if you want. Better than the one you've got."

"There could never be another bike as good."

Uncle Ray waved him off. "You're still missing my point. Invest in the boat. You'll make money—and money is power. Turn your worst day into your best."

The worst day of his life happened three years earlier. And selling the bike would be his worst mistake ever. "Sorry. Not happening."

Uncle Ray shook his head. "I don't think you've heard one thing I've said. Last night *changed* everything. Can't you see that?"

Uncle Ray waited. What? Did he expect Harley to reach under his shirt, pull the lanyard out and hand him Kemosabe's key? Or maybe tell him where he'd hidden the motorcycle's title?

"Do you have any idea what that motorcycle of yours is worth?"

It was priceless—and not for sale. Kemosabe was his ticket away from Uncle Ray, and his one real connection with his dad. It was more than that. Kemosabe *was* him. A huge part of who Harley really was. *Harley Davidson* Lotitto. It was the one thing about him that really mattered.

"You're pinned—and you don't even know it." Uncle Ray looked at him like Harley was something to be scraped off his shoe. "But come on. You need to see this boat up close." He elbowed open the pickup door and led the way down to the docks.

Sailboats. Seriously big cruisers. And an occasional fishing job. Slip after slip of gorgeous boats just begging to be taken out to sea.

"There she is."

A classic Maine lobster boat sat in the still water at dockside, its lines slack. High at the bow, low at the stern. The thing had fresh paint—hull and pilot house. The name *Deep Trouble* was painted across the transom in huge red letters. So this was it. The boat Uncle Ray had been obsessed with. The answer to all his problems. "Thirty-five feet long. Rebuilt Cummins diesel below the deck."

"Beautiful." And Harley meant it.

"Great lines, right? And look at the strength of that bow. This could be an icebreaker."

The beam in front looked massive and strong, like something from the hull of a Viking dragon ship.

"And it's mine." Uncle Ray bobbed his head, smiling the whole time.

Harley stared at him. "You actually bought it?"

"Couldn't miss the chance. And I got the first thirty days on the slip free. *Deep Trouble* belongs to me now."

"How?" Uncle Ray didn't have that kind of money—that was the big reason he'd wanted Harley to sell Kemosabe, right? "I thought the bank wasn't going to give you a loan."

"Those desk jockeys don't know the first thing about diving—or how a dive business operates. They want to see that the business is making big bucks before they give a loan—but if I were making big bucks, I wouldn't need the loan, right?" He laughed at his own joke. "I don't need the bank or their money."

"So how did you afford this?"

"Short-term loan from a short-tempered man." Ray jumped into the boat and strode to the helm. "I wanted you to see *Deep Trouble* for yourself. So you don't turn down my offer before you know what you're investing in."

"Hold on." Harley didn't like the sound of that short-tempered man thing. "You borrowed money from a *loan shark*?"

His uncle leaned back against the helm. "Picture this: We start taking dive charters again. You'll run the shop. I'll be taking the groups out. Hand over fist, baby. We'll be making dough hand over fist."

"So it *was* a loan shark?" Was he crazy?

"I'm a diver." Uncle Ray puffed out his chest a bit. "I know how to handle myself around sharks. Even great whites like Quinn Lochran."

Sheesh. Even he referred to the guy as a man-eater? "Two-legged sharks can be more dangerous than a great white, don't you think?"

Uncle Ray looked annoyed. "The guy is just a businessman, okay? So what if he's not listed with the Better Business Bureau? Everything with the loan was legal."

Harley frowned. "When do you have to pay the money back—and what happens if you're short?"

"Look," Uncle Ray said, "Uncle Ray's Rules, *number two*: I land on my feet. I always do. And I will this time too. I got plenty of time. I've got other ways to get the money, but I gotta know—like right now—if you're in or out. You'd be my silent partner."

Silent? Harley was pretty sure that meant he'd be expected to hand over the money—and then just keep his mouth shut. "I'm out. I was never in."

Uncle Ray shook his head. "My buddies say you look like me. Like you could be my kid or something. But you are all your dad."

"Why do you hate my dad?" The question just spilled out. Harley regretted asking it the moment he said it. But he did hate him, right? How else could he explain why he'd want Harley to sell the one thing that still made him feel connected to his dad? "Was it just the piggy-pile thing? That was it?"

"Fair question." Uncle Ray looked weirdly calm. "Your dad always made me look bad to our *dear* mom and dad."

He'd never met his grandma and grandpa, but his dad had told him stories about them that were so captivating that Harley felt like he did know them. He wished he could have met them.

"He was the *good* boy. Mommy's little lamb. He made me look like the black sheep. Believe me, *that* got old."

He went on to give example after example—and it all sounded so clichéd and "poor me." The more Uncle Ray talked, the more it seemed like he'd been the rebellious one—and if he'd fallen out of favor, it was all his doing.

"You know what I got when my parents died?" Uncle Ray held up a fist. "Nothing."

"And when your dad got his permanent new address at the cemetery, he left a nice trust for you, buddy-boy, but not a thing for his brother."

Which wasn't entirely true. Uncle Ray sold everything of Dad's he could get his hands on. Dad's Wide Glide—the motorcycle he drove when he'd taken Harley for countless rides while they built Kemosabe? Gone. Harley never saw a dime of that money. Uncle Ray might have sold Kemosabe, too, if Harley hadn't kept the key hidden until the lawyer stepped in. Uncle Ray would have gotten the life insurance payout too, if the lawyer hadn't protected Harley's inheritance with a trust fund.

"I built the Rockport Dive Company without help from any of them."

Definitely not true. The Blast Chamber tank refill station, the generator and outbuilding—all of it was from money Uncle Ray basically stole from Harley.

"You and my dad—weren't you ever close?"

Uncle Ray thought for a moment, then smiled. "I remember one time my senior year when we were really close." He held up his thumb and forefinger. "Our faces were about this far apart. Your dad's was turning blue, as I remember. Of course, I had my hands around his throat pretty good. But my dear old dad swooped in and put an end to that. Put an end to a lot of things, really. I left not long after."

The look on Uncle Ray's face said there was a lot more that he wasn't saying.

"I find it kind of ironic," Ray said. "My parents said I was reckless. I was living dangerously." He shrugged. "But here I am. Sole survivor of the Lotitto family."

Harley stared at him. *Sole survivor?* He reached for his wallet and pulled out his Rockport High school ID. "Phew."

Uncle Ray glanced at the ID, then at Harley. "What."

"I just wanted to make sure nothing changed. Last I checked, I was a Lotitto too."

"Yeah, yeah. You know what I meant."

Harley was pretty sure he did. Deep down, Uncle Ray didn't consider him to be family.

"But enough talk about the past," Uncle Ray said. "We have to look to the future." He kissed the tips of two fingers and tapped the hull. "Last chance. You invest, and you get a piece of the profits. You'll get a cut."

About the size of a paper cut, no doubt. "I'm keeping the bike. You'll have to find another 'silent' partner."

Somehow Uncle Ray's face seemed darker. "That bike is gone one way or another. I say we use it before you lose it."

"I'm *not* going to lose it. And I think you ought to get out of this loan while you've still—"

"Not interested in what you think," Uncle Ray said. "By passing up on this investment, you just proved how stupid you are. But you still owe me thirty-five Benjamins for the money missing from the register—and I need it before August 14."

So that was the date the loan was due? Only eight days left? No wonder Uncle Ray had put the full-court press on him all week. "I'll pay you every cent—but it will take months, not days."

"Which is why I got an appointment with the lawyer Monday. There's got to be a way to get money out of your trust fund."

Yeah, and if Uncle Ray was able to tap into the fund, he'd find reasons to keep doing it until the whole thing was gone.

Uncle Ray climbed out of the boat and headed to the pickup. "Gotta make another stop on the way back."

The wind blowing through the open windows was the only sound for the first couple of miles. Harley stole a glance his uncle's way on every left turn—when he was busy watching for traffic and wouldn't see Harley looking. Uncle Ray looked calm. Almost happy. Totally weird for a guy who owed money to a loan shark. If Uncle Ray was late on the payback, if he broke his promise like that, the shark might bust his legs. Harley wasn't sure why he cared, but did his uncle really know what he was getting into?

"Uncle Ray?"

His uncle gave him the Laser Ray.

He wanted to be honest—and careful with his tone. "I get it. You really want that boat. But don't you think it would have been best to wait on *Deep Trouble* . . . for a time when you wouldn't have to go to a loan shark?"

"No-siree-Bob." Uncle Ray didn't hesitate. Like he had absolutely no doubts. No second thoughts. "Wimps want things they never get. Uncle Ray's Rules, *number eight*: If you see something you want . . . take it."

"Not earn it?"

Uncle Ray laughed. "Taking it *is* earning it, boy. Remember that." He pulled into the liquor mart's parking lot. "Back in five."

Harley tagged along. Not that he wanted to be with Uncle Ray—or that his feelings about alcohol had changed. But it was a chance to do something good. He wandered the aisles, dropping back to put more distance between him and his uncle. What had the driver been drinking before crossing the centerline and hitting his dad's Ford? He picked up a bottle of vodka. Checked to be sure no employee was within sight . . . and let the bottle slip from his fingers. It crashed to the floor. "Oops."

The owner—or the manager—hustled toward him with one of those yellow *Piso Mojado* signs. He set up the folding, double-faced caution sign with one hand like this was a routine thing in the store. "You okay, son?"

Harley nodded—wearing his Mr. Innocent face. "I-I think so."

"Careful. Glass everywhere. I don't want anyone getting hurt."

Which is exactly why Harley dropped the bottle of hard liquor in the first place. *That* vodka wasn't going to hurt anybody now. It could never wreck a family.

"Accidents happen," the man said.

"Yeah, they do." But that particular bottle would never lead to a *car* accident. Harley felt just a tiny bit of pride in that. He pictured a Lockheed-Martin F-22 Raptor with painted insignias lining the fuselage around the cockpit for every enemy kill. Harley wasn't flying a fighter jet, but he did keep a tally of liquor bottles he'd taken out in his one-man war against alcohol. He had rows and rows of neatly drawn bottles on one of the walls inside his shed. And he'd add another hashmark when he got home today. With all the times he'd let a bottle slip, nobody ever figured out just how deliberate the accidents were. "Can I help you clean up?"

The man waved him off. "I got it."

Harley backed away and made his way back out to the truck. He leaned against the grill of the Silverado, staring at the liquor mart. He'd love ten minutes alone in the place. But for now, he'd have to settle for isolated, strategic kills. And there would absolutely be a next time.

Uncle Ray didn't say a word about the broken bottle. But he ranted about Kemosabe most of the way back to the shop. "You better hope that enemy of yours got all the payback on you that he wanted. Because if he didn't, he'll be back. Then what are you going to do, huh?"

"Scorza won't try it again."

That got Uncle Ray's attention. "You let the cops deal with this. You go after Scorza and you'll mess everything up."

Harley wasn't so sure things could get worse. And there wasn't time to wait for the police to figure things out. Harley knew who did this—and he'd have to take care of it. And if Uncle Ray was right about Scorza trying to damage Kemosabe again, Harley had to act fast.

Decision made. *Sorry, Ella, but I gotta deal with Scorza long before Monday.* And he'd take care of him after work tonight.

CHAPTER 9

Saturday, August 6, 5:30 p.m.

"HURRY, DAD." But there was no way they were going to make time going through Rockport on a Saturday while most of the shops were still open. Tourists crept along in their cars, craning their necks to take in the sights and look for parking spaces all at the same time. "He suckered me into going to Roy Moore's for change. When I came back—he'd closed up early and was gone. I still can't believe it."

"Sounds like he knew exactly what you were trying to do," Dad said.

"Totally." And Parker was pretty sure Harley was going to do something they'd all regret. Parker kept his eyes peeled for his friend. Harley would have taken 127 toward Gloucester—and Scorza's house. Part of him wished he'd hopped on his bike and given chase instead of asking Dad to drive him. At least he'd feel like he was physically doing something to catch Harley—and stop him from doing something stupid.

"How much of a lead does he have on us?"

Parker checked the apology text again. "I'm sure he was already on his way before he sent this. Maybe fifteen minutes. Twenty." It was too much time.

"Read me what he said—exactly."

Parker scrolled back.

"'Parks . . . sorry to ditch you. I texted Scorza. Denying everything. Stinkin' liar! I'm stopping by his house to make sure he doesn't come near Kemosabe again.'"

Dad nodded. Eyes on the road. "How far will Harley take this?"

"Farther than he thinks he will—which is what has me worried. Scorza will taunt him, push him until he takes a swing—or worse. Harley's going to get himself in trouble."

"And then Scorza's dad will file a complaint and the law gets involved."

Okay, Dad got it. "And honestly, Harley's on thin ice with his uncle. If Harley gets hauled in, you think his dear Uncle Ray will bail him out? Sometimes I think that guy is looking for an excuse to get rid of Harley."

They cleared the town limits, and Dad mashed the accelerator.

Parker strained to look ahead. Even after rounding the bend at Calvary Cemetery there was still no sign of Harley.

"Does he know you're coming after him?"

"Pretty sure he does. But he'd figure I'll be on my bike."

"So," Dad said. "He doesn't know you've told me anything."

Parker shook his head. But Harley would figure it out in a big fat hurry when he saw them drive up. Parker leaned forward just a bit. Searched the road ahead, practically willing himself to see Harley pedaling like crazy.

Dad reached over and gave Parker's knee a squeeze. "We'll find him."

Yeah, they would. But would they find him before he made a mess of everything?

CHAPTER 10

HARLEY'S LEGS BURNED FROM PUMPING so hard on the pedals, but it was nothing compared to the angry fire burning deep in his gut. Scorza stood on the driveway of their rented home wearing his number eight jersey and hosing down his Jeep Wrangler. The moment he saw Harley wheel into the driveway, a way-too-confident smirk creased his face.

"Harley Lotitto." Scorza dropped the hose and set his hands on his hips. "Come to see what my dad bought me?"

Orange body. Oversize tires. Spare tire mounted on the tailgate, wrapped in a new-looking cover with one of those Jeepy slogans written across it: *Don't follow me. I won't stop when you get stuck.*

Harley almost laughed at the idea. Harley would never follow Scorza anywhere. Not ever again. "I came to see *you*, barf bag. Not your Wrangler."

"It's a 2004," Scorza said. "Needs a little work, but my *dad* and I will have plenty of time to work on it before I'll have my license."

Already Scorza hit him with the dad-jab? In Harley's book, Scorza officially took the first swing. Harley was going to smack that smile off Scorza's face so hard, it wouldn't land for blocks. "You did it, right? Busted the window. Tossed in the smoke bombs."

Scorza shrugged. "Why? Because my best friend deserted me for a group of loser friends? Pretty weak motive."

"You stay away from Kemosabe."

If someone were watching from inside, Scorza would probably come off as being downright friendly. A regular sweet-tea kind of polite.

"You did it. Admit it."

Scorza had that smirk thing down to a science. "Unlike you, I'll get a football scholarship. If I get caught messing with your stupid motorcycle, I could lose that. Not worth the risk. And that antique probably won't even be running by the time you get your license."

Was he just trying to get Harley to take a swing at him? To jump the line of scrimmage early? Sometimes in a game an opponent would trash-talk him from the other side of the line. There were some who just had the ability to get through Harley's helmet and pads with their words. Their talk would penetrate all the way to a vault hidden deep inside him. The rage cage. And if Harley opened the door? The instant the center snapped the ball, that big-mouthed player would get a hit that would rattle his teeth—and shatter his nerve.

Scorza definitely had the gift of getting through—and had a set of keys to Harley's cage, it seemed. *Keep the cage locked, Harley. Keep it. Locked.*

"You stay away from my shed." Did the drapes move? Harley glanced at the windows again. "You know what I can do."

"Sounds like the *rage* is slipping out of the *cage*," Scorza said. "Better be careful, my friend."

"I am *not* your friend. And you're the one who needs to watch himself. If I even see you near that shed, I'll—"

"Do what?" Scorza didn't make any aggressive gestures. Didn't get in Harley's face. Had an almost eerie calm thing going on. "You come to my house—and get up in my face with your big talk. But you can't back it up, Lottie."

His annoying nickname for Harley since the rift between them grew to canyon size. But he wasn't about to show how it bothered him. "I'm giving you fair warning."

Scorza laughed. "You don't dare touch me. You know it—and I know it. You're running scared, Lottie."

"Me? Scared of you?"

"Oh yeah. Because you know in the middle of the night—when you're riding the sleepy town train and dreaming about Black Beauty—someone just might walk by your shed and start a *real* fire. That shed would go up in minutes. Bye-bye, Kemosabe."

Was Harley shaking? "Shut. Up."

"Yeah, all that work you did with your Daddy. Poof! Up in smoke."

Harley stepped into Scorza. Chest-bumped him. Hard.

Scorza raised both hands like he was totally innocent. "I don't want any trouble."

"Then you stay away—or I'm going to rip off your scholarship passing arm and beat you over the head with it."

The screen door burst open and Scorza's dad strode out of the house. Big guy—like he used to play for the NFL back in his day.

"I've heard just about enough." He glared at Harley. "Back off,

Lotitto. You heard my boy. If he says he didn't touch your motor-cycle, he didn't touch it. He's never lied to me."

His dad had no idea of half the things Scorza did.

An F-150 pickup roared up to the curb and the passenger door flew open. Parker? And his dad at the wheel. What? Parker told his dad where Harley was going? The two hustled toward them.

"You stay away from my boy," Mr. Scorza said—loud enough for even Mr. Buckman and Parks to hear.

"If he comes near my bike again," Harley said, just as Mr. Buckman and Parker chugged to a stop, "I'll make him live to regret it. I promise you that."

"You just threatened my son," Mr. Scorza said. "And you"—he pointed at Parker and his dad—"are my witnesses."

What?

Mr. Buckman put a hand on Harley's shoulder. "We should go."

"Not until Scorza admits he did this."

"Harley," Parker's dad said. "C'mon. Let's back away and talk about it."

Parker's dad was messing where he didn't belong. Harley gave Parker the side-eye. How could he snitch and get his dad involved?

"I know you did it." He stepped closer to Number 8, but Mr. Buckman held him back by the shoulders. Harley knew he was making a mistake—but he couldn't stop himself. "And you're going to admit it if I have to beat it out of you."

"That would be assault," Mr. Scorza said. He positioned him-self between his son and Harley. "Go. You're trespassing. Leave, now."

Harley strained to lock eyes with Scorza. "You even get close to that shed, and you'll wish you hadn't."

"More threats," Mr. Scorza said. Bryce leaned around his dad and smiled.

That was it. Harley broke free from Mr. Buckman's grip and plowed ahead. Mr. Scorza stepped into Harley, and they collided. Not real hard—but Mr. Scorza stumbled backward in a totally exaggerated way, like NBA players hoping to get a foul called on their opponent. "He hit me. You all are witnesses. That's battery!"

Parker's dad had Harley by the shoulders again, but with one arm across Harley's chest, pulling him back. "Easy, Harley." He spoke close to his ear. "They're baiting you. Walk away." But Harley couldn't look weak. Wouldn't that just be inviting Scorza to try again? His threat had to look real.

A police siren sounded—and close. Who'd called them? Parker already betrayed him by bringing his dad here. Did he call the police too?

Harley was still struggling against Mr. Buckman, but his heart wasn't in it.

The Gloucester cop strode up the lawn.

"Officer!" Mr. Scorza shouted. "This young man is trespassing. He threatened my son multiple times—and just attacked me. I want to file a complaint—and a restraining order."

Attacked? Restraining order? "I only—"

The cop grabbed Harley and had him up against the Wrangler. "Hands where I can see them. Now."

Harley obeyed. "This is crazy."

The cop pulled one of Harley's arms down. Cracked his wrist with a steel cuff. The loop swung around and ratcheted in place. "Now the other one." Harley lowered his other hand and the cop snugged both wrists good.

"I'm going to lead you to the car, and we're going to have a little talk." He spun Harley to face him and pointed at Mr. Buckman. "This your dad?"

Harley shook his head. "I don't have a dad." He shot a look at Parker. The guy he'd thought was his friend looked guilty as sin. He'd betrayed him—and he knew it.

"Got somebody I should call?"

Harley looked away from Parker. Kept his eyes on the cop's combat boots. "I got nobody. I'm on my own."

CHAPTER 11

RAY PULLED INTO A PARKING SLIP at the Cape Ann Marina fifteen minutes early. His feet automatically led him to the slip where *Deep Trouble* was securely tied with brand-new dock lines.

Mr. Lochran had requested the meeting—which did nothing to set Ray at ease. The loan wasn't due for eight days, so why the face-to-face? But Ray would show him he was on top of things. It was all good.

He had a good view of a huge chunk of the marina from here. It was easy to see if anybody was within earshot. Totally out in the open—and uniquely isolated. No wonder Lochran picked this spot to meet.

Lochran strode down the dock precisely on time. A big man. Massive shoulders. Arms like a tuna fisherman. And he could probably squeeze open a can of tuna with his bare hands, too. A man followed maybe twenty feet behind him. Wiry. Six inches shorter than Lochran, at least. But the guy was no lightweight. Weird that Lochran had a bodyguard smaller than he was. But something about the way Wiry-guy carried himself said he had ways of getting the job done other than sheer size and muscle. Right now, though, Ray needed to keep his head in the game. Ray stood to climb out of the boat as Lochran approached.

"You just got the boat. You need to enjoy every minute. Stay aboard." Lochran motioned him away from the gunwale and stood above him, leaning on a post. "I make it a habit to pay first-time customers a visit one week away from their deadline."

Did he emphasize the word *dead*—or was Ray imagining it?

"Any questions you have for me? Anything you need clarified?"

Ray shook his head. "I pay you one week from tomorrow. I'm good."

Lochran smiled. All mouth and teeth. The eyes didn't carry even a hint of friendliness. "You're *good*. Splendid. I must have gotten some bad information."

Ray didn't want to know. Didn't want to ask. But there was something about those eyes—like he was expected to ask the obvious. "Bad?"

Lochran nodded. "About that motorcycle that you practically had sold. What I heard? You don't even have it for sale yet. And you can't, because you don't have possession of it. A little technicality you failed to mention earlier."

Ray held up both hands. He did not like the way this was going. "Let me explain. I—"

"Ironically enough," Lochran said, "those three words are often the last words from the lips of men who have disappointed me. '*Let me explain.*'" Lochran put a mocking little quiver in his voice. "I can explain."

Lochran towered over him from where he stood on the dock. Likely a deliberate power move on his part. "If you have to explain *anything* to me, Mr. Lotitto, don't try to make off like everything is *good*."

Ray had no idea how the guy knew what he knew, but right now landing on his feet meant being totally honest with the guy. He gave him a version short enough to fit on an index card.

Lochran listened without interruption, his head nodding slightly like he was doing an inventory of the facts—and making sure nothing was missing.

"I wouldn't have borrowed the money from you without a solid backup plan—and a backup for the backup." He hoped he sounded positive enough without going all pie-in-the-sky on him. The truth was, Plan B was going to be dicey. And his Plan C would mean tapping the kid's trust fund. Both B and C would be a lot trickier to pull off than he'd thought his Plan A was. If only the stupid kid would have just agreed to sell the bike, Ray wouldn't need his backup plans at all.

"So, you'll have the motorcycle in your possession . . ."

"Tomorrow night. Guaranteed."

"Guaranteed, or you'll give me my money back, is that it?"

For some reason that struck Ray as funny. He tried to hide his smile, but honestly, the money-back guarantee comment was kind of hilarious coming from a loan shark. "You'll get your money back."

"I always do. With interest. Guaranteed." Lochran looked at him long and hard.

Ray looked back, just as hard. What was this, a staring contest or something? Ray's survival instincts warned him not to look away. Not to blink. It felt like his eyes were beginning to water, for Pete's sake.

Lochran seemed to be measuring him up. "I'll need to verify."

Good. Then he'd see Ray was the kind of guy who meant what he said. "A photo?"

Lochran shook his head. "In person. I'll be in touch—or my associate, Mike Ironwing." He pointed to the wiry guy.

Great name for a bodyguard. "You won't be disappointed." He'd wanted to sound confident, but there was a fine line between that and cocky. Had he crossed the line?

The guy stood there for a moment. "You know, Mr. Lotitto, I'm beginning to get a bad feeling about all this."

He wanted to say something to assure him, but he couldn't seem to think of anything. And the truth? He agreed with Lochran on that point. Ray was beginning to get a really bad feeling too.

CHAPTER 12

Saturday, August 6, 10:15 p.m.

ELLA WAS GOING TO MISS JELLY after her dad got their new home finished. Especially the talks deep into the night. The extra twin bed in her room just wouldn't look right without Jelly lying there in some crazy position. Right now, Jelly's back was on the mattress and her legs rested on the wall above her headboard in a perfect right angle. A string of multicolored lights around her bedroom window—her way of bringing a little Christmas into her room all year round—washed Jelly in a Candy Land of colors.

Parker had told them more about the fiasco between Harley and Scorza. That was bad enough—especially with the threat of a restraining order. But it was the rift between Harley and Parker that had Ella worried. "Do you think maybe Parker was exaggerating—or that he read Harley wrong?"

"I asked Parker that very question." Jelly bent her knees and let her feet walk up the wall above the headboard and back down. "He's afraid it's *worse* than he thinks. He's texted Harley like five times. No response."

Ella groaned. "I thought guys were supposed to get over stuff like this real quick." And they probably would have, if Harley wasn't wound up so tight on this. "Think they'll be okay?" That was the big question, right? Ella loved the four of them together. She couldn't imagine it being just three.

"Parker knows how to be a good friend," Jelly said. "He'll figure something out. But having said that . . ."

Ella waited as long as she could. "What?"

"I was just thinking, there's no reason why we can't help."

"Any ideas?"

"Get Grams to bake up a Blueberry Ghost Pie. Invite the boys over. Get them talking again."

It was definitely worth a shot. After all, who could resist the magic of Grams's Blueberry Ghost Pie?

She stared at the lights. Listened to the sound of the surf pounding the Headlands. "Ever stop to think how many things have happened since that sign showed up at the dive shop yesterday?"

Jelly was quiet for a moment. "The smoke bombs."

Which thankfully did no lasting damage. The two of them had been able to clean up her paintings and bring them back to her room.

"The missing money."

Right again. And the massive tension between Harley and his Uncle Ray over that—and the fact that they were at an absolute impasse on the whole "sell the bike and invest in the boat" scheme. Uncle Ray had asked the unthinkable of Harley and just wouldn't leave Harley alone about his "stupid" decision.

"Then there was Harley's ill-advised visit to Bryce Scorza's house."

"Which," Ella said, "ended with a trip to the police station and the promise of a restraining order."

"And the wall building between Parker and Harley—something we sure didn't see coming."

Ella agreed. "*Your world is about to change.* That's what the sign said, right?"

"Kinda spooky when you see how it's actually coming true," Jelly said. "And so fast."

Too fast. Things were changing with no warning. No chance to get out in front of it—or out of the way. They were getting steamrolled by the change. "Grams fears it's some kind of curse." Actually, Ella believed that may be a bigger part of the weirdness than they thought. "The words did appear to be in blood, right?"

"I saw some strange things happen in the Everglades," Jelly said. "There was a time I absolutely believed that curses were real—and powerful."

For the next hour Jelly told her all about her experiences in the Glades. About Wilson, who was almost as good at getting them out of danger as he was at getting them into it. Ella learned so much more about the Everglades Curse than she had from Parker. They talked about her sister, Maria—and all that had gone on with Clayton Kingman. They talked about Parker's choices, and how he put himself in harm's way to help his friends. She filled in so many details that Parker had left unsaid. Ella actually squealed with delight when Jelly told how she'd tried to sabotage Parker's plans.

The more they talked, the closer Ella felt they were in their beliefs—or maybe superstitions. They talked about the reality of demons, the evil of man, and the power of God. Jelly seemed to know more about God than Ella did, but still, it was nothing close to where Parker was at.

It was well after midnight and the conversation still showed no signs of slowing. Honestly, Ella was pretty sure they could talk all night.

The conversation came full circle—and they were back to Harley.

"He's got to be feeling so alone," Ella said. "I'm afraid he's pulling away."

Jelly agreed. "Somehow we have to get those boys back together."

And soon. Because right now the world was changing for all four of them—and Ella didn't like the direction it was going.

"I have the worst feeling," Ella said. "If we don't get things back to the way they should be—and soon . . ." She hesitated, knowing she shouldn't even say the words out loud. It was bad luck.

Jelly looked at her, eyes wide in agreement. "You don't have to say any more."

She was the sister Ella never had. A soul sister. They could even read each other's thoughts, it seemed. And clearly, they were on the same page. If they didn't get things back to the way they should be soon, they never would.

CHAPTER 13

RAY WATCHED THE KID BALL UP HIS BLANKET around his pillow and march down the stairs. He fell in line right behind him. "I told you to stay away from Scorza. And what did you do? The opposite."

The kid did the hard-of-hearing act.

"You get dumber by the day," Ray said. "You know that?"

Harley still didn't answer. He maneuvered around the dive shop displays, past the Blast Chamber, and unlocked the back door.

"I give you a chance to invest in the future—you turn it down. If that wasn't stupid enough, you get yourself hauled in by the police and put your entire future at risk."

The kid didn't even give him enough respect to look him in the eye. "My future is in that shed."

The problem was, it was Ray's future too. "Your ship finally came in, and you won't get on board."

84

"Oh well." The kid made a screwball face. "Guess I missed the boat."

"You mocking me, boy?" It was all he could do to keep from smacking the goofy expression off the punk's face. All in good time. "You trying to make me look like an idiot?"

Harley shook his head and pulled open the door. "You do that just fine without any help from me." He was out the door, then ducked his head back inside. "But . . . thanks for bringing me home from the police station. G'night." He slammed the door, and that was that.

Ray threw the dead bolt in place. *Fine.* The kid could stay out there for all he cared. He took a deep breath. The kid had blocked Ray's way to a better future every chance he got, hadn't he? But no more. *No stinkin' more.*

So, the smoke bombs hadn't been enough to get the job done. Lesson learned. He wouldn't have that problem with the next phase of his plan. And everything was in place. He'd pulled in the favors and put together a crew. Jack Kelsey was more than capable. And Vinny Torino? He was just the kind of guy you wanted in your corner in a clutch situation.

Everything was falling into place. Even the incident with Harley and the Scorza punk. Ray couldn't have asked for a better launch ramp for his meeting with the lawyer Monday morning. He'd show how his nephew was off the rails. A liability. There had to be some kind of loophole in that trust fund to pull out money for a legal fee fund. Hello, Plan C. In less than forty-eight hours he'd have the motorcycle—and his hand in the trust fund. He'd sell the bike fast. And maybe—no, absolutely—he'd get the money for the loan and pay it off early.

When was the last time Lochran had somebody pay back a loan

before the deadline? Ray would probably be the first. The loan shark would pick up some healthy respect for Ray, that was for sure. There'd be no standing on the dock over him anymore. He'd look Ray eye-to-eye after that. Ray's Rules *number fifteen*: *Don't let anyone disrespect you.* And Lochran was getting dangerously close to doing exactly that.

Ray stepped to the paned window and looked out over Rockport Harbor, then zeroed in on the shed. He had Plans B and C rolling simultaneously. He'd get the money he needed, and then some. "Sleep tight, kid. Keep that bike safe now." Ray chuckled at the thought. "If you can."

CHAPTER 14

BRYCE SHOULD HAVE BEEN in bed an hour ago, but he still felt too juiced up to sleep. The look on Harley's face when the cops hauled him away kept popping into his head. Was Harley in the police station right now? Was he spending the night? The way Bryce saw it, Harley Lotitto deserved everything he got. He'd walked right into it. Came angry and ready to do a little damage. But the joke of it all was that Harley was the only one who got hurt. He'd done it to himself.

Bryce peeled off his jersey and hung it on the hook behind his bedroom door. "Who's the barf bag now, Lottie?" He flopped onto his bed. Stared at the blackness of the ceiling. Just a few months ago Harley was his wingman. Bryce would tell him how far to run, and where to make a cut, and he'd do it.

Summer football camp had been a disaster. Sure, Bryce gave Harley a hard time. Threw the passes low, high, or way too close to a defender. He sure didn't make things easy on Harley. The problem was, Harley still made most of the catches. When he got slammed down on his hip pads he got right back up. It was like he was making the catches, not to make Bryce look good, but to spite him somehow. Every time Bryce gave him a sloppy handoff, the guy carried the ball like they were in a championship game instead of football camp.

A quarterback needed complete loyalty from his team. And clearly Lotitto found ways to undermine Bryce. When he called a play, Lotitto would roll his eyes. Grunt. And he never clapped as the huddle broke. It didn't take long for others to follow his lead.

But just hours ago he'd taught Lotitto that his attempted mutiny came with a price. Harley had looked like an out-of-control hothead to Gatorade and his dad . . . and definitely to the cop. Bryce wasn't done with Harley, either. He'd push him—and Bryce knew exactly where his ex-best friend's weak spots were. For some unexplainable reason, Black Beauty was one of them. Kemosabe was the other. And the motorcycle was where he'd focus. He'd send a message that Harley would know was from him—but could never prove.

If Harley reacted by breaking the restraining order, he'd get himself in a world of trouble. He might even be barred from team try-outs. He'd be doing community service instead. That would stop Harley from eroding team loyalty when football started.

But if Bryce did this right, Harley would realize soon enough that he couldn't win. He'd wave the white flag. Yeah, Harley would bury the hatchet and call for a truce. Then they could get back to where they were before. Bryce calling the plays—and Harley running them.

Harley was trapped. He could fight back or surrender—it really didn't matter. Either way, Bryce would get the MVP status he deserved.

Bryce had an idea of something he could do to Lotitto—in less than twenty-four hours. It was simple. It was reckless. And definitely a little crazy. But it would send a clear message. Bryce would land on his feet with this one . . . and he'd have Harley on his knees.

CHAPTER 15

PARKER STOOD ON THE DOCK, searching the T-wharf for a sign of his friends. While he watched, he prayed.

He'd sat with his mom and dad in church earlier that morning. But he just couldn't track with the sermon. His mind was on the way things had unraveled with Harley at Scorza's place. The way Harley had looked at him—like his friend had sold him out.

Anybody in the congregation who'd glanced his way probably had thought Parker was taking notes on the sermon like crazy. Not this time. He'd needed to talk to God—about a lot of things. And he did that best on paper.

He hadn't known Harley as his friend for all that long. But still, Parker had never seen him like this—and things weren't getting any better. Harley hadn't answered one text since the cop escorted him to the police car.

Harley was in some kind of invisible vise. Pressure from his uncle. From Scorza. And now the police. Personally, Parker had long ago come to believe Harley was naturally self-destructive. Without God in his own life, Parker would likely mess things up royally. And Harley didn't have God to lean on, look to, or learn from. Right now, he was pretty much on his own . . . and with the anger brewing inside, he was his own worst enemy. Parker had to patch things up with Harley. How else would he be able to truly help his friend?

God, throw me a lifeline here. Harley needs your help—and he doesn't even know it. Show me what to do, because I'm fresh out of ideas.

He was still writing when the sermon ended. He'd slipped his prayer into his Bible and scanned the congregation one more time for Jelly and Ella. Maybe they'd slept in. Again.

Mom had put her arm around him. "Why don't you see if the girls want to go out in the *Boy's Bomb* after lunch? Maybe Harley will go with you."

Had she been reading his mind—or his prayers? She smiled but didn't offer any explanation. And it didn't matter. Her idea sounded pretty good.

He sent out a group text:

I'm running out to Dry Salvages in the *Boy's Bomb*. Anyone else want to go? Jelly, you've been wanting pictures of the seals, right? I'll bring donuts from BayView Brew. Meet at the T-wharf. 3:00 p.m.

The girls had responded immediately. No surprise there. Jelly had been bugging him about going out to the Dry Salvages ever since she'd come to town. But it was, what, a good three miles outside the safety of Rockport Harbor? He'd need really, really calm seas to handle that trip with the little, 40-horsepower Mercury engine on the back of the *Boy's Bomb*.

Honestly? Leaving the safety of the harbor—and going that far from shore in the *Bomb*—was always dicey. But the seas seemed flat. The weather report looked steady. And the risk was worth the reward if Harley showed up.

Parker checked his phone again. Harley still hadn't responded in the almost three hours since he'd sent the text. Not even an emoji. *God, please. Please.*

He saw Jelly first. Walking the granite block edge overlooking the South Basin of the harbor. Cargo shorts. Oversize orange tour-guide-type fishing shirt. His, actually . . . the one he'd worn that day on Gator Hook Trail when he lived down in the Everglades. Sleeves rolled up and buttoned in place. She had a pack—likely filled with camera gear.

Ella walked beside her. Gypsy dress. Cowgirl boots. Laughing at something Jelly had said.

Parker smiled at the girls. *God, now bring Harley.*

Ella kicked off her boots the moment she got in the boat.

"Is he coming?" Jelly kept her voice down. "Have you heard anything?"

Parker checked his phone again. "Let's give him five more minutes." *Or ten.*

Ella slipped her boots back on. "I don't think he'll come without a little in-person push. Jelly? Let's go get him."

He liked that idea. "I'll wait here a few minutes before driving over—just in case he shows."

Jelly and Ella trotted up the ramp and disappeared.

Parker made sure the spare gas tank was full and all four life jackets were exactly where he'd kept them stowed. Double-checked the anchor and line. He checked under the seat. Flare gun. Mask. Snorkel. Fins. Dive knife. First aid kit. Extra transom plugs. Spare ignition key.

He fired up the motor. Untied the lines and coiled, looped, and hung them inside the boat from the cleats. He cruised slowly past the other slips, the yacht club, and swung wide around Eric and Maggie. The harbormasters were docking their newest boat, *Alert 1*. It was black with red and white accents.

The 25-foot Safe Boat was clearly built to handle rough weather. Self-draining decks. A 150-gallon gas tank. Twin 250 motors on the transom. The collar around the boat made it look unsinkable. Gunwale rails so strong that he doubted King Kong could rip them free. There were even decent cutouts in the gunwales for quick boarding—and to make it easier to pull aboard survivors from the water.

The thing had an aluminum center console built like Fort Knox—complete with a safety glass windshield and side windows. The console roof bristled with UHF and VHF radio antennas, a radar pod, search light, emergency lights, and a tow spool with who knew how many feet of cable. There were probably a couple of surface-to-air missiles tucked in there somewhere too. The best thing on the roof was the infrared camera—giving them the ability to see right through the fog.

"Eric . . . Maggie," Parker called. "That thing is gorgeous."

Maggie smiled and pointed ahead. "Eyes on the road, captain."

Parker made a quick course correction to keep from hitting a buoy. "I want a ride sometime."

"Too calm today," Eric said. "Pick a day when we can really have some fun."

Parker saluted. He'd definitely like that.

Maggie waved back. "Be safe out there, Parker."

Exactly what he planned to do. He tooled around the front of the T-wharf and the floating dock.

He spotted the girls right away, talking with Harley outside his shed. Ella's hands were moving as quickly as she talked, although Parker couldn't hear a word she was saying. She was definitely giving her best sales pitch. Harley's head was down. Hands jammed in his back pockets. It didn't look like he was planning to go anywhere.

Parker hit the horn and motioned for him to join them. It was worth a shot, right? Suddenly Ella grabbed one of Harley's arms—and Jelly the other. They tugged and pulled. He took a step, then another. Seconds later he was all in, jogging with them toward the nearest ladder leading down to a floating dock. Parker had the *Boy's Bomb* pulled up by the time they got there.

Within minutes they passed through the narrow channel between the breakwater off Bearskin Neck and the base of the Headlands.

The girls kept the conversation going—but there was probably more screaming and laughing from the spray than anything. Harley glanced his way more than once with a look Parker couldn't quite read. But he was on board—and that was something.

Even the flattest-looking ocean has waves. A deep pulse. Parker felt the slight rise and fall of the bow. The farther from the harbor they drove, the smaller the boat seemed to get. And lower to the water, too.

The word *islands* made the Salvages seem bigger than they were. They were more like two massive heaps of huge rocks—but out in the Atlantic, miles from shore. Little Salvages came first.

It wasn't just smaller than the other, but it was shorter, too. In low tide the cluster of black rocks hunkered low in the water—a haven for gulls and seals. In high tide, Little Salvages ducked underwater completely—but not by much. It held its breath, waiting to rip the hull wide open on an unsuspecting fishing boat or yacht. An old minesweeper had met its doom there. It was a wreck that Parker intended to explore—hopefully soon . . . and with Harley.

Dry Salvages kept its head above water even in high tide—which was probably how it got its name. And the island was bigger all around—but still there wasn't a tree or plant on either one of them. No beach to make an easy landing, either. How the seals got up there was a wonder.

Parker steered into the waters that separated the two islands and dropped anchor. The water was slightly calmer between the two. And Parker had no desire to push his luck by going on the open ocean side of the Dry Salvages.

The seals were out in droves. "We can't stay long," Parker said. Too much could change this far from shore. And if the seas got heavy, there'd be no getting back to the harbor quick. Not with the *Bomb* being at full weight capacity and powered only by the little 40-horse motor.

Harley stood and scanned the surface. Parker had a pretty good idea what he was on the lookout for.

"This is perfect." Jelly was already pulling her camera from the pack. "I'll get some great shots. And Harley . . . if you see a great white, let me know. I'd love to get a picture."

He gave her a half smile. "They're out here, you know. Some divers say the great whites stay over by Cape Cod because of all the seals there. Thirty or forty miles from here."

Parker wished that were true. But Eric and Maggie had set him straight on that one.

"But the way the seal population is growing out here at the Salvages," Harley said, "they'll be coming here for snacks."

That's right, Parker thought. *What's thirty miles to a great white?* Eric and Maggie had told him that nearby shark-detecting buoys had reported tagged great whites in the area.

"Wouldn't that be something if one came here to feed while I had my camera?" Jelly scanned the water like she might see a dorsal fin. "I would get some crazy-good shots."

"Crazy," Parker said. "I agree with that much." An average great white would be longer than the *Boy's Bomb*. A terrifying mind-picture. Especially when he thought about how thin the fiberglass hull really was.

Harley didn't say a word. With the motor off, things felt even more awkward between them. Parker had to patch things up between them . . . but how? With every minute that passed, it would only get harder.

"What would you do," Parker said, "if we were diving right here, and the shadow of a great white passed overhead?"

Harley looked at him for a long moment. "I'd warn my friend what was coming if I thought he didn't see it."

Parker felt like someone had tied a dock line around his stomach and cinched it tight.

"And I'd stick with my friend until we both got in the boat safely."

Okay, so it was time to talk about it. "I texted," Parker said. "I told you not to talk to Scorza. Told you I was coming."

"You didn't mention your dad would be there—and that you'd be bringing the cops."

"You think *we* brought the police?" Parker shook his head. "I was just as surprised as you were."

Harley nodded like he believed him. "I guess Mr. Scorza didn't waste any time."

"I'm really sorry for how it all turned out," Parker said. And it was the truth. How could he make Harley understand he'd been trying to keep him from hurting himself? Parker was pretty sure he couldn't. Not yet, anyway.

Harley shrugged. "Scorza deserves everything he got—and a whole lot more."

"You still believe he's the smoke-bomber?"

He gave a slight nod. "Oh, yeah. It was him."

Harley just wasn't seeing the whole picture. And this was the wrong time to argue with him. What Parker needed to do was meet Harley where he was at. "So, what's next?"

"Nothing. I have to stay away from him—the restraining order is for real." Harley looked over at Dry Salvages—but not like he was really seeing it. "And Mr. Barf Bag better stay away from me."

The way Parker saw it, Harley was a finisher. He may not start things, but he definitely knew how to finish them. Trouble was, he was liable to finish himself in the process.

"Well," Ella said, "you get yourself in more trouble with Scorza, and you're going to have to deal with Jelly and me." She made a fist. "Believe me, you don't need that kind of trouble. We're way scarier than a restraining order."

Harley raised both hands in mock terror. "I'll be good."

The laugh did them all good.

"My uncle thinks I'm an idiot for passing up the chance to buy in on his new dive charter boat, *Deep Trouble*." There was something about the way he said it. He didn't ask what any of them thought, but he was fishing, wasn't he?

"You sell that bike, buster," Ella had her fists up again, "and you better lace up your running shoes. You promised me a ride on that when you get your license."

"Honestly," Harley said, "that is the *only* reason I'm holding out." He dropped his head to hide his smile. "I just can't get Uncle Ray to understand how important it is for *you* to get that ride."

Ella slugged him in the arm. "Keep it up, Harley. I could slug your arm all day. I'll tattoo your arm with bruises."

"So," Harley said, "if I change my mind and buy into *Deep Trouble* with my Uncle Ray, I'll be in deep trouble with you. Is that it?"

"Precisely." Ella raised her chin slightly. "Your choice, Mr. Lotitto. Do you want to be in deep trouble with your uncle—or with me?"

Harley laughed. "No contest. You're a lot scarier than he is."

He earned another slug on the arm for that one. But it seemed to loosen him up even more. He told of how things were heating up between him and his uncle. About the loan shark—with only a week to pay. He told them about the trust fund, and how Uncle Ray intended to find a loophole to get at it so he could get the money back from the robbery—and cover legal fees.

Harley was having it harder than Parker had guessed. Harley hated his uncle—Parker was sure of that. But the strange thing? Harley seemed legit worried that Ray would get himself hurt by the loan shark if he didn't come up with some serious money—and fast.

"I don't see how he can do it," Harley said.

Jelly looked like she was processing that one.

Harley also told how he'd slept in the shed. How he was doing it again tonight—and every night until he was sure Scorza wouldn't try another stunt like the smoke bombs.

"But it's still covered with soot in there," Jelly said. "Sleep there again and you might end up in the ER with smoke inhalation."

And just like that, Jelly and Ella stitched together a plan to hose out and scrub the inside of the entire shed. Hopefully it would be dry by the time Harley went to bed.

Minutes later they pulled anchor, and headed back for Rockport Harbor. The uneasiness between him and Harley was shrinking, for sure, but it was still there. The closer they got to shore, the more Harley clammed up. Ella and Jelly laughed and chattered on, but Harley seemed more and more antsy. Tense. He coiled the bow line in his hands. Let it drop on the deck. Then started all over again. As they neared shore, Harley scanned the backside of Bearskin Neck. Probably looking for Scorza—or maybe smoke.

Parker liked the plan of cleaning the shed. It was a way to show support for Harley. Build a bridge. "We'll take down the signs." Road signs. Street signs. License plates. The inside walls of the shed were filled with them. "Bring them outside the shed and scrub them down. We'll have the Hangar looking better than new."

"A fresh start," Jelly said.

Definitely. And somehow it would give their friendship a new start too.

CHAPTER 16

CLEANING THE SHED TOOK A WHOLE LOT more effort—and time— than Parker had figured it would. But Harley seemed more like himself, and that made the work worth it all. The two of them unscrewed every one of the road signs and license plates from the walls. Jelly and Ella gave them a soap and water scrubbing, not just a hosing down. They propped them all along the backside of the dive shop to dry. Harley pocketed the cash and Kemosabe's title from the secret spot behind the No Passing sign. Nobody would have ever guessed how much money he had there.

"What's this all about?" Ella pointed at several lines of hash marks—actually they looked like small bottles—drawn in neat rows directly below where the Dead End sign had hung. An X was drawn through each bottle, giving it a skull-and-crossbones look.

Harley hesitated. "A little safety project I've been working on. Maybe I'll tell you sometime."

Ella angled her head slightly. "I'd like that."

But Harley didn't say another word. Clearly this wasn't the right time.

Soot covered the outside of Harley's massive chest of tools, which wasn't a big deal. But some of the drawers had been open, and way too many tools had a black film covering them now. Parker made a call to his Dad, and he was there minutes later. The three of them wheeled the chest out of the shed and wrestled it up a makeshift ramp and into the back of Dad's pickup.

It wasn't easy convincing Harley to let Parker take the tool chest home for a good cleaning. Parker didn't get the feeling it was about a lack of trust. More like Harley was still holding back a little . . . not wanting to be in Parker's debt or something. In the end, Harley agreed, which allowed him to focus on cleaning Kemosabe.

Parker screwed a piece of plywood over the broken window and cleaned up the shards of glass. How Harley had slept on the floor the night before was a mystery.

Kemosabe sat twenty feet from the shed, like it was watching the whole thing. Harley finished cleaning it just about the time the shed was done.

Before they had time to put anything back in the shed, Uncle Ray sauntered up and peered inside. "Remind me never to let you decorate the store, Harley. Looks like a ghost town." He laughed at his own stupid joke and held up a baseball bat. "A little house-warming gift."

Harley stared at him for a moment. "A Louisville Slugger? What am I supposed to do with this?"

"Nothing if your old football buddy shows up," Uncle Ray said. "And if he does, call me. Call the police. Call your cleaning crew here. But you stay away from him. He's got that restraining order—and that means the law is on his side."

Harley glared at him. "I'm not going to let him just—"

"You touch him again"—Uncle Ray stepped up to Harley, fully in his face—"and you're off to juvey or something worse. And then don't expect a lick of help from me." He gave Harley a two-finger poke in the forehead. "If they file a lawsuit, who do you think they're going to pull into court? Your *guardian*, hothead. And that would be me. They already got a legal advantage with that restraining order. I am not taking the fall for you. Got that?"

Somehow Parker wasn't surprised that Harley's uncle was only concerned with how this all impacted himself.

Harley worked his jaw muscles, but to his credit, he kept his mouth shut.

Jelly and Ella moved closer, like they didn't want to miss a word.

Uncle Ray crossed his arms. "If I find out you go anywhere near that kid—against my orders—you won't be sleeping in the shop—or the shed anymore. I'll put you in juvey myself. Message received?"

Harley kept his eyes focused on the ground. He moved his hands like he was catching a pass and pulling it in. "Received." His eyes flitted to Parker for an instant.

Parker expected him to look embarrassed. But what he saw looked a whole lot more like rage. Ella and Jelly didn't look too happy either.

"Hey, look at me when I talk to you." Uncle Ray pointed at Harley's eyes, then at his own. "Keep your peepers right here."

Harley raised his eyes, staring at his uncle through strands of hair hanging below his eyebrows. "If you don't want me using the bat, why bring it out?"

"Because I think you got an enemy out there. Maybe it's Scorza, maybe not. Anybody else—besides Scorza—tries something?" Uncle Ray thumped the bat on the floor. "You swing for the fence."

Amazing he was actually encouraging Harley to attack anybody.

Harley's uncle set the bat in the corner nearest the shed door. "It's right here if you need it."

"Nobody is going to mess with me or my motorcycle now— not with me sleeping in the shed."

"Depends on how bad somebody wants the bike—or wants to make you squirm. If it were me, I'd have removed whatever my enemy wanted so he couldn't get at me. I'd have sold the bike."

"You'd sell your mother if it got you ahead somehow."

Uncle Ray snickered. "A survivor does what he needs to do. And that's a lesson you'd do well to learn." He looked at Jelly and Ella like he just noticed them. "You kiddies have fun. Uncle Ray is already late to meet up with some friends in Gloucester." He patted the lump in his pocket. "Might even have me another party night." He dropped his cigarette stub and ground it good with his foot. "You sleeping out here again for sure?"

Harley nodded. "Maybe Parks will join me." He glanced Parker's way, but his face clouded immediately. "Forget it. This is my problem."

Uncle Ray walked toward the back door to the dive shop. "Just don't make it *my* problem. And be sure you lock this door before you hit the sack." He waved over his shoulder and disappeared.

There was no way Parker's mom and dad would let him do a

sleepover—especially just two nights after the incident. He could ask, sure. But that "Hold on" was putting his parents in a tough position to say no. "Sorry, Harley, I—"

"Forget it." He waved him off. "It's just that . . ." He stopped and clenched his jaw just a bit. "Forget it."

But he couldn't just leave it hanging out there. "It's just that *what*?"

Harley stormed over to Kemosabe. Swung a leg over and sat there for a second. "Ever notice how everybody seems to know what you need to do when you've got a problem—but they aren't around when it comes to actually helping?"

Ella sucked in her breath. "Harley Davidson Lotitto. That is *not* fair. We've all been helping, and you know it."

At least she could get some words out. Parker felt like he'd taken a punch to the gut.

"*Sorry* if I offended you." It was one of those totally lame apologies that really meant *I think you deserved exactly what I said, but I'll say I'm sorry if that makes you happy.*

"Now you're making it worse." Ella shook her head. "This isn't you. And if you ask me, nobody should be sleeping in this shed. Not you. Not Parker. Not until the police get whoever was behind all this."

"Scorza." Harley looked down again.

"That's your best guess. But we know it isn't safe to stay out here," Jelly said. "What if this isn't over? Don't you think it's kind of a big ask to drag Parker into this?"

Harley stared out over the North Basin. Not that he seemed to be looking at anything in particular. More like it was to avoid looking at his friends. "You're right. Definitely a *big ask*. I won't make that mistake again."

"Hold on," Parker said. "We're friends . . . which means there's no such thing as a big ask."

"I got this now," Harley said. "I don't need any more help."

"Harley . . ." Ella looked hurt. "What is *wrong* with you?"

Harley took the lanyard of keys from around his neck and fired Kemosabe up. "You just don't understand." And just like that Harley was like a boat cut free from its mooring. Adrift. Distant—and getting farther by the second. He took the key from his lanyard and fired Kemosabe up.

Parker had to try to salvage this somehow. "I'll talk to my mom and dad. I like the idea of sleeping in the Hangar tonight."

"Don't bother."

Ouch. Parker didn't want to show how much that hurt. "How about we let the shed dry out a bit, then I'll help you move your mattress down here."

Harley shook his head. Sat there revving the motorcycle over and over, then slammed it in gear. Loose gravel shot from the rear tire—banging the road signs propped against the building. The bike swerved slightly, but Harley got it back on track and up the ramp into the shed.

"Seriously." Jelly followed him inside. "Let us help you get your mattress down here so you don't knock over any of your uncle's precious T-shirt displays while lugging it out of the shop."

Harley cut the motor and put the key back around his neck. "You three have done enough." His voice cool. "I got it under control now."

But that wasn't how he looked. He didn't look in control at all.

CHAPTER 17

BRYCE SCORZA HATED WAITING—for pretty much anything. Staying in motion had always worked well for him. The instant the ball was snapped, he was moving. Whether handing off the ball or passing, he never stopped before hearing the ref's whistle. He was harder to sack that way.

But this time it was different. In order to do what he needed done, he'd have to stay absolutely still. The more he'd thought about it, the less he believed Harley would call for a truce. Bryce needed to rattle Lotitto's cage good. Do something that would shake him up enough to come after him again. Break the restraining order. And it wouldn't take much. Then the cops would haul Lotitto away for sure. Bryce would come out on top, like he always did. Lotitto deserved some payback for the way he'd ditched him for his new friends. For the way he divided the team. He'd send a don't-cross-me message to Lotitto—and to all the other guys on the team at the same time.

"You're one brilliant quarterback, Bryce Scorza. You call the plays on the field—and off." He smiled—and absolutely agreed with himself.

Bryce had made the perfect hiding place by rearranging a stack of lobster traps on Bradley Wharf earlier in the day—while Gatorade took the others out for a little boat ride. He was done long before the boat came back. His lobster trap hideout was way too close to the shed to risk being seen in the daylight, so he'd positioned himself under the support beams next to the boat ramp to wait for just the right time.

From that safe distance, he'd watched Gatorade, Black Beauty, and Everglades Girl help Lotitto clean the shed—then get picked up by Gatorade's mom. Minutes later, Bryce had found the perfect opportunity to wriggle into his hiding spot unnoticed. Now it was just a matter of waiting for the right moment to strike. From here he had a great view of Lotitto's shed—but he'd never be spotted in the dark. It was like Bryce had his own little rabbit hole. It would allow him to sneak out and do the deed quick, then get back into hiding and watch the reaction. It was like running a play and being a spectator in the stands all at the same time. The best of both worlds.

Lottie moving his mattress to the shed was an interesting twist. But Bryce would adapt. In fact, with him actually sleeping in the shed, things would be more interesting. Did Lotitto really think he could keep Bryce away from the bike just by sleeping next to it?

Gatorade's mom had been all smiles. Like picking up Gatorade and his friends was no bother. She hugged the girls. Even hugged Harley and whispered something in his ear. Bryce was glad he didn't have a mom breathing down his neck, knowing everything he did. Once Bryce went to his bedroom after dinner, Traci Trophy

Wife wouldn't be popping in to say good night. Especially not after he turned off his light. His stepmom stayed out of his business and out of his way. She'd be focused on Jaxon, her eight-year-old brat. Bryce didn't have to worry about Jaxon wandering into his room either. The kid knew better than to do that again. Bryce was actually relieved Jaxon wasn't a real DNA brother. The kid had zero ability to catch or throw a football—and even less desire to learn.

Dad wouldn't notice that he'd slipped out his window and biked to Rockport. He wouldn't even know if Bryce stayed out all night. Dad had regular hours working for an insurance company, but he also worked plenty of nights in some kind of second job. Bryce never got a good explanation for what his dad actually did those nights, but he wore a suit. Obviously he wasn't cleaning offices somewhere. The night work always meant he'd come home with cash, though, and that kept Traci Trophy smiling. Tonight, Dad was out. And when he did come home, he'd head right for his own bedroom—and he wouldn't stop to say good night to Bryce on the way. Parents probably didn't realize how well their kids knew their routines—and how to avoid getting caught.

Bryce should have made his hideout big enough to allow him to stretch. His shoulder ached from lying on his side. Lotitto had closed himself in the shed. Locked it from the inside too, no doubt. Lottie was so stinking sure that Bryce was behind the smoke bomb incident. Which was annoying. If he was going to get blamed for something, at least he ought to have the fun of actually doing it.

But Bryce was going to have fun tonight.

Even after the light inside the shed turned off, Bryce waited for what would have been two full quarters on the football field, hoping Harley would drift off to sleep. The North Basin of the harbor was still. Dark—except for flashes of moonlight glittering on the surface. A lone lobster boat chugged its way through Outer Harbor toward the T-wharf, sending ripples racing for opposite shores. What if the fishermen got loud and woke Lotitto? He needed to get this done. It was go time.

Bryce wriggled out of his hiding spot and slipped off his shoes. With Lotitto actually inside the shed, he'd have to be extra quiet. He crept as silently as a shadow, even across the gravel. He stopped at the windowless side of the shed and listened for any movement coming from inside. So far, so good.

He fished the tube of fire paste from his pocket, unscrewed the cap, and squeezed out giant, one-foot letters across the entire wall of the shed. Like petroleum jelly, the goop stuck to the wood siding perfectly.

BARF BAG

Lotitto would know exactly who sent the message—but wouldn't be able to prove a thing. He capped the tube and stepped back to admire his work.

And if anyone was a total barf bag, it was Harley. Hanging around with Gatorade—and Black Beauty—and likely telling Everglades Girl all kinds of bad things about him? Blaming Bryce for the smoke bomb stunt? Yeah, Harley was the real barf bag here—and he deserved whatever he got.

It wasn't like Bryce was going to burn down the shed or anything. Somebody would see the fire—or Bryce would use the Walmart phone to call in an anonymous tip. And Bryce would stick around long enough to make sure Lotitto got out of the shed okay. Nobody would get hurt, but this would cut Lotitto down to size quick.

Bryce reached for the stick lighter from his back pocket and flicked it on. It sounded way too loud. Had Lotitto heard it inside?

A diesel engine snapped his attention back to the Motif fishing shack.

The lobster boat had swung toward the floating platform and was reversing to pull alongside the eastern granite wall of Bradley Wharf. Two men aboard. One at the helm, the second at the stern holding a dock line.

Great. Harley took his finger off the lighter trigger. Of all the luck. The fishermen were docking . . . and right within easy view of the shed. If he set the letters on fire now, whoever was in the boat would see it—and maybe they'd put it out before the message had permanently burned in. Worse yet, they'd spot him—and this was the one play he wanted to run without spectators in the bleachers.

Okay, not game over—just a delay of game. He'd wait until the fishermen left. He crept back to the lobster traps and army-crawled into his spot—and just in time. The man with the dock line stepped off the boat gunwale to the wooden ladder running up the granite wall. Dark pants. Dark hoodie. Shoulders like the guy had pads under his sweatshirt. He tied the boat, bow and stern, like he'd done this a million times before.

The helmsman killed the engine, walked to the stern, and handed up what was clearly a gasoline can to Hoodie. Just by the way Helm-guy handled the can, it was clear the thing was full. Why were they unloading gasoline from a lobster boat? The boat had an inboard motor. Which meant it was most likely diesel. Why would somebody have a can of gasoline on a boat with a diesel motor?

Hoodie moved fast—but as quiet as if he wore moccasins. He disappeared around the far side of Lotitto's shed. A moment later he slipped back into sight. Hunkered over, the guy was clearly pouring a steady stream of gas along the base of the shed. Lights along the edge of the harbor reflected off the combustible liquid.

Bryce swore under his breath. He did not like this. Not one bit. He stayed absolutely still now—like his life depended on it. He didn't blink. Didn't swallow. Only his heart was moving—and it was beating at a tie-game-in-the-fourth-quarter pace.

Hoodie stepped away from the shed and set down the can. He struck a match. Tossed it. With a *woomph* the gas ignited, flames instantly stretching up three sides of the shed. Apparently, Hoodie hadn't doused the end with the shed doors. The fire paste ignited almost immediately. The words *BARF BAG* grew bright and glared at Bryce. He was going to get blamed for this—for the whole thing!

Hoodie ran past the traps—not ten feet from where Bryce held his breath. The man jumped from the granite wall into the boat, and both men disappeared into the pilot house shadows. All lights off—like the boat was parked for the night.

Lotitto was inside the shed. It was one thing to burn a message into the siding of the shed. But to let Lotitto burn inside? He couldn't do it. What if the cops traced it back to Bryce somehow? It would end Bryce's chances at too many things. No football now—or scholarship later. No career in the military. He'd get sent away—or locked away. No thanks.

He dug the Walmart phone from his pocket. The thing wasn't traceable, right? Within seconds he'd dialed 911 and whispered a hoarse warning about the fire to the operator, doing his best to disguise his voice.

The boat was still tied at the wharf. Why weren't they booking for the channel?

It wasn't just the gas burning now. The siding of the shed

caught. Black smoke billowed up the sides. *You've got to warn Lotitto. Get him out of there! Move, Bryce!*

He'd barely bellied halfway out of his hiding spot when the shed doors burst open. Dense smoke from inside rushed out, racing for the moon.

He expected Lotitto to run out screaming in terror or something . . . but it was a full three-count before he saw any movement at all. The rear tire of the motorcycle emerged—then Lotitto on the seat, holding the handlebars and pumping his legs like he was driving a football sled backwards. Down the ramp, clear of the shed.

Scorza would *not* have stayed in the burning shed long enough to grab anything or anyone. Lotitto was stupid. Way too obsessed with that motorcycle for his own good. Lottie started the bike and peeled out like a maniac, racing to the granite pier where Bryce lay dead still.

He stopped next to the tower of lobster traps, dropped the kickstand, and practically vaulted off the bike, turning the bike off but leaving the key in the ignition. He ran his hands frantically over the gas tank and seat. "You okay, Kemosabe?" He checked the fenders. Handlebars. Tires. As if he were making sure a spark hadn't landed anywhere. "I saved him, Dad." His voice was a shaky sob. "He's okay."

Did he really think he could talk to his dead dad?

"What in the—" Lotitto was looking at the shed now. "*Barf bag? Really?*" The words stood out like a flaming tattoo but were quickly being swallowed by the rising blaze. "Why would he do this, God?" His words rose above the growing roar of the flames. "I'm going to kill him! You know I'll do it!" He ran for the shed, pulled the phone from his pocket, and disappeared from sight around the corner. Reappeared seconds later with a hose, blasting at the base of the shed. The flames clapped and popped loud enough to drown most everything out.

There was no way Harley would save the thing. The fire was too intense. And there was no way Bryce was going to move now. He couldn't risk Lotitto catching him. He'd have to wait this out. Nobody would see him here, right? There was no way this fire could get passed off as a prank. With the gasoline? He'd get charged with arson. Maybe attempted murder. Bryce would deny being here. Deny long enough and loud enough, and people would believe him, right? It worked for politicians all the time.

The fire lit the area around the shed like a giant torch. Bryce was still in the shadows—and thanked his lucky stars his hiding spot was so small. He absolutely could not get spotted.

He gave a quick scan around him the best he could from such tight quarters. Hoodie was on the move again. He climbed out of the boat. Crept along the backside of the pile of traps. He stopped at the motorcycle, rocked it off its stand, and wheeled it toward the waiting lobster boat.

Wait, what?

The helmsman had a wooden ramp in place, running from the granite lip of the pier all the way onto the boat deck. With the tide as high as it was, the ramp wasn't nearly as steep as Bryce would have figured it would be.

They were stealing the motorcycle?

His back to the Motif fishing shack, the lobster traps, and the motorcycle, Lotitto was still playing junior firefighter. A losing battle for sure.

Both men eased the motorcycle down the ramp now—like they'd rehearsed the thing. So that was why Hoodie didn't gas the shed entrance? This was their plan the whole time—to smoke Lotitto out and grab his bike? What kind of enemies did Lottie have?

Sirens echoed across the bay from town. For an instant, Bryce thought of whistling for Lotitto. Warning him that his precious motorcycle was being stolen. But how would he ever explain why he'd been here in the first place—hiding among the lobster traps? And the goons boosting the motorcycle seemed like true professionals. Did he really want to draw their attention? What if they identified him? These guys were some seriously bad dudes, and Bryce wasn't going to put his head on the chopping block for some stupid motorcycle—or an ex-best friend.

No. Bryce had already done enough to help, right? Stuck his neck out there and called 911. Watched to make sure Lotitto got out of the shed safe. How many more heroics could one guy be expected to perform? Yeah, Bryce really was the hero here—and he'd done way more than enough. It wasn't like Harley was in any real danger now. In fact, Bryce was the one who'd be in danger if the lobster boat goons saw him.

Sit tight, Bryce. Wait this out. Maybe this was fate or something. What goes around, comes around, right? Maybe Lotitto was just getting what he deserved. Actually, Bryce was sure he was.

The motorcycle stood on the lobster boat deck now. The men secured it quickly with nylon ratchet straps and threw a tarp over it. The guys worked like a NASCAR pit crew. Hoodie patted his pockets. Searched the deck around the bike. "I lost it." He ran up the makeshift ramp and studied the ground all the way to where the bike had been parked moments before. He dropped to his knees and swept the rock and gravel with his hands.

The driver tossed the ramp over the side and fired up the diesels. "Come *now*, Kelsey—or swim to Gloucester."

Okay, so the big guy's name was Kelsey. Bryce wouldn't forget it. Kelsey did one more sweep, growled, and hustled back to the boat. He cast off the lines and pushed off. The boat quietly chugged into the shadows of the harbor even as the fire engine wheeled from Bearskin Neck onto the tiny back road leading to Bradley Wharf.

The reflections of the red lights clashed and fought each other across the surface of the water like they were in some massive scrimmage. Emergency lights from the fire truck, ambulance, and now even police cars lit the place up like it was high noon. And the shed was nothing more than a giant fireball now. Suddenly his hiding spot didn't seem nearly as safe as it did minutes before. If Lotitto noticed the bike gone—and ran over to investigate—he'd spot Bryce for sure.

Gotta get out of here. Right now. Firemen. Cops. Gawkers. A fireman wrestled the hose away from Lotitto and forced him away from the shed and toward his uncle—who was yelling about something.

This was his moment. While the chaos and confusion was at its peak, he'd slip out. Work his way behind the other sheds to Roy Moore's outdoor eating deck. Shinny between the buildings onto the street running down Bearskin Neck.

He'd be okay—once he got moving again. What had that Kelsey guy been searching for? Bryce might come back to look for it tomorrow. But for now, he needed a clean getaway. He had to get back to his bike—and back home to Gloucester. Would Harley tell the police about the flaming words on the shed? Would they come to question him? Probably. He wanted to be in his bedroom before they did.

In a sick way he admired the team who'd pulled off the heist. They'd executed their play perfectly. Scary good. First the smoke bombs, and now a legit arson hit? The two events had to be related. Harley had some enemies who were way beyond dangerous.

And now, in a way, Bryce was tied to them . . . because he was there. And with the word written in fire paste, it wouldn't be hard to place Bryce at the scene of the crime.

What if the arson goons found out he was an eyewitness? What would they do to him? He absolutely couldn't tell the police what he'd seen from his hiding spot. He might admit he wrote *BARF BAG*, but he'd tell them he left. He'd say he decided against lighting the words on fire and just went home. If the police believed he was at the scene when the goons did their work, word might get out through a dirty cop. He'd be dead.

What was the old saying? "Keep your friends close—and your enemies closer" or something like that. Bryce could run, but if the goons tracked him down somehow, he'd be at a deadly disadvantage if he didn't know who they were. His stomach got that hot, prickly feeling like it always did an hour before a game. If he wanted to steer clear of these guys, he'd have to find out who they were first. Bryce had to figure out who was targeting Lotitto—and make sure he didn't become a target too.

Which meant he had to get back to Gloucester before that lobster boat did. After they off-loaded Harley's motorcycle, he'd follow them. He'd get a piece of information that he was sure would prove to be worth solid gold—and maybe his own ticket out of jail. He'd find out where Kelsey and his friend, Helm-guy, took that motorcycle.

But first things first. Right now, he needed to do what he did best. Move—and without getting caught.

CHAPTER 18

ELLA WOKE TO THE DISTANT WAIL OF SIRENS. Sounded like a fire truck or paramedics. She opened her bedroom window and strained to get a fix on the direction. A fog was beginning to creep into town—and it wasn't making it easy to pinpoint the source of the sirens. One moment she was convinced it was coming from Bearskin Neck—and the next she wasn't so sure at all.

But an uneasy feeling woke from wherever it had been sleeping inside her. She grabbed for the necklace and closed her hand around the cross. "Jelly?"

"I hear it." Her friend swung out of bed and stood at the window.

Ella whipped off a text to Parker:

Hear those sirens? I hope they're not near Harley.

A reply dinged back almost immediately:

I can't reach him—he's MIA.

Ella's thumbs were a blur:

Could he sleep through the sirens?

Parker was almost as fast on the reply as Ella had been:

Exactly. They woke my dad up. We're going to check it out.
I got a bad feeling.

He had a bad feeling? It couldn't be anything as dreadful as the monster lurking in her mind.

Jelly pulled on her jeans. "We've got to get there."

Ella's thoughts exactly. She thumbed another note:

Pick us up in five?

Parker replied immediately, and Ella read his text aloud:

"'Sorry, we're heading straight to the wharf. Jelly's dad will come for you.'"

Apparently, all of them were just as concerned about Harley as she and Jelly were—which did nothing to ease her fears.

"We'll be right behind him." Jelly stepped into her shoes. "Let's go."

Ella slipped her dress over her head. Shoved her feet into her boots. She bolted from her room and flew down the stairs with Jelly a heartbeat behind her.

She scrawled a note to Grams and left it on the kitchen table where she'd see it. Grams would be worried sick if she woke up and found both girls gone. At least this way Grams would know where they were—and she could make a quick phone call to know they were okay.

Ella opened the front door and felt the heaviness of the fog almost as much as she saw it. Grams's superstitions seeped into her mind. How the sea smoke would claim a life on shore before it crept back out to sea. *Harley!* She clutched the cross pendant tighter.

CHAPTER 19

EVEN FROM A BLOCK AWAY, Parker could see that a police car had the entrance to Bearskin Neck completely blockaded. Dad veered down the T-wharf instead, tires screaming. The still waters of Rockport Harbor gave them a full view of the backside of Bearskin Neck—as much as the fog allowed—for the first time since they'd left the house.

Flames fully engulfed Harley's shed. Orange tentacles clawed for the night sky like the Hangar had been sacrificed in some pagan ritual. The fiery reflections on the water made it look like North Basin itself was on fire.

"Harley!" Was he trapped inside? "Harley!" Parker unclipped his seatbelt and reached for the door.

Dad grabbed his wrist. "Use your head. I'll park and be right behind you."

Like he knew Parker couldn't sit back when his friend was in danger.

"Pray, Dad!" Parker bolted from the passenger seat and ran around the foot of the harbor. Across the boat ramp. Then from rock to rock to the harbor retaining wall. The cop was stopping cars from going down Bearskin Neck, and Parker wasn't going to chance he'd stop people on foot. Nobody was going to be patrolling the route Parker took.

He didn't slow until he approached the fire truck nearest Harley's shed. Firemen were dousing everything within ten feet of the inferno. If the fire spread to the building, they'd have another Great Chicago Fire on their hands. The shops on Bearskin Neck were too close to each other.

"Harley!" *Where was he?*

Several skippers scrambled aboard their lobster boats moored in the North Basin. They weren't taking any chances of fiery ash landing on their decks or igniting coils of line. Diesel engines came to life as the men worked to get their boats to other parts of the harbor.

"Harley!" What was left of the shed roof collapsed, sending up fiery tracers. "God—please—don't let Harley still be in that shed!"

A pumper truck by the granite retaining wall snaked a feeder hose over the rock, sucking water right out of the harbor. A second crew of firemen doused the structure at the back of the dive shop that housed the oxygen and nitrogen tanks used to fill the dive tanks.

"Harley!" There was no sign of his friend.

Police had already formed a perimeter several shops away, forcing curious onlookers back.

Harley's Uncle Ray looked like he'd just rolled out of bed. He pressed close to the action, wearing basketball shorts, a sleeveless T, and flip-flops. "Forget the shed," he shouted. "Keep the hose on the dive shop!"

Parker scooted past the pumper truck, only to be blocked by a cop.

"Hold on there, partner."

Parker recognized him instantly. "Officer Greenwood—it's me, Parker."

"Too dangerous to get any closer, Parker. You have to—"

"Harley was in there! Sleeping in the shed!" Parker faked moving in one direction, then bolted in the other.

Greenwood was either really quick, or he anticipated the move. Strong arms wrapped around Parker and held him fast.

"He's not in the shed—and I prefer you didn't get any closer yourself."

Parker struggled against Greenwood's grip. "Where is he? Is he okay?"

Suddenly Parker's dad was there too. "Easy, son. Stop fighting him. Officer Greenwood, where's Harley?"

"Ambulance—in front of the dive shop." Greenwood released his grip. "A little smoke inhalation is all. But they'll have to take him in to check him out."

Parker glanced at his dad and instantly got a nod. He backtracked—away from the police line—and scooted between two buildings to get onto the street running through the heart of the Neck. Sure enough, an ambulance stood right in front of the Rockport Dive Company with lights blazing and the rear doors open wide.

Harley sat on a gurney, covered with soot. He did not look one bit happy. "Parker!" He motioned him over, coughing and hacking the entire time.

Parker pushed his way past gawkers. "I am so sorry . . . Harley
. . . I should have been with you."

"Forget it. Just take care of Kemosabe—that's all I care about.
They're making me go to the hospital, even though I'm fine."

How would he break the news to him? "But the shed—it's
gone. Like . . . to the ground."

"I rolled Kemosabe out in time—parked it right on Bradley
Wharf alongside the wall of lobster traps."

Thank you, God! If Harley's bike had been lost in the blaze,
there was no telling what he'd do.

"It was Scorza."

"You saw him?"

Harley shook his head. "*BARF BAG* was written on the side of
the Hangar in giant flaming letters. It was him. Who else would
use those words?"

Scorza torched the shed? This was insane. It was all going way
too far.

"Don't let Kemosabe out of your sight, Parks. Keep it safe."
Harley gripped his arm like he thought the paramedics might drag
him away before he finished. "Promise me."

"I promise. Nothing will happen to it. I'll stay with it until
you get back."

Harley broke into another coughing fit. "I'll have no place to
keep it. Get your dad to roll it up into his pickup. The key is still
in it—along with the lanyard and the spare. Just get it out of here.
Someplace safe."

He could do that—and it was a way to blaze a trail back to his
friend. "I'm on it."

"Go!" Harley released his grip. "Don't let my uncle talk you
into keeping it in the dive shop. You're the only one I trust."

Parker sprinted past the emergency vehicles and cut along the narrow passage separating Roy Moore's from the building next to it. He raced past small stacks of traps and came out at the foot of the granite pier jutting out to Motif Number 1. Here the stacks of traps were piled six feet high. Parker ran down one row and up the next.

No Kemosabe.

Maybe Harley actually parked it closer to the Motif building— or on the other side of it, where it would be more protected from sparks or spray from the fire hoses.

Parker ran around the building and back. *No.* He retraced his steps. Widened his search.

Nothing.

No. *No.* He gave the entire area a thorough scan. Firefighters focused the hose on the shed now—what was left of it. He could see the entire area clearly from the lights of the emergency vehicles. Cars. Traps. Shops. People. But no deeply chromed 1999 XL Sportster.

Kemosabe was gone.

CHAPTER 20

ELLA AND JELLY WERE AT THE CURB when Jelly's dad pulled up—and had the door open before he came to a complete stop. Jelly dove inside and Ella followed. "Go, go, go! We're in."

Her dad laid down the safety rules on the short drive. *Stay together. Don't go near the fire. Make sure your phones are on.* Just the kinds of things Ella imagined her bio-dad might say—if he'd loved her enough to be around.

Jelly's dad dropped them at the curb a block away. "I'll park the car and find you there soon." He pulled Jelly close and kissed the top of her head.

He turned to Ella as she shouldered open the door. "You be careful, hear?"

There was a strength in his eyes. An intensity. And Ella felt all the stronger for it. Jelly broke out into a run down the sidewalk. Ella did her best to keep up—which wasn't easy in her cowgirl boots.

They stopped in a sort of stunned silence at the entrance to the T-wharf. The sight across North Basin confirmed Ella's fears.

Jelly grabbed her arm and stepped off the sidewalk. "We've got to see if he's okay."

Instinctively Ella glanced up Broadway to check for traffic as they crossed the street—and stopped in her tracks. "Jelly!"

It was Scorza. Loading his bike into the bed of a pickup. An illuminated Lyft sign sat on the dashboard. What was *he* doing in Rockport at this hour? And why was he in such a hurry to leave that he couldn't just bike back to Gloucester?

But she knew. Harley had been right all along.

Jelly clutched her arm. "If we tell Harley . . ."

She didn't have to finish; Ella already knew. He'd do something stupid—and they'd take him away.

"What about Parker?" Jelly actually looked scared. "Do we tell him?"

"He'll tell Harley—you know it."

Jelly nodded, like she agreed . . . but was torn at the same time.

"We have to promise each other not to say a word about this." Ella clutched the cross in her hand and held out her pinky. Adding the cross would make this some kind of an unbreakable oath, right?

"Ahhh—I hate this! A long time ago I promised Parker I wouldn't keep secrets from him. How can I do this?"

"Think what will happen if you don't," Ella said. "They're boys. Which means they'll do something. They won't sit back—not after this. If Harley hurts Scorza and Parker is with him? They're both going down. C'mon. Pinky promise."

Jelly stared at Ella's hand for a moment, tears running down her cheeks. "We have to protect them, right? From themselves?"

Ella nodded. She wanted to just hook her pinky on Jelly's and seal the deal, then find Harley and Parker. But it couldn't be one-sided. Both of them would have to agree on this—and right now—or one of them would get weak and tell the boys.

"But if they find out we didn't tell them what we saw—what if they don't trust us anymore?"

"They'll get over it. Isn't that better than them doing something stupid that will land them in jail?"

Jelly groaned and raised her pinky. Real slow, like she was still fighting it inside. "You think we're going to regret this?"

Ella gave her a look like that was a ridiculous question. She locked her pinky with Jelly's. "We're lying to our best friends. Yeah, we'll regret it."

Ella already did.

CHAPTER 21

Sunday, August 7, 10:46 p.m.

THE MOMENT ANGELICA SAW PARKER—she knew something was terribly wrong. He was talking to his dad and Officer Greenwood—pointing toward the Motif. Uncle Ray was there too, looking totally annoyed.

Uncle Ray swore. And not just once. "I told him. I *told* him. Turn the chrome into cash—before you lose it all. Stupid kid."

Angelica looked at the smoldering heap of rubble that had been the shed. *The motorcycle . . . melted?* How could Bryce Scorza do *that?*

Parker brought her and Ella up to speed in seconds. Angelica grabbed her phone to give her dad a quick update. "And keep an eye out for a big Harley-Davidson motorcycle!" she told him.

Officer Greenwood hustled toward the lobster traps. "Show me where the bike was parked."

Angelica, Uncle Vaughn, Parker, and Ella followed.

Greenwood pulled out a flashlight. Inspected the ground. "It was here." He pointed to a pair of indentations. "That's from a kickstand." He glanced around. "And I don't know how anyone could have gotten it off the Neck without being seen. One way off—with an officer blocking the way."

Officer Greenwood excused himself, got on his radio, and had a quick conversation with someone. Uncle Ray drifted back to the shop—shouting orders at firefighters like he was the only one on the scene who knew what to do.

"This is going to kill Harley," Ella said.

Angelica was more worried about who *he* might kill.

Officer Greenwood was back. "I've notified the department. They'll be on the lookout. And no Harley-Davidson motorcycle drove off Bearskin Neck. I'll do a little cruising. See what I see."

She wanted to tell him about Scorza. What she'd seen. But clearly Scorza didn't have the motorcycle. Did he hide it? Or was he working with others? Obviously he was involved in this somehow.

Parker looked desperate. "What am I going to tell Harley?"

It seemed more like he was thinking aloud than expecting an answer.

Angelica's dad trotted up. "I saw a few people on the way and asked about the bike. Nobody has seen it. Or even heard it go by. And with the exhaust pipes on a Harley-Davidson, they would have heard it go by."

"So," Uncle Vaughn said, "you're thinking somebody might have put the bike in neutral and rolled it away, and maybe it's still close?"

"Exactly."

Angelica wanted to believe it was nearby—and that they'd find it fast. But if someone drove it away before the street was barricaded, they could be halfway to Boston by now. The truth was, with the sirens—and the chaos? Somebody could have started the bike—or just rolled it to a different spot—and nobody would've noticed.

"Let's divide up," Uncle Vaughn said. "Parker and I will take the Neck. We'll go from building to building. Check every corner big enough to hide a motorcycle."

Angelica's dad nodded. "I'll take the girls. We'll drive around town with our windows down. Maybe we'll hear it if we don't see it."

But Angelica got the feeling this wasn't about someone stealing Kemosabe to take a little joyride. This was way too choreographed.

An image of the sign that had been posted on the dive shop flashed into her head.

IT STARTS TODAY.

Apparently, whoever had started this wasn't finished yet.

CHAPTER 22

Sunday, August 7, 11:15 p.m.

BRYCE HAD SET THE LYFT DESTINATION for the Fisherman's Memorial in Gloucester. It was a shot in the dark. He could have gotten dropped closer to the north end of the bay, where most of the commercial fishing boats were moored or docked. By Gorton's fish packing plant. But so many of the boats that came to that end were bigger than the one he'd seen take the motorcycle. At least by the Fisherman's Memorial he'd have a good view of most boats heading into Gloucester Bay. He'd improvise from there.

The longer he rode in the second seat of the Ford Ranger, the more he doubted he'd see the mystery lobster boat at all. It had taken him too much time to get off Bearskin Neck. Too much time to get the ride to Gloucester. And the guy behind the wheel was absolutely ridiculous. He had to be driving ten under the limit the whole way. By the time they dropped down on Western Avenue, Bryce was ready to jump out.

Traffic backed up almost immediately. The bridge over Blynman Canal was upright, letting a couple of boats pass.

"How about I drop you here," the driver said. "Looks like the bridge is going to be up for a bit."

Bryce couldn't get out of the truck fast enough. He pulled his bike from the bed and raced toward the bridge. Hidden among the lobster traps the way he'd been, he hadn't noticed the name of the boat or even one number of its registration. All he knew was that it was white—like a thousand other lobster boats. But that didn't matter. He'd recognize the boat instantly. How many boats would be coming to shore with a tarp-covered cargo like that one had? One by one the cruisers and lobster boats motored by, but not one of them had a motorcycle on deck. The bridge lowered back in place. The traffic passed.

Had he missed the boat? Or was it still out there somewhere? He dumped his bike and paced along the waterfront, scanning for telltale green and red lights. He waited another ten minutes. Maybe fifteen. Nothing.

The boat could be anywhere. Maybe they hadn't been going to Gloucester. Maybe they were dropping the bike someplace where only the fish would find it—like three miles offshore. Like out at the Dry Salvages. Maybe Lotitto would be diving out there someday—probably with Gatorade—and he'd get a real surprise. A rusting motorcycle covered with seaweed and barnacles that looked an awful lot like the one he used to keep so protected in his shed. Bryce would pay good money to see the look on Lotitto's face. The guy would swallow his regulator.

But why would someone go to all that trouble to steal a bike only to destroy it? Only a hard-core enemy would do something like that. How many enemies could Lotitto have? No, the enemy angle made no sense. So the guy named Kelsey and his friend stole it for the money they'd get? Could the bike be worth enough for all the trouble they'd gone through to get it?

And it looked like the goons pulled it off. Got clean away. Harley was probably searching up and down the Neck right now. The police too. But they'd never find the bike there.

In a way, Lotitto was getting what he deserved. Bryce's idea was a little vandalism to the shed. But somehow, some kind of cosmic justice had been at work and Harley got a lot worse than that. Bryce would have been totally happy about it except for that one little thing. The message written in fire paste. Harley had seen it, and he would tell the police that Bryce was the only one who could have done it. Bryce was going to be questioned about being at the scene of the crime. He still didn't have a better idea than to deny he'd been there when the shed was hit by the pyro.

Which meant he'd better get back home—and fast. Shower off all scent of smoke. Throw his clothes in the laundry.

The unmistakable rumble of a motorcycle starting grabbed his attention. The thing was a good distance away—but the water had a way of allowing sound to travel. He peered inland. The sound was definitely coming from the direction of the Cape Ann Marina. It had to be Harley's bike!

So the boat had passed under the bridge before Bryce got there. Okay . . . at least he had a starting point to look for the bike. He had a feeling he'd desperately need that information before this all was over.

He wanted to swing his leg over his bike and pedal like a crazy man to the marina. But the goons were too good. They'd have Harley's motorcycle hidden away long before he got there.

Suddenly the sound of the motorcycle was gone. How long

had he heard the motor running? Thirty seconds? A minute? It couldn't have been much longer than that. Harley's motorcycle hadn't been moved far once it was off the boat. Either someone loaded it onto a truck or the thing was hidden close by—maybe right there at the marina.

Bryce was practically shaking. He was the only one who had any idea where the motorcycle was. It was like he had a super-power. How impressed would Everglades Girl be if she realized that? Lotitto, Gatorade, Black Beauty—none of them had any idea of Bryce's true abilities. The universe smiled on him. How else could he explain how he'd been at the right place at the right time to see the bike taken, and again at the right place and time to hear it being off-loaded?

Deep in his gut he knew he needed to find the motorcycle. For his own good or protection somehow—and he wasn't even sure what that meant. But he'd have to trust the superpower inside— even if he didn't understand it.

Yeah, he'd find the thing. He'd start his search tomorrow. But right now? He had to get home—fast. And get cleaned up and back in his room . . . before the police showed up.

CHAPTER 23

Sunday, August 7, 11:30 p.m.

THE LAST OF THE FIREMEN WERE PACKING UP when Ray felt his phone vibrate. Either it was the kid needing a ride home from the hospital, or the text he'd *really* been waiting for. Ray ducked inside the back door of the shop and checked the screen. Vinny Torino.

The horse is in the stable.

He read it twice, marveling at how the whole plan came together like clockwork. "You're a genius, Ray." He winked at himself in the reflection of the glass, then stepped back outside. The key was to keep himself in plain sight as much as possible. And stay loud. Those who didn't see him would hear him. Twenty witnesses could say he'd been at the scene the entire time. Not that anyone might suspect he had anything to do with the fire or the missing bike, but staying visible would guarantee nobody ever would.

Even he was impressed with how completely the shed was ruined. Charred rubble, most of it. Trails of smoke rose heavenward like the spirit of the shed itself was crying out to God. Which was a ridiculous thought.

The trouble was, the title for the motorcycle must have been hidden inside. There was no other place it could have been. Sherlock Holmes himself couldn't have searched Harley's room any better these last days before the fire. Ray had even combed the tank fill station room. But the loan clock was ticking, and they'd had to go through with the heist tonight. The missing title was the only little glitch in the plan. Ray wouldn't be able to sell the bike for nearly as much without proof of ownership.

Which meant he'd be coming up short—with only seven days until the loan was due. And the more he saw of Lochran, the creepier the guy got. Okay, so maybe the missing title was a big problem.

But the horse was in the stable now—and Ray would make something happen, right? Maybe some fat corporation would ask him to take a couple of their execs on a dive charter this week. There was nothing to worry about. And Ray had Plan C in motion too. He had an appointment with the lawyer in the morning, right? He'd find a way to tap the kid's trust fund. And he'd get the money for Lochran—on time or early.

One of the cops drove stakes in the ground and formed a twenty-foot perimeter around the shed with a roll of yellow *Police Line Do Not Cross* tape.

"Hey." Ray pointed at the tape. "You think this was more than an accident?"

"Not for me to say." The cop nodded at the charred rubble. "But for the shed to go this fast, there had to be an accelerant. I'm no expert, but it looks like the work of an arsonist to me."

Arson. Just the word suggested a high level of skill. Like

being certified as a master diver. Or having his captain's license. "Whoever did this must have really known what they were doing. Think it was a pro?"

The cop shrugged. "Not my call. But if his goal was to destroy the shed—fast . . . yeah, the guy was good."

Oh, he was good, all right. And that's why he'd come out on top. He always did. Title or no title. Dive charter or no dive charter. Getting into the trust fund the easy way or the hard way. Ray would find a way to get the money he needed.

CHAPTER 24

Sunday, August 7, 11:40 p.m.

PARKER STOOD ALONGSIDE HIS DAD on Bradley Wharf between stacks of lobster traps and the Motif fishing shack. The quick grid-pattern search of the Neck had turned up nothing. Uncle Sammy and the girls hadn't had any more success than Parker and his dad. Jelly's dad left to take the girls home. The police and fire trucks were gone.

Harley had asked Parker—begged him—to do one thing. Just one. And Parker had failed. How was he going to tell him Kemosabe was gone? And what would that do to their friendship? None of this would have happened if Parker had stayed in the shed overnight with him. Even with the fire, Harley or Parker—one of them—would have been with Kemosabe the entire time. Dad would have loaded it in his truck just like Harley asked, and it would be parked at their house by now.

A ghostly quiet had settled on the place. A light was on above the dive shop. A shadow swept past the window. Likely Harley's Uncle Ray. Why wasn't he at the hospital?

Harley had texted a half-dozen times . . . and Parker hadn't opened one of them. How was he supposed to tell him somebody had played Houdini with Kemosabe and made the 650-pound motorcycle completely disappear?

"You've got to answer him," Dad said.

"I was hoping to have some good news first." But the likelihood of that had grown impossibly slim. "And this isn't the kind of thing I want to tell him in a text." Although he'd hate to tell him in person even more.

Dad nodded. "What do you say we go together?"

But there was nothing that was going to make the news easier, was there? "Whoever took Kemosabe must have gotten it off the Neck before the fire department came."

"Maybe," Dad said. "But the way I understand it, Harley was still there dousing the shed. So . . . somebody drove it past Harley? How likely is that?"

Not likely at all.

Dad stood staring at Motif Number 1 and reached for the flashlight case on his belt. "Did you look in the windows?"

No. He hadn't. "But the shed was locked—I thought . . ." A wave of hope surged through him, and he sprinted for the iconic building, Dad following at an easy jog.

The shed was definitely locked tight, but they got enough of a view through the windows to rule out any possibility that someone had rolled the bike inside.

"Another dead end. But it was a good idea, Dad."

He nodded. "Ready to talk to Harley?"

Parker was pretty sure he'd never be ready. Not unless the

bike materialized as quick as it had disappeared. What if Harley snapped—went on some sort of justice rampage and hurt Scorza? They'd put him in some detention center for sure.

Parker stared at the water and kept thinking about what his dad had said about the impossibility of someone getting the bike past Harley. "Dad—what if nobody saw the bike leave the area—because it never did?"

"Talk to me."

"What if somebody rolled it right off the side of the granite pier? On the other side of the Motif? Nobody would have seen. And with the sirens and roar of the fire . . . who would hear the splash?"

Dad rushed to the edge of the granite block wall, training his flashlight into the dark waters below. The tide was in. The water deep. And the bottom was out of sight. "You could be onto something, Parker. Good thinking!"

That had to be the answer. "Will the saltwater wreck it?"

"The wiring will be shot. Likely the engine will have to be taken apart and cleaned . . . but he'll have his bike, and we'll get Kemosabe back to the way it was—just like new."

Parker wanted to believe that. Had to. "Can we get our gear—go down now?"

Dad stared into the dark waters. "If it's down there, we'll find it easier in daylight. And it will be a whole lot safer."

He was right. And the boats that had left the harbor would likely be returning. The idea of diving the area in the dark with boats passing overhead wasn't exactly inviting.

"The harbor is a no-dive zone, but I'll call the harbormasters. They'll work it out. We'll come back at first light," Dad said. "Maybe Harley will join us. But right now, we have to break the bad news to him."

Parker just hoped the bad news wouldn't break Harley.

CHAPTER 25

ELLA SAT ON THE EDGE OF HER BED and leaned into Grams like she used to as a little girl. "Why do people do such mean, cruel things?"

"The heart of man is desperately wicked, Ella-girl."

Jelly drew her feet onto the bed and pulled her covers to her chin like the events of the night had chilled her to the bone.

"But, Grams . . . what would drive someone to take the one thing Harley had that connected him to his dad?"

Grams eased her long fingers through Ella's hair. "Greed. Jealousy. They aren't called monsters for no reason."

Or could it be revenge? If they could figure out the motive, they'd have their man, wouldn't they? What if it was revenge? That would be just one more thing that pointed to Scorza. Or was that too obvious? Somehow, she couldn't picture even a bloodsucking leech like Bryce Scorza doing something this extreme.

She and Jelly told Grams all about the **IT STARTS TODAY** sign at the dive shop on Friday—and the growing list of things that had happened since. Grams gasped. Shook her head. Squeezed her eyes tight like she was trying to stop the images rolling in her head.

"You girls sleep now," Grams said. "You need the rest. Each day has more than enough evil for a body to deal with—and tomorrow will be no different."

Ella and Jelly whispered for a bit, but in the end, it seemed each was alone with her thoughts.

Whoever was behind this, they'd managed to pull off the impossible, hadn't they? Harley had been sleeping next to his bike, and still he hadn't been able to keep Kemosabe from getting stolen. And in all likelihood, whoever had taken it had done it while police and firefighters were there—or on their way. Was Scorza even capable of something that organized?

The real question was what Harley was capable of. How far would he go to get justice? But Ella knew the answer. Too far.

CHAPTER 26

THERE WERE TIMES IT WAS BETTER for Harley to keep his mouth shut when he was getting a lecture from Uncle Ray. And this was definitely one of those times. His uncle had been ranting the entire drive back from the hospital, covering the same ground he'd already beat to death.

Not once did he ask how Harley was feeling. *Do your lungs hurt? Is it hard to breathe?* Those were the types of things Parker's dad had asked when they came to the hospital to tell him about Kemosabe. Parker's dad *felt* Harley's pain. Anyone could see that. Uncle Ray just *added* pain. Piggy-piled it on. Not that he wanted his uncle's sympathy, but Harley would have been happier if Uncle Ray said nothing—good or bad. All his barrage of criticism did was remind Harley again and again of just how much he didn't belong here.

Uncle Ray kept the tirade going even as they got to the shop and headed up the stairs. Harley would have gladly slept in the shed—if there was anything left of it. Harley stood in his room. Leaned against the wall and stared. No pillow. No sheet. No blanket. No mattress. And definitely no peace. Uncle Ray followed him right into his bedroom.

"How many times did I tell you to turn that chrome into cash?"

Did he really want him to answer that? The guy had been like a parrot—the same tired lines over and over and over.

Uncle Ray paced the tiny room like a caged tiger. "And now it's gone. You'll never see that bike again—and if by some stroke of luck you do, it will probably be in no shape to sell. It'll be worthless."

The Ray-gun. That's what Harley called it when his uncle got like this. Just hitting him shot after shot where it hurt most—with laser accuracy.

"Stupid. That's what you are. You held on to that bike too tight. You were obsessed with it."

He was a fine one to call Harley obsessed. Uncle Ray was obsessed with money—or anything he could turn into money, especially if it was Harley's. And his whole thing with getting the dive charter boat? What was that if not obsessed?

"I gave you a chance to turn that motorcycle into a money-making investment. You could have put the money into the boat—started making some real money yourself."

Why? So he could save up and buy a nice motorcycle someday?

"Now you got nothing. No way to pay off your debt, either—or did you forget you still owe me $3,500 from the robbery?"

How could he forget? Uncle Ray was always shoving it in his face. *Keep your mouth shut, Harley. Wait him out. He's got to run out of gas soon.* But he'd already been going on for how long? But to argue with him—or question Uncle Ray's opinion—would fuel him for another twenty minutes. At least.

"You should listen to your Uncle Ray more often, boy. After that smoke bomb stunt, I saw this coming. I warned you to sell that bike before you lost it, didn't I?"

He absolutely did.

Uncle Ray leaned closer. "Didn't I?"

Give him a bone, Harley. He hated to, but Uncle Ray would lean in even more if he didn't get an answer to a direct question. "Oh, yeah. You definitely called it."

"Doggone right I did. I should get a booth at the next county fair or something. Remarkable Ray's Psychic Predictions. I could make a killing."

For a guy who claimed to see the future, couldn't he see how stupid it was to borrow from a loan shark?

"Here's another prediction—and I'll give it to you free of charge," Uncle Ray said. "You'll never see your precious motorcycle again."

Shut the parrot up. If Harley had a box of saltine crackers, he'd shove the whole thing down Uncle Ray's beak.

"Gone. The bike is gone."

Harley was going to prove him wrong on that.

"Admit it." Uncle Ray stopped pacing and stared at him. "Look me in the eyes, and say it."

The stupid repeat-what-I-just-said tactic. Harley had been to Parker's church a lot since the quarry incident. One Sunday they had a guest preacher who kept telling the audience what to say. "Turn to the person next to you and say . . ." It was always some lame-o comment. Harley hated that. Hated. Hated. Hated. It was a power move. Controlling. A preacher could feed his stupid ego by making a statement and getting a whole congregation to repeat it back like a bunch of mindless groupies. *Almost* a whole congregation—because Harley never did. Parker didn't either. And neither did his parents. It was one thing for Harley to stonewall a preacher, but do that to Uncle Ray?

"The bike," Uncle Ray said each word slow and deliberate. Hands on hips. Leaning close. "Is gone." His eyes got that bug-eyed stare thing going on. "Say it."

There were times he'd fought Uncle Ray. And he definitely would again in the future. But this wasn't the time. "The bike . . . is gone." For now. But not for good. He'd find it.

Uncle Ray grunted. "First smart thing you've said." He stood there for a second like he was trying to decide if he needed to have Harley repeat any other bits of his drivel. "I need some sleep." Uncle Ray turned and shuffled down the hall. "Big day tomorrow."

Right. The day he was going to try to break into Harley's trust fund.

Harley waited until he heard his uncle snoring in the other room before tiptoeing out of the house. He grabbed at the keys hanging from the leather lanyard around his neck. But there were no keys—and the truth of it hit him like a punch to the gut. Kemosabe's key—he'd left it in the ignition when he'd gone to fight the fire. Made it easy for whoever took it.

"You're an idiot, Harley." Why hadn't he moved Kemosabe after the smoke bombs? Hidden it at Parker's? He'd been so sure that sleeping by the motorcycle would be enough. "You messed things up good this time." Who needed Uncle Ray to beat him down with accusations? He could do it fine all by himself.

The Hangar looked like something out of a war movie. Just a blackened skeleton of the shed remained. No roof. No doors. Just some charred two-by-four uprights and a pile of rubble in the center. A mound, really. Like it was a freshly filled grave. For an instant, Harley pictured himself under the debris—and shook off the thought just as quick. But if Kemosabe was really gone, a whole chunk of Harley's future was buried now, wasn't it?

There wasn't enough left of the Hangar to leave any evidence of the words he'd seen blazing on the siding. *BARF BAG.* How could Scorza have done this? Back in the day, they'd done their fair share of vandalism together. But arson? Never. And if Scorza knew Harley was inside, the moment he lit that fire he'd added attempted murder to his unwritten rap sheet, right? And it wasn't like he stole a bicycle. It was a motorcycle . . . and that was a felony. Arson. Attempted murder. Grand theft. If he left evidence behind, he'd risked everything. His dreams of a football scholarship, for sure. The only place he'd play ball would be in the juvey detention center rec yard. Would Scorza risk everything—just to get at Harley? Apparently so. Besides, with Scorza's ego he probably was certain he wouldn't get caught. Which meant he was taking no risk at all.

Except for the fact that the words *BARF BAG* pinned him to the scene of the crime. And Harley was going to make him pay for his sins. But he had to play this smart.

Scorza wanted a fight. Was begging for it. And Harley would be walking right into the whole restraining order trap if he went after him. Harley was going to have to think this out. He might get only one chance at Scorza, and he'd have to make it count. Had Scorza taken Kemosabe? Of course he had. And Harley was going to get it back—one way or another.

Harley walked out to Motif Number 1. Checked the exact spot where he'd parked Kemosabe in such a rush earlier. He'd walked right into Scorza's trap—like it was some kind of pass pattern. As much as he knew the bike was gone, he had to see the spot for himself.

If Parker and his dad hadn't shown up Saturday—and Harley had been able to finish with Scorza—would things be different now? Scorza wouldn't have dared take the bike. Parker didn't want Harley to hurt himself by hurting Scorza. Obviously. But now Scorza had hurt Harley in a way that might never heal if they didn't get Kemosabe back.

Parker said he'd run immediately from the ambulance to the wharf to guard Kemosabe. He probably had. But still . . . if he'd slept in the shed with him, this never would have happened. Parker looked absolutely tortured to give him the bad news . . . but he'd just have to get used to it. There was going to be a lot more bad news before this was over. After Harley settled things with Scorza, there was no doubt he'd be taken into custody. And he couldn't count on Uncle Ray to bail him out this time. His uncle would sign whatever papers needed to get him put away in juvey for sure. One way or another, his friendship with Parker was going to end. And that meant he'd lose Ella, too. And Jelly.

He had to stop thinking this way. Not that it wasn't all true, but he had to keep a clear head. He was on his own, and he couldn't make a mistake. Right now, he had to find the bike. Parker's theory about Kemosabe being dumped in the harbor made a whole lot of sense.

The tide was still high. Harley stepped from granite block to block as he walked the perimeter of the Motif pier. The surface of the water was black—and dead calm. He turned on his flashlight app and studied the face of the granite wall dropping down to the water—looking for any kind of fresh scrape—or black paint. He scanned the water for any telltale bubbles that might still be escaping. Air could still be trapped in the exhaust pipes or under the bike somehow, right? He looked for any signs of oil or gasoline rising to the surface—leading him to his trusted friend.

"God . . . if you're as real as Parker makes you seem . . ." He wasn't even sure how to finish that. But if God was real, he already knew Harley's heart, right? Maybe he didn't have to try to put his thoughts into words. "You know, right, God? And I'm begging you."

He had to get some sleep. But he longed for dawn so he could strap on his tank and find Kemosabe. He'd bring it to Parker's. His tools were already there. He'd start taking it apart immediately. Clean every bit of saltwater off it. Replace the wiring. The ignition system. Everything electric. He'd save up for new gauges. But he'd have the bike—and that's all that mattered. It would be okay. It would. He'd reassemble it. Kemosabe, his trusted friend, would ride again.

But what if his bike wasn't in the bay?

The question gnawed at him. Wormed its way into his gut.

If Scorza hadn't rolled Kemosabe off the pier, he had it hidden somewhere. And Scorza would be dead-set determined not to tell Harley a thing—especially if Harley leaned on him. Getting physical with Scorza to make him talk would be his last resort. It wouldn't be easy, but Harley would have to keep his hands off his ex-best friend until they found the bike. Then he'd deal with him.

And he'd have to make it count—because he'd only get one shot at Scorza. After Harley finished with him, Officer Greenwood would lock him up. Because the only way to keep the XL Sportster safe was to make sure Scorza would be in no condition—or too scared—to touch Kemosabe again.

Harley left the wharf and found himself staring at the shed again. The burial mound. But this time it wasn't himself he imagined at the bottom of the charred grave. It was Scorza. And it felt good.

CHAPTER 27

Monday, August 8, 6:10 a.m.

PARKER WOKE BEFORE DAYLIGHT TO THE *DING* of a text notification.

Harley. It had to be. Which was good. He'd been way too quiet at the hospital. *God, break down the wall between us.* Parker rolled over and grabbed his phone.

He stared at the name. *Wilson.*

Hey, Bucky . . . Jelly told me you're having trouble with some pyro-dude up there. Want help?

What on earth was Jelly telling him? And it was too late for help now. The bike was gone.

Not sure there's anything we can do now.

Parker sent off the text and waited for Wilson's response.

We Miccosukee have ways to deal with guys like him.

Parker didn't doubt it. Had Jelly only told him about the smoke bombs—or was he up-to-date about last night?

Did you hear Kemosabe is gone?

Yep. Remember, Bucky, Miccosukees are good trackers.

Was he serious? Like he'd hop a bus or something? Not likely, but it was good to know his friend from Everglades City was still there—and still had his back.

You're only half Miccosukee—so that makes you only half a good tracker?

A smiling emoji popped up.

Parker fired back another response.

If we ever need your help, I know I can depend on you.

Wilson sent back a couple of thumbs-ups—and an icon of what looked like a machete. Exactly the kind of thing Parker would expect from Wilson.

His alarm was due to ring in seconds. He turned it off and hustled downstairs. He'd grab some breakfast and load the tanks into Dad's truck.

Dad was already in the kitchen with Mom. She scooped hot oatmeal into bowls. "You men need something hot in you," she said. "Especially you, Parker, if you're going in that water." She passed him a bowl of brown sugar.

Fifteen minutes later, they parked the pickup alongside the North Basin of Rockport Harbor—not thirty feet from where Harley's shed once stood. The sun had just barely said its official good morning, and the horizon still glowed with the remnants of dawn.

Harbormasters Eric and Maggie idled *Alert 1* just off Bradley Wharf. If the two were bothered about being out so early, it didn't show on their faces. They did what was needed—and then some.

Harley waited on the pocket of beach just below Roy Moore's. He already had his wet suit on. The black color suited the brooding look on his face. Ella and Jelly stood beside him. Parker was surprised to see them—but then again not. Ella hugged herself and clutched her cross pendant all at the same time.

"I have lights." Harley pointed to a pair of underwater flashlights but didn't look Parker in the eyes.

The lights were a good idea. The water still looked black. Parker studied his friend's face. Harley looked like he wanted to say something but was keeping his mouth shut instead. That only added to Parker's sense of how much he'd let Harley down. If they found the bike now, all that would change. Parker was sure of it. He prayed silently that it wouldn't be all scratched up from its trip to the bottom of the harbor.

Parker's dad planned to stay topside on the granite pier—along with El and Jelly—tracking their bubbles.

"When we find it, we stand it up on its tires," Harley said. "One of us on each side. Then we walk the bottom and roll it back to the beach. We'll figure out how to get it off the beach once we get there."

And Parker would stick with him. Bringing it to Dad's house. Hosing it down. Taking it apart piece by piece. Cleaning every bit of saltwater off it. By the time they had it back together, their friendship would be back too.

The two of them readied their gear like they were part of a pit crew out to break a team record. They waded into the shallow water off the beach until they were waist deep.

Parker glanced up at his dad. Locked eyes with him for a moment. Dad held his hands together as if in prayer—and pointed to Parker. *Yeah, definitely pray, Dad. We need all the help we can get.*

"Let's go." Harley flipped on his flashlight, shoved his regulator mouthpiece in place, and dropped below the surface.

Parker followed immediately.

The water was dark—but clear. The beam of their lights cut right through the black. They kept the lights sweeping from side to side, following the rock wall around the pier. The east side and south end of the pier were their only hopes, really. There was no way Scorza would have dumped the bike on the other side—in plain sight of anyone fighting the fire. Somebody would have seen the splash, even if they didn't hear it.

Fingers of icy water worked their way into his wet suit, searching for warm skin. What if this wasn't Scorza? What if it was Steadman? What if he was suited up himself—knowing they'd check the bottom around the Motif? What if he intended to finish the job he'd started at the quarry? But why risk coming back where anybody might recognize him? He was too smart for that, right? Or did he think he was too smart to get caught? Parker kept scanning ahead. To the side. And looking over his shoulder, just in case.

Clayton Kingman's face flashed in his mind. Now there was a guy who could pull something like this off. And he was the type who'd travel from the Everglades all the way up to Massachusetts for a chance to get even. But the attack was focused on Harley—not Parker. And according to Jelly, Kingman was still in jail—and not up for parole. That was a little fact he'd double-checked last night.

Which brought this back to Scorza—and the improbability of it all.

Parker kept the granite wall of Bradley Wharf in sight. Harley ran a snake pattern, closer and farther away to make sure they didn't miss the bike if it somehow rolled farther away from the wall—which seemed like an impossibility given the weight of the bike and how level the bottom really was.

The search proved as empty as the bubbles rising to the surface from Parker's mouthpiece. Clusters of seaweed. Lots of rock and sand. Snatches of rope. Bottles. Unidentifiable scraps of metal—rust blistering on all sides.

They glided silently side by side for the entire length of the granite pier. Harley motioned for them to backtrack—but farther away from the pier this time. The calm Parker had seen on his friend's face earlier was gone now. They widened their perimeter and searched up to a good twenty-five feet off the wall—definitely farther than anyone could've possibly ditched the bike. Harley motioned for them to round the pier and check the other side, but his eyes seemed to mirror the hopeless feeling Parker felt.

Twenty minutes later they were right back where they started.

Parker surfaced and pulled off his mask. His gimpy arm had never gained back more than sixty-five percent of the function he had before the alligator attack. After coming up empty-handed, his arm felt even weaker. Dad, Jelly, Ella—all of them were on the beach now. Nobody had to ask what they'd seen down there—or rather, what they hadn't seen. The answer was obvious.

Harley did not look good. His face looked pale, despite coming out of the cold water.

Parker wished he'd say something. Anything. Harley's brooding quiet was killing him. But Parker had no idea what to say himself.

Dad waded into the water to help both of them with their gear. Parker knew exactly what he was doing. This was about Parker's arm and how he'd struggle to remove his gear alone. Right now, Dad's assist only made him feel more helpless than he already was.

El and Jelly handed each of the boys a towel the moment they got to shore.

"We'll find it," Dad said—seemingly to no one in particular. "Now we have one less place to look, right?"

Right. But this was the one place that had been their best shot.

Uncle Ray sauntered up. Arms folded across his chest, he towered above them on the granite lip of the wharf. Not saying a word. Which was probably good, seeing the mood Harley was in.

"I've got that appointment this morning," Uncle Ray finally said. "So you'll be manning the shop, Harley."

Parker should have known the guy's silence wouldn't last.

Harley glared up at him through strands of wet hair. His eyes smoldering with hate. "I've got to look for my bike."

Uncle Ray shook his head. "Not before this"—he pointed at the remains of the shed—"is cleaned up. We could book a charter any day now, and this will be the meeting spot. Can't have an eyesore like that around."

Harley stared at the sand. His fists clenching and unclenching. To some it may have looked like he was trying to warm them. Get some numbness out. But Parker knew better.

"After that," Uncle Ray said, "look for the motorcycle. Stay out all night. Not that it will do you a lick of good. I already told you that thing is gone."

The idiot uncle turned on his heel and walked back toward the back door of his shop. Harley tore at his wet suit, pulling it off like it was his mortal enemy clinging to him.

Jelly stepped closer to Parker. "What do we do now?"

Like Parker had the answers. He had no idea what on earth they were going to do now. But they had to think of something—and fast. Harley was a time bomb . . . and Parker had no idea how little time was on the clock before he exploded—and did something they'd all regret.

CHAPTER 28

HARLEY WORKED THE DIVE SHOP ALONE ALL DAY. Rockport Dive Company opened for business at ten o'clock—exactly when Uncle Ray had the appointment with the lawyer. The fact that he hadn't come back yet probably meant he was drinking. Celebrating that he'd gotten access to the trust fund—or consoling himself that he'd failed. When he did come back, he'd be bragging or brooding. Harley lost either way.

The shop had been quiet, but being the only one on deck, it wasn't like he could leave—no matter how much he wanted to. Parker, Jelly, their dads, and Ella showed up just after Uncle Ray left for his appointment. Officer Greenwood gave them the green light to clean up the shed. The way Mr. Buckman explained it, the police had all the evidence they needed. The fire was definitely arson.

Harley could have told them that the moment he saw the blazing words *BARF BAG*. What he really needed was for the police to focus all efforts on finding Kemosabe. Which is what Harley would be doing if he wasn't stuck here. Part of him wanted to just lock up the shop and get at it. But if Uncle Ray came back and saw what he'd done, there would be trouble. He could live with the yelling and the lectures, but it was the underlying threat that had Harley worried. Sometimes it seemed that Uncle Ray *wanted* Harley to mess up so he could turn him over to the state. He could get relocated to Boston—or even farther. If that happened, Harley would never get Kemosabe back.

It was a balancing act. He had to let the police do their thing— and hope they had the tools or smarts to find his motorcycle. But they had limitations. They couldn't *force* Scorza to talk. It's not like they could waterboard him or something—even though he deserved it. As far as Harley knew, there were no witnesses to say Scorza was anywhere near Bearskin Neck last night. Would the police even question him based on Harley's gut feeling?

But if the police didn't turn up anything—and soon—Harley would have to do something to make Scorza talk. If he waited too long, his chances of rescuing Kemosabe would go way down. Oh yeah, definitely a balancing act.

He drifted to the fill station room and stood at the window overlooking the North Basin. The spot he'd always loved to sit at night to watch the harbor. But now all he could see was the five of them working on the cleanup. They were making great progress. The uprights were all down. Somewhere along the way a dumpster had been delivered. Definitely not something Uncle Ray had arranged—that was for sure. The five of them worked like ants. They grabbed charred debris by the hand and shovelful. The dumpster was almost filled, and the shed that he'd known as the Hangar was nearly all cleaned up. What was left of it, anyway.

Harley should feel grateful for all they were doing. But they didn't get it. Nobody did. He didn't care about the shed cleanup—no matter what Uncle Ray said. If they really wanted to help, they should be looking for the motorcycle.

The front door bell jangled, and Uncle Ray stormed in, cussing up a regular typhoon. So that answered one of Harley's questions. The trust fund was unbreakable. Good. Now Harley would have to deal with his uncle's foul mood.

"I'd love to take that lawyer out on a little dive trip," Uncle Ray said. "Out to the Dry Salvages—and leave *him* out to dry." He shook a white envelope big enough to hold legal documents without them being folded. "Ironclad. That's what he said this is." He shook the papers. "Well, we'll see about that. I'll find a loophole. There has to be something."

He stomped up the stairs and came back minutes later without the papers. "How are you going to pay back that $3,500? And by the fourteenth?"

There was no need to answer. He couldn't pay. Both of them knew that.

"I'll get into that trust fund if I have to sue you to do it. There's got to be some wiggle room."

If there was, Harley had no doubt his uncle would find it.

"I'm going out for a smoke." And just like that Uncle Ray was gone. No questions about how sales were that day in the shop. No thank you for manning the shop when he should be out looking. Not a word of encouragement about the chances of finding the bike.

The moment the door closed behind Uncle Ray, Harley bounded up the stairs. He'd never seen any documents about the trust. He just knew it existed. The papers had to do with his future—and something inside him desperately wanted to see them. As if maybe they would provide some kind of proof that he *had* a future . . . or at least the hope of one.

Uncle Ray's door was open a crack, and Harley stopped dead. Instantly he knew this was a trap. He knelt on the floor and inspected the open end of the door. And there it was. A paper-clip stood on end, propped against the open door. If he swung it open, the paperclip would drop to the floor without a sound—and Uncle Ray would know he'd been in his room. He'd learned the penalty for that when he was twelve.

Harley backed away from the door, nice and easy so the paper-clip didn't drop because of any vibrations. "Sorry, Uncle Ray. You're not going to have the pleasure of giving me the belt this time." Whatever was on those legal papers wasn't worth falling for the trap.

He eased down the stairs and made his way to the fill room. The shed was gone now. And somehow it seemed that all his freedom had been chucked into that dumpster too. His plans for escape. How many times had he told himself he could do this? Put up with Uncle Ray until he was eighteen. Then he'd fire up Kemosabe and make his getaway. Three years down. Three to go. But without his bike? He'd never make it alone.

Which meant he had to get Kemosabe back. He'd heard once that the first seventy-two hours were critical in a kidnapping. If the missing person wasn't found by then, likely they never would be. The way Harley saw it, what happened to Kemosabe, his trusted friend, was nothing short of an abduction.

Seventy-two hours. Harley wouldn't wait any longer than that. He'd give the police a chance to find it, and he'd look like crazy himself. But if by Wednesday night Kemosabe was still gone,

Harley would do this his way. And after he did what he did, there would be no going back to life the way it was.

On the bright side, he wouldn't have to deal with Uncle Ray anymore. Likely Harley would be in jail.

But if Kemosabe wasn't found, Harley had no future anyway. Scorza hadn't just robbed Harley of his motorcycle. He'd stolen his past. His future. His dreams. Oh, yeah . . . definitely his dreams. Which is why he'd get his ex-best friend to talk . . . or he'd end Scorza's dreams too.

CHAPTER 29

PARKER HAD NEVER WORKED SO HARD IN HIS LIFE. He'd felt helpless when it came to the actual search for Kemosabe, especially after the underwater angle turned out to be a bust. But cleaning up the shed was something he could do. Something measurable. And it meant Harley wouldn't have to waste daylight with the cleanup himself. And secretly, he'd hoped after the cleanup was done, maybe he'd be too tired to beat himself up for failing Harley.

Not finding the bike in the harbor was a huge setback. Parker had been so sure. Absolutely positive that God was going to answer that prayer and that he'd be helping Harley disassemble and clean the bike tonight. The only thing he'd be doing with Harley was keeping him from retaliating against Scorza . . . and he'd probably mess that up too.

Harley showed up in the back window of the dive shop a number of times. Probably wishing he could be helping. But he didn't venture outside once. Not to say thanks. Not to offer them a glass of water. Sure, the guy had a lot on his mind . . . but still. To Parker it was proof that the wall Harley was building around himself was getting taller.

The shed footprint was still there. A perfectly rectangular patch of clean ground surrounded by scorched earth. Dad made arrangements for the dumpster to be taken away, then left with Uncle Sammy. "Got something to pick up," he said.

Parker busied himself picking up their gear. Shovels. Sledges. Crowbar. Gloves. Rake. Broom.

"I'm going to see if I can get Harley out to see the job," Ella said. "I'm worried about him." She tapped on the back door. He didn't leave the shop, but talked with her in the doorway instead. When she turned their way, she looked more concerned than ever.

Jelly was on her the moment she got back. "How is he?"

"Not good." Ella didn't look so good herself. "It was his eyes. All I saw was anger. And determination. Like he's biding his time . . . waiting for something."

"Waiting . . . ?" Jelly let the question hang there.

Ella looked back at the dive shop. "To pay Scorza another visit." Jelly groaned.

"He can't get that out of his head," Parker said. "I know, I know. The whole *BARF BAG* thing he saw points to Scorza . . . but nothing else does. It makes no sense that Scorza would take that big a risk."

Ella and Jelly exchanged a look that was impossible to read.

"What?" He looked from one to the other. "Am I the only one who thinks this was too big for Scorza to pull off?"

Neither girl said a thing.

"If this is all connected—the smoke bombs, and then the fire,"

Parker said, "Scorza has masterminded multiple crimes—without getting caught. There's no way."

Again, that look passed between the girls. Like they could communicate without words as well as he and Harley did when they were diving. "Am I missing something?"

"Yes." Jelly grabbed a rag from her back pocket. She wiped his cheek. "You're a sooty mess."

He stepped back. "I'm serious."

"What you're missing," Ella said, "is a plan. Now that the shed is cleaned up, what do we do next?"

Okay. Both of them dodged his question. There was something they weren't telling him—and clearly they didn't intend to. But Ella was right. They needed a plan. There had to be something they could do to find the motorcycle. But Parker had no idea what.

CHAPTER 30

ANGELICA HATED BEING DISHONEST WITH PARKER. Everything he said made sense. This *did* seem too big for Scorza—at least that's what she probably would have thought if they hadn't spotted him grabbing the Lyft ride. The truth was, he probably couldn't have pulled it off alone. Maybe he had help from some diehard loyal players on the team. But if Parker knew what she and Ella knew? She was pretty sure he'd change his opinion.

And if he did, *then* what would he do?

Seeing him the way he was now—desperate to help Harley—he wouldn't keep it a secret from his friend. Then they'd both get themselves in trouble. She was sure of it.

But not telling someone the whole story was as bad as lying. She'd learned that when she covered for her sister, hadn't she? Hadn't she promised herself she would never do that again? No secrets?

Parker stood by a neat pile of tools, brushing himself off.

"I can't lie to him," she whispered to Ella.

Ella nodded like she understood. "And you can't protect him if you don't."

Ugh. The truth of it hit hard. She would have to choose, wouldn't she? Be honest or protect him? She couldn't have both. Or maybe she could put the decision off—she could hold her secret just a little bit longer.

CHAPTER 31

ELLA WAS THE FIRST TO NOTICE Parker's dad returning. He parked the truck and swung out of the cab.

"Your next job." He opened a box filled with leaflets he'd had printed. "Just picked them up."

Jelly held one up and read. "MISSING. 1999 Harley-Davidson XL Sportster. Black, lots of chrome. Custom gas tank with *Kemosabe* painted across."

There were more details. A Rockport Police phone number. A silhouette of a motorcycle. And a $500 reward for information that led to the recovery of the bike.

"Great idea." Parker looked at his dad. "But who pays the reward?"

"Let's just say some concerned citizens."

Jelly's dad exited the extended cab carrying a small bin filled with rolls of duct tape and heavy-duty staplers. "We got the go-ahead from Officer Greenwood. Your job is to canvas the area with posters. Bearskin Neck. Around town. The two of us"—he pointed to Parker's dad—"will cover Gloucester. Then we'll hit Pigeon Cove."

The towns north and south of Rockport. It was a good plan.

"Jelly and I will work as a team," Ella said.

Jelly looked like she loved that idea. "Parker, how about you take everything from Rockport Pizza up to the train station," Jelly said.

"The library," Parker said. "Police department. Fire station. And lots of light poles in between. Maybe Harley can help me after he closes shop." He stuffed a stapler and a roll of duct tape into the pockets of his cargo shorts.

"We'll take from Front Beach all the way to Atlantic Avenue," Jelly said. "The T-wharf. Yacht Club. Bearskin Neck. And as many shops as we can that will let us put one in their window."

The two men took off in the pickup. Honestly? It would be a good effort. Posters were a great idea. But Ella wasn't holding out a ton of hope. She didn't know why she felt it, but she had the definite sense Kemosabe would never be found. But at least the posters would keep them busy. Give them something to do so they felt like they were helping. And maybe it would give Harley more time to cool down—and to accept the inevitable. Kemosabe was gone forever. She just hoped to be there for him when he finally realized that. Maybe if she was with him, she could find a way to keep him from self-destructing somehow.

Parker tucked the stack of posters under one arm. "Think we can get it done by dark?"

"We'll be done," Ella said. "Right, Jelly?"

Jelly checked the time. "Way more than enough daylight. But

if you are worried you can't keep up, we'll give you a hand when we're done." She put on an innocent face—but Ella saw right through her.

Harley slipped out the back door of the dive shop at that moment. He paused at the spot where the shed was. Stared at it. Then he walked up to the three of them and picked up one of the posters. He read it without a word. His face serious. Dark.

Any illusions she had that the posters might give him hope vanished.

Parker explained the plan to Harley—about him joining Parker after he closed the shop at six. "You and I will have more ground to cover," he said. "So we've got the tougher job."

Maybe when it came to posting the Missing signs, sure. The really tough job was keeping the truth about Scorza a secret. But the girls would do it. One look at Harley's face told Ella they had no choice.

CHAPTER 32

BRYCE WAS TAKING A CHANCE going to Rockport today. But he needed to catch a break, and that usually meant taking a risk. He'd often felt that running a gutsy play had the potential for more yardage. Finding the motorcycle was goal one for him, and he wasn't going to find it sitting at home and playing it safe.

He pedaled hard. He could think better when he was on the move—and he had to be really clearheaded right now. He was hiding key information about the motorcycle heist, but he had to appear normal. Which was the real reason he brought his football, keeping it tucked under one arm.

His bike ride to Cape Ann Marina didn't turn up anything helpful. He didn't find the boat, either. Or if he did, he didn't recognize it. There were too many lobster boats—and he couldn't get close enough to the ones moored out on buoys to be sure of anything. For now, the marina was a dead end. He'd seen some nasty dudes steal it. What would they do if they found out there was an eyewitness? And Harley's rage cage thing? Bryce had to play this smart, and that meant he'd need leverage. Finding Harley's cycle could prove to be the ultimate get-out-of-jail card. It was the key to everything he wanted right now—especially keeping himself alive.

And the next place to search was Bradley Wharf. Clearly one of the goons had dropped something—and it was important enough that he'd delayed his getaway to look for it. Whatever the thing was, Bryce was going to find it. Hopefully it would somehow lead Bryce to the motorcycle.

Actually, what he really wanted right now was to fast-forward his life. To college—playing with a full-ride scholarship. Thousands of fans jumping and screaming when he walked onto the field. Or better yet, zoom ahead to when he'd join the Marines like his big brother.

"If you want to be Mr. Nice Guy, get a job like most everybody else does. But that wasn't for me." Those were Rocko's exact words to Bryce when he was home on leave. "I'm as mean as I want to be now—and people see me as a hero."

That actually sounded really good to Bryce. Football wasn't his end goal. It was a way to get strong. Get tough. Be mean. It was his personal training camp for the military. Then he'd be a real hero. Which was one reason he couldn't let the arson charge fall on him. Would they even let him in the Marines with that on his record?

Had Officer Greenwood bought the baloney Bryce fed him this morning? The guy had come to the house. Got permission from his dear stepmom to ask him a few questions. Traci Trophy Wife just stood there hugging her little mama's boy, Jaxon, while Greenwood asked question after question. And Bryce had answered.

"No, I didn't put smoke bombs in the shed Friday night."

"Yes, I went to Harley's shed Sunday night."

"Yes, I wrote *BARF BAG* on the shed in fire paste."

"No, sir, I didn't light it. I got cold feet. I heard something inside the shed and realized Harley was inside. Vandalism is one thing . . . but setting a fire—with someone inside? I'm not *that* stupid."

By the way his stepmom looked at him, even she saw through that one. And Bryce had noticed something else. She also seemed just a little bit scared of him—which was a nice bonus. Bryce was just that much more sure she wouldn't question what he did—or how late he stayed out.

Whatever Officer Greenwood was thinking, he was smart enough to keep it hidden well. He kept jotting notes. Circling back. Asking about specific times.

"Yes, sir, I went straight home. Gosh . . . you said the shed burned down? I have no idea how that happened. Is Harley okay?"

"No, sir, I only have the one phone."

"No, sir, I've never bought a second phone at Walmart—or anywhere else."

And that was the big moment. All he had to do was admit to making the 911 call. It would prove he didn't set the fire, right? But it would also prove he'd been there when the goons set the fire. If word got out? He'd be seen as a loose end. An eyewitness. The only thing that stood between them and prison. The guys who hauled away the motorcycle in the lobster boat were two men he never wanted to see again. Definitely mean—but not the hero type.

Greenwood actually played the 911 call on his phone for Bryce, watching his face the whole time. Naturally, Bryce denied making the call or recognizing the voice. But his dear stepmom moved Jaxon to her other side—so she was positioned between Bryce and Jaxon. What? Did she think he'd set fire to the brat's bedroom or something?

Greenwood saw her reaction. He had to. But Bryce wasn't admitting anything. And with no witnesses, what could the cop do, right? Greenwood left, but Bryce got the definite vibe the cop would be back.

If he was suspicious, and that showed up in his report . . . who else might see it? Bryce's claim of innocence might be a brick wall for the cop without any evidence. But Kelsey and that other goon? They didn't seem like the type who'd risk even the ghost of a chance there'd been a witness. That was the real reason he had to keep what he'd seen last night locked up in a vault. If the wrong guys found out, Bryce wouldn't have to worry about scholarships or a future in the military. He also wouldn't have to worry about how he'd celebrate his sixteenth birthday.

Bryce was never any good at defense. He was all about offense. He couldn't sit back and hope Greenwood wouldn't find a traffic or security cam somewhere that would show he was there when the fire started. He couldn't sit on the bench and pray the goons never got wind that someone may have seen the whole thing.

So he'd stay on offense. He'd find out where the motorcycle was—and fast. He'd lead Harley right to it, and the police investigation would be over. Kelsey and the other goon would crawl back into whatever cave they'd come from. Bryce could see it all play out in his head. He'd be Harley's hero. No more ex-friend. Harley would drop-kick Gatorade and be part of Bryce's huddle forever. They'd be running pass patterns on Front Beach like old times.

Bryce saw the first Missing poster near the fire station. The

closer he got to town, the more he saw. He stopped and pulled
one off a light post. He'd put it up in his bedroom as a souvenir.
The thing would brighten his day just looking at it. And he'd use
the phone number listed. He'd call in some bogus leads. Keep the
cops off the real trail until Bryce found the bike. If Bryce wasn't
the one who found it, Harley would never come crawling back to
him like a guilty puppy. And Bryce really wanted to see Harley
grovel. Just imagining it made him smile.

Bryce biked right down Bearskin Neck. Parked near Roy
Moore's and hustled down the walkway leading to the patio out
back. Harley's shed was gone—like totally cleaned up.

"That was fast," he said to no one.

He hoped to find what he was looking for and get out of
Rockport fast. No sign of Lotitto—or his friends—which was
good.

His hiding spot among the lobster traps was still there. Which
gave him all the bearings he needed. Whatever the guy dropped
had to be between him and where the boat was parked, right?
Actually, it could be anywhere around the shed itself. Or maybe it
had dropped into the water when they were loading the motorcycle
onto the lobster boat. But this is where the goon kept looking—
and it's where Bryce needed to concentrate.

He stood right where Lotitto had parked the motorcycle before
running back to fight the fire. Bryce searched the ground as he
walked to where the ramp had been propped. Nothing.

Bryce retraced his steps. Scanned more carefully now. Especially
checking the crevices between granite blocks. He toed and swept
the gravel with his foot. Moved a couple lobster traps that he
hadn't remembered from last night and peered close to the ground.
He stood and looked back to the east side of the wharf, replaying

the scene from the night before. He walked to the edge of the granite retaining wall, then did it all over again.

He held out his football like a divining rod, sweeping it back and forth above the ground like it had the power to point him to whatever he wasn't seeing.

He got the gnawing feeling he wasn't alone. *Is somebody watching me?* He broke off the search for a moment and did a slow 360. There were tourists on the Tuna Wharf, but none looking his way. He scanned Outer Basin. Sailboats moored, nose into the wind. No Officer Greenwood sitting in the cockpit of one of them with a pair of binoculars and a walkie-talkie. Which was a good thing. How would Bryce have explained himself?

He was the only soul on Bradley Wharf. He scanned across the inlet to the North Basin. T-wharf had traffic, but nobody who appeared to be watching him.

"Shake it off, Scorza." It was pregame jitters or something. Nothing more than that. "Get the job done and get out of here." Hearing his own voice boosted his confidence a bit.

The lobster traps. Had anybody moved one of the stacks? Bryce grabbed the top one off the pile nearest to where the motorcycle had been parked. He set it to one side. Grabbed the second. Then the third. The ground below the last trap looked clear, but he lifted the boxy thing anyway. Something rattled inside the trap, clattering to a stop inside the wire cage.

It was silver—like stainless steel—and would easily fit in the palm of his hand. Bryce's heart spiked. "You're amazing, Bryce Scorza!" He heard fans cheering in his head even as he shook the trap and angled it until the object fell to the ground. He ditched the lobster trap, snatched up a very new-looking pocketknife, and examined it. *Cut Through the Clutter* was screened in orange ink on one side of the handle.

He flipped it over—and stared. *PORT KNOX Storage—Gloucester.* "Bryce Scorza," he practically shouted, "you are a genius!"

"If that were true, you wouldn't be here."

Bryce balled the knife in his fist and whirled to face Everglades Girl—with Black Beauty coming up right behind her.

Everglades smiled. "Didn't mean to scare the big football hero."

Bryce waved her off. "I should be used to fans stalking me by now."

Black Beauty pointed at his football. "The chances of us becoming fans are about as high—"

"As you trading that football," Everglades Girl said, "for a Frisbee."

Bryce gave her a once-over. Tour guide shirt. Cargo shorts. Some sort of hiking shoes. Cap from someplace in the Glades. Tiny. Tough. He couldn't help but smile. "Not a fan? Yet here you are following me. Again."

"I wouldn't follow you out of a burning building." She glanced back to where the shed had been. "Speaking of burning buildings . . . what were you *thinking*? You could have killed Harley with that fire."

"I didn't start that fire. I wrote the *BARF BAG* thing, but that was it. I was probably back in my bed before that fire started."

The two girls looked at each other like they weren't buying it.

"You were *here*." Everglades stepped right up to him. The girl was fearless.

Deny. Deny. Deny. "You're both delusional. Especially you, Everglades."

"You're confusing delusional with dangerous. And we *are* dangerous." She made a muscle. "Strong as a gator. And as quick as a snake." She feinted a jab at his face.

He instinctively jerked backward and kicked himself for it.

"Oh yeah," Everglades said. "Incredibly fast. Remember that, Mr. Scorza."

Was he smiling? He had to be. The girls really thought they could intimidate him? Entertain him—yeah. They were better than a circus act. But intimidate? Not a chance.

"Harley thinks it was you," Beauty said. "And if *I* were you, I'd give him back his motorcycle before he gets his hands on you."

"I'm telling you, I had nothing to do with whatever happened to his bike."

Everglades stepped closer. "Yet here you are—right where his bike was before it was stolen. Sure looks like you're returning to the scene of the crime."

"Hey, I didn't touch his bike. I didn't torch his shed. I already told the police everything I know."

"Right." Everglades glared at him. "You told the cops whatever you felt you needed to say to get off the hook."

Quick. Fearless. And she was smart, too. "I got nothing to hide."

"Really?" Everglades pointed to his fist. "Show us what you picked up there."

Beauty stepped up beside her. Shoulder to shoulder. What he wouldn't give to have an offensive line as protective of him as these two were of Harley and Gatorade.

"Open your hand, Scorza," Beauty said. "Unless of course you *do* have something to hide."

To not show them would absolutely make it look like he was guilty as sin. But to let them inspect it would give them the clue that may actually help them find the motorcycle. Maybe if he only showed them one side of the knife.

He opened his fist and bounced the knife on his palm so it would be impossible to read any of the words on it. He closed his fingers over it again. "Just a cheap pocketknife I found. A piece of junk."

"You're holding it awfully tight for something with no value." Everglades snapped her fingers and held out her palm. "Let's see it."

Not something he could let happen. "You want to see it?" He hauled back and threw it far out into the harbor. "Be my guest." He swept his hand toward the harbor.

Everglades gasped. "Bryce Scorza!"

Hearing her say his full name was kind of nice—even though she looked spitting mad.

"I can't believe you did that!"

He kissed his pointer finger and touched the bicep on his passing arm. "Believe it, girl. That was a seventy-five-yard throw—at least. I could have thrown it farther if I wanted."

Everglades Girl shook her head. "That could have been a clue."

"Clue nothing. Probably some kid dropped it."

Everglades stared out over the water like she was willing the thing to rise to the surface.

Bryce leaned in close enough to whisper. "It's gone, Everglades."

"Just like you should be." She whirled to face him. "If Harley finds you here—"

"I'm not afraid of Lottie." Okay, maybe that was a tiny stretch of the truth.

"Then you're incredibly stupid," Beauty said. "You think that restraining order will stop him? You need to tell him where that motorcycle is."

Bryce spread his hand out on his chest. "I didn't take it. I swear. I'm actually looking for the motorcycle—just like everyone else."

Everglades frowned. "Why are you looking for it?"

"There's a nice reward, for one."

"Like the guy who has a Jeep Wrangler before he gets his driver's license really needs the money," Beauty said. "Look, we saw you getting into that Lyft truck—and that was long after the fire was blazing."

Okay, that wasn't good. Not one bit. He did his best to put on a confused face. "What?"

"Cut the act, Mr. Scorza," Everglades said. "You were still in town when the shed went up in flames. Either you started it—or you know who did."

They were sharp. And he needed to get sharper. Spin his story just right so it all made sense.

"My advice?" Everglades stepped closer. "Tell us what you know. You really don't want Harley to get his hands on you."

Hold on. Bryce needed to think. Were the girls tipping him off so *he* wouldn't get hurt? Not a chance. They'd probably love to see him get decked. This was about *Harley's* protection. If Bryce told them what he knew—and that led to finding the motorcycle— maybe they figured Harley would back off. "I think it's *you* two who don't want Harley to get his hands on me."

Bullseye. He saw it in Beauty's face immediately.

"If Harley comes near me, he's breaking the restraining order. What will happen to him then?"

Beauty's eyes darted from Bryce to Everglades and back.

He had them on the ropes. "And if he touches me—I mean, if he even puts a finger on me—they'll take him away. We all know that."

"Tell us." Everglades was using her tough girl voice again. But there was no real muscle behind it.

"I did write *BARF BAG* on the shed wall—in fire paste. But once I realized Harley was sleeping in the shed, I didn't light it. End of story."

"You didn't see the fire truck?" Beauty said. "Didn't hear the sirens?"

Don't let them know you saw the fire. Deny. "Yeah, I saw the fire truck. It was in a hurry, so you'll excuse me if I didn't ask where it was going. Somebody could have been choking on a slice of pizza for all I knew."

Everglades Girl looked frustrated. "Okay, Mr. Scorza. Why the big rush to get out of town last night?"

"It was late. I had to get home." Bryce shrugged. "I didn't want to get grounded."

"You really expect us to believe you never saw the fire *and* were in such a humongous hurry to get home?" Everglades Girl was back, taking another wild swing.

But he could handle it. "Like I told you, I was in a hurry. That's *why* I called for the Lyft ride instead of just taking my bike." Use their own arguments against them. It worked on his dad all the time. "Thank you for helping me prove my point."

Bryce scooted past them. He needed to get out of here before Harley showed up.

Suddenly the football got knocked free from his hand. The thing hit the ground hard and did a herky-jerky dance for the granite wall. Bryce scrambled after it, nearly diving to catch it before it end-over-ended to the water below.

Both girls stood there each with a seriously smug look on their face. "Fumble," Everglades said. "Looks like I'm two for two." She made a muscle—and instantly spun her hand around like a snake striking him again.

Right. Strong and quick. The girl was maddening—and amazing. He held up the football. "But the quarterback recovered it. Remember that."

Everglades nodded. "*After* he fumbled."

He had the sense that he'd been here way too long. He'd gotten what he needed—a massive clue to where the motorcycle might be. But it had come at a cost. The girls had caught him in the exact spot where the bike had been standing. And they knew he was still in town when the fire was raging. Both of those would give Officer Greenwood plenty of reason to come back and question him.

Just act like you've done nothing wrong and have nothing to hide, Bryce.

"Why don't you tell us what you *really* know," Everglades said.

The girl was a firecracker with a short fuse. An M80. Small package with a big boom. What he wouldn't give to have her on his team. Maybe if he found the motorcycle, he'd get a twofer. He'd get Harley back, and maybe he'd get Everglades Girl to see him in a new light.

He may have lost a little yardage on this play by the girls seeing him. But finding the knife? That put him in a *really* good field position. He wished he had some kind of snappy comeback. Something to get their minds off what he knew—but wasn't saying. But after just standing there and staring at them way too long, nothing came. He turned and headed for Roy Moore's deck—and his bike.

"Hey!" Everglades Girl again. "Where do you think you're going?"

Wouldn't they like to know. "To earn that $500."

CHAPTER 33

BEFORE SEEING SCORZA, Angelica felt a level of hope rising with each flyer they'd stapled to a wooden post or taped on a shop window. Nobody could walk the Neck and not know a motorcycle was missing. But after the last flyer was up—and suddenly there was nothing to do but wait? It felt more like her balloon of hope had a small leak.

And after talking with Bryce Scorza, what was left of the air in her balloon was gone. She watched him stride across the deck behind Roy Moore's and disappear between the buildings.

"Scorza is like a human tick," Ella said. "He gets under your skin. Causes problems. Do you believe that guy?"

"Not as much as he hopes we do," Angelica said. "What if Scorza *is* behind everything, like Harley thinks? I mean, it makes sense, right?"

"Stealing a motorcycle and burning a shed makes absolutely no sense, girl."

Angelica shrugged. "The thing I don't get? What's the motive? I mean, why go to all this trouble? If Scorza *is* the guy—and he gets caught? Arson? Grand theft? Attempted murder if he knew Harley was sleeping in the shed when he set it on fire? They could try him as an adult."

"People do crazy things when they're angry," Ella said. "Look at road rage. Somebody gets cut off—and the next thing you know he's shooting at the other guy's car."

"So you think Scorza is still ticked that Harley ditched him as a friend? You think he wants payback—for that?"

Ella shrugged. "Why not? He's an egomaniac—or a narcissist. He sees his old friend Harley hanging out with Parker. It makes him really mad. Or maybe he's just plain mean."

"Actually," Angelica said, "I think it's both. His pride is hurt, so he wants to hurt Harley."

Ella seemed to be processing that for a moment. "And the thing is, when he hurts Harley, he hurts all of us."

True enough.

"So," Ella said, "how much of his story do you believe?"

That was easy. "He was here. He did the fire paste. And I believe he left. But not as early as he claims he did. Do you think he started the fire?"

Ella nodded. "Now I do. Don't you?"

Angelica definitely did. "But he had to have help making Kemosabe disappear—or he hid that thing really close." But where? And how did he get past Harley? It just wasn't fitting together. "That pocketknife must have been awfully important to risk coming back for it." She stared at the area where he'd thrown the knife. The thing likely got swallowed by silt on the bottom. It was gone for sure.

Ella frowned. "Now what?"

What *could* they do? "We know Scorza started the fire—but the one piece of evidence that could have proved something has been pitched into Rockport Harbor."

"No—what do we do about Harley?" Ella said. "Can you imagine what would happen if we tell him what just happened here?"

"There would be no stopping him, restraining order or no restraining order." But keeping this from him didn't feel right either. "I wish we could tell Parker."

"You know he'd tell Harley. He'd say it would be dishonest not to. He's a prisoner to his own integrity."

Angelica wouldn't go so far as to say he was a prisoner, but his need to do the right thing could put him in a bad spot, couldn't it? "If Harley raced off to deal with Scorza, who do you think would be right there, trying to stop him?" Parker would be involved. "I could call Officer Greenwood, though. Tell him what just happened."

"That Bryce Scorza was on a public wharf, found a pocketknife, and then threw it into the water?" Ella shook her head. "What does it prove—besides the fact that he's a litterbug?"

Angelica giggled at that. "Yes, probably nothing. But I have to tell someone. Greenwood would be safe. There'd be no way he'd tell Harley—or Parker."

"Well, after you do that," Ella said, "we need a new strategy. I think we need to take a lesson from Scorza's fans."

Angelica snorted. "What fans? How can a guy like that—"

"I say we follow him," Ella said. "But at a distance. We could get lucky. Maybe he'll lead us right to the bike."

It was a shot in the dark, but it was something.

"So, back to the boys." Ella held out her hand. "They can never hear about us finding Scorza here—or the knife. Agreed?"

Angelica stared at Ella's hand, then grabbed it and gave it a single pump. Angelica was on a roll now. More like a backward slide. Keeping more secrets from Parker. She hated doing that. Actually, that wasn't quite accurate. She hated *herself* for doing that.

CHAPTER 34

HARLEY CLOSED THE SHOP, locked up the money from the register in the safe, and set off for Rockport Pizza. There were Missing posters everywhere—each one a reminder of just how much he'd lost.

To not meet them when they'd texted him about dinner would have been a mistake. He had to keep them off the trail of what he really intended to do. If they caught the scent, they'd be all over him to stay away from Scorza. They'd want him to give his word that he'd leave Scorza alone. But he definitely wasn't going to make a promise he absolutely knew he wouldn't keep.

And after he refused to make the promises, they'd make it tougher for him to deal with Scorza the way he needed to. One of them would always be on him.

Each one was tricky in their own way. Jelly? She could sniff out a lie—and wasn't afraid to confront. Parker? He'd do whatever he needed to stop Harley—in the name of protecting him—even if that meant getting his dad to help. Harley didn't want that happening again. Ella? She was human sodium pentothal. Truth serum. If she started asking him the right questions, he didn't have the ability to do anything but tell her the truth. She's the one who worried him most.

He had to keep them from knowing what was really going on in his head. He needed his friends—now more than ever. He knew that. But if the bike wasn't found—and soon—he'd lose them anyway, wouldn't he? Because when he dealt with Scorza, they'd be gone. In a way, maybe it was easier to think of them as gone now.

Harley stopped on the sidewalk just outside Rockport Pizza. The others were already at a booth. Jelly and Ella shared a bench seat. Parker sat opposite and a little sideways, his back against the wall. Harley was no good as an actor, but he needed to get a whole lot better. Now. He steeled himself for what he needed to do, then stepped inside Rockport Pizza like he was walking onstage.

The smell reminded him instantly of his dad and all the times they'd worked on Kemosabe with an open box of pizza between them. *Don't go there, Harley. Not now.* He pushed the thought out of his head.

Act natural. Smile. He slid onto the bench seat, with his back to the street. A large pizza sat dead center on the table. Half cheese, half cheese and pineapple. Ella and Jelly were all about the small talk. Obviously, Harley wasn't the only one acting at the moment. *Just be yourself, Harley.* The problem with that strategy right now? He had no idea who that was.

"What?" He pointed at Jelly's plate. "You're actually eating pizza? Does that mean you're finally getting tired of PB and J?" It was a lame comment, but right now it was the best he could do.

She shook her head. "I'm just having pizza so you all don't get jealous of my PB and J."

It cut the tension—at least for the moment. But the longer they sat there eating and talking, the more Harley felt on edge. Parker, Ella, Jelly. It seemed that each tried to act like they weren't watching him. Like they weren't analyzing everything he said and every reaction to what they said.

Harley had the weird feeling that both Ella and Jelly were holding out on him. Not telling him something. But what? Or maybe he was getting a little paranoid. Actually, Harley was the one holding the little secret about what he'd do to Scorza on Wednesday night.

"Crime victims sometimes blame themselves," Jelly said. "They say things like, 'I shouldn't have been out that late at night. I shouldn't have gone alone.' But it's wrong thinking."

So now she was trying to psychoanalyze him or something? Talk about being obvious. "Kemosabe is gone," Harley said. "And it is absolutely, 100 percent my fault."

Ella watched him from across the table. "How do you figure?"

He glanced at Parker. "I should have never let you know I was going to Scorza's Saturday. That's all on me. If you and your dad hadn't stopped me from putting the fear of God into him, he would have never dared come back last night."

Parker stared at the table like he knew Harley was right.

"If I'd had five more minutes alone with Scorza—you know where I'd be right now? Sitting on Kemosabe."

"Wrong." Ella pointed at him with a slice of cheese and pineapple. "You'd be sitting in jail. Parker and his dad kept you from messing everything up."

It made no sense to argue. "At least I'd still have my bike." Okay, he'd said way too much. *Stick with the plan, Harley.*

For a moment nobody said a word—which was way more than just awkward. Harley took another bite of pizza. Maybe if he kept his mouth full, he wouldn't talk so stinking much.

"With all these reward posters around town," Ella said, "somebody's going to call with a tip."

"Right." Jelly put on an overly optimistic face. "What are the chances that Scorza—or anybody else—got that motorcycle off Bearskin Neck without somebody seeing *something*?"

Jelly seemed to be in some kind of junior detective mode. "How long after you parked Kemosabe by the lobster traps before the fire truck pulled up and blocked the access road behind the shops?"

"A couple minutes. Maybe less. I rocked it up onto its stand, then ran for the hose."

"So," Jelly said, "if Scorza took the bike, he would have had to roll it right past you—or the fire engine."

Exactly what bothered Harley. "And there were volunteer firemen all over—and more pulling up."

"What about rolling it between buildings," Parker said. "Could he have done that—then rolled it right down the street and off the Neck?"

Harley shrugged. "I've never tried. But how did he get it past *me*? He'd have rolled it right past the shed. And if it was after I was hauled off to the ambulance, same thing. The ambulance was parked like right in front of the dive shop. I had a clear view down the Neck. How could I have missed someone kidnapping Kemosabe?" The truth was, there was so much chaos going on, there was a very real chance he could have missed it—and he hated himself for it.

"Well, now we know he didn't roll it off into the water," Jelly said, "so he must have used all the confusion to roll it right past people."

Ella nodded. "Which is why those posters are going to turn up something."

Harley wanted to believe it. But he wasn't going to stand around with his hands in his pockets waiting for the phone to ring. He'd mapped out his own plan those hours in the shop this afternoon when Uncle Ray was out and the customers were scarce. He'd start with a phone call to Scorza. Not a text. Nothing in writing that could be used against him later. He'd keep the call short so Scorza couldn't motion anyone over to listen in or record it. And he wouldn't need long to say what he needed to say. *Tell me where to find the bike, and I'll drop this. But if I come to you, I'll drop you.*

"We have to figure this out—and fast," Jelly said. "With every day that passes, our chances get slimmer."

"Oh, *that* was helpful." But Harley already knew how fast the clock was moving. And deep inside, he absolutely feared it was already too late.

"I'm just saying—"

Harley waved her off. "I shouldn't have said that. I'm sorry." And he meant it. He definitely had to be more careful.

Parker took a massive bite of pizza. "We've got to start thinking like Scorza—or whoever took the bike."

"It was Scorza—and I've played enough football with him to know how he thinks." All three of them were looking at him now—like they expected him to psychoanalyze his ex-best friend. "Scorza acts first. Thinks later." That little trait had worked well for him on the football field. Not always so well off.

"So for now," Jelly said, "let's assume Harley is right. This was Scorza. What does he plan to do with the bike?"

Scorza always had to win. To come out on top. He was way too much like Uncle Ray in that way. "Make sure I never see it again."

"What better way to hurt you," Ella said. "The guy's a pig."

"If Scorza wants to make sure you never get the bike—how would he do that?" Jelly stared at her pizza like it held the answers.

"He'd dump it somewhere," Harley said. "Maybe hide it until things cool down a bit, then take it someplace and ditch it where it will never be found." Maybe he *would* roll it into the water someplace.

"A quarry," Parker said.

There were dozens of flooded quarries on Cape Ann. If Scorza dumped it in one of them, Harley would never find it.

"Even if a diver found it a month later—it would have been in the water too long," Parker said. "Right?"

Harley shrugged.

"We are not going to let Scorza win," Ella said. "I guarantee he won't be smiling when this is all over."

"If he is, I'll smack that smile off his face." Harley cringed inside. This was not the type of thing he wanted to say aloud. He should have brought duct tape.

"Mr. Lotitto," El said, "have you been playing football without a helmet lately?"

Harley just shook his head.

"Because you're talking like a guy who's taken a few too many hits to the noggin."

He smiled slightly.

"We're going to find that bike," Ella said. "But we have to be smart about this."

If she thought her confidence would rub off on him, she'd guessed wrong. But he'd play along.

She studied his face. "Promise me you won't do something stupid."

Exactly where he didn't want this conversation going. And he'd done it to himself by shooting off his mouth. "Stupid was when I thought he was my friend, once upon a time. Stupid was thinking that all I had to do to keep Kemosabe safe was sleep next to it. So don't worry, Ella. No more stupid for me. From now on . . ." *Here you go again, Harley. Stop. Shut your mouth.*

Where was the duct tape when he needed it? Harley shook his head. "Don't you worry. I'm going to play this smart." But by the looks on their faces, his acting wasn't up to par.

The rumble of a motorcycle cruising down the block made all four of them stop dead. But it only took a couple seconds—if that—for Harley to know it wasn't Kemosabe.

"Is it . . . ?" Jelly stared out the storefront windows.

He shook his head without even turning to look.

"It's a Harley-Davidson . . . but not Kemosabe. Wrong pipes." Jelly gave him a look like it was strange he knew his bike's voice.

"We've made some decisions while you were at work," Ella said. "The police will be tracking down calls the posters generate, right? Meanwhile, Jelly and I will search online for 1999 XL Sportsters for sale."

He was kind of impressed she remembered the model and year.

"Or people selling parts for them," Jelly said.

Harley dropped his pizza on the floor—hoping it looked like an accident. He bent to pick it up. He didn't trust himself to keep a poker face—and couldn't let them see a hint of what he was feeling. He wanted to scream. Rip the table away from the wall and send it flying through the front window. If Scorza even *tried* taking Kemosabe apart, he would take Scorza apart, piece by piece. *Pull it together, Harley. Pull it. Together.*

Harley sat back up. "I really appreciate what you're doing. They're good ideas, every one of them." He tried to say it like he meant it. "But do you have any idea how many Harleys are out there or how many people might be selling parts? Millions."

"But not for that year. That model," Jelly said. "And I'll narrow the search to Cape Ann."

It was worth a shot. "Leave no stone unturned, right?"

"Exactly," Ella said. "What about you, Harley? What's your plan?"

Here it was. What they'd been fishing for the whole time. They'd probably worked it all out before he got here. *Find out if he's planning to visit Scorza—and stop him.* "Uncle Ray isn't letting me off work to search. So each day—the minute we close—I'm going to keep checking the Neck. I don't think he could have moved it beyond that."

"And I'll check everywhere I can until you're off work," Parker said. "And until then we'll make the dive shop our base of operations. Any new intel we get, we funnel it through Harley."

He saw right through them. Parker was the designated driver, so to speak. He was to be the one who kept Harley far from Scorza. He'd be checking in on him all day—and planned to stay close after work. Of course. Well, he'd let Parker think he had everything under control—until the 72 hours were up Wednesday night. If they still hadn't found Kemosabe, Harley would do this his way. Then Parker would suddenly realize he wasn't in control of Harley at all . . . but it would be too late to stop him.

He wanted Parker, Ella, and Jelly for friends. And he needed them even more than he wanted them. But if he didn't get Kemosabe back, he'd do something awful. And he'd lose the best friends he'd ever had. It was like Scorza wasn't done stealing from him. First the motorcycle. Soon his friends. Scorza was robbing him of everything he cared about.

This waiting around was nuts. He had to get the information out of Scorza, one way or another. "How long do you think he'd wait for things to cool down before he moves it from wherever he's hidden it?"

"A week or two, at least," Ella looked to the others like she expected everyone to nod their heads.

Would Scorza wait that long? Maybe. But Harley sure wouldn't. It would be hard enough to wait until Wednesday. If they didn't find Kemosabe by then, he'd be paying Scorza that late-night visit. And after that? Harley would go to jail.

CHAPTER 35

IN THE NEARLY 72 HOURS THAT HAD PASSED since Kemosabe went missing, and especially the last forty-eight hours since the four of them met at Rockport Pizza, a lot had happened.

A lot of *nothing*.

The way Parker heard things, the police followed up on calls that came in to the number listed on the poster. People claimed to have heard or seen the bike up in Pigeon Cove, Newburyport, and beyond. But no Kemosabe.

Parker kept to the plan of searching Bearskin Neck. He knew every shop—and every narrow alleyway pass between them. He'd looked in every window, tried every lock. Even looked for motorcycle tracks every place that wasn't paved.

Harley had joined him Tuesday after work—which set Parker more on edge than ever. Not that Harley wasn't a help. But he was getting harder. Quieter. More distant. Not a zoned-out kind of thing. His mind was definitely busy someplace—but he just wasn't telling Parker where.

It didn't help that Harley had found another cardboard sign on the door this morning. It was in the shape of a cross with the words **KEEMO—SOBBY** written in marker with a hand-drawn emoji of a crying smiley face. Directly below it were the words **REST IN PIECES**.

Parker was at the dive shop when Officer Greenwood took it to check for prints. Harley insisted there was no need. He knew who did it. "I hope Scorza made an extra cross. His family may need it."

That got him an in-your-face lecture from his Uncle Ray—even with the cop and Parker right there.

"You stay away from that kid," Uncle Ray said. "That's not a request. And if you're not going to follow my orders, then we got a whole different problem to deal with."

Which showed how much Uncle Ray didn't know him. Giving Harley a direct order like that would likely have the opposite effect.

"After we close shop I got some work to do on *Deep Trouble* to outfit it for dive tours," Uncle Ray said. "I'll give you two hours to do more searching with your buddy here, but by eight o'clock sharp I need you right back here to run some errands for me."

Parker had been pretty sure Uncle Ray intended to keep him too busy to pay any visits to Scorza's house.

Parker was back minutes before Harley turned the bolt on the dive shop—and his friend looked like he'd locked himself up at the same time. Brooding. That was a vocab word Parker had never used in his life. But it was the one that popped in his mind when he saw Harley's face. Jelly or Ella could probably read him better—and he wished they were here. But to Parker, Harley had the face of one bent on revenge. He had to get his mind on the search, not payback.

"I've been thinking about that sign from this morning," Parker said. "And I talked to Jelly and Ella about it too. What if it's a clue?"

"To who wrote it?" Harley shook his head like the whole thing was obvious.

"No. To what he plans to do. *Pieces.* That's what the sign said. He's going to take it apart. That's how he'll get it off the Neck. One piece at a time."

"You think he's going to set up a table at the Farmer's Market or something?" There was no missing the sarcasm in his voice.

"No, I don't think he's that stupid—and I don't think you are either, okay?" Maybe Parker said it a little too harshly, but Harley was being ridiculous. "He wants to get the bike someplace safer. That's the only way he can make sure you never find it."

Harley didn't say a word for a long moment. "He's taunting me. Showing me the ball—and daring me to strip it from him."

That actually made a lot of sense. "So how about we post ourselves where we can see anyone coming or going from the Neck—until you have to do that stuff for your uncle."

Harley stared at the ground. "He's got an Uber lined up for me to make some deliveries."

"Okay," Parker said. "I say we grab something from Top Dog. We take it to go and do some serious people watching."

Harley shrugged like he really had no opinion. No plan of his own. "Whatever you think." He raised his head for a moment, glancing at Parker through strands of hair. But his eyes harbored a dark determination.

The look lasted only a split second. But more than enough time to alarm Parker even more. *Dear God . . . help me to help him.* If eyes were really windows to the soul, then Harley had traveled someplace terrifying. And he was pulling away.

"After the errands, just text me," Parker said. "You can come over to my house and we'll hang out, okay?"

"I'll do my best." Harley said the right words, but there was no conviction behind them.

The way Parker saw it? Harley had his own plans—and Parker wasn't part of them. How was Parker supposed to stop him now?

CHAPTER 36

OVER THE LAST TWO DAYS, Ella had transformed Grams's kitchen into some kind of investigation headquarters. Right now, Parker's mom was there. Grams. And Jelly, of course.

Ella put Mrs. Buckman and Grams in charge of searching for Harley-Davidson motorcycle parts. Grams on her old laptop computer, Mrs. Buckman on her phone. Ella and Jelly used their phones to search for Harley XL Sportsters for sale anywhere from Newburyport to Boston.

And there were plenty.

But a quick check of the posted photos eliminated every single one of them.

By far the tougher job was tracking down the parts, but to their credit, the women weren't complaining.

"I'm not sure I even know what I'm looking for," Grams said. "But I'm focusing on that fancy gas tank Harley had."

With the name Kemosabe custom painted across the side, it was probably the one part of the bike that would never be put up for sale, but Ella didn't want to discourage her.

"Ladies," Mrs. Buckman said, "would you be okay if I prayed—aloud—about this?"

Prayer was probably exactly what they needed.

"A fine idea," Grams said. "We need a little divine intervention here. I was just thinking I ought to bring some petitions to the Lord myself."

Honestly, Ella wasn't so sure any of Grams's prayers would make a difference. She was a pretty loosey-goosey mix of superstition, tradition, and a wide variety of Bible verses and quotes from who knew where. One minute she could be speaking to Ella, the next she was talking to God. Or a dead relative. Sometimes Ella had to keep her eyes on Grams just to get a clue as to who she was addressing.

Google satellite view. That was Grams's approach to prayer, it seemed. God was way up there somewhere looking down on mankind. If a person wanted to get His attention, they'd need to raise their voice a bit.

But Mrs. Buckman was different. A "follower of Christ" was how she described herself. But that didn't begin to describe what Ella saw in her. Parker's mom was what Ella imagined a true believer would be like.

"God knows where Harley's bike is," Mrs. Buckman said. She closed her eyes and paused. Was she trying to figure out what she wanted to say—or maybe focusing on the fact that she was bringing a request to almighty God? Ella couldn't say. Ella bowed her head with the others but kept her eyes open to watch her.

Mrs. Buckman asked God to lead them. To help them—or the

police—find the bike when the time was right. She didn't raise her voice. If anything, her voice got softer. Like God was sitting close.

She'd barely prayed a couple minutes before she stopped all of a sudden. *Was that it? Was Mrs. Buckman done?* Grams could go on and on with her prayers.

Mrs. Buckman's eyes were still closed. But tighter. She raised her face toward the ceiling—but was still silent.

Okay, there was a time when Ella would have thought the whole thing was a little weird and she would have made tracks for the back door. But not now. Something in her wanted more.

"Oh, Father," Mrs. Buckman's voice was even softer now. "And now about our Harley." God *had* to be close—because even someone in the next room wouldn't be able to hear what she was praying.

Passion. That was the word that came to Ella's mind. There was passion now in the things she asked God for—and not a word was about the motorcycle.

"He's hurting—bad. Worse than he'll let anyone see."

Ella believed that with all her heart.

"He wants to be a man, wants to be strong, but he has no idea that true strength comes from knowing his own weakness—and relying on You."

Grams raised her hands . . . swaying and kind of moaning the way she did sometimes.

"He's in trouble now. I feel it, Lord."

Ella reached for the silver cross. Clutched it between both hands. It was like Parker's mom had looked into Ella's soul and seen her deepest fears.

"He's lost his way—and he's losing hope. He thinks he's alone . . . even though he's not. He can't see it. He's in danger, and he doesn't even know it—or maybe he doesn't care." Tears ran down Mrs. Buckman's cheeks. Was it some kind of premonition she had? Yet every word resonated with Ella's heart.

Jelly's eyes opened a slit, and she looked directly at Ella. If Ella were to pull out her watercolors and paint that face on canvas, it would be the picture of fear. Was she really that afraid—or was she mirroring what she saw on Ella's face? Jelly leaned close and hugged Ella. One of them was trembling—but Ella couldn't be sure if it was her or Jelly. Maybe they both were.

"I don't know why You make some young men the way you do. Impulsive. Quick to take action—even when they suspect they're making a terrible mistake."

And that *was* Harley, wasn't it? He was restless that way. More than that. Reckless. Exactly how were Ella and Jelly supposed to keep Harley from hurting himself—and dragging Parker in after him?

"He's on the edge, Father—without much of a foothold. Oh, Jesus . . . keep him from going off the deep end."

Ella squeezed her eyes shut, sending fresh tears down her cheeks. "Or if that's too much to ask," she whispered, "protect him when he does."

CHAPTER 37

BRYCE SAT ON A STACK OF LOBSTER TRAPS near the Cape Ann Marina and checked the time. He could hop on his bike, make it home to grab dinner, and be back within thirty-five minutes. Forty at the most. He hated to leave. What if he missed the goons if they showed up to check on the bike? He should have packed something to eat. *Idiot.*

Port Knox Storage sat directly across the street. From Bryce's vantage point, he could see the entire storage facility: two low buildings sitting parallel to each other, fifteen steel garage doors in each one—each large enough to drive his Jeep Wrangler inside. Plenty of room for Harley's motorcycle. Each garage door from the one building faced a twin in the other, with a paved alley in between.

Bryce had replayed the timing from Sunday night in his mind—when he heard Kemosabe. The motorcycle couldn't have been running for more than a minute—so as long as it hadn't been moved since then, the thing was close. He'd already searched the marina good on Monday. Now he had his money on Port Knox Storage. Why else would that Kelsey guy stall their escape to look for the pocketknife?

He'd spent most of the day yesterday—and all day today—at his post or patrolling within easy view. Nine times people came to the storage facility. Every time somebody did, Bryce straddled his bike and took a casual ride right down the center alley of the place. He even wore his jersey. The last thing he'd wanted to do was look like he was sneaking around. That would get him suspicious looks right away. He timed his ride past the units just right. The garage door was open each time with an easy view inside. Bikes. Boxes. Furniture. But no Harley-Davidson.

He'd sketched the layout of two buildings and drawn a big X through the nine spaces where he absolutely knew the motorcycle *wasn't* hidden. That left 21 spaces to check. And he'd check every one of them if he had to.

Bryce had plenty of time to think, too. Yes, Beauty and Everglades Girl had caught him red-handed at the worst possible time. And yes, he'd had to answer a bunch more questions from Officer Greenwood. But he'd stuck to his original story. "No, sir, I never saw the fire. No, sir, I have no idea how it started." He was pretty sure the cop still didn't buy it any more than he did the first time he questioned him. But he never hauled him into the station. So that was a good sign.

He'd wrestled with the idea of just telling the police officer what he knew. The cop came across as the kind of guy he could trust. But if Bryce did that, the police would probably open every unit in Port Knox until *they* found the bike. They'd get the credit—not

Bryce. There'd be no reason for Harley to come crawling back to him in total gratitude. No reason for Everglades to worship the ground he walked on. There was really no decision to make. He was going to stick with the plan. He'd watch Port Knox or break into every unit if he had to. But he was going to find that bike.

Time was the problem. He couldn't just watch the place day after day—hoping he could rule out more units. He had a sense that there wasn't that much time on the clock. But he'd prepared for that.

Last night he'd made a run to the Building Center right there in Gloucester. He picked up a beefy pair of bolt cutters and a half-dozen heavy-duty padlocks. The keyed type, not combination. Apparently, that was where most of the people renting the units at Port Knox bought their locks. They were exactly the same kind. And he picked up one can of black spray paint. Money wasn't a problem. His dad always left his keys and a big ol' wad of cash on the bathroom counter at night. Bryce made it a habit to lighten his dad's load by a twenty now and then. He'd built a little emergency stash of his own. Which paid off big. When he went to the hardware store, he used cash—and had all he needed. Before heading home, he'd pedaled directly to Port Knox and found a place to hide his purchases where nobody would notice.

He'd done well. Planned everything out. He deserved a little dinner break. And getting some fuel in his gut now was just plain smart. Because tonight he'd open a unit or two—just to test things out. He might even check more if things went well. Maybe he'd get lucky. And if something went south and he had to make a run for it, he'd be glad his tank wasn't empty.

CHAPTER 38

RAY CLIMBED ABOARD *DEEP TROUBLE* at the Cape Ann Marina a full thirty minutes early. Quinn Lochran wasn't the kind of guy one kept waiting. Besides, Ray needed a drink or two just to calm the jitters. He pulled a flask out of the cabin and took a quick pull on it.

He'd also brought Vinny Torino and Jack Kelsey. If Lochran could bring a bodyguard, Ray could bring two. Not that he'd let on that the boys were with him. Lochran wouldn't like that. But Vinny and Kelsey were posted three slips down, dressed like fishermen. They'd brought tools and busied themselves with some bogus repair on the deck of another lobster boat. Far enough away where Lochran wouldn't worry about them eavesdropping. But Ray was pretty sure that Lochran—or his *associate*, Mike Ironwing— wouldn't try anything cute with witnesses around.

But even if they did, Kelsey and Vinny were ready. They weren't just carrying hand tools in that toolbox. Vinny had his Glock. Kelsey his Springfield Hellcat. Both were expert shots. Ray hadn't gotten where he was by taking unnecessary chances, right? He smiled to himself. Felt way more confident for this meeting. He had the motorcycle. He had the men.

There was only one little problem. Yes, the Plan B heist went perfectly. But there'd been only one nibble on the bike—and the guy wasn't coming to see it until tomorrow morning. If he bought, all was well. Ray would get a huge chunk of what he'd need to pay off the loan early. But what if the guy didn't buy when he found out Ray didn't have the title for the bike? The loan was due in four days, and Plan C wasn't going well at all. According to the lawyer, the trust was made out of Kevlar. It couldn't be penetrated. Period. There was absolutely no provision in the trust to pay out Harley's $3,500 debt.

The lawyer's exact words? "The trust does not exist to cover Harley's expenses—no matter who he owes, no matter how much. If it was that easy to access the money, what was to stop Harley from making a bunch of frivolous purchases and running up a pile of debt?" It was all Ray could do to keep from running his fist up the guy's frivolous nose.

But Ray's Plan C wasn't dead in the water. There was one more layer to it. What if the kid got himself in serious legal trouble? Surely the lawyer would let Ray tap the trust fund to keep the kid out of jail. And if the kid got himself in a big enough jam, wouldn't it make sense to hit the trust for maybe fifty big ones so he could set up a reserve for legal fees? And Ray would set *himself* up as Harley's legal counsel . . . which meant he could access the money whenever he pleased.

Ray would put a call in to the lawyer in the morning . . . because Harley was going to get himself in a *whole* lot of trouble while he was doing Ray's "errands" tonight. And young Harley wouldn't be with his friends, so he'd have no alibi. Everything was set.

Ray was good for the money. Lochran would have to see that. Ray just might need a bit more time.

Vinny fired up the cordless drill. Revved it a couple times. His signal to let Ray know that Lochran had arrived.

Ray wanted to climb back on the dock to level the playing field between him and Lochran a bit. But he thought better of it and watched Lochran walk down the pier. Ironwing was there, trailing by twenty feet again. And he stopped a full boat slip before *Deep Trouble* and waited like he was some Secret Service agent on security detail.

Lochran stood over him again, leaning on the very same post as last time.

Ray wasted no time explaining his situation and why he may need an extension. To ask for the extra week before he was even sure he needed it was risky. But to wait until the loan was due to ask for an extension? That would be suicide.

Lochran was quiet for several seconds after Ray finished his spiel. The man shook his head slightly and clucked his tongue. "Ray, Ray, Ray. I'm disappointed."

"Hey," Ray said, "I may not even need an extension. We lost the title in the shed fire, and that's making the sale a little trickier. It's just a tiny glitch."

Lochran looked him dead in the eyes. "A tiny glitch. Let's take a little tour through history, shall we? There was that glitch that caused the fire on the Apollo 1 simulator. Three astronauts died." His voice steady. Low. "Remember the story of the missing nuclear submarine, the USS Scorpion back in 1968? A routine mission— but then there was a tiny *glitch*. All 99 crew members lost. Glitches take down commercial planes . . . and sink pretty little lobster boats. Tiny glitches get people killed, Ray."

The guy had watched too many mobster movies or something. "Look, you'll get every penny of what I owe you. I just wanted to let you know there could be a delay. I want to be totally honest and up front with you."

"Up front and honest," Lochran said. "Good qualities. So if you're so concerned about being completely truthful with me, when were you going to tell me that you brought two friends with you tonight? The ones who helped steal the bike in the first place, I presume?" He nodded his head in the direction of Vinny and Kelsey.

"Oh, they had some work to do on—"

"Stop." Lochran stared him down for a moment. "Now, Mr. Up-Front-and-Honest, I'm going to tell you how this is going to work, all right?"

Ray nodded.

"You will take me to the motorcycle. Now," Lochran said. "I'm going to need to verify if anything you're telling is the truth or not. Next, there will be no extension on your loan. You have four days. And your payment just went up by twenty grand."

"What?" Ray wanted to throttle the guy. He stopped before saying another word. *Keep your mouth shut, Ray. Play this smart.*

"Ten for even *asking* for an extension. Ten for bringing your men to a private meeting." Lochran didn't shout. In fact, he spoke so quiet Ray had to step closer just to hear him clearly. "The penalty for not playing by my rules is never cheap. And if you say one more word, the amount will climb again."

The arrogant weasel. Maybe Lochran should be the one who walked a little more carefully. If he really expected Ray to come up with that kind of money in four days—or four weeks—maybe Lochran was the one who'd need to be looking over his shoulder. "How am I supposed to come up with that kind of money in four days?"

"That really isn't my problem, Ray," Lochran said. But this is just a little thing, right? And you've already assured me how good you are at working out tiny *glitches*."

What on earth was he going to do? Honestly, if Ironwing wasn't on the pier Ray would pull Lochran off the dock and—

"Mr. Lotitto, do you know what I was thinking as I walked up this pier—and read the name *Deep Trouble* on the back of your boat?"

He didn't care what the man thought.

"I was thinking, *Poor Ray. I hope he doesn't find himself in another kind of deep trouble before this is over.*" Lochran shrugged. "For your sake, let's hope it was a random thought . . . and not a premonition."

CHAPTER 39

THE FOUR SECURITY CAMERAS at Port Knox Storage had been Bryce's first priority. Were they just the type that kept a recording going that could be played back if there was a burglary? Or was somebody in an office somewhere actually watching a live feed from the cameras? There was no office on the property, and Bryce was willing to bet the owner wasn't paying a guy to sit around somewhere else and watch four monitors around the clock. But none of that mattered: he had to make sure there were no pictures of him breaking into storage units.

The owners of the place stored a ladder behind the second building—which was mighty thoughtful of them. From there, the can of spray paint did the rest. He wore an old COVID mask, a sweatshirt over his jersey, and kept his hoodie up. He gave the lens of each camera an even coating of flat black. Once it dried, nobody would notice. He put the ladder away and took off for the Cape Ann Marina across the street. If somebody was actually monitoring the cameras, he'd know soon.

When no cops showed up, he mounted up and biked down the alley between the two buildings that made up Port Knox Storage like he owned the place. No hoodie or COVID mask needed. *If you don't want to raise suspicions, act like you don't have anything to hide.* There was nobody there at the moment, and that helped.

He'd already checked his diagram of the units and picked one of the twenty-one unknowns at random. He took the bolt cutter out of hiding and used the thing to snap the padlock on the rolling garage door. It was no harder than biting a half-frozen Snickers candy bar in half. Cutting through the hardened steel shackle actually felt really good. It reminded him that he was strong. Invincible. When this was all over, maybe he'd swing by regularly and cut some locks if he had nothing better to do.

Bryce lifted the door. Empty. Instead of dropping the door and securing a new lock in place, he got the idea to make this unit his base of operations—at least for tonight. It beat leaving his bike out in the open. If he had to make a run for it, he'd have nothing holding him back. He stepped inside and pulled his bike in after him.

Only twenty units to go.

He gave a quick check to be sure the coast was clear, then casually walked to the building directly opposite him and cut the lock. The unit was packed, but it didn't take thirty seconds to realize this was another dead end. He slipped back to his base unit, dropped the bolt cutters, and picked up one of the new locks. A minute later he'd locked the dead-end unit across from him. Whoever rented this space would have a nice surprise when they found their key didn't work. He picked up the busted lock off the ground and hustled it back to his headquarters, closing the garage door behind him. So far so good.

He put an X through both units on his sketch and made a quick decision about which lock he'd snap next. He lifted the door a couple inches and listened. The sound of a car echoed down the alley. He eased the door back down an inch and waited.

The car passed Bryce's hiding spot—and then a second car followed immediately afterward. They stopped a unit or two past his. Doors slammed, and instinctively Bryce counted every one of them. There were at least five people there. Which stunk because with a crew that size, likely they were going to be moving a lot of things in or out of a unit. Bryce would be stuck in his hideout until they finished, and he may not get as far tonight as he'd hoped.

He dropped to the ground and peered out the narrow opening at the bottom of the door. A Chevy Silverado pickup in front. A black Hummer parked behind it. A garage door on the other side of the alley rolled open—but the Hummer blocked Bryce from seeing inside.

A man stood in the center of the alley—where he could keep an eye on everything. He was built a little like that new running back at football camp. Karl David. Not huge, but the guy was quick. He could find a hole where there was none. Hard to tackle, and hard on the tackler. David was fearless. Could match up against a guy with fifty more pounds on him—and would absolutely punish the guy. David sent more guys limping back to the bench than any other player Bryce knew. And this guy standing in the alley gave off that same vibe. He had the look about him that said you'd better not mess with him. That's when Bryce noticed the bulge along his waistline just above his back pocket. The guy was packing? What kind of mover carries a gun?

Another man stepped out from between the two vehicles. Instantly Bryce recognized him. Kelsey—the guy who'd torched the shed, grabbed the motorcycle, and dropped his pocketknife. Another guy joined him. Bryce was sure he was the guy who'd been at the helm of the lobster boat.

Bryce was practically shaking. Excitement? Fear? Who cared? He'd found the missing bike! It had to be in that unit. "Bryce Scorza, you are brilliant," he whispered. "You've found what the cops couldn't." *But what was the deal with the armed escort?*

Kelsey glared at the man standing in the middle of the alley. "Looks like your boss is satisfied, Ironleg."

"Iron*wing*, Mr. Kelsey." There was something totally creepy about the expression on the guy's face. "But I think you knew that. If the name is too hard to remember, just call me *sir*."

Kelsey made a show of spitting, then climbed back into the second seat of the Silverado.

Helm guy hadn't moved. He jerked his thumb toward his own chest. "I'm Vinny Torino." The guy was built like the Hummer. "And believe me, I got *no* problem remembering your name, Mr. Ironwing." He raised his chin a bit and smiled. "I'll be seeing you."

Ironwing shrugged. "I doubt it. Not until it's too late, anyway."

Vinny Torino laughed it off and disappeared between the two vehicles.

The storage unit door on the other side of the Hummer rolled down in place with a bang. Ironwing did one quick scan of the area, then swung into the driver's seat of the Hummer.

Bryce eased his rolling door back down that last inch and shinnied deeper into the unit. He stood motionless for a good five minutes after he'd heard both vehicles pull away. He needed the time to think.

He'd open the other unit. Just to be sure the motorcycle was there. And he'd have to figure out exactly how to tell Harley Lotitto. He'd want to milk this for all it was worth—but he couldn't sit on the information long. What if he waited until tomorrow to tell Lotitto—but Kelsey or Torino or Ironwing moved the motorcycle before that? He'd bring Lotitto to an empty unit. That definitely wouldn't work. Which meant Bryce needed to change his plans. He'd have to move the bike.

Bryce raised the garage door. Checked both ways down the alley. Stared at the unit the goons had just locked tight. He'd roll Kemosabe right back here to his headquarters. He'd pop a new lock on the door, and nobody would even guess where it was. He'd be in control. He'd call the plays from there. Bryce smiled. He was so far out ahead of everyone else that they couldn't even see him. It was like he was going into the fourth quarter with a five-touchdown lead.

For just an instant he thought of his dad. Would he be proud? Oh, yeah. He'd call him a chip off the old block—or something like that. But this wasn't the kind of thing he could tell him yet. When it was all over, maybe he'd talk his dad into going out for breakfast or something. Just the two of them. He'd give him the inside scoop, start to finish. His dad would look at him with respect. Pride. Maybe they'd make a regular thing of the breakfasts.

But breakfast would have to wait. Right now he had work to do. "Keep your head in the game, Scorza."

He rehearsed the whole thing in his mind—just like he would before running a play on the field. He'd have to go fast. Cut the lock. Move the bike. Lock both units. He could do it in under five minutes. And Bryce would have the only key.

Kelsey, Torino, Ironwing, and whoever the hired muscle worked for would have a huge surprise the next time they came to see the motorcycle. Bryce did not want to be anywhere within five miles of Port Knox when that happened.

Bryce grabbed the bolt cutters. Bounced on the balls of his feet a bit to work off the jitters. And really, there was nothing to be nervous about. Besides cutting a few locks, he'd really done nothing all that wrong—or even dangerous. Yet.

CHAPTER 40

HARLEY SAT IN THE BACK SEAT OF THE UBER and crossed off the first item on the list from Uncle Ray. What was the story with all the deliveries? Why not have the customers come to the store to make the pickups? Uncle Ray couldn't possibly get them to add a *Don't Drink and Dive* T-shirt to the order if they weren't in the store, right?

But he knew what this was all about. This was Uncle Ray's way of keeping Harley busy. Uncle Ray wanted to be sure Harley didn't have time to pay Scorza a visit. It would be bad for business, isn't that what he kept saying? So, the Uber driver was pretty much his babysitter. The way Harley saw things, it didn't matter how many deliveries Uncle Ray gave him. He'd be paying his ex-best friend a visit tonight. And he'd find out what Scorza had done with Kemosabe.

Uncle Ray thought he was smart. He'd paid for the Uber up

front—and had worked out the entire route with him. What he hadn't figured was that in addition to the packages, Harley had brought his bike along. He'd asked the driver at the last minute. "After the last stop, I think I'd like to just bike home—if it's okay with you. And if there's more time on the meter—consider it a bonus if you keep it between the two of us." The driver was happy with that deal, and the bike fit easily in the back of his SUV.

A business card holder was mounted where a passenger could grab a card. Tony Bernardi. Harley pocketed one, just in case. Uncle Ray had tipped the guy well and paid for a full ninety minutes. Bernardi was happy enough to wait at each house while Harley went to the door with the package. A special-order prescription mask for one customer. A repaired regulator kit for another. The first two drop-offs were in Rockport. The next, Pigeon Cove. The last couple were in Gloucester.

It was after nine when Harley dropped off the final package in Gloucester. "We made great time, Mr. Bernardi. I'll just take my bike and ride from here."

"You're the boss."

Harley definitely was. The guy pulled into the public parking lot on the waterfront, and in less than a minute he was gone. Harley stood there with his bike. Part of him wanted to just sit out on the docks by the lobster boats. If only he could turn back time. He'd have moved Kemosabe after the smoke bombs. To Parker's house, for sure. Someplace Scorza wouldn't have found it.

But Harley had messed up. Hadn't expected Scorza to outmaneuver him like he had. Harley had to stop looking back—and only look forward now. He had to stick with what he knew to be true—and not get lost in the rearview mirror. And the truth was, the police weren't going to find Kemosabe. Seventy-two hours . . .

and no leads? To put any hope in the Rockport PD would be stupid. And his friends could keep searching online for Kemosabe—or body parts—but they'd have more luck reeling in a 400-pound tuna on ten-pound test line. The job was too big. Harley had to accept that—and stop depending on others to find his motorcycle.

Tonight was his one chance to find out where Kemosabe was hidden. He'd lure Scorza outside somehow. Ring the doorbell and drag him out of the house if he had to. And if Scorza didn't start talking—fast—he'd have to pound the information out of him. Hit fast. Hit hard. Hit to inflict maximum pain. How many minutes would he have before the police showed up? Hopefully enough. Because after tonight he'd be arrested—and probably wouldn't be going home again. Finding Kemosabe would make it all worth it, though. And it might be his ticket to freedom—if he could prove Scorza stole it.

He swung a leg over his bike and pushed off. He was going to do this. Yet deep inside he knew he was making a mistake. What would Parker do? He'd pray. That was fine for him, but Harley didn't exactly know how one connected with God that way. Ella would be disappointed in him, wouldn't she? But maybe she and Jelly would understand why he had to do this, right? At least they'd see he wasn't afraid to fight for what was right.

When the police took Harley away, would he still be able to be friends with them? He hoped to God that he could. He needed them. But he had to do the very thing all of them had been trying to keep him from doing. What other choice did he have? Isn't that why he'd been pulling away from the three of them these last few days? Hadn't he been trying to get along without them somehow, knowing he was probably going to lose them anyway?

The whole thing was a gamble. If he avoided Scorza, he'd keep the friends he valued most—but lose the only thing he treasured. The one thing that connected him with his dad. He'd lose his dad all over again—and he'd be farther away than ever. It was like that grave would be twelve feet deep instead of six.

"God . . . I need some help." What was he thinking? That he could just talk to God like Parker did? That he could just ask God to work all this impossible mess out somehow? No . . . he was on his own here.

He was only a half mile from Scorza's now. "Last chance, Harley. Play it safe. Keep your friends—but say goodbye to Kemosabe? Say goodbye to the future Dad was trying to give you? Say goodbye to who you really are—your identity?" He thought about that for a moment. "Or do you take the gamble? Do you ignore the impossible odds? Do you take a chance that Scorza will spill his guts and tell the truth . . . that you'll get the bike back, yet somehow keep your friends—and your freedom—in the process? Do you dare risk everything . . . for the chance to have it all?"

But he knew the answer. He'd known all along. "Let's do this, Harley. Roll the dice."

CHAPTER 41

ANGELICA WANTED TO MOVE. Hated sitting around doing nothing but watching Scorza's house. But she promised she'd stay put. They had a perfect view from about a hundred feet away. And now that it was dark, there was no chance they'd be seen. A security light lit the driveway from a second-story eave on the house. Scorza's Jeep Wrangler was parked right in the middle of it, like it was onstage basking in a spotlight.

Dad had dropped them off just before dark, and he was coming back before ten o'clock. He'd laid down the ground rules and had grilled her and Ella about following them to the letter. Under no condition were they to leave their post. They weren't to step one foot closer to Scorza's house—no matter what happened. If Harley showed up, they could shout to him from where they were, but they weren't to risk getting in the middle of something. Angelica and Ella agreed to everything. To break the ground rules would break trust—and she could kiss goodbye the leeway he'd given them. Worse than that, she'd disappoint her dad . . . something she absolutely would not do. Not after all he'd done for her.

Bryce Scorza arrived home just minutes after Dad had pulled away.

"Looks like he just won the Super Bowl," Ella said. "What's that all about?"

Scorza swung off his bike and dropped it on the front lawn. He raised both fists over his head and did a little victory dance around the Wrangler parked on the driveway—watching his own reflection in the windows. Angelica wished she'd caught it on video. But who could she show? "The guy is completely vain."

Ella agreed. "It's like he thinks he has an audience of fans even when he doesn't."

"So," Angelica teased, "you're still not a fan?"

"No more than you."

A light turned on in an upstairs room a minute after he went inside. Since then, everything had been quiet. And boring.

It was after nine thirty when Ella nudged her and pointed. Someone walked toward Scorza's house. Dark pants. Dark hoodie—with hood pulled up far enough to shadow the entire face. It was definitely too warm out for a sweatshirt. A guy would only dress like that if he didn't want to be seen. But his build was a dead giveaway. "Harley?"

Angelica's heart sank. It absolutely was. "I had sooo hoped he wouldn't."

Ella pulled out her phone. "If we can't go to him, at least we can text him. Let him know we're here. I don't think he'll do anything if he thinks we're here." Her thumbs flew across the screen.

Harley turned onto the drive, then hesitated for just a moment once he got even with the Wrangler.

"What's he up to?"

Angelica had no idea, but she didn't like the looks of it.

He pulled something out of his pocket—then suddenly used it on the hood. "It looks like he's writing something on the hood with a marker." But even from this far Angelica could hear a metal-on-metal scratching noise. "Harley, no! Has he answered yet?"

Ella shook her head.

"I'm calling him," Angelica said. She whipped out her phone and dialed. It went right to voicemail.

Harley hunkered at the driver's side door like he was fumbling with the lock. An instant later he leaped inside.

Angelica watched, stunned. "What is he *doing*?"

"We have to stop him," Ella said. But that would mean leaving their post—and doing what she promised she wouldn't. The truth was, she stood frozen . . . like she couldn't move even if she wanted to.

The Wrangler roared to life, suddenly backing down the driveway. "Harley, no!" Angelica didn't dare shout. Scorza would look out his window. He'd call the police.

Harley threw the Wrangler in gear and lurched forward, nearly hitting the curb before straightening out and racing down the middle of the street. He gave the horn a double tap.

Ella was on her feet—phone to her ear. "I'm trying him again. He's got to ditch that car before the police catch him."

Angelica dialed Parker. It was instinct. But what could he do? What could any of them do? Nobody could blame Scorza for ruining Harley's life now. He was doing a terrific job of it all by himself.

CHAPTER 42

PARKER DUG HIS PHONE OUT OF HIS POCKET, hoping it was Harley.

"Do you know where Harley is—right now?" Jelly's voice, definitely stressed.

"I haven't seen him in over an hour. He's probably still making deliveries for his uncle. He's going to call when he—"

"He did something really stupid." She filled him in on every gut-twisting detail.

Stealing Scorza's Jeep? That was grand theft auto, right? On top of breaking the boundaries of the restraining order? Not good. Not good at all.

"He's lost it, Parker," she said. "He went right over the edge."

And Parker hadn't been there to stop him. He'd only had two jobs to do, right? *Find Kemosabe. Keep Harley from doing something stupid.* Parker had failed on both counts.

"What will happen to him?" There was a desperation in Jelly's voice.

Parker was pretty sure she knew exactly what was going to happen. "He's going to get arrested," Parker said. "And this time they won't go easy on him."

"My dad is coming. I gotta go. We'll look for Harley," she said. "If we don't find him in fifteen minutes, I'll ask my dad to drive us to the dive shop."

"I'll talk to my mom and dad. We'll meet you there." Parker needed to see Harley. To ask him why he did it—without even giving Parker a chance to talk him out of it. Not that it would do any good now. But still. "We have to find him—before the police do."

CHAPTER 43

HARLEY REHEARSED EVERYTHING IN HIS MIND, like he was running a pass pattern. Only he wasn't. He was going to drag Scorza out of the house and beat the truth out of him. He cut through the Walgreens parking lot, picturing the whole thing. Scorza would be on his knees—admitting everything.

"Harley!"

He hit the brakes and glanced over. "Grams?"

She stood by the door of her Camry, motioning him over. "I can't tell you how happy I am to see you!" She looked heavenward. "God sent me an angel!"

He circled around and hopped off his bike.

"My key is *not* working. At first, I thought it was the little battery inside, but the key isn't going into the slot, either." She waggled the keys in front of him. "This is making no sense."

He glanced at the car. "Mind if I try?"

"I wish you would. And I'll bake you a Blueberry Ghost Pie if you get it open."

He pressed the unlock button on the remote, scanning the parking lot as he did. A set of headlights blinked two aisles over. "Ah, Grams? This isn't your car—unless you've gone back to strapping Ella into a baby car seat."

She looked in the rear side window and beamed. "Lord Almighty! Right make and model, wrong address."

He aimed the remote toward Grams's car and hit the emergency button this time just long enough for Grams to get a bead on where it was.

Grams pulled him into a hug. "You earned yourself a pie, young man. And a ride home, too. You shouldn't be out all hours. And where are the girls?"

He shook his head. "Not with me."

"They said they were helping you with something."

He didn't want to get them in trouble, but obviously Grams got her wires crossed—or the girls were totally bamboozling her. Maybe he wasn't the only one with a hidden agenda.

She started toward her car. "Let's get your bike loaded in—"

"I can't." He said it way too fast to come off as casual as he wanted. "I have to stop somewhere."

"You just show the way and I'll—"

"No . . . I have to pay someone a visit."

She looked at him like she knew. "Harley. Anger is a demon. You let that devil ride along with you and soon he'll want to drive."

"I have to do this."

A siren wailed—and not far away. A second one answered—but from a different direction.

"Hear that?" Grams shook her head. "It's a sign. You're not

supposed to do whatever it is you think you need to do. Let me drive you home."

The sirens seemed to be converging—and right in the direction he was headed. "Thanks—and I'm sorry. Grams, I'm going." He backed away.

She shook her head. "Son, you're already gone."

He mounted his bike on the run and pedaled like a crazy man. He stopped a block from Scorza's and watched the first police car roar up. What was going on?

What if somebody had phoned in a tip to the Missing hotline? Would Scorza be that stupid, to hide the motorcycle at his house? On the other hand, who would have suspected he'd bring it home, right? But how on earth did he get Kemosabe past him—and all the way here?

Scorza ran out the front door—along with his dad. Using lots of hand motions, they were explaining something to the cop, pointing at the empty driveway. If the police suspected Scorza had Kemosabe stashed there, they sure were in no hurry to slap cuffs on him. Something didn't feel right about all this. And where was Scorza's Wrangler?

"Get out of here, Harley." He spoke aloud to himself. "Make it quick."

He whipped his bike around and rode off in the opposite direction. He took the next corner and hadn't gone two blocks before he saw the Wrangler smashed into a tree halfway up somebody's front lawn. He pedaled up to it, fishtailed to a stop, and dropped his bike.

The driver's door was open—with nobody inside. Unbelievably the motor was still running. What if the gas line got ruptured in the crash? What if it caught fire—or blew up? Someone could get hurt. Harley reached inside and turned off the ignition, pocketing the keys.

The airbags hadn't deployed, so maybe the hit wasn't as bad as it looked. Still, whoever was driving could be injured. Wandering around dazed or something. He flipped on the flashlight app and scanned the steering wheel for blood. Nothing. Then the front seat. Nothing but a black hoodie—inside out. The light picked up a name written in Sharpie on the tag. *Harley.*

What was his sweatshirt doing in Scorza's Wrangler?

Almost instantly the pieces flew into place. "I'm being set up." Scorza had swiped his hoodie somehow. Faked his Wrangler being stolen . . . and planted the evidence inside. He was one step behind Scorza . . . *again.*

"Get out of here, Harley," he said out loud again. His heart was beating in his ears. He swept the flashlight around the inside of the Jeep one more quick time to be sure no other incriminating evidence was left behind. He panned across the entire dashboard— and saw letters scratched into the hood.

"No."

He swung the light onto the hood. *BARF BAG*—in big letters—and right down to the metal. How would he explain his way out of this? He had to get back home—fast. Maybe if he got there quick enough the timeline wouldn't work. It would prove he didn't do this.

Harley pulled the hoodie on and grabbed his bike. He mounted on the fly and scooted between two parked cars and onto the middle of the road.

He saw the headlights too late. Harley swerved as the driver slammed on the breaks, tires screaming. Harley glanced off the bumper. Rolled a couple of times, then got right back up on his feet again. He stared into the headlights for an instant, then grabbed his bike off the ground. He ran next to his bike for several steps before jumping on and pedaling like crazy.

His adrenaline fueled his legs for two blocks before he worked out his next move. Skidding to a stop, he whipped out his phone—and the card from the Uber driver.

The guy answered on the first ring—way before Harley had a chance to catch his breath. "Need . . . pickup . . . fast . . . Mr. Bernardi. Where you . . . just dropped me."

CHAPTER 44

Wednesday, August 10, 10:05 p.m.

JELLY'S DAD BROKE THE SILENCE. "Everybody okay?"

Ella still held the passenger seat in front of her in a two-handed death grip. She was definitely a little shaken up by the screeching stop. But she was massively rattled by who she'd seen rolling across the pavement before disappearing again. "I'm okay."

"Me too." Jelly's voice sounded shaky.

Mr. Malnatti shifted into park and killed the ignition. Threw on his emergency flashers. "I'm going to take a look at the Jeep, make sure nobody is inside."

Ella and Jelly unbuckled and were two steps behind him.

"Don't touch anything," he said. "You don't want your prints on this." He took a quick look inside.

"Did you see . . . ?" Ella couldn't finish.

"Harley's face?"

Ella nodded. He'd looked terrified. And younger somehow.

Like he was just a kid who had gotten in way over his head and didn't know how to get to the shallow end of the pool.

"Look at that." Mr. Malnatti pointed at the writing on the hood. "*BARF BAG.*"

"Oh, Harley!" Ella wouldn't have believed he did it if she hadn't seen the whole thing with her own eyes. "There's no way they won't know who was behind this."

"He parked his bike a few blocks away," Jelly said, "stole the Wrangler, and drove it right back to where he'd left his bike. Probably thought he'd get away clean by not driving the Jeep long enough for the police to catch him."

Her theory made sense to Ella. "And he deliberately rammed the thing into a tree to even the score up a bit."

Jelly's dad phoned 911 and gave the location of the Wrangler. He disconnected and stood for a second with his hands on his hips. "Nobody was hurt. So no reason we need to stay here."

Which was a relief. There was no way she wanted to answer the questions the cop would ask her. Like if she'd gotten a clear look at the car thief's face.

"Still want me to drive you to the dive shop?"

Ella looked at Jelly. Her friend nodded. "Parker will be there. And Harley will end up there too . . . if the police don't get him first. We've got to talk to him."

Ella was pretty sure Jelly wasn't going to snitch on Harley any more than Ella would, but with *BARF BAG* written across the hood, Scorza would know exactly who did it.

Ella dialed Harley the moment she got back in the car. She was almost surprised to hear him pick up. "Harley!" She put him on speakerphone. "I'm in the car with Jelly and her dad. Where are you?"

For a moment all she heard was wind—like he was moving fast. "On my way home." His voice a desperate kind of whisper—and breathing hard. "I'm in trouble. I mean big, big trouble."

"A little late to figure that out. What were you thinking?" Ella fought back tears. "Stealing Scorza's Wrangler? Scratching *BARF BAG* into the hood? This isn't the Harley I know."

"Whoa, whoa, whoa," Harley said. "That wasn't me. I've been framed by Scorza."

Instantly Ella felt the hot rush of anger. She saw it in Jelly's face too. "Because you were doing deliveries tonight for your Uncle Ray?"

"Right. Right."

"And you didn't steal the Wrangler."

"I swear . . . it wasn't me. I admit, I was going to his house to shake him up a little. To make him tell me where he'd taken Kemosabe. But when I got near his house, I saw the police and I left."

Ella wanted to throw the phone out the window. Or onto the floorboards and stomp the living daylights out of it. "You are such a liar!"

"What?"

Harley had betrayed her. It made her want to scream. "You're lying—to me."

"And to me, too," Jelly shouted.

Ella gripped the phone harder. "I thought we were better friends than that." He'd wrecked everything now. Everything. "Well, no more."

"Honest, I'm telling you the t—"

"Save it for the judge, Mr. Lotitto." She held the phone up in front of her face and shouted into it. "Ella and I were staking out Scorza's house—and we saw you steal the Wrangler."

TIM SHOEMAKER

"I nev—"

"Stop. Lying. That was us who nearly ran over you—when you were racing from the crashed Wrangler. I saw your face. Are you going to deny that, too?"

Only the muffled sound of wind answered. Harley didn't say a word.

"Are you still there?" Ella waited. Jelly leaned closer, like she didn't want to miss a word.

"You gotta believe me, I—"

"Are you going to deny that was you we almost ran over?" Ella could not believe this. Jelly looked just as incredulous. "We saw you. Right there in our headlights. When did you turn into such a pathological liar, Harley? You're pathetic."

"Listen—would you just listen?" There was a desperation in his voice. Despair. "Just a couple months ago one of my best friends was so concerned about injustice—and for good reason. And now—without hearing his full side of the story—she's already playing Lady Justice and judged her friend guilty?"

Did he really think he could talk his way out of this? "Ex-friend, Mr. Lotitto." It spilled out of Ella's mouth fast. "She's judged her *ex*-friend . . . because no *real* friend of hers would lie to her like that." And just as quick as the words left her lips, regret swept in.

"Roger that." Harley was silent for a moment. "I guess I know where I stand now." His voice hard.

How dare he try to turn this around on her. "And where is *that*, Mr. Lotitto?"

"Nowhere . . . and definitely alone." He disconnected.

His words—or maybe it was his defeated tone when he spoke

them—sliced right through her. Which made her even more angry. "I can't believe that guy."

Jelly's dad glanced at her in the rearview mirror. "You two made that point pretty clear to him."

"He had it coming," Jelly said. "And he hung up on us, Dad."

Again, Mr. Malnatti's eyes met Ella's in the mirror. "Only after you two gave up on him."

CHAPTER 45

HARLEY PULLED HIS BIKE FROM THE BACK of Mr. Bernardi's Uber behind the dive shop, his thoughts on Ella. So, she didn't believe him. There hadn't been one ounce of respect in her voice. How could a friend believe the worst about him? Didn't she think that he might have the decency not to lie to her? He took out his key and slipped inside through the back door. Uncle Ray was stomping around upstairs like he was wearing lead boots. Harley didn't flip on the light. He didn't need it—and really didn't want Uncle Ray knowing he was back.

If there was someplace else Harley could go right now, he'd leave. If only Kemosabe was still parked in the Hangar. He'd fire him up and ride and ride and ride—even without a license. He lifted his bike over his head and hung it from hooks he'd screwed into the beams stretching the length of the fill station room. Maybe he could just sleep on the floor by the fill station tonight.

THE DEEP END

His foot kicked something—an empty beer can by the way it clattered across the wood planking.

"Is that you?" Uncle Ray pounded down the stairs, swearing the whole time. "I just got off the phone with the police."

Uncle Ray flipped on the shop lights. Black jeans. Black T-shirt. Dark eyes. "They're on their way. Did you really boost Scorza's Wrangler?"

Did he really want to hear Harley's side of it?

Uncle Ray stood in the doorway to the back room, hands on hips. "What am I going to do with you, huh?"

Was he really supposed to answer that?

"Look at me when I talk to you."

Harley didn't raise his head. Just his eyes.

"Mr. Tough Guy," Uncle Ray said. "I see the hate in your eyes—and honestly, I'm glad. Because the feeling is mutual, kid. And you're going to need some fight in you if you're going to survive wherever they send you. I'm done with you. Finished. Finito. Terminado."

As if using different languages would make it so much more clear to Harley. But what bothered Harley most is that he should have felt something. Fear. Remorse. Anything. But he was numb. Like somebody had injected a double dose of anesthesia to the emotional center of his brain.

"Why do you think I gave you all those deliveries, huh? It was to keep you busy. Keep you away from that Scorza kid."

Another Uncle Ray scheme that didn't work out like he planned.

"And to think I offered you a chance to have a piece of this business." Uncle Ray's eyes got that bulging thing going, like the pressure of all that anger inside his skull forced his eyeballs out of their sockets that much more. How angry would he have to

233

be before his eyeballs actually popped out of his head? Harley imagined what that would—

"You selfish, inconsiderate brat. I give you a roof over your head. Give you a job. And this is how you show your gratitude? You had to keep your precious motorcycle—and you lost it anyway. I tell you to stay away from Scorza—and you go anyway. I get no respect from you."

Harley didn't care if Uncle Ray believed him or not. But Ella? Jelly? Would Parker think he was lying too?

A police car pulled up in front of the shop. Harley tried to steady his own breathing. To get ready for what was coming next. An officer tapped on the door.

Uncle Ray leaned in close. "Your dad would roll over in his grave to see how you've turned out."

It was like his uncle was baiting him to take a swing at him—with the cop right there looking through the glass. Harley jammed his hands in his pockets instead.

Uncle Ray glared at him for a moment, then turned for the front door. "Let's go, tough guy."

Without another word, Uncle Ray unlocked the door and stepped outside.

Harley followed, but he had the sense that he wasn't on his feet. He was falling. Away from this place. His friends. Everything he loved. He was alone . . . growing more distant by the minute . . . and there was nothing he could do to stop it.

Small clusters of people stood a safe distance away. Tourists, probably. They were always walking Bearskin Neck, even late into the night. And then he saw them. Ella and Jelly, staring at him like they were looking at a monster. Jelly's dad stood behind them, hands on their shoulders. And Parker—along with his mom and dad—was hurrying toward the girls. Harley already knew what Ella and Jelly thought of him—and avoided their eyes. He groaned at the thought of Mr. Buckman thinking he was a punk criminal or something.

Parker was his only hope right now. He chanced a look at his friend. Parker's face. Not disgust. More like pity. Apologetic. Which meant he'd judged him too. Even Parks thought Harley stole the Wrangler? Oh, yeah. Harley was alone.

And that anesthesia must have been some pretty strong medicine, because he still didn't feel a thing. He couldn't look at Parker's mom and dad. He was pretty sure they'd be no different than the others.

"Here's your car thief," Uncle Ray said to the cop. "I can't handle him anymore."

The cop motioned for him to place his hands on the sides of the car and spread his legs—right there . . . with everyone gawking. He got a quick pat-down. The cop lowered one of Harley's wrists behind his back and ratcheted a pair of cuffs on him even as he recited the Miranda rights to him. Harley slowly lowered the other hand for the cop to secure.

He looked at Parker one more time. Saw what looked like pain on his face. The cop placed a hand on Harley's head and directed him into the back seat of the police car.

Harley had prayed on the way to Scorza's tonight. He'd admitted he needed help, anyway. Well, *that* sure paid off. The cop drove to the circle at the end of the Neck and looped back. Ray stood in front of the shop, arms folded across his chest like he still had more rant in him. Jelly's dad had his arms around the two girls—who both seemed to be crying. Like Harley had died or something.

Actually? Maybe he had.

CHAPTER 46

PARKER WATCHED THE POLICE CAR DRIVE OUT OF SIGHT down the Neck. The way Harley looked at him when they put him in the car wasn't something Parker was likely to forget. Like he figured Parker didn't believe him, and the fact crushed Harley. And then when he drove past after doing the circle at the end? He hadn't even looked Parker's way. This wasn't the Harley he knew.

"You're sure you saw him," Parker said. "I mean you're sure it was him?"

"Parker," Jelly said. "He was right there in our headlights—plain as day."

Ella nodded. "And guilty as sin."

"You saw the blood on Harley's face," Jelly said.

He did. It looked dry and sticky—like the flow had stopped—but there was enough on his forehead to show he'd taken a good hit to the head.

"It was either from the accident—or when he spilled his bike on the street. It was him all right. What, you think he had a stunt double or something?"

Parker didn't know what to think. He believed Harley would rough up Scorza, given the chance, but steal his Wrangler? In a way it made sense . . . an eye for an eye, right?

"He had a head injury," Dad said. "He should be checked out."

Uncle Ray marched across the street to where they stood. "I can't trust the kid anymore. And business is tough enough without all the legal fees he's going to run up."

"About that," Dad said. "How are you going to post bail?"

"I won't. Not tonight. It'll do him good to spend the night in a lockup."

Parker couldn't imagine his dad doing something like that.

"His head." Dad pointed at his own forehead. "Is somebody going to check that out?"

"I have no idea," Ray said. "Maybe smacking the steering wheel knocked some sense into him.

"And tomorrow I'll talk to the lawyer. Again." Ray Lotitto spat the words out. "The kid has a trust fund. I need to be able to tap into that. There will be Scorza's car to repair too. This is a mess."

It definitely was. And the way Parker saw it? Harley had nobody to help him get things cleaned up.

CHAPTER 47

HARLEY HAD ONLY GRABBED SNATCHES of sleep the night before at the police station. And he sure hadn't caught a wink of shut-eye after Uncle Ray picked him up in the morning. Harley stood in the back of the dive shop. The filling station room. He stared out over Rockport Harbor. Uncle Ray was still at the lawyer's, trying to pry his way into Harley's trust fund. Another thing from his dad he was going to lose. Uncle Ray had given Harley charge of the dive shop. It had been so quiet, Harley actually checked to be sure the sign at the front door was flipped to the OPEN side.

Ella never texted—or stopped in. Same with Jelly. He scrolled through the texts with Parker again.

Home yet?

                              Yeah. Uncle Ray posted bail
                              for me this morning.

How's your head?

He'd thought about how to answer that for a minute or two. If Parker was talking about the cut, that was one thing. But if he wanted to know what he was thinking? That would be a whole lot more complicated. In the end, he settled on the split he'd picked up after tangling with Mr. Malnatti's bumper.

```
I'll live.
                                    Your uncle there?
Not at the moment.
                                    I'm stopping by.
Don't bother.
```

Harley had paused before sending that one. That wasn't what he really wanted . . . but there was anger in him. Growing stronger. A monster, really. Stomping around in the cage deep inside him. Picking at the lock. Testing its strength against the bars. The truth was, Harley wanted to punish. To hurt. To let others know the pain he was feeling.

```
                        I heard Jelly and Ella's
                        side of the story. Now I
                        want to hear yours.
```

Honestly, hadn't Parker already made up his mind?

```
Why?
```

Seconds later Parker was back.

```
                        Anybody who makes a decision
                        without hearing both sides
```

```
                          is playing the fool. I read
                          something like that
                          somewhere.
```

If Harley knew Parker, it was probably in the Bible. But what Harley really wanted to hear? *I know you didn't do this. There must be some mistake. Somebody set you up for this.* Any one of those would have been nice.

The fact was, Parker believed Harley had stolen the Wrangler too. He was just looking for an explanation as to *why* Harley did it, so he could understand him better? No thanks. If that's what his friends really believed about him . . . then fine. He wasn't going to defend himself.

But the truth? He wanted his friends back. Needed them. Yet he was so stinkin' angry—or full of stubborn pride—he couldn't bring himself to say that. He needed them to make the first move. None of this meeting him halfway stuff. Parker needed to meet him all the way—something that would probably never happen. There was too much distance now. It seemed Harley was still free-falling.

Harley sent one last text.

```
I've got nothing to say.
I gambled. I lost. I'm the fool.
I'd rather you not be here right now.
```

He'd lost everything. Harley was the biggest fool on Cape Ann. A fool for thinking he could really have a life without his dad. A fool for thinking his uncle had an ounce of care for him somewhere deep inside. A fool for thinking he could be lucky enough to have friends like Ella and Parker and Jelly. A fool for thinking that they might believe the best in him . . . not the worst. A fool for thinking somehow all this might work out. A fool for thinking he would find Kemosabe. And most definitely a fool for thinking God cared—even though Harley would be the first to admit he wasn't really good enough for God to care about. Somehow, he'd hoped God was different. *You're definitely the fool, Harley.*

The question now was what Harley was going to do. Uncle Ray made it clear before he left for the lawyer's that he was done. He'd be turning Harley over to the state, however that worked. Uncle Ray would do it too. With breaking the restraining order and grand theft auto charges? Harley wasn't going to be placed with some nice family who just wanted to help him out. He'd be in a juvenile detention center somewhere. Or he'd get stuck in the home of some family that was only interested in helping themselves to the money the state would offer . . . not helping Harley.

One way or the other, he'd be leaving this town he loved . . . and moving to hell. And he'd make that visit to Scorza's house before he left. Not to find out what he did with Kemosabe. Even Harley had to admit the bike was probably long gone. But he'd let the rage out of the cage when he got Scorza alone. Scorza would live to regret the day he messed with Kemosabe . . . but he wouldn't live long.

Harley had always dreamed that Kemosabe was his ticket away from Uncle Ray. That somehow it was his dad's way of helping him escape. There would be no escaping on Kemosabe now. No music from those straight pipes. No comfort from the vibrations flowing through him that made him one with his bike.

But Harley couldn't become part of the system. Maybe he could run. Make his way south. To Florida. Where he could live outside all year round. He had some money . . . but how long would it last? Maybe he could make it all the way to the Everglades. Where Parker had lived before. Maybe he could find the friend Parker and Jelly left down there. Maybe he could call Wilson if he really needed some help.

If he ran, at least he'd be calling the shots. He wouldn't be the new kid to target at some detention center. And he wouldn't be sent to another home with a beer-guzzling man running the place like a dictator.

How long before he got sent away? Harley had no idea. But he wouldn't just let it happen. He needed to disappear—and do it in a way where he'd never be found. There really was no other way out of this. Maybe come back in ten years and see if there was anything left of his trust fund.

"You're alone, Harley." So incredibly alone. There was no light at the end of this tunnel. For there to be light, the tunnel would have to end. But there was no end to the tunnel he was in. Right now, all he could see was the dark.

CHAPTER 48

BRYCE PEDALED TO CAPE ANN MARINA after lunch, wearing Harley's lanyard around his neck. Harley had made the dumb mistake of leaving the key in the ignition when he rescued Kemosabe from the burning shed. And the spare key was with it, which meant Bryce now had the only keys to the motorcycle that existed. Bryce wasn't going to lose the keys. He kept the lanyard tucked inside his jersey. The keys would open all kinds of doors for him—at least that had been his plan.

It was amazing how one day could change everything. Bryce had done what nobody else had been able to do: find the motorcycle. And it was safely stashed in the empty storage unit. Last night he'd planned to get up this morning and see Harley. He'd amaze him—and Everglades Girl—with the stories of his heroics. Harley would have had his motorcycle by now, all thanks to Bryce. Right now, the two of them should have been running pass patterns on Front Beach.

But Harley's joyride in Bryce's Wrangler changed all that. Not that it was the end of the world or anything. His dad would get it fixed—or buy him another one. But Harley had totally messed with him again. And this one was unforgivable.

Even worse, Bryce wasn't so sure Harley was done. The guy was so stinkin' sure Bryce had taken Kemosabe, he was willing to go to jail to get even. Stealing the Wrangler proved that. But would he do more? Would he ambush him somewhere, maybe bust his hands or find some other way to ruin Bryce's future? That's what Bryce would do if it was the other way around.

Bryce dropped his bike and sat on the pile of lobster traps across the street from Port Knox Storage. He took the lanyard off and bounced the motorcycle key in the palm of his hand. He reviewed the decisions he'd been wrestling with all morning.

No, he wasn't going to return the motorcycle to Harley. In fact, he was going to do everything he could to make sure Harley never sat on it again. Bryce would take the thing apart, piece by piece. Some would be donated to dumpsters. Others to Gloucester Bay. He'd keep the gas tank, though, as a souvenir. With the name *Kemosabe* custom painted across it? It would look nice in his bedroom. And he'd keep the ignition key as kind of a trophy. A badge of honor. He'd wear it under his jersey to school. And for every football game—just like Harley used to do. It would be a constant reminder of what happens when people mess with him. Bryce smiled. He liked that idea.

But Bryce couldn't delay this game any longer. What if the manager of Port Knox Storage rented out the empty unit? They'd discover the bike, call the police, and the game would be over.

Second decision? He'd have to stay clear of Harley until they locked him up or took him away for good. Bryce had to protect his passing arm. His hands. His future. Which is why he'd been so cooperative with the police when they questioned him this morning. And he'd testify before a jury that he'd seen Harley from his second-story window. He saw Harley's face. Saw him steal the Wrangler—even though Bryce hadn't seen any of it. The quicker they locked Lotitto up for good, the safer Bryce would be.

And the third decision had to do with his safety too. Kelsey and Torino looked like nasty dudes, and that Ironwing guy seemed even worse. There were already plenty of people on the lookout for this bike—and now there'd be at least three more. But these guys were in a whole new league. They were *not* the type to mess with. So he'd play it really safe. Watch his back. Limit the number of times he allowed himself to go to the storage unit. And it was one more reason to get the cycle taken apart and out of there as quick as he could. He'd need to pick up some tools today. And he'd start the disassembly tomorrow. Get it done and never go back. Finish the job before the guys realized the bike had been stolen from them.

But eventually they would find out, right? They'd go to their storage unit—and find it empty. Then what? Would they look for him? Track him down somehow? That's what was really gnawing at him. He kept going over it, like he'd missed something important. He'd spray-painted the security cams before breaking into the units—so a review of the tapes would show nothing. So why the twisting in his gut?

He couldn't shake the thought that he'd made a mistake. Bryce climbed off the lobster traps, swung a leg over his bike, and rode across the street. He had nothing to hide, right? To anybody who might happen to see him, he was just a kid riding his bike. Minding his own business. Enjoying the last bits of summer before school started.

He pedaled down the alley between the buildings lazy-slow. Nothing looked out of place with the unit where he'd found the motorcycle—or the one he'd stashed the bike in now. Both of them had the locks in place like nothing had ever happened.

A quick glance at one of the security cameras showed nobody was onto him yet. The thing still had the flat black coating. So what was making his gut tell him to go hide someplace?

He pedaled to the end of the alley, did a wide loop, and headed back. Like he'd done every time someone had come to drop off something in their storage unit. He'd done that, what, nearly ten times? And it had paid off. He'd known which ones not to bother breaking into.

Suddenly it hit him. "Bryce . . . you bonehead." He knew exactly what he'd done wrong . . . and he'd botched it good. When they discovered the motorcycle was missing, they'd demand to review the security cameras—which would show no break-ins . . . just like he'd planned. But the recordings *would* show someone riding down the alley over and over again in the days just before the cameras went black. Every time someone opened a unit. They'd know immediately he'd been casing the place with the intent to break in.

Sweat broke out on his forehead. Down his spine. He hadn't even worn a cap. They'd have a clear view of his face. And there was more. He was wearing his Rockport High School football jersey with his number eight blazed across it. How hard would it be to find out his name—and where he lived?

They would find him. And when they did? He was dead.

CHAPTER 49

RAY CLIMBED INTO HIS SILVERADO and slammed the door. He started the engine to get the AC going but didn't leave his parking spot. He needed to think.

If he had his way, every lawyer would be shipped off to Siberia. Someplace as cold outside as lawyers were inside. The trust was locked up tighter than Harley's shed used to be. The lawyer insisted there was no loophole that allowed for Ray to access funds.

Even if the kid owed him $3,500 because he didn't lock up the store.

Even if the kid was costing him money to post bail—with more legal fees to come.

Even if the kid committed heavy-duty crimes—like grand theft auto.

Even if there would be damages to pay for the messed-up Wrangler.

All Ray's careful planning—which he'd executed perfectly—and for what? For some stupid lawyer to say the "trust doesn't allow for blah, blah, blah." Honestly, he'd been so sure the whole Wrangler stunt would clinch things. It should have been the master key to open the trust. What was the point of holding money for the kid's future if he ended up in jail—which was where he was going. Well, juvenile jail, at least.

That much he got the inside scoop on. Next week he'd be free of the kid for good. Ray might even help him pack. All he had left now could fit in a backpack. Ray chuckled. Pictured his nephew being hauled off to juvey. Wouldn't his dearly departed brother be proud.

But this was no time to celebrate. The loan—with the added 20K penalty—was due Sunday. Three days. And he had no way to get that money. None. Sure, Kelsey had an appointment to show the bike to a hot prospect at this very moment. But even if the guy paid cash and drove it off today, Ray would be at least twenty grand short. That stinkin' penalty was ridiculous. *Impossible.*

"Use your head, Ray. You always come out on top. You just gotta figure this out." He could sell the Silverado, right? But it wasn't worth no twenty grand—even if he could pull off a miracle and sell it quick enough. And then what was he supposed to do for wheels?

Ray needed that trust money. Now. He had a copy of the trust. Maybe it was time he read the thing—start to finish. He'd find something. The tiniest little hole was all he needed. He'd suck funds out of that trust with a straw if he had to.

His phone vibrated. Kelsey's name popped up on the screen. Good. He could use a little good news. Maybe if he gave Lochran half the money two days early, he'd extend the loan another couple days on the back end.

He answered the call. "Done deal?"

"We've been double-crossed, Ray. The key on the lock didn't work. I got the property manager over here with a set of bolt cutters. The space is empty, man."

It couldn't be. "You got the right unit?"

"For sure. There was a lock sitting on the floor inside—and it had been cut. Our key fit it."

Ray swore. Again and again. "Lochran was the only one who knew the location."

"And his bodyguard, Ironwing. They set you up, man."

The Silverado's tires screamed as he roared out of the lawyer's parking lot. "I'm there in five. Wait for me. I'm calling Lochran now. He's got some fancy explaining to do."

"Got that right." Kelsey disconnected.

Ray blew a stop sign. Headed for the bridge. Ray was a survivor. He landed on his feet. He always did. He would this time too. "You watch and see, Mr. Quinn Lochran." He'd give him a piece of his mind—and a knuckle sandwich once he got past Ironwing.

He scrolled through his contacts and jabbed the one simply listed *Genie*. That's the way Ray had looked at Lochran when he'd met him the first time—a genie . . . granting the kind of wishes that only happen when you've got piles of dough. Well, Lochran was going to wish he'd never double-crossed Ray Lotitto.

CHAPTER 50

ELLA SET GRAMS'S BLUEBERRY GHOST PIE on the kitchen table. Jelly and Parker each took a slice, but without Harley there filling his plate, it just didn't seem the same.

"Are we all agreed that our online search for Kemosabe is so far a lost cause?" Ella scanned the faces—all looking as glum as she felt. Nobody disagreed. Four days since it was stolen—and not a trace of it had been found. The police had chased down several bogus leads, according to the update Parker's dad got from Officer Greenwood.

"And are we all agreed," Jelly said, "that Harley is a lost cause too?"

That set off a serious debate with Parker. The guy couldn't accept the obvious. Jelly and Ella hit him with solid logic—and everything pointed to Harley being a liar.

"We saw him steal the Wrangler—right from Scorza's driveway,"

Ella said. "Saw him making his escape after he crashed it. Positive ID, for sure. And Jelly's dad collided into him. Saw his face clearly looking right into the headlights. That's three eyewitnesses. And you're basing his innocence on what, exactly?"

"I just don't think he did it," Parker said finally.

"Grams saw him in the Walgreens parking lot, probably minutes before he stole it," Jelly said. "She actually talked to him. Harley was right there in Gloucester. Do you have any actual facts that would prove it wasn't Harley?"

"Maybe Parker thinks Harley's got an evil twin," Ella said. "*That's* probably who we saw."

"Okay, okay," Parker said. "I don't have any hard evidence, if that's what you want. It's just a gut feeling."

Jelly looked almost apologetic. "You want to believe him. I wish I could too. But we have to face the hard truth."

Parker didn't say a word. He poked at his pie with his fork.

"And there's something else we haven't talked about. We all know Scorza left his Wrangler keys at the dive shop. We all know Harley hid those keys from him."

Ella had forgotten all about that. But it all fit, didn't it? "He said he would do something with those keys eventually."

"And last night he did," Jelly said. "We heard they found the Wrangler keys in his pocket, right? How do you explain all that?"

Parker shook his head. "I can't."

"And when we called him, he blamed it on Scorza," Ella said. "He never told us anything to make us believe he hadn't taken the Wrangler and scratched *BARF BAG* onto the hood."

"He never really told me his side of it," Parker said. "That's the problem."

"There *is* no other side to it," Jelly said. "And *that's* the problem."

Grams leaned against the kitchen counter. "It does look bad for our Harley. But I've lived long enough to know that sometimes there are explanations that make all the difference. Reasons that we would have never guessed."

Was she siding with Parker now? "There is no explanation—no excuse for what Harley did. Sometimes the obvious answer is the right one."

"It often is," Grams said. "But sometimes not."

Ella wasn't going to argue. Not with Grams. The room was quiet for a few moments.

"We tried to help him," Ella said. "We did. But when a guy won't take your help—and he can't seem to help himself—he's a lost cause."

"Ella," Grams said. "You're angry. You feel betrayed. It's because you care about him so much. We all do. But we have to be mighty careful before we label him as a lost cause."

"And what would *you* call him, Grams?" Ella said it a little sharper than she should have.

Grams looked at her for a long moment. "Not a lost cause, Ella-girl. Just . . . lost. The boy is lost." She let that hang out there for a moment. "And I don't think he feels there's a soul on God's green earth who is there for him. Nobody to offer him a hand. Not even to point the way."

Jelly lowered her head. Stared at the table. Parker sat with fork in hand, his pie untouched.

"His momma abandoned him as a child." Grams still kept her eyes on Ella. "You of all people ought to cut him a little slack for that."

Okay, that one stung a bit. "But I didn't get a restraining order slapped on me. And I haven't been out stealing cars and taking them for joyrides."

"Child." Grams clucked her tongue. "You were surrounded with love—your entire life. Harley had that until a few short years ago. Now he lives with that pig of an uncle. Do you have any idea what that must be like?"

"So you're saying the hard breaks he's gotten in life give him an excuse to do the awful things he's done? You raised me to be responsible for my choices—not blame it on my past."

Grams got a sad look in her eyes. "You're right, Ella-girl. Harley's past doesn't earn him a pass for wrong behavior. But by golly it ought to earn him a bit more compassion from his friends."

Parker closed his eyes. Sat still as death. Only his lips moved. And Ella knew the guy was praying again. For Harley, no doubt. Or was it for her? That actually made her want to sew his lips shut.

"So what do we do?" Jelly broke the silence. "If he keeps lying to us—I mean, what *can* we do, right?"

Ella nodded, but she kept her eyes on Parker.

"I'll go see him," Parker said.

"Exactly what do you expect to hear that will make anything he's done okay?" Ella was pretty sure she had him there.

He shook his head. "I'm going in with zero expectations. That's the whole point of hearing him out, right?"

The four of them together . . . everything had been perfect. But Harley had thrown it away. For what? They hadn't just lost him; Parker was getting weird too. It seemed he was siding with Harley—even with all the evidence against him. Harley was ruining everything.

"I keep seeing the watercolor you did," Parker said. "Harley and I on Humpback Rock. That's the friend I want back. He needs our help . . . but I have no idea how to reach him."

"He lied to us. To *me*." And in that moment, she'd found the dead center of her hurt. "How could he do that?"

Grams stepped over and wrapped Ella in her arms. She motioned Jelly into the circle too.

A lump burned in Ella's throat. "Friends don't lie to friends—no matter how bad the truth is. How could he, Grams? How could he?" Maybe Ella would never know.

Parker was standing now. He took a step away from them.

Jelly must have noticed it too. "You leaving?"

"I need some advice. I've got to talk to my parents. Thanks for the pie, Grams."

He still hadn't touched it.

"Are you coming back?"

Parker shook his head. "After I talk to my mom and dad, there's someone I need to find." He slipped out the side door and shut it tight.

"I hope he wasn't talking about Harley," Ella said. "He won't find him."

"Ella-girl," Grams said. "Have a little faith."

What was the point? "You said it yourself, Grams. Harley is lost."

CHAPTER 51

AFTER TALKING WITH HIS MOM AND DAD, Parker felt he had some direction. A starting point with Harley, anyway. He actually wished his parents were coming with him to do the talking. But his parents had already done plenty—and they were pretty amazing. They'd also given him an incredible amount of leash over the last week—something he appreciated more than he could say. And somehow, he sensed this was something he needed to do. It was something Harley needed him to do, anyway.

He'd have gotten to the Rockport Dive Company a lot faster on his bike than he did on foot. But he needed the extra time. To think. And to pray.

Parker walked up Bearskin Neck and cut off on the back road to Bradley Wharf. Harley hadn't answered any of Parker's texts. Obviously, the dive shop was closed now. Maybe he'd talk to him if he threw pebbles against his bedroom window.

The sun had set behind him, and the world in front of him got darker by the minute. As it turned out, Parker didn't have to throw anything against Harley's window. He was there, behind the shop. Sitting on an old lobster trap he'd set smack-dab in the middle of where his shed stood less than a week ago.

Parker slowed his pace. Harley sat there, slump-shouldered, staring out over Rockport Harbor.

"Harley?"

He gave Parker a sideways glance, then focused on the harbor again.

Parker grabbed a nearby lobster trap and set it next to Harley's. Sat next to him in silence for a couple of minutes. "Tell me what happened."

Harley picked up a charred remnant of the shed they'd missed in the cleanup. He tossed it in an end-over-end throw that splashed into the darkened waters of the harbor. "You know what happened. You think you do, anyway."

"Tell me your version."

Harley shook his head. His jaw set.

"I'm your friend."

Again the side-eye. "Are you?"

"Yeah—and when a friend is in trouble he goes to his friends. You should have come to me—"

"Instead of going to Gloucester, is that it?"

"I guess so." This wasn't going how he'd pictured it. He started out with the words Mom had given him. But he'd just gotten off track, hadn't he?

"There's no point to you being here, Parks."

"Look, help me out here," Parker said. "That last thing didn't come out right. Tell me what happened in Gloucester. You made some deliveries. And we both figured your uncle was trying to keep you too busy to go to Scorza's."

Harley sighed. Threw something else into the harbor. The ripples spread wider and wider, but he still didn't say a word.

Keep quiet, Parker. Let him talk. He had to resist the urge to fill in the quiet with a stupid question that might make things worse.

A minute of awkward silence passed. Harley looked out over the harbor. "I'd given the police, the posters, and the internet searches a full seventy-two hours. But they didn't turn up a thing. I didn't dare wait longer. I knew Scorza was behind this. And I was going to get the truth out of him. So I convinced the Uber driver to let me bring my bike. After the last delivery in Gloucester, I told the driver I'd pedal home—sent the guy on his way. That's when I headed for Scorza's. I was going to *make* him tell me what he did."

"Why didn't you call me?"

Harley gave him a long look. "So you could talk me out of it? Or race in with your dad and stop me? I don't think so. This was my last chance. My only chance. Because once I broke that restraining order, I knew there'd be no going back."

Parker stood. Plowed his hands through his hair. The guy did it to himself. "Harley . . . why?"

"The chances of Kemosabe being found were getting slim. I had to know I'd tried everything I could to find him. Even if that meant stepping into trouble. I kept thinking my friend needed me to do this for him."

Parker was not buying that line. "You thought *I* needed you to—"

"Kemosabe," Harley interrupted. "The name means 'trusted friend,' remember?"

"You did it for your motorcycle?"

Harley didn't answer for a half minute. "Sounds stupid. But that bike was a friend to me. And a guy doesn't abandon his friends—even when he has no idea where his friend is at."

Ouch. So that's how Harley saw the situation.

"And I was going to Scorza's for my dad, too."

A lobster boat motored into the harbor. Pulled up to its buoy. "You may have to explain that one to me."

He gave a single nod. "We built that together. He wanted me to have that. If I'd have sold it—like Uncle Ray wanted me to— I would have dishonored him."

Parker could see that.

"And when the bike was taken, I would have dishonored him if I didn't do everything in my power to find it. Get it back. My willingness to fight for it was a way of showing him how much I loved that gift. And the one who gave it."

He had a way of making what he'd done sound noble. "So you stole the Wrangler—not to get even or to show Scorza how it felt to lose something he loved. You were trying to pressure him into telling you where he hid Kemosabe—but you lost control and hit that tree. Is that it?"

Harley stared at him. "That's not it at all. I didn't go there to steal anything. I was going to beat the tar out of Scorza. You still think I stole the Wrangler—and that I lied to you and Jelly and Ella."

This is crazy. He should have stuck to his plan to listen more and talk less.

"You didn't come to hear my side, Parks. You came to try to understand why I did what you *think* I did."

"You're saying you didn't take the Wrangler?"

"I'm not saying anything now." Harley shook his head. Stood. "You think I've been lying? Thanks, Parks."

He strode for the back door of the dive shop.

"Harley, talk to me! C'mon."

He whirled around. "I'm done talking."

"You're not playing fair."

"Says the Christian who had me judged before even hearing me out."

Okay, now *that* was making Parker mad. "You haven't told me your side—so what am I supposed to do?"

Harley grabbed the doorknob. Pulled open the door. "If somebody told me you stole a car, I wouldn't believe it—no matter who told me it was true. Not until you told me yourself. I guess I had a whole lot higher view of you than you did of me."

Had. He said *had*. Like the friendship was history.

"See ya, Parks."

Maybe the friendship *was* gone. "Harley, I need a do-over here. Let me try again."

Harley stepped inside, then spun to face him. "I'll send you a postcard from juvey—unless I get out of here before they take me." He closed the door, and the light turned off in the fill station room.

Parker stood there—not sure what to do next. "God, help me. I messed it up again." Grams was right. Harley was lost. More than Parker had even guessed. And now he'd just pushed Harley farther away.

CHAPTER 52

RAY SAT IN THE CABIN OF *DEEP TROUBLE* waiting for Lochran to show. Ray's tough-guy phone call hadn't worked out quite the way he'd expected. He'd wanted to slam Lochran. He'd gotten himself slam-dunked instead. The guy was scary smart. And always seemed to be a step ahead of Ray.

What started as a phone call accusing Lochran of double-crossing him morphed into a shameless begging for a chance to work out a new plan. Lochran made no promises, but advised him not to run—and to meet him at the boat at 10:45.

Honestly, he might have run—if not for what he'd found in the trust fund. Plan A had been to get Harley to sell the bike—and he'd pay off the loan. No problem. Plan B was to take the bike from Harley and sell it on the side. Plan C was about tapping the trust fund for "legal fees." All of them had sounded so good. So foolproof. But now Plans A, B, and C were all dead in the water—or sinking. Nothing had worked. Not one of the plans would give him access to the kind of money he needed now. Until he found the loophole. Now he had a Plan D. And it kind of scared him. The plan was a ray of light—but terrifyingly dark at the same time.

He'd been on his fourth beer when he saw it. He read the paragraph over and over. It was the only chance he had. It was his salvation. Now he just had to sell it to the loan shark.

Lochran's Hummer pulled into the lot at exactly 10:45. Ironwing walked to the pier ahead of his boss this time—and clearly on high alert.

"Where are those guys hiding?" Ironwing kept scanning the nearby boats even as he asked.

"Not here," Ray said. And he was telling the truth. "I just want to talk—and float another plan by you."

Ironwing hopped lightly onto the boat and checked the cabin. A moment later he ducked back out and climbed to the dock. "Clear."

"I told you. I'm alone."

"More than you realize, Mr. Lotitto," Lochran said. "Now, we need to have a serious chat."

Ray motioned him aboard the boat. "I've got something to show you."

Lochran smiled. "I'll look at it from here, thank you. I've learned it's a lot easier to get into *deep trouble* than it is to get out of it. But that's more your department right now, I believe."

"I'm sorry for accusing you of taking the bike," Ray said. And he meant it. "Somebody else took it—and I'll find out who."

Lochran shook his head. "I'm already working on that. You need to stay focused. And you've got some serious money to rustle up—by Sunday. You said you had a plan, that you were willing to pay added penalties."

Penalties nothing. It was a ransom Lochran expected. Ray was buying his life back. "Right." Ray held up the trust agreement. "Read the paragraph I circled."

Lochran took the paperwork. Focused on the page for longer than Ray could hold his breath. Then the loan shark looked over the top of the agreement directly at Ray as if he was assessing whether Ray really intended to follow through. "Exactly how much is this trust worth?"

"Half a mil—as of a couple days ago."

"You know I can verify that," Lochran said. "So if you're not shooting straight with me on this . . ."

"Do it. Verify. I got it right from the lawyer's mouth. So with the penalties, I owe you forty grand. I'll do my part before the loan is due . . . and then the payout is a done deal. A sure thing. Once I go through all the legal hoops, I'll have all the money I need. And you'll get every penny I owe you."

"But you'll be late."

"Yeah, but—"

"There are no extensions," Lochran said. "And those legal hoops you mention could drag on for weeks, I suspect. Thank you, but no. I think our business is done here, Mr. Lotitto." He stepped off the dock onto *Deep Trouble*'s gunwale and jumped down onto the deck.

Ironwing untied the dock lines, tossed them into the boat and followed his boss aboard the boat like he'd known exactly where this was going all along.

"Hold on," Ray said. "What are we doing?"

"You're going to take us for a boat ride, Ray. It won't take long. Somewhere outside Gloucester Harbor. Start her up."

Ironwing stepped closer in a way that made Ray's knees feel absolutely weak. He knew exactly where this was going. Ray went to the helm. Fired up the Cummings diesel. "Listen, I've got two more days."

"And no way to pay." Lochran shook his head. "Comes a time when a businessman needs to know when to cut his losses. And you, my friend, are a loss. But not a total loss. You'll serve as a good reminder to others who might be tempted to be late."

"Wait a sec." Ray landed on his feet, right? He needed to make this happen—right now. And he was going to get one shot at this. "I'll have the money. Slap on extra interest. Another penalty. You saw the trust agreement. If something happens to the kid, I'm the *only* relative. That makes me the beneficiary of the whole shebang."

Lochran held his gaze. "Half."

Two hundred and fifty thousand? That was the price? Ray would have paid the whole thing to save his skin. But this way he'd still have two hundred fifty left. And he'd have a boat. A dive shop. He'd be on Easy Street. "Deal."

"And we still have a deadline," Lochran said.

What? "But it will take weeks—"

Lochran held up one hand. "I understand the legalities will take some time. But the wheels must be in motion. The deed done."

Meaning Harley would have to have a terrible accident by Sunday.

"Verifiable proof. And I'm moving up the due date."

Ray's mouth went dry. "When."

"Twenty-four hours."

He could hardly breathe.

"If I give you more than that, you're liable to run. But my associate will find you—and he is very skilled at making cold feet a permanent condition."

Ironwing smiled—like he was picturing Ray with actual cold feet. The kind with a toe tag.

Ray nodded. Lochran was right. If Ray was willing to do this in two days, he could do it in one. Kelsey or Vinny would help—and he'd cut them in. He'd get this nasty thing over with—and he'd be free of Lochran—and Ironwing—forever.

"Do we have an understanding?"

"Yes, sir." Why he added *sir* to the end, he had no idea. The guy just had that effect on him.

"Eleven o'clock p.m. Tomorrow. We'll meet right here. You'll have proof, or you'll take us for a little boat ride. Don't disappoint me again."

Ray wouldn't dream of it. "Twenty-four hours. Right here." That gave him tonight to come up with a plan. And tomorrow . . . to execute.

CHAPTER 53

PARKER SAT ACROSS FROM HIS DAD at the breakfast table. Last night had been agonizing. He'd told his parents how he'd bombed the conversation with Harley. Confessed he didn't know what to do next. And they'd asked him to sleep on it. Pray on it. So Parker did . . . at least the praying part. He wasn't sure how much sleep he'd gotten.

"So," Dad said, "what are you thinking this morning, son?"

Mom breezed into the kitchen and took a seat.

"I keep coming back to the same thing—wondering if there's something I'm missing. Something Harley didn't tell me—or didn't get a chance to. I feel like really hearing his side of the story might change things—even though I have no idea how."

"Hearing someone before judging them is always a good idea," Dad said. "Anything else?"

"Yeah. Two things, really." But they were just feelings. "I think you were right, Mom. Jelly told me that you prayed when you were with her and Ella and Grams. Something in your prayer stuck with her. About Harley being in deep water or something. I absolutely believe it's true. He's in way over his head—and he's got no life jacket. I have a feeling this is going to get worse somehow—fast."

"Do you have a sense"—Dad seemed to be searching for the right words—"of any idea of what that might be?"

"Either he's going to get taken away, put into the foster system—or juvey. Or he's going to run before they do. But either way, he won't be in Rockport anymore. If we don't do something, we'll lose him."

Tears welled in Mom's eyes. "I love that boy. I pray for him every day."

"He's put up a wall between us. I have no idea what I'm supposed to do to get around it. I've been praying God will show me—and give me the courage to do whatever it is."

Mom and Dad listened. If they had an idea, they were careful to keep it from showing on their faces.

"I just feel my first step is to talk with him again. Just the two of us. Today."

"Maybe let *him* talk this time," Dad said.

Parker couldn't agree more.

"We're proud of you," Mom said. "You know that?"

He definitely did—even when he wasn't so proud of himself.

Mom rested her arms on the table and leaned closer. "You said there were two things you were thinking."

Parker shrugged. "It's just that none of this makes sense, you know? It's too big. How could Scorza pull this off? To make a big motorcycle like that disappear without a trace? I don't think he's that good. Dumping the bike off the wharf and into the harbor would sound like him. An impulse kind of thing. But to ghost it away? He'd have to have that all planned out—and have help."

Both his dad and mom seemed to be tracking with him. Neither of them looked at him like he was crazy.

"Harley is so sure it's Scorza, but too much doesn't fit. I mean, how did he know Harley would pull the bike out of the shed and park it there? I say Friday night with the smoke bombs was just a trial run. A dress rehearsal. Whoever did this learned whatever they needed to know. And Sunday night they were ready."

A look passed between his parents.

"What. You think I've seen too many movies?"

Mom reached over and rubbed his arm. "Officer Greenwood said nearly the same thing to your dad earlier in the week. He was convinced Bryce Scorza wasn't the mastermind behind this."

"So," Parker said, "what does this mean?"

Dad smiled. "Greenwood is smart. He's onto something. And God will help him figure this out."

But it could be too late for Harley. "Does he think Harley stole the Wrangler?"

Dad shook his head. "He wouldn't say. The Gloucester police think so. But something about the way Greenwood was talking tells me he thinks there's more to it."

Okay. That was good. "But what do we do—like right now— for Harley?"

"We're all going to pray together," Dad said. "And then you're going to follow through on what was on your heart when you walked into the kitchen this morning. That sense you got after you'd prayed."

Parker met his eyes. "I need to get Harley to open up. We're missing something."

Dad nodded.

"And I need to stay close. Harley is self-destructing."

"We're all self-destructive, Parker," Dad said. "I believe that with all my heart. If not for God's influence in my life, I'd have ruined myself a thousand times over." He paused, maybe to let that sink in. "And a scary thought? Our Harley is largely on his own. He doesn't have God in his life."

But Harley had a friend who did. "So . . . I'll stick to him like a life jacket. Maybe help keep him from doing something self-destructive and stupid." And somehow, with God's help, he'd keep his friend from going under for good.

CHAPTER 54

Friday, August 12, 3:00 p.m.

BRYCE CHECKED HIS BACKPACK. Padlock key for the storage unit. Screwdrivers. Socket set. Matches. Knife. Four heavy-duty garbage bags. The construction garbage type—three mils thick, forty-two-gallon capacity. He'd take apart what he could. Bag it up. Make at least one dumpster run. He added a hammer to the pack. What he couldn't take off, he'd crater.

Shouldering the pack, he grabbed his football and mounted his bike. He'd even worn his jersey. He'd gone back and forth on the decision, but in the end, he'd opted to wear it. The important thing right now was to act normal in every way. To look totally casual. Like he wasn't hiding something that a ton of people were looking for. Which was harder to do than it seemed. Between the police and the thugs, an awful lot of those people carried guns.

Jaxon was on the driveway coloring some white planter box with permanent markers. Trophy Traci was in her own world, scrolling on her phone. She was in for a messy surprise if she would get a life and pry her eyes from the screen. Bryce steered around them both.

"I'll be late," Bryce said. "Don't wait up to tuck me in."

She didn't look up. "Okay, have fun."

Exactly what he intended to do.

He scanned the block in both directions. Lots of parked cars and a few trucks. But nobody sitting inside watching for him. Honestly? He'd probably been worried for nothing. Even if somebody did look at the Port Knox surveillance videos, what were the chances they'd look back far enough to spot him? Once they realized he was smart enough to paint over the security cameras, would they have bothered to look at the earlier footage? Nobody would guess he'd made the stupid mistake to let himself get recorded over and over again.

Bryce pedaled down his street and headed for Western Avenue. He'd take the bridge over Blynman Canal and be at the Cape Ann Marina within fifteen minutes. He'd camp out there until he was sure no cars were at Port Knox. Then he'd sweep in and get to work.

An old F-150 pulled away from the curb, heading his way. Okay, so maybe all the cars hadn't been empty. It didn't mean anything. He made a quick turn at the end of the block, just in case. The sand-colored pickup kept going straight.

"You're spooking yourself, Bryce," he said. He made another few turns and got himself back on course. He hadn't gone two blocks before he saw the tan pickup truck again. Coming from a different direction, but headed for the same intersection.

Turn or keep straight—turn or keep straight? Bryce coasted for a moment—gripping the handlebars with one hand, the football with the other. He powered right through—like he was rushing into the end zone for a touchdown. He glanced at the driver, but whoever it was held a map against the steering wheel, blocking Bryce's view.

Okay. So, the guy was just lost. And if he was using a map, he had to be a geezer. "You're imagining things, Scorza. Just jumpy is all." Saying it out loud boosted his confidence. He pulled onto Western and put some muscle into the pedals. The ride to the waterfront was largely downhill, so he let nature do its thing. In seconds his tires were humming.

Boats lined up in the harbor, waiting for the bridge to lift and let them pass. Cars sped up like they knew they'd get stuck for fifteen minutes if they didn't step on it. He chanced another shoulder check. Tan pickup . . . two cars behind him. Coincidence—or was the guy tailing him?

Bryce made like he was pushing hard to make the bridge, and the truck rolled right along with traffic and passed him. The instant the truck's front tires hit the steel bridge, Harley braked hard and slid to a stop.

"Yeah!" Bryce raised the football and shook it at the pickup— now on the other side of Blynman Canal. "Kids aren't as dumb as you thought."

The bridge rose, and the pickup kept going. Didn't even tap the brakes. Bryce watched until it drove out of sight. If the guy was really following him, he would have pulled over, right?

"You're getting paranoid, Bryce." The truth was, he had nothing to worry about. But still, he wasn't going to make multiple trips to Port Knox. Every time he went there, he'd be taking a chance. He had to be smart. So today was it. One and done. He'd slice and dice it. Pull off anything he could. Dent what he couldn't remove. Then, if the paint was still on the security cameras, he'd roll the bike behind the second building, baptize the thing with gas, and throw a match. It would be easy enough to boost a spare tank of gas from the back end of some boat in the marina.

Even after the bridge was back down in place and he was on his way again, he found himself watching traffic more, and giving every side street a double take. No sand-colored F-150. And no Hummer or Silverado either.

He wheeled into the Cape Ann Marina parking lot, went to the docks, and walked to the end of one of them. Nothing looked out of place. He had a good view of Port Knox, and he hadn't seen a single car or truck pull in or out. He watched a full fifteen minutes, and still nothing.

Bryce casually made his way back to his bike. He slipped the lanyard off from around his neck and stared at the ignition key for Harley's motorcycle. Was he going to do this or not? As much as he tried to convince himself he was just playing it safe, he knew better. He was stalling now. Running down the clock. He wrapped the lanyard around the post of his bike seat and secured it tight. "Okay, Brycie-boy. It's go time."

Once he made the decision, he couldn't get to the storage unit fast enough. The alley was empty. Perfect. And the security cameras still had their black coating.

He biked to his unit, laid his bike down, and dug inside his pack until he found the padlock key. A silver pickup pulled into the far end of the alley. Silverado. His stomach did a tuck and roll. Was it the same truck he'd seen at Port Knox when he'd discovered Kemosabe?

Run. Every instinct inside him told him to take off in the opposite direction. But if he did, he'd look totally guilty, right?

The Silverado slowed a couple of bays down and started a three-point turn like he was going to back up to one of the garage doors. The glare off the guy's side window made it impossible to get a good look at who was inside.

Bryce kept his head down, like he was trying to unlock the padlock on his unit, but his peripheral vision was on the door of that Silverado. If it flew open and somebody headed his way, he'd race for the open end of the alley. He turned his bike around and leaned it on the garage door, just in case. He'd have a faster start without the bike—but in the long run the bike would get him the distance he'd need. He shed his pack. Leaving the pack might pick him up a fraction of a second—which might make all the difference. There was nothing in there that could be traced back to him. He propped the football on his pack.

The Silverado stayed in that position. Not quite backed up square to any one garage door. Just sitting there, blocking the entire alley. Was the guy on his phone?

Okay, he had to think. If this was even the same Silverado that he'd seen Wednesday night, the guy probably wasn't suspicious of Bryce. What did he have? Did he even know the motorcycle was gone? If so, would he have gone back far enough in the security tapes to even spot Bryce? Unlikely. Bryce just had to keep from doing something stupid and obvious—like bolt in panic.

Stay. And stay cool. He made the decision and pretended to play with the lock. But with every second that passed the uneasy feeling grew. Okay . . . time for a new tactic. He'd leave real casual-like, and sit it out at Cape Ann Marina. He'd come back when the truck left. He tucked the key deep in his pocket.

"Having a little trouble with that lock?"

Bryce whirled to face a voice that had come from the other

direction. Kelsey. Definitely one of the guys from Wednesday night—no more than ten feet away. The tan pickup was parked across the alley at the far end of Port Knox—the driver's door hanging wide open.

Play it cool—or run?

"Let me help you with that."

Okay, this guy was fishing. One slipup—and he'd know Bryce was the guy. "Wrong key, that's all. Gotta go home and get the right one."

Kelsey stopped not two feet away. "You sure?"

"Yep." He should have run the instant he saw the Silverado. *Play it cool, Bryce.*

"How about you let me have a try?"

Bryce shook his head. "It'll give me an excuse to get a snack." He picked up the football. Tucked it under his arm.

"You've brought nothing to store in the space—and you sure can't haul much out on your bike." Kelsey made an exaggerated show of looking at the pack and the ground around it. "What you got in the lockup?"

"An ATV." It was the first thing that popped in his head. "Just going to do a little work on it." He shook the pack to make the tools jangle a bit.

"Really. What kind of ATV?"

"Honda." Bryce had a Honda lawnmower—not an all-terrain vehicle.

"Sweet." Kelsey nodded. "What model? The XJ250—or the LE350?"

Eenie-meenie-miny-mo. "250. I think. I'll ask my dad."

Kelsey stepped into Bryce—his hands out to his sides like he was ready to stop him if he tried to bolt. "Honda don't make either model. How about we see what's *really* inside?"

Bryce took a step back and spun like he would to avoid getting sacked. He slammed into the guy from the Silverado. Instantly two sets of strong arms wrapped around him like steel straps.

He thrashed and fought to free himself. He threw an elbow and connected with someone's ribs, but the grip didn't loosen a bit.

Kelsey dropped back and threw a roundhouse punch with lightning speed. Bryce tried to duck, but all he could do was turn his head to the side. The blow hit with incredible force. Like Bryce was playing on frozen turf—without a helmet—and he'd been sacked by a 250-pound linebacker.

Kelsey grabbed a handful of Bryce's T-shirt right at the neck and slugged him again. The blow caught him on the cheekbone just below his eye. There must have been a nerve there directly connected to Bryce's knees. They buckled. The ball slipped from his fingers and tumbled across the alley.

"Key. Now."

Bryce reached for his pocket with a hand that shook way too much to be his own. He found the key, pulled it out, and opened his fist. Kelsey snatched it up and slid it easily into the padlock.

"Well, lookee there." Kelsey smiled. "I guess you had the right key after all."

The guy holding him from behind still hadn't let up. Bryce had to get out of here before they confirmed he was the one who'd stolen the motorcycle from them. The strength was returning to his knees.

Kelsey peeled off the padlock and gave the garage door an upward jerk. The door followed Kelsey's orders like it knew what he'd do to those who didn't react quick enough.

Now. Bryce dropped into a crouch position and bent forward, lifting the guy holding him right off the ground. He bucked and twisted, but the instant the guy released him, Kelsey was back. The goon swept Bryce's feet right out from under him. He landed on his hip. Hard.

Kelsey rolled him to his back. Drove a knee into his gut. "I can do this all day, kid. That what you want?"

Bryce couldn't breathe. Couldn't say a word.

Suddenly Silverado guy ratcheted an oversize nylon tie around Bryce's ankles—allowing him to get a good look at the guy.

Lotitto's uncle?

What was going on here? Pieces flew into place. Harley hated his uncle—and from all he'd heard, the feeling was mutual. His uncle stole the bike—which was enough of a shock. But what about the guys with the guns? Something big was going on here, and how it turned out for Bryce would depend on how he played the next few minutes.

Kelsey grabbed Bryce's arm and dragged him inside the storage unit, next to the motorcycle.

Mr. Lotitto rolled Bryce's bicycle inside and dropped the garage door in place. Flicked on a flashlight, and inspected the motorcycle. "Perfect. Not a scratch." He towered over Bryce. "What were you going to do with the tools? Take it apart? What kind of friend are you anyway?"

What kind of uncle was he—doing what he was doing? Or was this whole thing some way to scam their insurance? Claim the motorcycle was stolen. Get a check from the insurance company. And sell the bike on the side. He'd double his money.

"I always land on my feet." Lotitto slapped Kelsey on the back. "Right? I mean, how many times have I said that?"

Kelsey snickered. "And you're going to keep doing that, too."

Lotitto did a little dance. "Got that right. I'm going to get that money for Lochran. And you and I will make good too. And someday we might even show Lochran just how much he underestimated us."

"Oh, yeah," Kelsey growled. "Ironwing, too."

This was not sounding like an insurance scam. Bryce shouldn't be hearing this. None of it. Why didn't they at least cover their faces so he could never point them out in a lineup? But he knew why.

Kelsey grabbed the back of Bryce's shirt and pulled him roughly to his knees. "Hands behind your back."

Bryce obeyed. Maybe if he did everything they said, they'd let him go.

Kelsey secured Bryce's wrists with another nylon tie. "So, what do we do with this one?"

Mr. Lotitto looked at him long and hard. "That is going to depend on him. You know, he could be a big help to us. He may even be our salvation, if he's smart. Then you and I would be awfully grateful, right, Mr. Kelsey?"

"And looking for a way to show that gratitude too." Kelsey snickered. "We take care of our own."

Okay, they were giving him a chance, right? "Look," Bryce said. "I'll do whatever you want me to do. Honest."

Kelsey swung a leg over the motorcycle and gripped the handlebars. "What a bike. No wonder the kid didn't know what to do with himself when he lost it."

"So, Mr. Scorza," Lotitto said. "You and young Harley were best friends once upon a time. Still feel that way?"

Normally he would have hidden how he really felt about

Harley. But now? He had to tell the truth, and he felt that was exactly what they wanted to hear. "I hate him. Look, I know he's your nephew, but after what he did to my Wrangler last night? I was going to destroy his bike."

Mr. Lotitto seemed to be processing that. "Looking for some payback, is that it?"

"Yeah . . . definitely." Bryce could whine. Grovel. Plead for his life. But he was pretty sure that wouldn't help him one bit right now. They needed to see strength. They had to know that he could do whatever they wanted him to do. He was the star quarterback. The guy who was headed for a scholarship someday. Definitely the military. "He messed with me at football camp—had more guys following him than me. I'm the quarterback. I'm the team leader. Not him."

"Sounds like that ugly green monster is alive and well in you, Mr. Scorza."

Maybe he *was* jealous. "When I found the bike, I wanted to be the hero. Make Harley crawl back to me. Now I want to hurt him. Bad."

Ray Lotitto clucked his tongue. "And now we've ruined your big plan to get even with him. A pity, really. You were so close."

For some reason Harley's uncle wanted to be rid of him as much as Bryce did. "I don't suppose you'd let me rip the bike apart—and pretend you never saw me, right?"

Kelsey laughed. "He's got guts. Maybe we should let him help us."

"I'll do it." Bryce blurted it out. "Anything. I'll do it."

Mr. Lotitto squatted down next to him. "You know, I'm beginning to believe you would."

Bryce angled his head to look Harley's uncle in the eyes with the one eye that wasn't swelling shut. "I can do whatever you need."

"Let me tell you a story, Mr. Scorza."

Ray Lotitto talked of a good man who bent over backwards to help an orphan boy. And he only asked one thing of the boy: to invest in his business. The boy was ungrateful for all the man did for him, and he flat-out refused, forcing the good man to take a big loan from a bad man. There were some setbacks—none of them the fault of the good man. When the loan shark slapped colossal penalties on the good man—with the threat of death—he knew there was only one way to get the money. There was a trust fund that would pass to the boy when he was twenty-five . . . or to the guardian if the ungrateful orphan met an untimely death himself.

Bryce felt a growing panic rising inside him. Harley's uncle intended to kill him?

"So, Mr. Scorza, you tell me how this story ends." Mr. Lotitto raised his eyebrows as if he actually expected him to do it.

"Okay . . ." Bryce glanced back at Kelsey—who was leaning in with obvious interest. "The, uh, good man had no choice. He was between a rock and a hard place. And the orphan kid still didn't show him respect. I mean, he like totally was in his guardian's face with his attitude." Was he saying the right things? He paused and searched Mr. Lotitto's face.

"Go on."

"The bad loan shark was leaning hard on the guardian. And he had to do something about him. But the guardian needed help. He had a right-hand man who would help him. The guy was strong as a linebacker—and quick too. Not the kind of guy anybody would mess with."

Kelsey roared with laughter. "I'm loving this story, kid."

"And even as good and smart and strong and quick as the

guardian and his good right-hand man were, they knew the loan shark was dangerous. But then they met a kid who hated the orphan's ungrateful guts as much as they did. He promised to help them—and that he'd keep his mouth shut. And the good man decided to give him a chance." Bryce swallowed. "And he was glad he did. Really glad. The orphan got what was coming to him. And the kid did what he was told—and never said a word about it. He got a football scholarship—and the good man and his strong friend came to every game. And they all lived happily ever after."

Kelsey clapped him on the back. "If the football scholarship doesn't work out, you really ought to consider being a writer. You got real potential, kid."

At least he was talking like Bryce had a future. A chance to make it out of this alive.

"You do understand the ungrateful orphan is going to have an unfortunate accident," Mr. Lotitto said.

Bryce nodded.

"And we can make it a double accident . . . or not. It depends if you're going to work with us or not."

"I'll do anything you say," Bryce said. "Anything." And the scary thing? He meant it.

Mr. Lotitto looked at him long and hard. "Okay, there are a couple things I need to do. And I'm going to keep you here—with duct tape over your mouth so you don't cry for help or anything stupid like that."

"Do it," Bryce said. "I won't let you down."

Lotitto checked Bryce's pockets and confiscated his phone. "We'll be back within the hour. And then you're going to make a phone call—and you'll do exactly as I say. Agreed?"

He'd be setting Harley up for something awful, wouldn't he?

But Harley deserved it in a way. He'd turned his back on Bryce, hadn't he? No, the Wrangler stunt was worse than that. He'd *attacked* Bryce when his back was turned.

"Agreed." Harley couldn't treat others like junk and expect not to get trashed himself, right? "You're the coach—and I'll run your plays."

Lotitto smiled. Looked at Kelsey like he wanted to be sure his right-hand man felt the same way.

Seal the deal, Bryce. This is your last chance. You don't want them changing their minds after they leave. "And can I say one more thing?"

Lotitto gave him the nod.

"Harley is out of control. He thinks I took his precious motorcycle. And when he finally figures his bike is never coming back? He's probably going to try to kill me—if I don't stop him first. I *want* to do this."

Harley's uncle folded his arms across his chest. "Okay, son. You've earned yourself a chance. Welcome to the team."

CHAPTER 55

Friday, August 12, 4:00 p.m.

ANGELICA SAT ON THE ROCKS OF THE BREAKWATER with a box of donuts from BayView Brew. Something about being out here along the coast usually calmed her mind. Not so much today.

Ella stood behind her easel, working on a watercolor she hadn't touched all week since the smoke bombs in the shed. Ella "processed with paints." That's the way she put it, anyway. Right now, she attacked the canvas with the brush more than stroked it. Whatever processing she was doing, it wasn't doing a thing to calm her. She rinsed her brush, stuck it in her hair, and took a step back.

"I need to stop." Ella pulled out her phone and scrolled through it. "I'm going to ruin the canvas if I don't. Something's off with me."

"It's not you," Angelica said. "It's Harley. He messed up, and it's messing with your head."

They'd both agreed to give Harley his space. Hopefully he'd

come around and stop lying to them. But if he didn't, well, Angelica would chalk it up to him not being who she thought he was. It crushed her to say it, but if he could lie through his teeth like that, he wasn't the kind of friend she wanted anyway. Ella talked like she was in total agreement, but Angelica wasn't so sure. There were times she didn't seem nearly as ready to do the hard thing: pull away from Harley. But Angelica was absolutely sure they needed to distance themselves from him. Totally convinced.

She just wished Parker felt the same way. He seemed so bull-headed determined to get through to Harley. To protect Harley from himself. Which was making her job a lot tougher.

"I talked to Wilson this morning," Angelica said.

"And you waited until now to mention that?"

She'd been trying to forget the conversation. At least part of it. "The guy never seems to worry about anything, you know? But he's worried about Parker."

"Ha. Tell him to get in line."

"Crazy thing? He doesn't think Scorza is a real player in this."

Ella dumped her rinse water. Shook the container. "What would he know?"

"Here's his take on things: The night Kemosabe was taken, the shed had been torched just so Harley would roll the bike far away from the flames. And the pyro *knew* Harley was inside—otherwise why not just break into the shed and roll out the bike?"

"Okay."

"They were taking a chance Harley would wake up and get the motorcycle out all right. Which probably says they were okay if Harley didn't."

Ella stopped putting her gear away. "He said that?"

Angelica nodded. "It was what he said next that really made me think. 'Better be careful. It's a really small step from being okay with someone dying . . . and making them dead.'"

"Scorza wouldn't go that far," Ella said.

"I told him that. He agreed—which is why he said we're looking at the wrong guy. She lowered her voice, imitating Wilson. 'Be careful you're not chasing the wrong enemy. When you do, your real enemy will get his knife in your back.' Those were his exact words."

Ella stared at her for a long moment. "So if this isn't two ex-friends in some kind of war, what is it? I mean, what other enemy does Harley have?"

"Besides you?" Angelica smiled.

"I'm not his enemy—but I sure wouldn't call myself his friend right now, either."

"Wilson asked if I wanted him to grab a bus and get up here. He's still kicking himself for not coming up when the whole thing happened with Steadman."

"What did you tell him?"

"That I thought he'd need to take a plane if he really wanted to be here in time to help. But he can't do that, of course."

"Too expensive?"

Angelica shook her head. "He says he'd never get a machete on the plane—or any of the other 'tools' he'd bring."

Ella laughed. "That's just what we need. One more guy who thinks he has to save the world."

"'Keep an eye on Bucky,'" he said. "'If he's set on helping Harley, he may be in more danger than he knows.'"

Ella reached for her cross this time. "I hope he's wrong about the danger. But it sounds like he knows Parker."

Ella was right about that. Parker was the kind of guy who'd

reach out to help a friend—and get pulled down in the process. For an instant her mind replayed a clip she'd done her best to keep locked tight. Parker's hand stretched out over the water—to take the pictures Angelica had pressured him to take. Suddenly, Dillinger was there—and the monster gator had Parker's arm, pulling him into the black waters. Then there was the way he'd risked his neck to find Angelica's sister when everyone thought she was lost in the Glades. And two months ago? He'd ended up on the bottom of the quarry when he'd tried to help Ella. Angelica loved his heart—but it was way too big for his body. "Somehow I have to keep that boy from doing something stupid."

"You really think you can do that?"

Truthfully . . . it didn't seem she could. Not if he wouldn't listen to her. "I'll do what I can."

Ella finished folding the easel and packing it in a duffel. "I'm going to give this canvas another five minutes to dry." She picked up her phone and started scrolling.

Angelica's mind drifted to Parker. He'd been processing things. She could tell. And usually that happened just before he did something crazy.

"Check this out." Ella motioned her closer. Held out her phone so Angelica could see the YouTube clip she'd cued up. The clip was titled simply, "Be Careful Who You Tie Yourself To."

The clip was animated, showing a pair of climbers going up some steep mountainside. The two were tethered together by a rope. Suddenly a bird flew around the head of the lead climber. He swatted at it over and over—even though his partner kept telling him to focus on the climb. With one mighty swing, the leader lost his balance and tumbled off the side of the mountain—taking the more cautious climber with him. The video may have been developed for some business reason, but it depicted the boys' situation perfectly.

"I have this awful feeling," Ella said, "that Harley isn't done doing stupid things. He's going over the side, and he's going to pull Parker right down with him."

Angelica's feelings exactly. "I'm going to call Parker. Again." She'd probably talked with him or texted five times today already. Every time he'd seemed distracted.

She dialed and put it on speaker the moment he answered. "Ella and I are here on the breakwater. We've got a donut from BayView Brew with your name on it."

"I stopped in the dive shop. Harley's working it alone today, but he still won't talk. He's definitely pushing me away."

Like Parker had been doing to her all day. It was like he hadn't even heard her offer for him to join them.

"He asked to be left alone for a while, so I left. But he still hasn't told me his side of the story."

"Maybe," Ella said, "it's because there is no other side to tell. We saw what we saw, Parker."

He didn't answer right away. "I just don't know why he wouldn't admit it. Not even to me. Why not just be real?"

"Maybe what you're finally seeing," Angelica said, "*is* the real Harley. Where are you?"

"In the *Bomb*."

The wind had picked up some. Angelica looked beyond the breakwater to Sandy Bay and the horizon line beyond. "The swells look kind of big for the boat out there. And there's definitely a fog bank moving in."

"Don't worry. I'm not going out past the breakwater," Parker said. "I'm just tooling around the harbor."

Thinking. He always seemed to think his clearest when out on the water. She should have figured he'd be in the *Boy's Bomb*. Ella pointed to the teal skiff cruising the Outer Harbor near the channel inlet. Angelica nodded. "We see you now. Want some company, skipper?"

There was a pause. Enough time for him to have answered the simple question twice. Like the signal to the cell tower got swallowed by the fog on the way out—or back. "Not this time, Jelly."

Ella exchanged a look with her. Obviously she didn't like Parker's answer any more than Angelica did.

"I'm still thinking about things," he said. "Sorry." Like maybe he guessed how much his words stung.

There was a time when she'd ride along with him . . . and he'd think out loud. Run things by her. But she needed to keep it light, not put him on a guilt trip. "Imagine how much more productive you'll be with two super-thinking girls like Ella and me to bounce things off. We could be at the T-wharf by the time you get there."

"Next time," he said.

What was going on with him?

"I keep running through this in my head," Parker said. "What if he's telling the truth? He admitted he wanted to put some hurt on Scorza that night. To pressure him into telling what had happened to Kemosabe."

"See?" The whole thing was so obvious to Angelica. "He practically confessed to stealing the Wrangler right there. What better way to put some hurt on Scorza?"

"That's just it," Parker said. "He was talking about *physically* pounding Scorza until he talked. He couldn't get a confession by stealing the car. Harley wasn't out for payback . . . he wanted answers. So, what if he *didn't* steal the Wrangler?"

"Then who did?"

"Maybe Scorza himself—to make Harley look bad."

Ella dropped her head in her hands. "Parker . . . you're trying to make Cinderella's slipper fit on the wrong foot. Angelica and I *saw* him leave the Wrangler . . . we *saw* his face."

"I know, I know," Parker said. "I keep getting hung up on that, too. But why would he tell me he had planned to beat the tar out of Scorza, but deny stealing the car? Beating up Scorza would have been a lot worse, don't you think?"

"Parker," Ella said, "I think you're thinking too much about this."

"I'm just saying, why would he lie? What if he's telling the truth?"

Ella pantomimed tearing her own hair out.

Angelica couldn't have agreed more. The guy made her crazy sometimes. He definitely needed a couple of super-thinking girls to keep his theories on the positive side of the sanity spectrum. "My dad saw him too, remember?"

"Yeah, then there's that. I just can't figure it out—but I have to." The sound of the motor was the only thing Angelica heard for maybe the next ten seconds. "Harley's made his mind up about something."

"Yeah," Ella said. "Like he's not going to tell us the truth."

The pitch of the motor changed, like he was slowing down. Sure enough. The *Boy's Bomb* was no longer throwing a wake. Even from here she could see Parker stand. He faced the open ocean. "Look, everything Harley has known and cared about is gone. He's only out of jail on bail. Unless his uncle is bluffing, Harley is going to be a ward of the state—or go to a juvenile detention center. He won't take this lying down."

Ella's hand went up to the Navajo cross around her neck again. "You think he'll try to get at Scorza again?"

"That's just it. I don't know. That could be part of it. Or maybe . . ."

"Maybe *what*?"

"I don't know," Parker said. "He's going to do something really stupid."

She watched him pace the short deck of the *Boy's Bomb*. "He's got nothing to gain by doing that, Parker."

"Nothing to lose either."

So it all came down to one big question. "What are you going to do?"

Parker paused. "Get ready for what I've got to do next. I guess that's what I've been trying to do while I'm out here."

Angelica did not like the sound of that.

Ella gave her the raised-eyebrows nod. She used her hands to pantomime two climbers on a steep incline.

"I thought I might phone my Grandpa," Parker said. "You know he's coming out here in another week or so."

Jelly wished he were here now. Maybe he could help Parker see the obvious.

"I just want to do the right thing." Parker was staring out the channel again, toward the open sea. "I'm just not sure what the right thing is. But something tells me I need to stay close to Harley. Like, the minute he gets off work I need to be there. Make him tell me his side of the story. From there I'll play it by ear."

Parker and his integrity. His sense of doing what was right. It just wasn't always safe. The guy could be maddening. "Parker." She spoke softly. Sometimes a quiet word was heard more clearly than a loud one. "Harley's a good guy. I know how much you like him.

We all do. But he's done some bad things. And there's a price to pay. You can't protect him from the legal system."

"I totally agree," Parker said. "I just want to protect him from himself."

Angelica wanted to scream.

Ella looked just as exasperated. She snatched the phone from Angelica. "But Parker, while you're out protecting Harley . . . who's going to protect you?"

CHAPTER 56

PARKER LET THE *BOY'S BOMB* DRIFT. The waves entering through the channel were definitely bigger now. They bullied the skiff back, like they were warning him not to mess with them.

His grandpa answered the phone, and over the next twenty minutes Parker filled him in on all that had happened with Harley over the last week—and what had happened *to* him. How the evidence looked like Harley had stolen the Wrangler in retaliation, but Parker just felt there was something he wasn't seeing. How Harley was pulling away, but Parker couldn't shake the sense that Harley needed his friends now more than ever. He told his grandpa how he believed Harley was in trouble, and if Parker didn't do something, his friend was headed for disaster.

"Everyone has a push point," Grandpa said. "Something that— if given enough pressure—has the power to send them someplace dark. Deadly. Someplace they never want to go. Off the deep end."

"Kemosabe was Harley's push point," Parker said. "His weakness."

Grandpa was quiet for a moment. "I'd guess it was more than that. The loss of his dad. That's why Kemosabe means so much to him. It's the root of his push point."

Parker found himself staring right into the water. "You think I have a push point?"

"We all do, Parker."

"If I do . . . I have no idea what it is."

"And you don't need to. Just pray your enemy doesn't discover it."

An icy chill flashed down his back, despite the warm air. "Harley's enemy found his push point, didn't he?" It really wasn't a question.

"Mmmm-hmm." Grandpa paused. "Sounds like your friend is in trouble, Parker. He's going to need you—even if he doesn't realize that yet."

"I don't want to mess this up. So . . . what do I do, Grandpa?"

The *Boy's Bomb* drifted another twenty feet before he answered. "Do you believe God has a plan for you? For Harley?"

Where was he going with this? "Well, yeah. I guess."

"So . . . do you think the almighty God of the universe is big enough or strong enough to carry you through—even if you mess up?"

"Well, when you put it like *that* . . ."

"There is no other way to put it, Parker. If we make some little mistake—or big one—that doesn't mess up His plans. The Word says His plans can't be *thwarted*—which is a great word, by the way."

But *still*. Parker had already messed things up good, hadn't he?

"You got yourself in a bad spot in the Glades—with that psycho

Kingman and that monster gator. There was only one reason you didn't die. Was it because Wilson was with you? Or maybe because you had that gator stick of yours?"

Parker's mind did a quick flashback. He'd been in the *Boy's Bomb* like he was at this moment . . . but the boat was going down. Kingman had his shotgun on them. And Goliath was waiting below in the water . . . ready to make an easy meal out of them. "Only God could have saved us."

"And what about just a couple months ago? You and Harley weighted down and plummeting to the bottom of the quarry with empty air tanks? Why didn't you two die?"

God had rescued them. No doubt about it. "It wasn't our day to die."

"Because?"

"God had a plan."

"And that plan couldn't be thwarted," Grandpa said. "And it still can't. Think of your life as a story, Parker. What happened in the Glades, and the quarry—and what's happening now. They're just bad chapters in a really good book."

The boat was drifting dangerously close to the rocks. Parker fired up the Merc and trolled deeper into the Outer Basin of Rockport Harbor. The thought of God having his whole life planned should have made him feel great. But there was a part of him that pushed back on that a bit. "If God has this whole story of our life planned out . . . what about our own dreams, Grandpa?"

"I'm glad you have dreams, Parker. God gives you dreams too. God has a way of weaving many of our dreams into His plans. Some fit with His plans. Some don't. Sometimes He gives us our dreams, and sometimes . . ."

Parker waited. Nothing. He glanced at the screen for a moment to see if he'd lost the connection. Grandpa was still there. Harley's dreams had all been wrapped up in Kemosabe, hadn't they? And now it was gone. "Sometimes he gives us our dreams, and sometimes *what*?" He thought of Harley and the lost bike. "He crushes them?"

"You know what?" Grandpa paused like he was thinking. "I'm going to let you think about it for a bit. How about we talk about it when I get there for that visit?"

Honestly? Parker didn't want to wait. He wanted the answer key now. "Sounds like you want me to work for that answer a bit more."

Grandpa laughed. "I think you'll take it more to heart if you do. But let me say this in the meantime: After all you've been through, you should remember that only God can truly keep us safe. You stay close to Him, Parker. Remember what He's done for you. And remember He has a plan that can't be what . . . what's that word?"

"Thwarted."

"That's it. Knowing God's got this will build your trust in Him. And that trust will give you the courage to do the right thing . . . whatever it is."

That still didn't help him know what to do to help Harley—besides listening. Parker looked out through the channel running between the Headlands and the breakwater. The waves were squaring their shoulders. Puffing out their chest. Rolling in with more swagger.

"This is important," Grandpa said. "I'm going to get off the phone to give you time to chew on it. I've got a spooky feeling I can't seem to shake."

Parker kept his mouth shut for a good ten count. But Grandpa didn't say a word. *That was it?* "Grandpa, you're not going to leave me hanging here, are you? What is it you feel?"

Another long pause.

"That I need to be praying for my grandson. Right about now."

Okay, this was getting just a little bit *too* creepy.

"Parker? You work on building that trust and courage, you hear me? Because I have the sense that whatever job God has for you next"—the volume of Grandpa's voice had dropped so low that Parker pressed his phone harder against his ear—"ain't for no weakling."

CHAPTER 57

HARLEY'S PHONE CONTINUED TO RING while he stared at the screen. There was no name, and the phone number wasn't one he recognized. Maybe the police wanted to know his shirt size so they could outfit him for juvey. Nah, probably not. But he was curious. And the phone kept ringing. He hesitated, then connected and raised it to his ear.

"Harley—don't hang up."

"Scorza?" The rage inside flared immediately.

"Just listen, I need to talk to you," Scorza said. The words spilled out of his ex-friend. How he'd written *BARF BAG* on the side of the shed. How he'd accidently seen the goons who set the fire. How they had taken the motorcycle away by lobster boat.

Harley stood there, stunned. "Of course . . . I couldn't figure out how they got it past me. That's brilliant."

"These guys are super smart, Harley. Like in a different league."

"So why are you telling me this? Why aren't you talking to the police?"

"That's what I'm trying to tell you. I found Kemosabe."

Harley's heart suddenly dropped its muffler. He could feel it thumping. "Where?"

"Just shut up and listen. I don't have much time." Scorza quickly explained how he'd witnessed the heist and wanted to be the hero by finding Kemosabe. How he believed that could patch up their friendship. "And I found it—and was going to bring you there today." He explained his change of heart after what Harley did to the Wrangler last night, how he'd wanted to destroy Kemosabe instead. But before he got back to the bike, he'd been spotted. Got clocked good by the guy who started the shed on fire. Broke away. He was hiding in Gloucester right now. Near the water.

But they knew where he lived. If he called the police, the goons would know he'd told—and there'd be payback. But if Harley "discovered" the bike himself . . . nobody would guess Scorza had told his mortal enemy . . . the guy who'd just trashed his Wrangler.

Harley wanted to defend himself on the Wrangler thing—but wasn't going to interrupt. Not until he found out where the motorcycle was.

"Don't you see?" Scorza sounded desperate. "If you find Kemosabe and they don't think I snitched, there's no reason for them to go after me."

It actually made sense. And it fit. Scorza wasn't doing this for Harley—he was all about protecting himself. "Why are they doing this to me?"

"I overheard something before I broke away," Scorza said. "Taking the bike wasn't about you. It was about your uncle."

"What?"

"He owes somebody money or something. That's why they took your bike—to get their money. You've got to 'find' your bike in a way that has nothing that could point to me. You have to promise me that."

Suddenly everything made sense. Scorza was telling the truth. And he was scared. "Just tell me where it is."

"Not over the phone. These guys are good. I'm not even using my own phone. This is a Walmart special. But if they're watching you—and they see you happen to discover the bike after talking on the phone? They could think it was me. I won't chance it."

Harley was so close. *So* close. But right now, his ex-friend was the key, and his connection with Scorza was shaky. If he got spooked, he'd go back into hiding and Harley would never get the bike. "How am I going to discover the bike if I don't know where to look?"

"We'll meet, but where nobody could possibly see us—someplace I'd never normally go. But we've got to do it now—before these goons decide to move Kemosabe, and it's gone for good."

Absolutely right. "Where? When?"

"I've got cash on me."

He always did. But what did that have to do with—

"I'm hiding out in a lobster boat. And I'm going to pay the guy to take me to the Dry Salvages. I'll be there in an hour. You be there."

"Hold on . . . how am I supposed to get there? My uncle has a boat in Gloucester, but I couldn't get there and out to the Salvages that quick." And Uncle Ray wouldn't take him anyway. Not after he'd refused to help his uncle buy his boat.

"You can't tell anybody about this conversation. Definitely not your uncle. Take Gatorade's boat."

He could, couldn't he? He knew where Parks kept a key stashed under the storage seat. Weird, he'd been blamed for stealing a car that he hadn't touched. Now he was going to steal a boat. Sure, why not? He was going to become the thief everybody already thought he was.

"You anchor between the Little Salvages and Dry Salvages. I'll be in the cabin of a lobster boat. If it looks like you're not alone, I won't even put my head up. I'll tell him to keep going. Got it?"

"Got it."

"You tell nobody. I'm going out on a limb for you, Harley."

No, he was protecting himself. But Harley didn't care. He had one last shot at finding Kemosabe before the motorcycle disappeared forever. "I'll close the store early—like, right now. I'll get the boat one way or another."

"And you never, ever tell anybody where you got this information. Agreed?"

"Agreed. And, Scorza . . . I owe you. Big."

"You got that right. Help me pull this off so the goons stop looking for me—and we'll call it even."

Harley flipped the OPEN sign on the front door to GONE DIVING. "I'm on my way. Don't stand me up—or you'll regret it."

Scorza laughed. "I'll be there. You just focus on what you've got to do—or you'll get us both killed."

CHAPTER 58

RAY TOOK THE PHONE FROM SCORZA. "You done good, kid."

The eager-to-please quarterback grinned. With one eye nearly swollen shut, the smile was hilarious. Pitifully lopsided.

"Now, you and me and Mr. Kelsey are going to get in his pickup. We're going to the marina and we're going to get in my boat." He liked the sound of that. *My* boat. And it was all his—or would be soon. "You're not going to cry out. You're not going to signal anybody. You're not going to do a single thing to attract any attention. You got that?"

The stupid kid nodded. "I'm part of the team, right?"

And if he believed that, he'd definitely had one too many concussions. "As long as you run the plays right."

Ray pulled out his phone. Dialed Vinny. Gave him the change of plans. "Kelsey and I—and the new kid on the team—are going to take care of Harley. You need to make the motorcycle disappear.

For good. And right now." With the money he'd get from the trust fund, anything he'd get for the bike would be chump change. And they definitely couldn't risk the theft being traced back to Ray. "Take that bike for a long ride off a short pier, Vinny. Nobody can ever find it." He gave Vinny the storage unit number and told him where he'd hidden the key.

"It'll be done before you get back," Vinny said. "I got just the place—and won't nobody find it for a hundred years."

Ray ended the call and pocketed his phone. So far so good. "Now, Mr. Scorza. I'm going to trust you—and we're going to cut those nylon ties." He nodded to Kelsey, who pulled out a knife.

"We'll dump your bike in the bed of my truck. The motorcycle will be gone before we get back. There will be no reason for you to ever come back to this lockup—got that?"

The football jock nodded. "When we get back, I'll grab my bike and ride straight home."

Ray gave him a nod. "And when this is all over, you're not going to say a word about this to anybody. Can you do that?"

"Count on it."

Kelsey cut the last nylon tie and the kid rubbed the deep indentations on his ankles and wrists.

Ray picked up the football and tossed it to him. "You've got the ball, quarterback. What play are you going to call?"

"Whatever the coach tells me to," he said. "I follow the instructions, and we all get what we want, right?" Again, that melonhead smile.

"Right." And the really hysterical thing about the kid wasn't the silly grin. It was the fact that he truly believed the coach would let him walk off the field when the game was over.

CHAPTER 59

ANGELICA WATCHED WHILE HER DAD finished getting ready for work. Parker had turned her down. He'd actually wanted to be alone rather than take her out in the *Boy's Bomb*. That was a first, wasn't it? When they'd lived in Chokoloskee he was always trying to get her to go for a ride with him—or with him and Wilson. Did he really not want her company while he was sorting out his thoughts? More likely he didn't want her to know what he was really thinking.

"Sorry about taking this shift tonight, sweetie." Dad buttoned the shirt on his National Park Service uniform. "Wish I could have whipped up some dinner for us before I left. Please tell me you'll do something more than another PB and J for yourself."

He knew her well, but probably not as well as he thought. "What can I say? I'm a PB and Jelly kind of girl forever."

Dad laughed. "PB, huh? I'm betting that's just a phase."

"Don't put money on that." She smiled. "You'll lose."

"You're crazy, you know that?" He folded her in his arms and hugged her tight.

His strength felt marvelous. A "don't-let-me-go" sort of good. "I *am* crazy, Dad. Maybe even head-over-heels crazy." And she was okay with that. "I just hope he . . ."

He looked in the mirror—but right at her. "Just hope he what?"

She'd definitely said too much already. "Not going there, Dad. Not this time. But can I ask you something?"

"Shoot."

"What *is* it with boys? I mean, why can't they just play it safe sometimes? Listen to reason?"

He sat on the counter, took her hands in his, and looked her in the eyes. "A dad couldn't be prouder of his girl, you know that? And I love how you want to be the protector. Ever since Mom left . . ."

Maybe he didn't want to go where he was headed either.

"It's a strength of yours," Dad said. "But every strength can be a weakness, too. You can't control everything."

"He's still trying to help Harley—"

"Parker?"

She nodded. And then she caught him up on pretty much everything she hadn't already told him, probably repeating some of it too. But he acted like he was in no rush—even though she knew he had to get on the road. The traffic going into Boston would be getting thick as fog.

"Harley is his friend," Dad said. "And Harley's in trouble. When a friend is in trouble, a guy like Parker is going to be there. That's one of his strengths too."

"But it's going to get him in trouble, Dad. Harley is *gone*.

Stealing Scorza's car is proof. He's off the trail—in the swamp somewhere—and I think Parker still thinks he can save him."

"And you'd rather see him do what, exactly?"

Something about his tone soothed her. Calmed her. "I just want him to stay safe."

He thought about that a couple seconds. "We all want that. I guarantee you Parker wants that more than anybody. But it sounds like you want him to *play* everything safe. Staying safe and playing it safe are two different things. Sometimes playing it safe isn't the best way to stay safe at all. Parker isn't going to do something without talking to his parents, right?"

True. He was good about that kind of stuff.

Dad opened a drawer and scooped up his key ring, loose change—and something silver that looked all too familiar.

She stopped his hand before he could stuff everything in his pocket. "Where did you get that?" She grabbed the pocketknife. *Cut Through the Clutter* screened in orange ink along the handle. She flipped it over. *PORT KNOX Storage—Gloucester.*

"It was a little gift when I rented the unit for all our stuff from the move. Once we get a place, I'll—"

"Wait, this could be important," Angelica said. She told him about Scorza finding the exact same knife where Kemosabe disappeared. "Or it may be nothing."

"Hang on to it," he said. "Maybe we should call Officer Greenwood. Let him decide if it's important or not." He kissed the top of her head. "Gotta run now. Call my mobile and we can keep talking on my way in."

She shook her head. "I'm good, Dad." He'd already given her plenty to think about. "I'm going to Ella's anyway." She held up the knife. "And I'm going to call this in."

Which is exactly what she did the instant he pulled out of the driveway.

"Port Knox Storage," Greenwood said. "I know exactly where the place is."

"You think this is important?" She hoped it was. But the more she thought about it the less important it seemed. Even Scorza didn't seem to think it meant anything—or he wouldn't have tossed the knife into the harbor.

"I'll put this at the top of the list, and we'll find out," Greenwood said. "Since the storage place is in Gloucester, I'll make a phone call to the Gloucester PD and see if they can do a little snooping around. How's that?"

Angelica couldn't ask for more. "Perfect."

"OK, I'll give a call right now. Anything else?"

Yeah, could you stop Parker from doing something stupid? "Yeah," she said. "But I think it's way out of your jurisdiction."

Officer Greenwood laughed. "Well, call me if something changes."

She desperately hoped she wouldn't have to call him. There'd already been way too many changes—and she wasn't sure she could bear any more.

CHAPTER 60

IT HAD BEEN NEARLY AN HOUR since Parker had talked to his grandpa, and he'd honestly tried to keep his eyes on the truth of God's having a plan. At first, it was tough to stay focused. But as he thought about God and the ways He'd been there before, Parker felt his confidence in God rise. And his own worries about not knowing what to do shrunk just a bit.

"God . . . I want your plan. What do I do?" Parker wasn't sure what he'd expected to happen. But he didn't hear a voice or see some mysterious hand writing a message on the hull of a sailboat or something. But there were two words that kept popping up in his mind. *Stay close.*

Okay . . . stay close to God—or to Harley?

Probably both. And if he was going to have a shot at Harley, he'd need to get to the dive shop before he closed—and not let him out of his sight.

Parker phoned his mom on the drive back to his boat slip. Told her what he'd been thinking—and how more than ever he believed he needed to stay close to Harley. "Can we have him over for dinner?"

Mom actually sounded really happy about that. She'd worked in Boston today—and his parents had driven into the city together. "Dad and I should be home by six thirty. He'll be as happy to have Harley for dinner as I am. Is spaghetti okay? With chocolate milk?"

Like she had to ask. "See you soon, Mom."

He pulled into his slip next to Steadman's Whaler and secured the dock lines. Cut the motor. Wiped the spray off the seats and helm and gunwales. His mind drifted to Harley. He'd be off work in less than an hour—and Parker would be waiting for him. He couldn't shed the sense that there was something he wasn't seeing—and maybe Harley wasn't either.

"Show me the way, God." He didn't always close his eyes when he prayed. But this time he did. He didn't want to see anything or anyone else. Nothing that might distract him. Nothing that made it hard to focus like he needed to. "Show me the way."

He opened his eyes to the sound of someone pounding down the aluminum ramp from the top of the T-wharf to the floating docks in the South Basin. *Harley?*

The guy who seemed to be pushing Parker away all day— was actually running toward him? Even then, Parker wasn't sure if Harley was glad to see him or not. Had he closed the shop early? His face looked absolutely haunted. And Parker thought of Grandpa's words again. This was Harley's moment. He'd hit the push point. He was on the edge—and whatever Parker did right now would either send him over that precipice—or give him a lifeline. *God . . . help me help him.*

"Parks." Harley sounded like he'd sprinted all the way from the dive shop. "I need your boat." He looked dead serious.

"For what?"

His eyes flicked toward the Outer Harbor for just a fraction of a second. "I can't tell you."

CHAPTER 61

Friday, August 12, 5:20 p.m.

HOW WAS HARLEY SUPPOSED TO CONVINCE Parker to let him take his boat? "Trust me." *That was the best he could do?* Ella and Jelly already thought he was a car thief. Would Parker really be any different?

"The swells are getting bigger. Even I wouldn't go out of the harbor in the *Bomb* right now. Where do you need to go?"

But he *had* to leave the harbor. "I can't tell you that either."

"How'd you even know I'd be here?"

Okay, Parker was going to figure this out. Harley had to be completely honest—or he'd break trust for sure. "I didn't."

Parker's eyes narrowed a bit. "So . . . you were going to just take the boat if I wasn't here?"

"Borrow it for a little while. I'll pay back the gas I use." Even then Harley knew Parker wasn't going to do it. Parker pulled the key from the ignition. Balled it up in his fist.

"I got a phone call, okay?" Harley scanned the shore. Was somebody watching? Making sure he wasn't telling a soul? "Somebody saw Kemosabe. *Saw* it being taken. Found out where it's hidden. They'll only tell me if I meet them. Please—just give me the keys and walk away. There are some very bad people involved in this. Someone might even be watching me now. Don't say a word to anyone about what I just told you. Promise."

Parker's eyes got pretty wide even though Harley had barely told him a thing. "Do you hear yourself, Harley? This sounds like a trap. You can't go meet anyone. Not alone, especially with the size of the waves outside the harbor. The whole idea sounds insane. Let's go to the harbormasters' office. Eric or Maggie will—"

"No—nobody can know." Harley could pull Parks out of the boat. Grab his keys. Toss Parker in the water and take off. Or he could tell him just enough so this wouldn't turn into a fight. Could he trust him with his secret? He knew he could. "It was Scorza. He won't do anything to me. He doesn't have what it takes—and even he knows that."

Parker seemed to be weighing his words. Harley had never had a friend like him. Not ever. A guy who would do just about anything to help someone in trouble. Harley was banking on that quality rising to the top right now.

"Where?"

"Dry Salvages."

"Are you crazy?" Parker shook his head. "Too dangerous in this boat. Too far off shore. The swells are too big."

"I'm running out of time. It's my last chance, Parks. If I don't do this, right now, I'll always—"

"You go out there by yourself in this boat and you may not make it back."

How could Harley make him understand? "If I don't find Kemosabe, I don't care what happens to me."

Parker stared at him like he couldn't believe it. "Well, you *should* care. Your friends sure care what happens to you. Your dad did."

He didn't *get* it. "Don't talk about my dad. I'm doing this *for* my dad, did you ever think of that? That was our project. If I lose Kemosabe . . . I'm nothing."

"Are you hearing yourself, Harley? Life isn't about what you own or don't own. That stuff doesn't define us—or it shouldn't."

"I got no time for this now," Harley said. "I need a boat."

Parker looked torn. Like he was cracking on the whole you-can't-go-out-in-this-weather thing. "You have to go into this with your eyes open. It's super risky."

Harley could see that Parks was considering saying yes. "Well, let me take Steadman's boat, then. I bet you know where the key is."

Parker looked at the bigger boat like he was tempted. "Nah, I know how my boat handles in rough water—and I've got plenty of gas."

Harley hopped into the *Boy's Bomb*. "Thanks, Parks. I owe you. Give me the key."

"Two conditions. No, make that three."

Harley undid the bow line and dropped it on the deck. "Name them."

"First, somebody needs to know. Going out there with growing swells? And there's a fog bank anchored a couple miles out just waiting to come in." He shook his head. "Nobody is going out of this harbor without telling someone. I have to call my parents."

"*You'll* know, Parks. Why get your parents involved? So if I'm not back by dark you can—"

Parker shook his head. "That's my second condition. I'm going with."

"No—you *can't* do that." Harley gave him the quick rundown. He had to be alone or Scorza would tell the lobster boat to keep going.

"Call him," Parker said. "Tell him the seas are too dangerous— and that I have to drive or you might not even make it to the rendezvous."

Harley was wasting too much time arguing. The truth was, he could use the help. The idea of taking anything this small out of the protected harbor—unless the seas were flat—was not something he felt confident to do. He'd have water over the bow before he got halfway to the Salvages. And he really didn't want to have to push Parker into the water to get the *Boy's Bomb*. He pulled out the phone. "If this blows the deal, I'm going to . . ."

Parker smiled. "You'll *what*."

"Go back to Plan A." Harley smiled back and grabbed his phone. Scrolled back to the last call he'd received. "You'll be going for a swim."

CHAPTER 62

BRYCE SCORZA'S WALMART PHONE RANG from Mr. Lotitto's pocket. He met Mr. Lotitto's steely eyes. "Nobody has this number—honest. Just let it go."

Ray Lotitto stared at the number on the screen. "It's Harley—which means there's a problem." He cocked his head slightly. "You'll take it. And you'll be on speaker. Play this smart, Mr. Scorza. Like the big game rides on how you handle this."

Bryce had followed every instruction so far. He'd helped the guy named Vinny load Kemosabe into an old panel van before leaving Port Knox. Bryce slid inside the Silverado without a fight. He could have run the moment they parked at the marina—and neither of them would have caught him. But they knew where he lived. And they'd get him eventually. So he'd walked between them all the way to the boat like they truly were all on the same team. And he wasn't going to mess things up now. No, the way to play this was to show

Lotitto and Kelsey that they could trust him completely. That he was no threat to them. The phone call was one more opportunity to prove it. That was how he'd come out of this in one piece.

He connected. "Harley?"

"I have a problem." Harley explained Gatorade insisting to go with—and about the growing waves. Those two were going to mess everything up. But Mr. Lotitto didn't look a bit rattled. His eyes narrowed, like he was processing how this variable might change things. He smiled and pulled the cap off a Sharpie. He scrounged around for something to write on. He pulled up Bryce's sleeve and settled for his forearm.

Bryce read the message and looked at Lotitto to see if he was serious. The man nodded.

"Okay," Bryce said. "Gatorade comes with. But neither of you tells another soul about why you're leaving the harbor—or I won't tell you a thing about where Kemosabe is. You're only getting one shot at this."

Mr. Lotitto was writing furiously again while Harley swore neither of them would say a word.

"You're being watched," Bryce said. "You know that, right? One of the guys from the team is doing me a favor."

There was a hesitation. "I don't see anyone."

"Good thing. Because if you did, we're done right now. He doesn't know what's going on, and he's not asking questions." Bryce read the next line on his own arm. He nodded like he understood enough of what they expected of him. "The instant I get off the phone I'm calling him. And he's going to need to see you leave your phones on the dock. If you don't, don't bother going to the Salvages. I won't be there."

Harley didn't answer for a few seconds. "What if we have boat problems? I mean, no phones . . . that's not even safe."

"There's nothing safe about any of this, Harley. The waves and the weather are the least of your worries. Believe me, if you mess this up, you'll never see Kemosabe again. These guys could move it anytime—and it'll be gone forever. Think about that."

Ray Lotitto smiled. Winked at him. Like he was part of the team.

"You hold your phones up so the guy with binoculars has a clear view of them—and let him see you leave them on the dock. Got it?"

Bryce was absolutely sure Harley got it all right. He was taking the bait. He'd be out in the open ocean, miles from shore. Like a couple of birds, Harley and Gatorade would be flying out to sea, not realizing it was a trap. Bryce wrestled inside, just a little. It was obvious Mr. Lotitto and Kelsey had no intention of letting Harley or Gatorade back to shore—unless they were floating facedown. Did he want to be part of this?

But he already *was* part of it. Nothing could change that now. Right now, he had to adapt. Scramble a bit to keep from getting sacked. Because unless he wanted to sleep with the fishes himself, he had to do exactly what he was told.

"You'd better get going, Harley," Bryce said. "The clock is ticking. If we drive by and you aren't anchored there, we're not circling around until you do."

Honestly, it felt really good to be calling the plays again. He was telling Harley what to do, and the running back was jumping. Harley should have never crossed him. If he hadn't, Bryce wouldn't have been in the lobster traps and seen the motorcycle heist. And Bryce wouldn't be in the bad field position he was in now. This was Harley's fault—and he was only getting what he'd probably deserved all along. No . . . not probably. Definitely.

Mr. Lotitto drew his finger across his own throat like it was a knife.

End this call, now. Bryce nodded. "I'm hanging up, Harley. Then I'm tossing this phone into the water. So there'll be no more calls. I'm on my way . . . so you'd better get moving."

"The minute I hang up we'll be flying to Dry Salvages," Harley said. "We'll leave our phones on the pier. And Scorza—I really appreciate this, even if you're only doing it to protect yourself."

It was a little late for Harley to start appreciating him.

"I owe you, Scorza," Harley said. "I'll remember this—what you're doing—for the rest of my life."

Which would be a lot shorter than Harley expected, if everything Bryce's gut told him was true. That was an absolutely intense thought. Bryce couldn't possibly get his head wrapped around it. But he didn't have to now. He'd save those thoughts for later. And the truth? Lotitto was already dead to him months ago. Right now, Bryce had something way more important to focus on. His *own* survival.

He disconnected—and looked up at the coach.

Mr. Lotitto nodded his approval, pointed at the phone—and then at the water.

Harley pitched the phone over the side. The thing dropped like a stone.

There was one interesting side benefit to this whole morbid thing. Bryce would be rid of the one friend who'd turned on him. And as a bonus, he'd see the ultimate payback to Gatorade, the guy who had turned Harley against him. All that with one little phone call.

Two birds.

One big stone.

CHAPTER 63

"DO YOU THINK SCORZA WAS TELLING US the truth—about somebody from the football team watching us?" Parker scanned the shoreline. "I mean, who would he get to do that—especially if he's really running from the muscle that did this? I think he's bluffing."

"We're not taking a chance." Harley grabbed the dry bag from under the seat. He held it high so anyone watching would see. He made a deliberate show of dropping his phone inside. "Now yours, Parks."

"I have to tell my parents—you know I do." He'd worked too hard to build trust. He wasn't going to toss it all to the wind because of Scorza's paranoia.

"What if someone is watching? I can't let you blow this."

Parker dropped to his knees. Got low like he was checking a connection on the gas tank. "Nobody will see me make the call from down here. I'm doing this." He tapped his mom's contact.

She'd be on her way home with Dad now—and she was more likely to have the phone on and nearby. By the look on Harley's face, Parker would have to make this quick.

Her phone went to voicemail immediately. *What was he supposed to do now?* At the tone, he gave a fifteen-second explanation of the sudden change of plans. He'd be late for dinner. Had to help Harley. This was his one shot at finding Kemosabe. He mentioned that there was a loan shark—and how Harley wasn't the target after all. They were leaving the harbor—and leaving their phones behind.

"I'm so sorry, Mom and Dad! We'll leave a note in a dry bag on the dock with exactly where we're going." Parker glanced up at Harley—who gave a quick nod.

"If we're not back by the time you get here—you'll know where to find us. I'll be careful, but we have to go—now." Parker disconnected and tried to get a visual on just how big the waves were getting. It was impossible to tell from here.

"Scorza is already on his way," Harley said. "We should have left five minutes ago."

Parker hunkered over the phone and whipped off a text to Jelly. Harley was so busy scribbling out a note to put in the sea bag with the phones that he didn't seem to notice.

Parker tossed the phone to Harley.

Harley held it high enough for anybody watching them to see it, dropped it in the sea bag, and placed the whole thing on the dock. Parker undid the stern line and fired up the Merc. Harley pushed them away from the dock.

Harley kept a watch shoreward as they raced past the yacht club. The farther they got from the dock, the more he seemed to loosen up.

"You think Scorza is telling the truth—that this is about your uncle, not you?"

"Makes sense, doesn't it?"

It definitely did. A whole lot more than all this having to do with Scorza out to nail Harley.

"He sounded scared, Parks. Here's my theory. This is about the loan shark. My uncle owes him money—and the shark took the bike hostage."

"To make sure he pays?"

Harley nodded. "Something like that. And if he's late—and he will be—my bike is gone. So we find out where it is—and get it before it's gone for good."

Parker slid the throttle all the way forward. He cut a straight line for the channel past the sailboats moored in the Outer Harbor.

"There was a third thing I needed to take you out there," Parker said. "Remember?"

Harley smiled slightly. "I thought you forgot."

Not hardly. "You're going to tell me what happened last night. Your side of the story. And I mean everything."

"I can do that. Get ready for a ride."

He could say the same thing to Harley. Even in the short time since he'd been on the phone with his grandpa, the seas had picked up. And he was not liking the looks of it. *God, help us.*

CHAPTER 64

"I CAN'T BELIEVE PARKER IS FALLING FOR THIS," Angelica said. Okay, it came out a whole lot more like a rant. "We *saw* Harley steal the Wrangler last night. Saw him running from it after he wrapped it around the tree. Harley is guilty as sin, and Parker refuses to see what he doesn't want to see."

Grams put a pitcher of sweet tea on the kitchen table and set glasses in front of the girls.

Ella started pouring the tea. "I think if Harley claimed he'd never left Rockport Wednesday night, Parker would believe him."

"Well, then you send young Parker to me," Grams said. "And I'll set him straight. I didn't just see Harley in Gloucester. I talked to him. He even teased me a bit after I'd been trying to open the wrong car. I just wish he'd taken my offer to give him a ride home.

He was determined to see someone, and it didn't take a crystal ball to know who he was talking about."

Grams looked troubled. Like she held herself responsible for not stopping him.

"I warned him not to do what he was planning to do. And then there were the sirens. One from this side of town. Another from the other side. I told Harley the sirens were a sign. An omen. This wasn't going to end well. He was polite and all, but firm. So he mounted his bike and went on his way."

Ella looked at Angelica, her eyes wide like she'd just realized something. "Hold on a sec. Grams—you said you heard the sirens—*while* Harley was there?"

Grams nodded. "He'd been helping me. I told you that."

"But you didn't mention the sirens before. We heard the sirens not even a minute *after* the Wrangler was stolen."

Angelica stood. "Any idea what time it was? Your receipt from Walgreens—do you have it?"

Grams pointed to the kitchen counter. Ella was there before Angelica, leafing through a handful of receipts. She found it—and held it up for Angelica to see. "Look at the time stamp."

Angelica read it but couldn't believe it. "How can this be? We *saw* him get in that Wrangler."

"But technically, we didn't see his face, right?" Ella shook her head. "We saw his hoodie. What if *everything* Harley was telling us was true? What if someone else was wearing that hoodie?"

"So then," Angelica continued Ella's train of thought, "Harley only saw the Wrangler *after* it crashed and checked to see if someone was hurt inside—just like we were going to do when we saw the Jeep."

"Somebody wanted it to look like Harley stole that car and crashed it," Grams said. "But why?"

He would get the blame, that was for sure. But it had to be more than that.

"Oh, no." Ella put her head in her hands. "What else has he been telling us the truth about—and we haven't believed him?"

Angelica pulled up Parker's text again.

```
Harley didn't lie. Can't explain it all now. Ray borrowed
from loan shark but can't pay. Shark sent some bad dudes to
steal Kemosabe as partial payment. Witness called Harley—knows
where bike is but scared of shark. Will only meet offshore
where nobody will see. Taking Harley in Bomb now.
```

"Something isn't adding up." Angelica tried to put her finger on it. "I'm not sure . . . I'm just not sure . . ."

"Think out loud," Ella said. "Talk it through."

Angelica nodded. "Okay, why would a loan shark steal the motorcycle? If he's anything like the ones in the movies, the guy borrowing the money pays up—on time—or else."

Ella and Grams nodded.

"How would the shark even know about the bike unless someone told him—and who would do that?" Angelica was on her feet now. Pacing. "And *why* would a loan shark go to all that trouble? *He* didn't have the money problems."

"Uncle Ray was the one who needed the cash," Ella said.

"Right," Angelica said. "Uncle Ray wanted Harley to sell the bike so he could pay off the loan shark for *Deep Trouble*. When Harley refused, his uncle's money problems didn't go away." How many times had Harley shared his uncle's code of living with them? "Ray's Rules *number whatever*: *If you see something you want, take it.*"

Ella sucked in her breath. "He hired someone to steal the motorcycle. And he used the feud with Scorza to keep everyone looking in the wrong direction."

Harley had been focused on Scorza, when his real enemy was right there the whole time. "If this person actually knows where Kemosabe is—that means Uncle Ray never got it sold. Which means he still has money problems—but bigger now. He owes a loan shark, who expects his money on time—or else."

Ella was on her feet now too. "So that explains why Uncle Ray went after Harley's trust fund. He said Harley was out of control and there were legal expenses, right? What if he helped fuel those along?"

Grams grabbed her hand as she passed. "What are you saying, Ella-girl?"

"The keys for the Wrangler were at the dive shop, right? Uncle Ray had just as much access to the keys as Harley. Ray could have had somebody else steal it. But he set it up to make Harley look guilty. His uncle even had him doing errands in Gloucester, right? So Harley's legal fees mount—and Uncle Ray figures as guardian he'll surely be allowed to take money out of the trust fund. And he'll get the money he needs for the loan shark somehow at the same time."

"But that doesn't happen," Angelica said. "Harley laughed about it, right? Said the lawyer told them the trust fund was unbreakable. Uncle Ray hit another dead end. First the motorcycle doesn't sell—then he can't get his hands on the trust. So he's stuck. Out of options."

Ella looked excited now. "Uncle Ray owes a lot of money to a really, really bad guy. *He's* the one in danger. Not Harley. And that means Parker isn't in danger either."

Angelica felt an overwhelming sense of relief. She hugged Ella. The two of them jumped together like all the cares of the world had just melted off their shoulders.

"His Uncle Ray is reaping what he sowed, if you ask me." Ella beamed.

"Ray's Rules"—Angelica lowered her voice to mimic the man— "I make my own luck."

Ella took a few steps with the Uncle Ray swagger. "I always land on my feet."

Angelica loved her impersonation. "Not this time, Uncle Ray."

Both girls burst into laughter.

"Girls," Grams said. "Something isn't right. What makes you think he's just going to roll over? If I know that man, right now he's working on a plan to get the money he needs. Every penny of it."

Their little celebration fizzled. Ella looked serious. "You think he'll sell the dive shop?"

"A decent man would," Grams said. "*If you see something you want . . . take it.* Does that sound like the thinking of an upright man? And if he was the one who was behind the shed fire . . . he knew Harley was sleeping inside. Ray Lotitto was willing to risk his nephew's life to get what he wanted. That man has got a heart of stone."

She was right. "We have to think more like him," Angelica said. "He'd keep looking for a way to get the money, right up until the end. That's why he kept going back to the lawyer . . . looking for a loophole in that trust fund."

The three of them were quiet for what seemed like a minute. Maybe more.

Suddenly Ella gasped. "No. No. No." She grabbed the cross with both hands. "I just had a horrible thought. Tell me I'm way off base—please."

Angelica stared at her. "Tell us."

"Harley has no other family—other than his uncle—right?" Her eyes were panicky. "What if something happens to Harley? Who would get all the money from the trust fund?"

Angelica's stomach tightened. *Dear God. Dear God. Dear God.* "That's it. He found the loophole. If something happens to Harley, all Ray's money problems go away. He's going to look for a way to—"

"Meeting up with the witness!" Ella wailed. "It's a trap! Harley isn't out of danger—he's headed directly into its jaws!"

And Parker was taking him there. Angelica shot a text off to Parker and Harley, her hands absolutely shaking.

`Call me!! Total 911 emergency!!`

Ella cried out like she was in pain. "But would his uncle do something that . . . monstrous? Harley is all the family he's got."

"Ray Lotitto hates that boy," Grams said. "I see it in his eyes. Hate is a monster; it surely is."

Angelica stared at her screen, willing it to light up with a response from one of the boys. "Why aren't they answering?"

She fired off another text.

`Ella and I need help—please!!`

If Parker thought Angelica needed help, nothing would stop him from answering. Unless, of course, he couldn't.

CHAPTER 65

Friday, August 12, 6:25 p.m.

OKAY, SO THE SWELLS WERE BIGGER than Harley would have guessed. And the drive slower. He scooted to the front seat—as if that would really help him spot Dry Salvages. What if they missed the rendezvous? "Are we getting close?"

Parker strained to see through the fog. Checked his compass on the helm. "Think so."

The *Bomb* took a gulp over the bow.

"Move to the back!" Parks motioned to him. "Gotta keep our nose up."

Even after he scrambled to the back, they still got slapped with spray. The swells got longer. Deeper. A glance at Parker proved he was probably as scared as Harley was. "Can the *Bomb* handle this?"

Parks flashed him a weak smile. "He's never let me down yet. This is nothing."

For it being no big deal, Parker definitely was on high alert.

One knee on the seat, he hunkered over the helm. Taking the spray in the face rather than taking his eyes off the water. It wasn't a one-handed steering cruise. He goosed the throttle and muscled the wheel to keep water from breaking over the bow again. Swinging left, then right, Parks took each wave where it seemed weakest. Like Harley running the ball through the defensive line.

Harley would have felt a lot better riding in something bigger. "Are you wishing we'd taken Steadman's boat?"

"I'm wishing we were at Rockport House of Pizza."

He wasn't the only one. Even the wind seemed determined to push them toward shore. To make Harley second-guess his decision. Its hollow voice steadily rumbled in his ears, as if warning them to turn back. Three or four inches of seawater had gathered in the back of the boat. It sloshed around the stern like it was frantically searching for a way to get back into the ocean.

"We going to make it?" Harley was only half-joking.

"Just keep your eyes peeled. I'm not liking the fog."

Harley looked back—and wished he hadn't. There was no sign of shore behind them. Parker kept checking the compass and making adjustments to the wheel.

And as they drove, Harley told him everything. What really happened Wednesday night with the Wrangler. The fights with Uncle Ray. And most of all his hopes that they'd get Kemosabe back. Parks listened. Nodded. And from all Harley could tell? He totally believed him. Harley may not have realized until that moment just how much he needed his friend.

"I felt like I was in quicksand," Harley said. "I couldn't sit back and do nothing. But the more I tried to make things happen . . . the more I struggled . . . the deeper I sank."

Parker glanced at him—then got his eyes back on the waves

rolling for the bow. "Well, you're not alone anymore. And Ella and Jelly will be on board once they hear the whole story."

Harley had been an idiot to pull away from Parker like he had. "I had some dreams, you know? And then somebody stole them."

"Dreams." Parker seemed to lock on to that word. "Look . . . dreams are good, but they're not everything. You have to hold on to them loosely, you know. If your dreams aren't working out, you can't just throw away everything—"

"You're saying you don't have dreams?"

Parker worked the wheel hard but took more spray over the bow anyway. "No, I have dreams. It's just that sometimes God gives us what we were hoping for, and other times we have to stop trying to make our dreams happen, you know?"

No, Harley didn't know. The only thing he was sure of was that you had to fight and hold on to what was yours—or else somebody would take it away. "My dad found that bike. We built it. He wanted me to have it for a reason."

"Yeah," Parker said. "Because he loved you. And he wanted to spend time with you. The fact that it would be something you could use for years was a total bonus."

"Exactly. He wanted a better future for me."

Parker hesitated. "I totally get that you didn't sell it for your uncle. I wouldn't have done that either. But after the bike was gone, your dad wouldn't want you to throw away your future to get it back." Parker checked the compass. "What if the police weren't at Scorza's when you got there? What if you'd gotten your hands on him like you wanted to? Ever since Kemosabe was taken, it's like you've had a death wish or something. I can't believe your dad would've wanted any of that for you."

Parker was right. Deep down, Harley knew it. But all that with Scorza was over now. And he was so close to finding Kemosabe.

"All I'm saying is that our dreams can't become more important than the one who gave us the dream—whether that's a parent, or ourselves, or even God."

Harley's dad definitely wouldn't have wanted him to go after Scorza like he had. Was Harley putting Kemosabe ahead of the one who gave it to him in the first place?

"Sometimes God gives us our dreams," Parker said. "And sometimes . . ."

"Sometimes He doesn't, right?"

"Maybe that's it," Parker said. "My grandpa was talking to me about it . . . but he didn't finish. Wanted me to think about it."

"I don't know a thing about God giving us our dreams," Harley said. "Seems better at snatching them away."

"There's got to be more to it than that." Parker turned the bow sharp to avoid the biggest wave Harley had seen since they'd left the harbor.

"I'm glad you're driving." What would have happened if Harley had taken the *Bomb* out by himself? He'd be swimming by now. And with the water at what, sixty-five degrees? It wouldn't take long for hypothermia to set in. "You couldn't pay me enough to drive out of the harbor with seas like this."

"Me neither." Parker flashed him a smile.

Harley was pretty sure that was the honest truth. But Parker would do it for a friend for free. He would never push Parker away again. Not ever.

"C'mon, baby!" Parker encouraged the *Bomb* on. "You can do it."

Harley had never really understood the fascination with a boat. Uncle Ray would testify to that. But watching Parker, he got it.

Parks wasn't just driving the boat; he'd become part of it. The very same way Harley was part of Kemosabe when he fired it up. So maybe what Kemosabe was to Harley, the *Boy's Bomb* was to Parker.

God—Parker's God—if You're up there . . . bring Kemosabe back to me. He didn't say it aloud, but if God was God, He could hear Harley's thoughts, right?

"Pull the transom plug," Parker said. "We've got enough speed—let's see if we can lose some of this water."

The *Bomb* wasn't big enough for a bilge pump. So they had to either bail or try the little plug trick. Harley gave it a twist, bracing himself so he didn't roll out the back of the boat. Sure enough, the water started draining.

"If we drop our speed, get the plug in fast."

Harley closed his fist around the plug—and an incredible thought swept through his head. Parker was risking the thing in life *he* treasured most—so his friend could get back what he treasured most. He'd never had a friend like that. And he might not for long if Uncle Ray carried out his threat to have Harley put back in the system.

Parker let out a whoop. "Little Salvages to port—and Dry Salvages dead ahead."

Little Salvages barely peeked above the surface between swells. The tide was nearly to the highest point, and within minutes all traces of the rocks of the seal refuge would duck below the surface. But like a mine, the thing would be skulking just below the surface, ready to rip the bottom off a boat that wasn't watching their depth charts.

"Scorza told you to anchor, right?"

Harley nodded. He screwed in the transom plug, staggered to

the front of the boat, and pulled the anchor from the cubby under the bow. Five minutes later their anchor was set and holding firm.

Parker stood and shook off the jitters. "Well, that was fun."

"So is football. And I feel about as beat-up as I do after a game."

They both laughed the way people do after they've had a close call—and lived to talk about it.

The Dry Salvages . . . dark rocks looming above the swells. How seals got up there, Harley had no idea. He was pretty sure a human would find it impossible.

Harley scanned as far as the fog would allow.

"Think he'll show?" Parker stood beside him, totally soaked.

With the fog and waves . . . Harley wasn't so sure anymore. "He's got to. I'd hate to think we did this for nothing."

Parker glanced his way. "It's never for nothing. This is about doing everything we can to get Kemosabe back."

Kemosabe. *Trusted friend.* Harley slung his arm around Parker's shoulders. He'd already got him back—even if they never found the motorcycle.

CHAPTER 66

ELLA STOOD ON THE T-WHARF looking over the empty spot in Steadman's slip below. No *Boy's Bomb*. No boys. Somehow she'd hoped—against all logic—that they wouldn't have left. Or that maybe once they'd seen the waves outside the breakwater, they would've turned back. "Going out in these conditions . . . what were they thinking?"

"You're assuming they *were* thinking." Jelly checked her phone again. "Nothing. Boys can be so incredibly stupid—you know that?"

She definitely knew it. An ominous picture was forming on the canvas in her mind. All grays and blacks. Ella couldn't make out what was coming to life in the painting, but the brush strokes were quick. Deliberate.

Grams had driven them by the dive shop. Only the neon lights around the showroom were on. The front door was locked. For a moment, Ella had pictured the cardboard sign Harley had shown them only a week ago.

IT STARTS TODAY.

Yeah, it had started, all right. And now there was no stopping it. She checked the time. "The Buckmans should be here any minute." Jelly had called them on the drive over. She gave them a quick rundown of their suspicions . . . about Uncle Ray and his desperation for the money from Harley's trust fund. Mr. Buckman told them to rendezvous at the T-wharf. In the meantime, he was going to make some calls. And he'd probably do a whole lot of praying too. Ella was sure they'd know what to do when they got here—or they'd think of something.

The harbormasters' office light was off. Ella wasn't sure what they could have done anyway. The fog alone would make it hard to find the boys. Sure, they had the night vision setup to see through it, but they wouldn't even know where to start looking.

"I feel so helpless." Ella stared out into the harbor. The edges of Motif Number 1 on Bradley Wharf were softened by the fog. And there was nothing visible beyond that. The fishing shack could have been the last thing on earth for how it stood there all alone in the vapors.

Harley and Parker were out there. Somewhere. How on earth would they find their way back? Were they really going into a trap?

Jelly dialed Parker's number and held it up to her ear. "Pick up, pick up, pick up."

Ella gripped Jelly's arm. "Listen!" Ringing. Definitely a phone. She zeroed in on a sea bag sitting on the dock next to Parker's boat slip. "They went out in this fog—and didn't bring their phones? Are they insane?"

Jelly sprinted for the ramp—and Ella pulled out all the stops to keep up. Together they undid the seal and dumped the contents on the dock. Two phones—and a note in Harley's writing.

"No, no, no." Tears blurred Ella's vision. "The Dry Salvages—in this weather—in the *Bomb*?" She clutched the silver cross.

"They're in trouble," Jelly said. "I feel it." She whipped out her phone and stabbed at Uncle Vaughn's number in her favorites. "I'm calling Parker's dad. He needs to know about the Salvages. He'll know what to do."

"Harley and his fixation with that bike," Ella wailed. "He's been set up—and blinded by his obsession. He's gone over the edge, Jelly!"

"And he dragged his best friend with him."

CHAPTER 67

DEEP TROUBLE SLICED THROUGH THE WAVES like the boat relished the rougher waters. White spray broke hard to port and starboard—as if wanting to get out of the way of the bow. White foam trailed *Deep Trouble*, swirling in confusion and chaos like it didn't know what hit it. The boat was just like Ray. He always plowed through. Those who didn't get out of his way were left tumbling in his wake.

He was the captain of his own ship. The old cliché made him smile. Because within the hour he'd do everything he needed to do to make sure *Deep Trouble* truly was all his. He'd get Lochran the action step he needed to back off and wait for his share of the trust fund. Once Lochran saw the lengths Ray would go to to get what he wanted, maybe it would give the loan shark second thoughts about threatening him again.

Lady Luck was smiling on him. Even the fog was a good omen.

There would be no witnesses from shore or sea. There was no god up in the skies with his hands on everything. No being who controlled who lived or died—and when. Too many people believed in that kind of stuff. They were praying when they should be planning. Had their eyes closed when they should be wide open. They stayed on their knees when they should be getting back up on their feet and getting out from under the piggy-pile of life. They looked for answers in an ancient book instead of writing their own book and living by their own rules. They were suckers. Delusional fools.

In reality, Ray was as close to being a god as a human could be. Sometimes he believed he could actually read people's faces and know what they were thinking. If that wasn't godlike, what was? Ray mapped the path for his own life—and he sure as sea-spray controlled the lives of others. He'd prove that soon.

Ray didn't bother binding Scorza's ankles or wrists. It completed the illusion that they'd truly accepted him as part of the team. The kid was so gullible it made Ray want to double over with laughter. But he'd save the guffaws for when he shared celebration drinks with Kelsey and Vinny later tonight. By now Vinny had dumped the motorcycle someplace where only the fish would find it.

"Almost there," Ray said. "So let's talk about our game plan."

Scorza held one side of the pilot house to steady himself, his eyes locked on the coach.

"Two scenarios, the way I see it." Ray glanced from Scorza to Kelsey, and back. "There will be a report of a terrible accident. Harley Lotitto—and his new friend Parker Buckman—took a skiff out way too far from shore when there was fog and building seas. They'd somehow forced Harley's ex-best friend aboard. They

believed he was involved with the theft of Harley's motorcycle—
and they took him out to the Salvages to scare him into talking.
Everybody knew they hated each other . . . but nobody guessed
Harley would take it that far—not even his dear uncle. Somehow
the boat got clipped in the fog and went down. Tragically, all three
boys perished."

Fear rose in Scorza's eyes. Exactly what Ray wanted.

"The grieving Uncle Ray inherited a trust fund," Kelsey said,
"and promptly donated half of it to charity."

That did make Ray smile. Surely Lochran had a bogus charity
he'd set up just to take in large sums of money like that. By donat-
ing half, nobody would ever suspect he was greedy to get the boy's
inheritance.

"Y-you said there were two scenarios," Scorza said. "What's the
second one?"

Ray rode the trough of a deep swell and rose to the top of the
next wave. "The way I see the second one play out, Harley Lotitto
and Parker Buckman went out to the Dry Salvages based on a tip
they got. Harley was desperate for any information leading to
the discovery of his stolen bike, and he must have convinced the
Buckman kid to chance the weather. Somewhere along the way
they got clipped—and weren't seen until their bodies washed up
on shore. Tragic loss."

"And what if Harley called someone and told them it was me
who wanted to meet them out here?"

Ray gave Scorza the side-eye. "You deny it. And there is no
proof. We didn't use your phone, did we?"

Scorza shook his head.

"We were looking out for you from the beginning," Ray said.
"Nobody wants to see you hurt. You've got a bright football career

ahead of you. But the decision is yours as to which scenario we go with."

Scorza thumped his chest with the football. "What do I need to do to convince you to run the second play?"

Ray acted like he needed to give that some thought. "I'll expect your help. If you have a hand in this, it will make Kelsey and me just that much more sure that you'll keep your mouth closed."

"I'll do it," Scorza said. "Count on me, coach. I can do this. I want to."

Ray leaned over and clapped him on the shoulder. "All right, son. I'll tell you what I want you to do. And I'll give you one more chance to back out. Sound fair?"

Scorza nodded.

"Maneuvering between Little Salvages and Dry Salvages will be tricky in a boat this size," Ray said. "Unless of course our target isn't moving."

"That's why you had me tell him to set their anchor."

Ray smiled. "You're sharp. Your job will be to make sure they don't fire up their motor, cut their anchor line, and scoot away. We want that target to stay put. Which means you're going to have to be on board the *Boy's Bomb* to do that."

Over the next few minutes Ray went over the details. Scorza nodded. Asked the right questions.

"Then you get clear of the boat and tread water while we make sure the deed is done," Ray said. "After that we'll pick you up, drive back to Gloucester, and park *Deep Trouble*. And you'll never speak of this again. You'll have a hand in this—and will be just as guilty as we are. So if you squeal, you'll be hurting yourself, too. You'll be an accessory; you understand that, right?"

Scorza acted like he was talking to a recruiter. "I can do this. You watch and see."

The kid was remarkably without any look of fear now. No dread for what he was being asked to do. In a way, Scorza had more of Ray's DNA than his own flesh-and-blood nephew seemed to have. Scorza saw himself as a survivor. A land-on-his-feet kind of guy. Even now Scorza paced the working deck of *Deep Trouble* like he was on the sidelines of a football field—waiting for the defensive team to get the ball back to him. There was an eagerness to him. Not the kind that says *let's just get this over with*. It was more like he couldn't wait to get in the game.

The kid was definitely more like Ray than he knew—except he lacked the street smarts. He certainly couldn't read others the way Ray could. Because Scorza clearly had no idea that Ray had zero intention of letting him out of this alive.

CHAPTER 68

THE WAY PARKER SAW IT? A foghorn was the saddest sound in the world. Mournful. The word *horn* shouldn't even be in the name. It didn't sound brassy like a trumpet—or any other horn he'd ever heard. It was only capable of playing two creepy tones: one a gasp, the other a groan. Instead of bringing comfort, the deep voice of the foghorn brought a hopeless feeling that he couldn't shake. It spoke in slow, two-word sentences.

You're—lost.

Give—up.

You're—doomed.

No—hope.

The seas were slightly calmer between Little Salvages and Dry Salvages, but the wind had shifted. Now it was coming out of the northeast, and the swells were deepening. The *Boy's Bomb* tugged at its anchor like it didn't want to be chained to the bottom, miles from shore. At least when they headed back to the harbor they'd be going with the waves. Less spray, maybe, but they'd have to be extra careful they didn't bury their nose riding the face of the swells.

"You think he'll show?" Harley scanned to the south, toward Gloucester.

Parker didn't know what to think. But who would Scorza have convinced to take him out in this fog? "I don't trust him."

Harley laughed. "I said I believed his story. I didn't say I trusted him."

Parker wasn't sure they should believe any story from someone they didn't trust. He wished they had their phones. Reception might be iffy so far from shore, but he'd feel a lot better knowing they had a way of reaching help if they needed it.

Something still bothered Parker. "Who took Scorza's Wrangler for a joyride—and set it up to look like it was you?"

"I figured it was Scorza himself," Harley said. "But he still thinks I did it. It's a mystery."

"Who'd benefit most by you being blamed?"

Harley snorted. "That's easy. Uncle Ray. To get me out of his hair. To get at the trust fund."

That actually made a whole lot of sense to Parker. "Because he has a very big loan to pay off to some very bad guys." Why hadn't he thought of that earlier?

"Well, his little plan backfired," Harley said, "because the lawyer made that trust bulletproof. The only way Uncle Ray is getting at that trust fund is over my dead body."

Suddenly Parker got a really uneasy feeling—and it had nothing to do with the waves or the foghorn. "Okay . . . hear me out on something. Your uncle still owes that money. If he doesn't pay it back . . . what happens to him?"

Harley shrugged. "I honestly don't care."

"But *he* does." Parker didn't even want to suggest the scary thoughts creeping into his head. Harley would have to put it together himself . . . but maybe with a little help. "Where can he get the money?"

"He can't," Harley said. "I wouldn't sell Kemosabe. And the lawyer wouldn't break the trust. He's out of options—and the clock is running. He's got until Sunday."

More pieces moved into place. "So, two days left . . . and your uncle is just going to give up?"

Harley grinned. "Maybe he's robbing a convenience store at this very minute. That'd be rich. I could visit him in jail. Or not."

"I'm serious." Parker hesitated. "What about that trust? Are you sure there is no way for him to get his hands on all that money—legally?"

"I told you," Harley said. "Over my dead . . ."

Harley whirled to face Parker. "Even he wouldn't go that far. No way."

Parker raised both hands. "Sorry. It was a stupid thought. I had to get it out there." And he kicked himself for it. Harley had already lost his dad, and now Parker had hinted that his uncle might be trying to kill him. *Idiot.*

A wave hitting Dry Salvage exploded into a geyser of spray.

"From day one Uncle Ray has stolen everything from me that he could get his hands on." Harley shook his head. "But I'd like to think that deep down, maybe really deep down . . ."

A white lobster fishing boat nosed through the fog. Only registration numbers were on the bow. If the boat had a name, it must have been painted on the transom. The boat stopped a good hundred feet away. Maybe more.

"This could be it," Harley said. "Either they're scoping us out to be sure we're alone—or it's just a lobster boat looking for its next buoy."

Parker strained to see. Reflections off the pilot house windows blocked his view of whoever was at the helm. A figure stepped around the corner of the pilot house. "Scorza." Even from here they could see that one of his eyes was nearly swollen shut. Maybe he had been telling the truth more than Parker gave him credit for.

Harley waved—and Scorza signaled back by raising his football in one hand. "Okay, Parks. This is it."

The lobster boat belched out a cloud of diesel smoke and headed straight for them.

CHAPTER 69

BRYCE FELT LIKE HE'D BEEN STUCK in the longest halftime ever. But the game was starting again, and Scorza had the ball. He'd show Harley's uncle—and Kelsey—what he could do. They'd be glad they had him on the team.

He should have been more nervous. But he didn't feel that at all. Just wanted to make this play happen—and get some serious yardage. On the field every player had a role. Each one just had to do his part right. That's how games were won. And this was just like football. All Bryce had to do was his little part. There was no crime there. Harley's uncle and Kelsey had the truly nasty jobs.

Bryce would definitely follow his brother into the Marines one day. And maybe today was a little practice for real combat someday. A good soldier followed orders. A good soldier sometimes had to sacrifice a life to save a more important one. Bryce was getting it right on both counts. He was important . . . he had a future. Something to live for. Harley had neither.

Harley stood on deck. Feet spread wide to keep his balance while the undersized boat Gatorade owned bobbed and hiccuped in the waves.

Bryce glanced back at Harley's uncle.

The coach gave him a wink and a nod. "You ready?"

"I got this." Bryce held the football at the laces and kissed the tip of it.

Harley's uncle slowed as he approached Gatorade's skiff. "Okay, I'll get you close—and you'll have to jump."

"You say jump"—Bryce worked his way along the cabin and crawled toward the bow—"and I'll ask how high."

He couldn't see Harley's uncle through the glare of the glass now, but Kelsey leaned around the cabin, smiling. They both liked him. He could tell. And now that he had the ball? They were going to like him even more when they saw what he could do.

CHAPTER 70

THE WHITE LOBSTER BOAT EASED CLOSER. Parker left the helm and joined Harley along the starboard side to keep the big lobster boat from bumping them. Whoever was captaining the thing knew what he was doing, and he worked his forward and reverse expertly to bring the boat close enough for Scorza to jump aboard.

The bow towered over them, rocking up and down in a sawing motion as the captain inched closer.

Scorza still held the football, smiling. "Permission to come aboard?"

Like this is all a game. Parker gave Harley the side-eye. "I thought you said he sounded scared on the phone?"

Harley grunted.

Parker looked at the height Scorza would be dropping from. "We got to soften his landing a bit."

"I really don't care if he twists an ankle."

"Neither do I. I just don't want him cracking the fiberglass hull."
Harley flashed him a quick grin and held one hand up toward
Scorza. "Are you coming or not?"

Scorza tucked the football under his arm and leaped off the
bow—and into the arms of Harley and Parker. The three of them
tumbled to the deck. The lobster boat was already backing away
from the *Boy's Bomb*.

"Thanks, captain!" Scorza waved the ball at the lobster boat.
"You won't regret this!"

"Wait," Parker said. "He's not giving you a ride back? I thought
you were scared to be seen with Harley."

"He'll be back when I signal him." Scorza braced himself on
the helm and dropped into the driver's seat. "Sorry, I have to sit
for a sec."

The lobster boat kept reversing, likely wanting to be clear of
the Dry Salvages before swinging around. Parker watched the distance between the boats grow. "That captain must be half-crazy
to drive you out here in the fog. How much did you have to pay
him?"

Scorza held his gaze for a moment with his good eye. "I sold
him my soul."

Which was a strange answer to a simple question. The lobster
boat captain must have eased off on the throttle. The boat just
sat there idling about fifty yards off the *Bomb's* starboard side. It
took on the ghostly appearance of some kind of phantom vessel.
The white sides of the lobster boat seemed to dissolve into the fog.

"Okay . . . you're here," Harley said. "And there's nobody
around. Just like you wanted. So . . . where's Kemosabe?"

"Sit down," Scorza said. "Too much rocking going on. It's making me seasick."

Harley and Parker sat.

"I told you I found the bike," Scorza said. "And I moved it to a safe place. Honestly, I was going to call you up. Tell you where it was. Get the whole friendship thing going again. But then you took the Wrangler—and that got me really hot. I mean *really*. Hot."

"That wasn't me," Harley said.

Scorza held up one hand. "Right. Whatever. So I went back to Kemosabe—with tools. I was going to take it apart. Get my revenge. But instead, I got caught by the same guys I'd seen take it the night of the shed fire."

"Wait," Harley said. "You told me you got away."

"Well, I did. I'm here, right?" Scorza stared at Harley. "But I couldn't save me and the bike. They got your motorcycle back."

Parker watched Harley's face. This was not the same story Scorza had told Harley earlier, right? What was going on?

"You said Kemosabe was safe."

"Was." Scorza said. "*Was*. And you'd have had it back already if you hadn't messed with my Jeep. There were two of them. They cinched nylon straps on my ankles and wrists. I thought I was a goner. Then they called a third guy to bring a van. They said they were going to dump your bike in the sea where you'd never find it. But they had trouble getting the bike in the van—so they cut the straps so I could help them load it—."

"So Kemosabe got taken away again—and you helped them load it?" Harley was on his feet—looking like he was ready to pitch Scorza over the side.

"You going to let me finish?" Scorza seemed to be enjoying this. "Sit."

Harley looked at Parker like he wasn't sure what to do. But to his credit, he sat.

"The instant that bike was inside the van and strapped in place, one of the goons fired up the truck and took off. Before the other two could get straps on me, I bolted. Didn't stop until I got to the waterfront."

Harley's face was dark. His fists clenched. "You lied."

Scorza smiled—and there was nothing friendly about it. It was the kind of smile he'd have after throwing a touchdown pass to seal the opposition's loss.

"Then why are we here?" Parker swung his arm toward the Dry Salvages. "Why the big secret meeting if Kemosabe is gone forever?"

"Two reasons." Scorza held the football high over his head to signal the lobster boat. Immediately the boat started their way. "First, I wanted to see your face the moment you knew you'd never see that motorcycle again."

Harley grabbed two fistfuls of his own hair. His whole face—the picture of agony.

"And the second reason? I came to save a life."

Harley stood. He planted both hands on the helm and leaned close to Scorza's face. "By telling me Kemosabe is absolutely gone? How is that saving my life?"

"I never said I was saving *your* life," Scorza said. "I'm saving mine. It was a trade, really. My life for yours."

Harley shook his head. "What are you *talking* about?"

The sound of the lobster boat's diesel motor carried across the waves. The boat was coming right at them again, but fast. Parker tried to see through the window of the cabin—to see if the captain of the thing even saw them. "Uh, if you're going to make your turn, captain, this would be the time."

But the lobster boat showed no sign of altering its course. Thirty yards away. Parker eyed it. He was not liking this. Not one bit. "Harley . . . the anchor."

"Pull it in?"

"No time. Release the line—let it go. We gotta move!" Parker motioned to Scorza. "Out of my seat. That captain is crazy."

Harley stretched over the bow, working at the knot on the anchor line. "The knot is too tight!"

"Knife under the seat," Parker shouted. "Cut it!"

Scorza scooted out of Parker's spot—his football tucked under one arm. Parker reached for the key. *Gone.*

"Looking for these?" Scorza held up the key ring like he was ready to throw a Hail Mary.

"No!" Parker lunged—but Scorza launched them high and far. The keys hit the gray waters and disappeared. The lobster boat was building speed. "You got a death wish or something?" The boat was now twenty yards and closing fast. "He's going to ram us!"

"He wants *you* two," Scorza said. "Not me!" Still clutching his beloved football, he dove over the side.

Ten yards.

Harley gave up on the bow line—there was no point. He stared at Parker, wild-eyed.

No time for life jackets. The lobster boat looked like a battleship bearing down on them.

"Jump!"

Harley rolled off the bow. Parker leaped for the stern. Even as he did, the world dropped into slow motion. Someone leaning out the port side of the lobster boat pointing at the *Bomb* like they were helping the captain stay on course. The lobster boat's bow rising with a swell—so high over the side of the *Bomb*—and dropping like the blade of a guillotine. Parker's foot was on the transom, and he pushed off with all his strength even as the bow crashed down on the skiff with a sickening crack. The hull broke in two. The front end disappeared around the bow of the lobster boat.

Parker hit the water—immediately caught in the churning aftershocks of the lobster boat's wake. Over and over he tumbled underwater—losing all sense of up and down. He opened his eyes—and clawed for daylight.

CHAPTER 71

ANGELICA FOLLOWED UNCLE VAUGHN'S INSTRUCTIONS to the letter. He'd been as alarmed as she was to learn where Parker had intended to take the *Boy's Bomb*. She paced the pier next to *Alert 1*, the harbormasters' boat. Fog choked the channel from sight. But even from here she could hear some pretty big rollers pounding against the breakwater. The *Bomb* wasn't built for seas like that.

Parker's dad had promised to call the harbormasters the instant Angelica got off the phone with him. All they could do was wait now—and pray they got to the boys in time. This waiting was driving her crazy. Angelica rehearsed her pitch. They had to let her ride in the boat to find the boys.

Parker's dad and mom roared halfway down the T-wharf and whipped into an open parking spot. The two of them ran toward Angelica and Ella. His dad still wore his National Park Service uniform—and his mom was totally dressed for the office. By the serious look on their faces, they sensed the boys were in as much trouble as she believed they were.

The harbormasters pulled up an instant later. Eric and Maggie hustled for the dock. Likely they knew better than anybody that the seas were too heavy for the *Boy's Bomb* and the water too cold if the skiff got swamped or capsized.

"Hurry," Angelica whispered. "Please hurry."

Ella locked one arm with hers. The other hand massaged the cross around her neck.

Eric and Maggie swung onto the boat—and into a smooth routine for making ready to head to sea.

Parker's dad stood at the very edge of the dock like he was ready to jump aboard as well. "Got room for a National Park ranger?"

Maybe it was the uniform. Maybe they understood a parent's desperation. Eric motioned him aboard.

"What about us?" Whatever pitch Angelica had rehearsed in her mind was gone. "Please?"

"No," Eric and Maggie answered together. Eric was in the pilot house. The twin 250s roared to life.

Mrs. Buckman wrapped her arms around Angelica.

Ella stood on the very edge of the dock. "Wouldn't an extra set of eyes be useful?"

Maggie shook her head. "It will be a rough ride. You're a minor. We'd need a parent's permiss—"

"I don't have a dad or a mom. I already called Grams, and she was okay with it—as long as I'm with my second dad . . . Mr. Buckman." She pointed toward the Outer Harbor. "See that seal—there in the middle of the channel?"

Angelica glanced toward the fog-choked Outer Harbor. There was no way Ella could see that far, right?

"Can't even see the channel from here," Eric said. "We've got to go."

"*I* can see it," Ella said. "I'm an artist. I notice everything."

Ella was bluffing, but Angelica wasn't going to snitch. Not with everything that was at stake. She only wished she'd thought of it herself.

"You *need* me with this fog." Ella leaped into the boat. Grabbed a handrail behind the pilot house and hung on like she dared them to pry her loose.

"You're slowing us down," Eric said. "We need to get out there."

"And you need me. Please. I-I need to be there. I said some awful things to Harley—and I was wrong. I have to help."

Maggie looked at Eric. She didn't say a word, but she must have communicated something.

"Life jacket. On." Eric pointed to the padded seat behind the center console. "Sit down. Hold tight."

Maggie tossed Ella a life vest. "He won't be taking it slow."

"Mrs. Buckman," Angelica struggled to break free. "What about me?"

Parker's mom didn't let loose. "You know they can't. Shouldn't. And they need room for the boys if . . ."

If something has gone wrong. Angelica didn't need Mrs. Buckman to finish . . . and she was right. "Just find them, Ella!"

Maggie cast off the lines and pushed *Alert 1* away from the dock.

Eric took off like his hair was on fire.

"Ella!" Angelica held up her phone. "Text updates!"

Did Ella hear her over the sound of the motors? Angelica couldn't be sure. The boat was moving too fast to tell if she'd nodded—and she never waved to show she'd heard. But waving was likely impossible. Ella was hanging on too tight.

CHAPTER 72

PARKER STRUGGLED TO KEEP HIS HEAD above water. He kicked off his shoes. "Harley!"

The entire back half of the *Boy's Bomb* was gone. Dragged below the angry waters by the weight of the motor. Shards of teal-painted fiberglass and chunks of debris floated everywhere. The front half of the hull bobbed upside down in the water a good fifteen yards away. "Harley!"

A bloody hand rose from the far side of the overturned bow.

"He's alive! Thank you, God! Thank you!" Parker's words came out in choking sputters. "How bad are you hurt?"

Harley raised himself high enough for Parker to see his face. "No pain. I'm good." He slipped back down behind the hull, out of sight.

Parker hoped he was good, but he was bleeding, right? Maybe the cold numbed him. Or maybe he was in shock. He did a quick damage assessment on himself, thanking God he'd escaped a direct impact when they got rammed.

Scorza was no more than ten yards away in the other direction—with Parker in the middle. The jock clutched the ball with both hands like it was his personal flotation device.

The lobster boat leaned in a hard U-turn. That's when Parker saw the name. *Deep Trouble.* Harley's uncle stood at the helm, bringing the boat about. Had he lost control and hit the *Bomb* by accident? Parker knew the answer, but he still couldn't believe it. He scissors-kicked to keep on top of the swells.

Scorza's words streaked through his head. *He wants you two, not me!*

He wants you two. *He wants.* Oh, yeah. This was about Uncle Ray—and what he wanted. What he wanted so badly that he was willing to steal to get it. Take their very lives, if that's what was needed.

Even now Ray Lotitto's crewman shouted something to the captain. Pointed their way. *Deep Trouble* was definitely bearing down on them too fast to pick up survivors.

"Jesus," Parker cried, "help us!" Harley's uncle was coming back to finish what he'd started.

CHAPTER 73

ELLA CAUGHT A FACE FULL OF SPRAY seconds after they'd raced through the channel and into the open sea. She tightened her grip. Mr. Buckman sat beside her, one hand gripping the pole next to him and the other locked onto the pole closest to her. His arm stretched in front of her like a human safety harness.

Eric held the wheel steady and throttled forward. This close, the twin motors behind her sounded more like jet engines. "We're in for a little turbulence," he said. "Buckle your seat belts."

Ella wished there *were* belts. The boys were insane to come out here in Parker's boat. It was too small. They were risking their lives—for a motorcycle? Instantly she knew that wasn't completely true. *Harley* was gambling it all for a motorcycle. Parker was risking his neck for a friend.

The silver cross slapped against the outside of her life jacket. Grams would have said it was an omen. A warning to hold it tight

357

and pull it close. To pray. She barely managed to tuck it inside the life jacket instead. She needed both hands to hold on right now.

Alert 1 smacked an incoming swell, shooting a wall of spray in all directions. Ella didn't dare let go to wipe her eyes.

Maggie called back to them. "You want me to ask Eric to take it down a notch?"

Ella shook her head. "Don't worry about me. The faster we get there, the better."

"It's going to be a wet ride." Maggie smiled. "You're going to get a Sandy Bay soaking."

Saltwater in the face didn't bother Ella a bit. Actually, she welcomed it. Nobody would see her tears.

CHAPTER 74

IMPULSE TOLD PARKER TO SWIM TO HARLEY, to the protection of the only part of the *Bomb* that was afloat. Instinct also told him he'd only be making it easier for Ray Lotitto to pick them off with *Deep Trouble.*

The lobster boat was maybe half a football field away now—and getting closer by the second. Angry smoke snorted from its exhaust stack.

"Keep distance between us," Parker shouted to Harley—then Scorza. "He'll have to target us one at a time. Wait until the last second—then dive fast and deep until they pass over."

Harley raised one hand and signaled with an okay sign. Scorza shook his head, still clutching the ball. "I'm not the target. I'll just wait until he picks me up."

Total scumbag. But if Scorza really wasn't a target, swimming to him was the safest place to be. He struck out in sloppy, heavy strokes. His cargo shorts felt like an anchor now—but there was no time to shed them. *Deep Trouble* was thirty yards away.

Only Harley's nose and eyes were above the surface. He clutched the half-submerged edge of the *Bomb*, looking ready to duck and dive when the boat got close enough.

Parker switched to a frantic breast stroke so he could keep his eye on *Deep Trouble*. Scorza was no more than twelve feet away.

"Hey, get away from me," Scorza shouted. "Back off!"

Parker ignored him and pushed hard to get close. Ray chose his target—and veered right for Parker and Scorza.

Scorza held up the ball. "Coach . . . it's me! It's me!" He used the ball for a pointer now. "Harley is behind the wreckage—over there."

Parker stopped swimming. Treaded water for a second. Gauging the distance from him to the boat—the speed—and when to go under.

Ray's crewman stood at the side like before. Guiding the captain right at them. Shouting. "Time for a haircut, boys!"

"Scorza, you gotta dive!"

Parker drew in a couple quick breaths, piked, and dove. Eyes wide open, he clawed and kicked for the darkness of the depths. *Deep Trouble's* diesel roared in his ears. He wasn't getting deep fast enough. Suddenly the boat passed over him. He tucked in his legs, fearing the prop or rudder would cripple him good.

A swirl of current tumbled him around and upside-down. The black silhouette of the lobster boat passed overhead like a massive great white. *Thank you, God!* Parker kicked for daylight, lungs convulsing for air.

He broke the surface, choking—sucking in air. Coughing, gasping for more. *Deep Trouble* was seventy feet away. Already beginning to blend in with the fog. Harley's Uncle Ray busy at the wheel. Kelsey continued scanning the water off the stern—but not Parker's way.

"Don't let him see me, God!" A swell lifted Parker, but he ducked under so his head wouldn't show.

"Ahh, ahh, ahh." Not words. But agonized whining.

Parker struggled to pinpoint where the voice was coming from. Scorza rose up on a wave, not twenty feet away. Eyes wild. Football floating loose. Arm outstretched—with an extra joint in the forearm . . . like he had two elbows. White bone gleamed nearly as bright as the sea foam. Blood wept from the torn flesh.

Fog swallowed *Deep Trouble* completely. Parker struck out for Scorza—grabbing the football on the way.

"He h-hit me," Scorza said. "My p-passing arm! How bad is it?"

"Not good." Parker stuffed the football under Scorza's jersey. The ball bobbed up to the neckline, working like a built-in life jacket. "Don't lose the ball—it'll keep you afloat." But that wouldn't do much good if Scorza bled out. "Still have your shoes?"

"Wha—?"

"I need one." Parker ducked underwater, grabbed one of Scorza's flailing legs. Ripped off his shoe and burst back to the surface. Immediately he pulled at the laces. Once he had enough length he wrapped it above Scorza's elbow—shoe and all. "Keep this tourniquet on, hear me?"

"Is h-he c-coming back?"

Parker heard the diesel motor, but couldn't tell where it was at with all the fog. "Yes. Can you stay afloat?"

"Y-you gotta save me." He grabbed Parker's shirt with his good hand. "This was your fault."

The weight was too much. Parker struggled to keep his mouth clear of the water. "Your legs, can you kick?"

"You gotta get me to shore."

They were way too far from land for that to happen. "Your legs—broke or not?"

"Not."

He checked over his shoulder. No sign of *Deep Trouble*. The teal hull of the *Bomb* was just within sight. Barely. Harley's hand slapped into view and slid off the boat bottom, leaving a trail of blood. It swung into view again, and slipped off—like he was trying to get a grip but couldn't manage it. How much blood had he lost? "I have to help Harley now."

"Leave him. His uncle's going to finish him off anyway." Scorza gripped Parker's shirt tighter. "You're with me now."

No. Parker was never with Scorza. "Listen to me. They're going to keep coming back until they're sure we're *all* dead. You got that?"

"I'm doing what they said," Scorza said. "They're going to let me live. You help me and I'll put in a good word to them for you."

Parker struggled to keep his head above water, but Scorza's death grip on his shirt wasn't making that easy. "You do what *I* tell you—and maybe *you* will live, got it?" A wave pushed him right into Scorza's busted arm.

"Owwww . . . " Scorza's eyes looked wild.

Parker had to get free of Scorza's grip. He boosted himself up with the help of a wave, then used his arms and the following downward momentum to force himself deep. Scorza released the shirt. Parker pulled it over his head and let the thing drift toward the bottom. He surfaced, feeling much lighter—but even more exposed to the cold.

Coming up behind Scorza—and staying clear of his good arm—Parker grabbed the football and stuffed it under the front of Scorza's jersey. The thing bubbled to the surface and clocked Scorza in the chin.

Scorza gave a little cry of pain.

"Float on your belly," Parker told him. "The ball will help keep afloat. When you need air, give a kick, fill your lungs, and drop back down. Kick your other shoe off."

"Wha?"

"Arms out to your side. Eyes closed. If *Deep Trouble* spots you, you've got to make them think you're dead and floating. Got it?"

Scorza grabbed for him, but Parker swished back out of reach. "I'm going to help Harley. You'll be okay—just do this, got it?"

"Harley's d-dead. I saw him go under. Didn't come up."

He was lying. Had to be. Parker scanned for the hull. Couldn't see if Harley's hand was still holding there or not. "I have to check."

"I-I'm bleeding. Sharks."

Not something Parker wanted to think about right now. "Yeah. Great whites, b—"

"You g-g-gotta help me!" Scorza then said something Parker couldn't make out. It dissolved into a pitiful sound. *Whimpering.*

"Great whites love seals. But seals don't wear jerseys, Scorza. Let's hope the sharks see your number and look for a seal instead. Do what I said. Play dead."

Parker pushed away.

Scorza lay there, arms outstretched—but his good eye wasn't closed. "I h-hope you drown out here, G-Gatorade! I hope a shark tears you apart so I can watch."

Parker couldn't get away from this guy fast enough. "See ya."

"At your f-funeral!"

The cold was numbing his legs. Arms. The throbbing diesel of *Deep Trouble* sounded louder now. The thing was close—but where? He worked the breast stroke for all he was worth, constantly scanning the edges of the fog for a sign of the boat approaching. "Harley!"

The foghorn groaned. *He's—lost.*

Parker pushed harder. Fighting the wind. Waves. And the cold that was pressing in on all sides. "Harley!"

Only the foghorn answered . . . relentless with its pessimistic predictions. *You're—next.*

"Harley!" His friend's hand was visible for an instant. Then gone again. Spray blinded him for a moment, and the waves seemed obsessed with keeping Parker away. He ducked underwater and thrust himself toward the floating piece of the *Bomb*'s wreckage, praying he'd get there in time.

CHAPTER 75

ELLA WAS SOAKED. She angled herself to see the water as best she could, without actually leaving her seat. Everybody aboard scanned for the *Boy's Bomb*. If Ella could make something happen by the force of her will, she'd see the boat bobbing at its anchor, both boys inside waving.

"God, please." She whispered the words. Not that it mattered. Nobody could have heard a word she said. Plus, she probably wasn't the only one praying right now. Parker's dad, for sure. Maybe they all were. She never really had time for God unless she was in trouble. Did that make her some kind of hypocrite for praying now? Prayer just wasn't her thing. That was Parker's go-to. Was he praying now? Would it do him any good? The cross under her vest dug in. Like it was reminding her it was there. "God . . . please."

Maggie was on the radio to someone. "Fog is getting thicker."

Great. It wasn't Ella's imagination. So that's what she got for praying?

"We'll have to slow up a bit." Eric eased back on the throttle. "Sorry about that."

Ella got it. She really did. Her brain had been screaming for them to slow down since they'd left the channel. But her heart had been crying something very different. *Go faster. Go faster. Please . . . just a little bit faster.*

CHAPTER 76

"HARLEY!" PARKER PUSHED THE LAST FEW strokes to the wrecked bow of the *Boy's Bomb*. "Harley!"

He scooted around from the other side. "G-g-good to see you, Parks!" His lips were a purply blue. Likely the same shade Parker's were right now. "He's c-coming around a-g-gain."

"How b-bad are you hurt?"

Harley held up his hand. "Nice little g-gash. Everything else okay."

At least no broken bones. "H-have you tried going under this th-thing?"

Harley gave him a doubting look. "Hide under a s-sinking boat. G-good thinking."

"The bow has built-in flotation. And there's p-probably air underneath. We could go under and—"

"Parks!" Harley pointed to *Deep Trouble*, materializing like a ghost ship out of the fog.

They saw Kelsey, standing to one side of the pilot house while he scanned the surface of the water.

They stayed low behind the bow. "God, don't let them see us. Make them go away. Please." Parker reached under the flipped hull. "There's air under there. We slip under, got it?" It was worth a shot.

They ducked below the surface together. Parker traced his hand along the familiar lines of the *Bomb*, and surfaced underneath.

Black, except for the light filtering in from under the sides— and not much room—but he could breathe. Harley surfaced an instant later. He sucked in a couple of shaky breaths of air. "Think they saw us?"

There was no way to be sure. "If it s-sounds like they're going to r-ram us again—"

"We g-go deep," Harley said.

"Right." How long could they keep doing this? "But we'll need to be quicker." Which was getting harder to imagine with the way the cold was making his limbs work in slow motion. Clothes might help him survive longer. Air trapped in pants could help him float. Maybe keep him from hypothermia a bit longer. But it would slow him down—and right now if he didn't dodge *Deep Trouble* quick enough, he wouldn't live long enough to die of hypothermia. "I'm going to lose some clothes. F-faster in my skivvies."

"I already did," Harley said.

Parker ducked underwater so he could tug off his cargo shorts and socks. It took two breaths to do it. Each time he went under it sounded like *Deep Trouble* had halved the distance between them.

The lobster boat rumbled closer. But not at ramming speed this time. More like they were doing a careful search.

"I was s-so stupid," Harley said. "Uncle Ray stole K-Kemosabe.

I tried so hard to get it back that I threw away m-my life. Yours, too."

"God is with us," Parker said. "And if we're to m-make it—nothing can thwart His plans."

Deep Trouble sounded close enough to board. If only they could do that. Just climb over the side, send Uncle Ray and Kelsey for a swim, and find some blankets.

"Think th-they'll g-guess we're under here?"

Parker put a finger to his lips. "I'm praying they don't."

"Parker," Harley whispered. "Pray harder."

CHAPTER 77

RAY HAD RUN A SLOW CIRCLE AROUND THE WRECKAGE, with a wide perimeter. No sign of the boys. Now he wanted one more cruise through the heart of the debris field, just to be sure.

"I think we got 'em," Kelsey said. "Like picking off fish in a bucket, right?"

"I land on my feet," Ray said. "And I'm going to come down hard on Lochran's toes next."

Word would get out quickly enough. Somebody would see the wreckage. They'd call the Coast Guard. It wouldn't be hard for Lochran to verify a skiff had been found—and there were no survivors. He'd know Ray was good for the money. The loan shark would wait for the trust to pay out. Ray would give him his half, the man would be out of his life, and Ray would have his life back. For just a second the thought of some kind of payback flashed in his mind. Maybe if they had the right opportunity—or rather created it—he and Kelsey and Vinny would deal with Ironwing and Lochran. Give them a taste of their own medicine.

One thing Ray had learned? Never deal with a loan shark again. And he wouldn't have to. He'd have enough money to live on Easy Street for the rest of his life. He'd move down to the Bahamas— or someplace he could live cheaply and run dive charters all year round. He'd be sitting pretty.

"Thanks, big brother." All this time he'd resented his brother— and his brat of a nephew. But Ray had worked it all around to his own advantage. His brother had left everything to Harley—but Ray would get it all anyway. Once again Ray proved what a survivor he was. How he came out on top.

"Mission accomplished." Kelsey clapped him on the back. "I only wish Lochran was in the little boat with the boys—and his triggerman Ironwing."

Ray couldn't agree more. "We'll fix them yet." He'd find a way. He promised himself that.

"Now what?"

Ray grazed the half-submerged section of hull that still remained afloat. "We give it five more minutes. Just to be sure." He hadn't gotten where he was by being careless.

He steered *Deep Trouble* in a tight circle and dropped it in neutral. He walked the inside perimeter of the boat. Slow. Scanning. Watching the waves rise and drop in all directions. There were no signs of life.

He kept a weather eye on Little Salvages. At least where he knew they sat below the high tide line. A telltale cresting of waves showed some of the rocks were still dangerously close to the surface. The waves seemed determined to send *Deep Trouble* right into the middle of it.

371

Ray shifted back in gear. He swung the boat around and headed for Dry Salvages, then made a nice, lazy loop and headed back into the floating wreckage. That one section of the *Bomb*'s hull caught his eye. Not that it was a problem. Not at all. In fact, it would be a help. If a skipper saw that, they'd get the whole Coast Guard thing going.

It's just that his adrenaline was still pumping—and the whole thing had ended too soon. It had been too easy. He goosed the gas and headed right for the chunk of wreckage. It was tempting that way. Like seeing fresh roadkill when he was driving the Silverado. Nothing huge. But a squirrel. Rabbit. Turtle. Hey, even a dog or cat. If he saw one plastered on the road, he liked to put his tread marks on the carcass as well. Liked the little hiccup he felt going over it.

The chunk of wreckage beckoned him in the same way. Ray slid the throttle forward. "I'm going to give that thing a little love smack from *Deep Trouble*, and then let's bring this back to the slip. We got some celebrating to do."

"Aye, aye, cap." Kelsey gave him a grin and a mock salute.

With the kid gone, he'd just locked in total ownership of the boat. With the other two boys gone, he'd eliminated the witnesses. He'd pay off Lochran—and still be sitting on a small fortune from the kid's trust fund. He'd called the shots and made it happen.

The teal bow section from the skiff moved slower than the waves. Like an iceberg. It was an easy target. Ray hit it square—and with momentum. He felt the thing underneath his hull, tumbling and rolling the entire length of *Deep Trouble*. The skiff remnant slammed the underside of the stern with more force than Ray would have expected, making *Deep Trouble* shudder for an instant. It was like the *Boy's Bomb* still had some life in it and was hitting back.

The busted skiff spun and twisted in the backwash of *Deep Trouble* like it couldn't figure up from down. He checked ahead of them again. The nasty trap of Little Salvages lay dead ahead. "Let's go home, Kelsey!"

Ray turned the wheel—and instantly knew there was a problem. The boat didn't respond. "What the—?"

He spun the wheel. Nothing. Swells broke over Little Salvages no more than twenty yards from them. The diesel was still running—but without steering what good would that do?

"I got no steering!" Ray slammed the controls into reverse. Throttled hard. The diesel protested loudly. Forward motion slowed; then a wave broke over the stern. "That stinking little skiff hull must have jammed up our rudder!"

Kelsey rushed forward as if gauging the distance to the rocks from the front windows. "Drop anchor?"

Too late for that. They'd have to get lucky. Time it right. "We'll catch a big wave and ride over the top."

CHAPTER 78

PARKER STAYED UNDERWATER AND held himself there. One more second. One more second. Parker fought the urge to burst to the surface. Every second underwater gave him a better chance that he wouldn't be seen. With frantic reaching, pulling, and kicking—he broke the surface and gasped in a blast of air.

Harley was already there. "I thought you were d-dead, bro. I thought you were out of the game."

Deep Trouble looked translucent . . . no longer solid. Like the fog and the boat were melding into one. Kelsey and Ray were focused on the waters in front of them, not behind. Kelsey pointed ahead, like he was suggesting a route to circle back. "This isn't over yet."

The last remnant of the *Boy's Bomb* was smaller now. *Deep Trouble* had taken another bite out of him like a great white might take a chunk out of a seal. The *Bomb* spun slowly, the tip of the bow nearly straight up, exposing the empty insides for a moment before yawning back down to the water.

"There's still a p-pocket of air underneath," Parker said. "Let's w-wait him out under there." And hope he sees no need to ram it again. Parker's gimpy arm felt almost useless. He slipped underwater and frog-kicked as far as his breath allowed him. If Kelsey or Ray looked back, he didn't want to be easy to spot.

He surfaced five feet from what was left of his boat. *Deep Trouble* was no longer in sight, but he could still hear the engine—especially when his ears dipped below the surface. His arms weren't working well enough in the cold water to do the crawl now. He managed a sloppy breast stroke that brought him to the side of the boat. He ducked underneath.

The pocket of air was smaller, but the two of them managed.

"W-we give it f-five minutes a-after we hear n-no motor," Parker said. "Then we climb on the hull the best we can and ride this baby to land."

"F-five m-minutes," Harley said. "Then home."

Parker prayed they could actually make it to shore. That the hypothermia wouldn't get them first.

CHAPTER 79

THE WIND CAUGHT *DEEP TROUBLE* and swung her sideways now, ten yards from where the highest point of Little Salvages crowned between swells. Too close. Too. Close.

"We need a big wave to carry us over!" They could do it, right? Get on the other side of Little Salvages and drop anchor. Throw on a mask and go over the side to fix the rudder.

"Hold on!" *Deep Trouble* slammed against the rock—with the sickening sound of splitting wood. The impact ripped the wheel from Ray's grip and smacked him against the port side gunwale. Kelsey wasn't as lucky. He was thrown from the boat and disappeared below the waves.

Almost immediately *Deep Trouble* listed to the port side. Seconds later the diesel coughed to a stop. Ray crawled to the lower cabin on all fours to grab the storm suit. Water was already filling the cabin—and rising fast.

CHAPTER 80

ELLA SAW THE PIECE OF WRECKAGE almost at the same time as Parker's dad cried out.

"No!" He pointed to a piece of teal fiberglass floating on the surface, driven by the waves.

Within seconds it seemed a debris field materialized out of the fog. Seat cushions. Dock bumpers. Life jackets.

"Taking a position," Maggie said. Immediately she was on the radio with the Coast Guard, giving their latitude and longitude. Then she radioed for rescue vehicles to get to the T-wharf and stand by.

All four of them searched the water—especially when a swell gave them the extra height to extend their view. Ella held on to the rail behind the pilot house to steady herself.

"Lousy fog," Eric muttered. "Going to make it hard for swimmers to see us." He glanced at Ella. Must have seen the despair in her eyes. "But it won't slow us down. We'll find them. I've got night vision here." He checked the infrared screen. "And you've got those eyes that can see seals in the fog, right?"

They'd need Superman's X-ray vision.

Scraps of fiberglass littered the area and would probably get lodged in the jetty or wash up on the beaches of Rockport before morning. Ella couldn't bear the thought. A large chunk tumbled in the swells. The helm—with the steering wheel clearly visible. The thing rolled, and for an instant she saw the wood name plaque Parker had carved long before they'd moved to Rockport. *Boy's Bomb*. All hope that this was some other unlucky boat was dashed.

Eric passed close to the helm, but kept scanning.

The piece of wreckage rolled and spun in the waves. Hopelessness seemed to be twisting and turning her the same way. She'd never felt so helpless. Sensing the boys needed help—but having no idea what she could do.

"Text home." Mr. Buckman kept his eyes on the water. "Tell them to pray hard!"

Ella's fingers flew over her screen, wet from spray. She sent the text off with a picture of the flotsam . . . and a desperate prayer of her own.

CHAPTER 81

Friday, August 12, 7:17 p.m.

ANGELICA SWIPED OPEN THE TEXT AND WAILED, holding it out for Parker's mom to see.

Finding bits and pieces of *Boy's Bomb* but no boys. PRAY HARD.

They clutched each other. His mom prayed aloud with a fervency like Angelica had never heard before.

Angelica prayed too . . . just a simple three-word prayer, over and over.

"God save them."

"God save them."

CHAPTER 82

HARLEY DID HIS BEST TO HOLD ON to what was left of the *Bomb*'s bow, but his fingers weren't working so well. "When is he g-going to l-leave?"

Every time his ears dipped below the surface of the water, he heard the echoing sound of a boat engine. Clearly Uncle Ray was combing the area, making sure they were dead.

"W-we w-wait l-little l-longer."

Parker was right. If they tried to leave now, they'd be easy targets. *Deep Trouble* would plow right over them. The cold had thickened their blood or something. Harley could tell he'd be as nimble as a log out in the water.

He fought the urge to slip out from under the hull—just to see where *Deep Trouble* was.

"Two m-minutes," Parker said. "Then g-gotta m-move."

Harley had no idea how they were going to swim to shore. He could hardly feel his legs.

CHAPTER 83

ELLA LOCKED ON TO EVERY PIECE OF DEBRIS she saw, hoping Harley or Parker would be holding on for dear life. The harbormasters' radio crackled to life. Ella couldn't quite make anything out that made sense. Obviously, it took a trained ear to catch what was said—because both Maggie and Eric took their eyes off the water and stared at the receiver for an instant.

Eric turned to them and explained, "A lobster boat from the harbor—*After Five*—just picked up a survivor not a hundred yards from us. They're racing him back to the T-wharf."

"Did they say who it is?" Ella blurted out. "His name?"

Eric shook his head. "It's a boy. No ID on him, and he's too cold to speak clearly enough for them to understand."

"They only saw *one*?" Parker's dad asked.

"Waves like this"—Maggie nodded toward the water—"they likely got separated. Let's keep a sharp lookout now. We'll find him."

They had to. Dear God in heaven . . . they had to.

CHAPTER 84

ANGELICA HEARD THE SIRENS before the rescue vehicles rumbled down the T-wharf. Paramedics. Fire Department. Police. It didn't take long to catch the report that a lobster boat was bringing in a survivor.

A survivor. As in one.

Reluctantly Mrs. Buckman and Angelica moved to the side when the medics wheeled a gurney down the ramp to the raft floating off the end of the T-wharf.

A blue lobster boat roared into the channel through the fog. He didn't slow, but set the moored sailboats to lurching in its wake. Only as he approached the Tuna Wharf did he show signs of cutting his speed. The boat pulled up to the float off the T-wharf and threw lines to the rescue workers on the scene.

A figure huddled in the pilot house, sitting on a lobster trap. A blanket was wrapped around him and formed a hood over his head. Instantly medics were on board, checking him out. Angelica strained to catch a glimpse. Parker's mom did the same.

One of the medics slid the blanket off the survivor's head.

"Bryce Scorza?" What was he even doing out there?

Mrs. Buckman held her tighter, her prayers rising heavenward.

Angelica checked her phone. No new texts. "Find them, Ella. Find them."

Scorza was on the gurney now, and three paramedics walked him up the ramp. One in front. Two pushing from the back. Clearly, he was injured. Angelica broke free from Parker's mom. Met Scorza just as they got him onto the T-wharf. "Did you see Parker—and Harley?"

He nodded. "I knew where his motorcycle was—and met to tell him. But we got hit by a boat in the fog. Gatorade's boat split in two. Just broke to pieces."

Angelica couldn't breathe. "Where are they?"

"Harley never surfaced. He's gone."

No. Dear God . . . no! "Parker—did you see Parker?"

Scorza nodded. "I held him up as long as I could. But he wanted to find Harley. He fought me off—and with my arm busted like this I couldn't stop him. I tried, I tried, I—"

"Easy, partner." The paramedic at the head of the gurney placed a hand on Scorza's shoulder. "We'll get you to the hospital and they'll get your arm back together. And a search and rescue effort is underway. They'll find your friends."

Scorza shook his head. "You can call off the rescue team. Parker went under—and he never came up."

Angelica whirled to meet Mrs. Buckman's eyes. "He's lying. He's lying! Parker can't die. He's supposed to . . ."

Parker's mom wrapped Angelica in her arms. Where Mrs. Buckman found the strength, Angelica had no idea. Because all Angelica felt now was weak . . . like she'd been crushed along with the *Boy's Bomb*.

CHAPTER 85

DEEP TROUBLE WAS CLOSE. Just sitting there. That's definitely the way it sounded. Parker feared they'd long passed the point where there was any hope of swimming to shore. But maybe if they got their limbs moving again. Maybe. The problem with hypothermia was that staying still actually increased the chances for survival. The more they moved their limbs, the more blood would pump away from their body core to their arms and legs. Blood coursing through their hands and arms and feet would cool faster— accelerating the danger of hypothermia. But they'd have to try to swim for shore anyway. If they stayed in hiding too long, they'd die for sure.

"C-can't wait l-longer," Parker said. "N-now-r-never."

"R-right b-behind you. P-pray f-first?"

Totally weird to hear Harley reminding him to pray. And he did. Nothing fancy. "G-God h-help us. Y-You're the only one w-who can." Sounded kind of Star Wars-ish, but it was the best he could do.

"L-let's go." Parker slipped his head underwater and ducked around the hull, surfacing slowly—and hoping nobody aboard *Deep Trouble* spotted them.

CHAPTER 86

ELLA STARED AT THE FLOATING CHUNK of the *Boy's Bomb* hull. The bow piece was scraped up something fierce. Had they hit a rock—or had a boat hit them in the fog? Long scuffs of white paint scarring the cracked fiberglass answered her question. They had to have been hit by a much bigger boat.

Eric held *Alert 1* in place, drifting right along with the debris field.

Suddenly a head surfaced to one side of the shattered hull. Another popped up next to him.

"Parker!" Ella shrieked and pointed. "Harley!"

Mr. Buckman whooped for joy.

The boys looked as startled to see the harbormaster boat as Ella was to see them. Stiff grins broke out on their faces—which looked incredibly blue. Parker raised his purple hand in a wave even as Eric swung the boat toward them.

Maggie rushed to the collar that rimmed the boat. Parker's dad joined her at the molded notch designed for easy exit and entry— or for fishing people out of the water.

Eric pulled alongside the boys with the precision that could only come from years of experience.

"Easy now," Maggie said. "We got you." In seconds Maggie and Mr. Buckman had both boys aboard. Immediately blankets were out and wrapped around them.

Send Jelly a text. The thought popped in her head. She absolutely didn't want Jelly or Parker's mom to suffer for one more minute. And she had to share this incredible joy with someone.

She whipped off the message. Sent it. She flipped to her camera app and captured pictures of the boys safely aboard *Alert 1*. She'd send those too—but first she had some major thanking God to do.

CHAPTER 87

THE PARAMEDIC TRUCK PULLED AWAY WITH SCORZA INSIDE just seconds before Angelica's phone dinged. She read the text through tear-filled eyes.

> Found both boys under same piece of wreckage!! Bodies blue!!

Bodies? Bodies! "God, no!"

Parker's mom read over her shoulder. She wailed and dropped to her knees.

Maybe Angelica could have talked Parker out of going to the Dry Salvages—if he'd have only told her what was going on. Maybe if she hadn't been so focused on protecting him, he wouldn't have shut her out the way he did. "Parker . . . what have you done?" He'd ruined everything—and it was her fault.

What if Ella sent another text with more details? Angelica couldn't bear the thought. Wished she hadn't opened this one.

She hurled her phone high out over the Outer Harbor. The thing dropped into the water and disappeared with barely a splash. An instant later the water's surface appeared unchanged . . . like Angelica's phone had absolutely no effect on it. But the last text it delivered would change her life forever.

CHAPTER 88

PARKER COULDN'T STOP SHIVERING. After Maggie finished bandaging Harley's gash and her EMT checks, she rewrapped Parker and Harley in dry blankets. Sat them on the seat directly behind the console section.

"You'll live." She smiled. "Believe me, we've seen lots worse." She joined Eric up front. "Let's get these boys home."

Ella and Dad gripped the handrails on either side of Parker and Harley and formed a wall around them—further shielding them from wind. Parker had so much he wanted to say. To Dad. Harley. To Jelly when they saw her. Maybe when his cheeks weren't so numb, he'd be able to say everything on his heart. Right now, he couldn't stop silently thanking God.

Maggie was on the radio, talking to paramedics on shore. "Got a couple of live ones here."

"Repeat, *Alert 1*," a voice crackled back. "Other survivor insisted all hands lost."

"Negative," Eric said. "The lost have been found."

And being found never felt so good. "Eric . . . Maggie . . . thank you," Parker said.

"I know you've been wanting a ride in this thing," Eric said. "But I never expected you to go this far to get one."

All of them laughed—and even that seemed to warm him up a bit.

"You definitely picked a good day for it, though." Eric eased the throttle forward. "The ride back will definitely be fun."

Harley shook his head and grinned at Parker. "I have never had such a great day in all my life."

"You found out Kemosabe is definitely gone," Parker said. "You call that a good day?" Truth was, Parker pretty much felt the same way—even though the *Boy's Bomb* was lost forever too.

"I think I've known it was hopeless from the beginning. The way I see it right now?" He gave Parker the side-eye. "I may have lost Kemosabe . . . but I didn't lose my trusted friend."

Parker smiled back. Oh, yeah. It was a good day.

CHAPTER 89

IN ALL THE EXCITEMENT, Ella had completely forgotten to send the follow-up rescue photos to Jelly. She managed to whip them off minutes after Eric headed for shore. She'd never seen anyone drive a boat with more skill than Eric did. She expected they'd take more of a pounding from the waves, but he climbed up one swell, then skimmed down the other side, goosing the gas or turning the wheel at just the right moment to keep the nose from burying itself. He made the tricky drive look easy—and had a smile on his face the entire time. They all did.

Ella leaned in closely to Harley just like Mr. Buckman was to Parker. It was about transferring all the heat they could to the boys. Ella had a million questions—but there would be time for questions and celebration later. Right now? She wanted to take it all in. There was a part of her that couldn't believe the boys were really okay. Another part of her marveled at how good they looked.

She thought of her desperate *God save them* prayer. God had heard her. And what had happened was nothing short of a miracle. "God . . . thank You. More than I can say."

An SOS came over the radio. Another boat in distress—and it didn't sound good.

"We'll get you to shore," Eric said, "and go out again. We'll find them."

Ella didn't doubt that. Not after she'd seen them in action. She imagined the celebration going on at the T-wharf—and wanted to be there. Even as they entered the channel, the flashing lights from fire trucks, police cars, and other rescue vehicles gave the fog a cotton-candy-happy glow.

By the time Eric reached the Tuna Wharf, he eased back on the throttle and dropped it into neutral. The *Alert 1*'s wake rolled past like it couldn't wait to bring the good news to everyone on shore. *After Five* was just pulling away from the floating platform off the T-wharf and into the North Basin.

Maggie was back, checking the boys. "You're both doing terrific."

Mr. Buckman put his arm around Ella's shoulder and pulled her close. She was pretty sure she knew exactly what he was feeling.

Eric throttled forward, and the scene at the T-wharf slid into sharp focus. Rescue workers stood at the top of the T-wharf and on the float. But there seemed to be more confusion than celebration. And with another boat out there somewhere in distress, that made sense.

"All right, boys," Eric called over his shoulder. "Feel strong enough to stand?"

Parker and Harley stood together, arms raised high as *Alert 1* pulled alongside the float.

Suddenly the crowd of rescue workers exploded into cheers and applause. Jelly and Parker's mom went from sobbing to stunned—then screaming in like a half second. Jelly broke free and stormed the ramp going down to the float.

"That's more like it," Eric said.

Oh, yeah. *Way* more like it. And this celebration wasn't going to end anytime soon.

EPILOGUE

Sunday, August 14, 2:00 p.m.

THE NEXT DAY AND A HALF KEPT PARKER BUSY—along with Harley, Jelly, and Ella. Bits and pieces of the bigger story drifted in. Kind of like the debris from the *Boy's Bomb* that washed up on shore with the tides. Jelly was the one who walked from Front Beach to the Headlands as the tide shifted from high to low—Saturday and Sunday—like she was on a scavenger hunt for all things *Boy's Bomb*. Ella joined her. But Parker didn't want any part of it. Seeing scraps of the *Boy's Bomb*—each one a reminder that he'd never take that boat out on the water again? No thanks.

But the *Boy's Bomb* went down swinging—and didn't go alone. As it turned out, a piece of the boat got lodged in *Deep Trouble's* rudder—and Ray Lotitto had lost all ability to steer. The big lobster boat lived up to its name and ended up in *really* deep trouble. The waves slammed them up against Little Salvages, and the boat he'd schemed so hard to get . . . sank to the bottom of Sandy Bay instead. Earlier in the summer Parker had learned a lot about God and justice. How God saw every hidden thing and dealt with it in His way—and in His time. Parker felt the sinking of *Deep Trouble* was just one more example of God's justice at work. The boat Ray Lotitto planned to use for dive charters . . . would now be a wreck for divers to explore.

Harley's uncle was picked up by the Coast Guard as he clung to a channel marker buoy. Officer Greenwood was waiting for him when they got him to shore. The way Parker heard it? Harley's Uncle Ray confessed to everything—even the three counts of attempted murder. Now that all hopes of him paying the loan shark were gone, it seemed he felt there was no safer place for him to be than in jail.

Uncle Ray's crewman—the guy who pointed the way for Ray to run them over? Turns out his name was Jack Kelsey—and he hadn't been found. Not that the police weren't looking for him. Parker's theory was that the guy had made it to shore—and kept going. If he was smart, he wouldn't stop until he was a thousand miles away.

Uncle Ray wouldn't divulge the name of the third man in his crew—or where the guy had dumped Kemosabe. But the bike was gone for real this time. He joked that the only things riding that Harley-Davidson now were starfish and barnacles. There was nothing in it for Harley's uncle to say more than that. And by not snitching on his friend, he guaranteed the bike would never be found. It seemed he took special joy in the belief that it would hurt Harley bad. But Harley wasn't quite the easy target he'd been.

Rather than sleeping above the dive shop, Harley had been bunking at Parker's the last two nights. By the time everyone went home and they hit the sack Friday night, both of them were asleep in seconds. But Saturday they talked late into the night—and early into the morning. Harley told him all about his dad—and how Parker's dad reminded Harley of him. He talked about Kemosabe, and how he'd made peace with the bike's being gone.

"The way I see it, Parks? I have my dad's DNA. He's part of me—and nobody can take that away." He went on to explain how he saw things differently now. Yes, his dad had rebuilt the bike with him for his future . . . but what he was really doing was preparing Harley for his future just by spending time with him.

"My dad loved me, Parks. Kemosabe was just a gift he gave me. I was making the motorcycle as important as my dad. The real gift my dad gave me was giving me so much of himself. He wasn't just building Kemosabe with me. He was building *me*. Does that make sense?"

Oh yeah. It made huge sense. There was something about being in a dark room that made it easy to talk. The breeze coming in through the open window and the sound of the breakers crashing on the Headlands helped too. They talked about their rescue and the *Boy's Bomb*. How they were going to miss going out in it. They talked about God. The reality of heaven, hell, and the Good News. The reality of Harley's need—everyone's need, really—for a rescuer.

The desperate, teetering-on-the-edge guy Harley had been in the days before the *Boy's Bomb* sank was gone. He seemed relaxed now. Balanced. He'd accepted Kemosabe as lost forever . . . and was choosing to focus instead on the things he still had: three friends who'd proved they would go to some pretty extreme lengths to be there for him. That's how he explained it to Parker late last night. His words played over and over in Parker's head, even after Harley had fallen asleep. "I'd be dead without you, Parker. If I'd gone out to the Dry Salvages by myself . . . I'd be dead."

"We'd both have been dead without God's help," Parker said. "And that's the truth."

Harley didn't answer, but his silence seemed to say that deep down he believed that too. God had been there for Parker in a huge way. More than ever, he believed God had a plan for his life. And Harley's. And God could be trusted to work out those plans if they let him. Even getting rammed by a lobster boat—miles from shore—couldn't thwart God's plans.

And in church this morning, Harley was really listening. He'd turned off his phone before sitting in the pew—like he wanted to show he was serious about not missing a thing. The girls had been there with Grams too.

After lunch, Parker and Harley caught up with Ella and Jelly. They met on the breakwater off Bearskin Neck around a box of donuts. The granite blocks made great natural chairs—and they all found a spot.

"What will happen to you, Harley?" Ella asked the question they'd all been wondering about. With his uncle in jail without bond, the state wasn't going to let a minor like him live on his own.

"The Rockport Dive Company will close—and the landlord will find somebody new to lease the spot." He smiled, like the idea of being without a home or a job didn't bother him. But Parker knew better. "Somehow, I'm going to stay in Rockport. The social worker said she understands—and believes she'll work something out. In the meantime, I'm staying with Parks."

Ella smiled. "The poor Buckmans. Jelly and I will send them a sympathy card. And flowers. And—"

Harley grabbed her donut, took a bite out of it, and gave it back.

Jelly looked like she had something she wanted to say. But she stalled for a bit. Maybe she wasn't sure it was the right time. She looked out over Sandy Bay. "I'm sorry we never found your motorcycle."

"Me too," Harley said. "But you all tried. The flyers. The stakeout."

"Yeah," Jelly said. "That stakeout was a *really* great idea. That's what led me to accuse you of stealing Scorza's Wrangler."

Harley laughed and grabbed a new donut from the box. "I gotta admit, the evidence against me was pretty convincing." His face grew serious. "And the truth was, if I had gotten my hands on Scorza that night? I might be in jail now too. I was so close to ruining everything. I was on the ledge, you know?"

"You were *off* the ledge, Mr. Lotitto," Ella said. "Like in a total free fall. I was afraid we'd never catch you."

Harley stared at the granite at his feet. "I was afraid nobody would try."

"Which goes to show just how stupid boys can be." Ella reached over and snagged a hunk of his donut. "And if you *ever* shut your friends out again? You'll be soooo sorry." She made a fist and shook it at him.

"Never again," Harley said. He was smiling, but it looked like he meant every word. "Last night Parks and I were talking. We wished we could have had you two girls in the conversation too— but it was pretty late to call."

Okay, Harley was up to something . . . and a glance from him told Parker to play along.

"You should have called anyway." Jelly looked excited that the guys had even thought of phoning them. "Seriously, I wish you had! We could have put it on speakerphone. We were up really late talking ourselves."

"Actually, we *tried* calling you, Jelly—but we had some kind of weird connection." Harley put on an innocent face and shrugged. "I mean it sounded totally garbled, like the phone was underwater."

Parker couldn't hold back the laughter any longer. Harley laughed so hard his face got all red and tears formed in the corners of his eyes.

Jelly snatched what was left of his donut and tossed it to the seagulls. "Very funny, wise guy. When I *do* get a new phone, you'll be lucky if I don't have your calls blocked."

There was plenty of speculation about what was going to happen to Bryce Scorza. He was still in the hospital after surgery. Paramedics had called him a wonder for somehow using his shoe—in heavy swells—to make a tourniquet for his own arm. The break required some screws to fix—and nobody was sure what that would do to his passing game in the long run. But the way things looked right now, he wouldn't even be passing a bowl of mashed potatoes for a long time.

And nobody knew where things would go with Scorza and the police, either. At the very least—and by his own admission—he'd been in possession of the stolen motorcycle—at least for a day. He hadn't called the police or made any attempt to return it. That wasn't good. And his part in going along with Uncle Ray—even throwing the key to the *Boy's Bomb* into the deep so they couldn't avoid the collision? Scorza kept claiming he was the real victim in the whole thing. It was anybody's guess how that was going to play out, but Scorza's dad supposedly had some shady Boston lawyer working on it already.

"Think you'll ever get another motorcycle?" Ella's question hung there for a moment.

Harley nodded. "Definitely. And it will be a 1999 XL Sportster. I'll get a new job. I'll save up. And if the motorcycle needs a little work, that's fine. I've still got the tools. Parks will help me—and your dad, right?"

He was absolutely right on that.

"What about you, Parker?" Jelly looked at him. "You've never lived near the water without a boat."

Parker shrugged. "I'd like to think I'll find a new one." But like Harley finding a new motorcycle, it wouldn't be cheap—and it would probably take a long time. He thought of the talk he'd had with his grandpa just days before. About God having a plan for him . . . and how he'd weave Parker's own dreams in and out of it. "Sometimes God gives us our dreams. And sometimes . . ." It seemed the natural way to finish the statement was *and sometimes not*. But that didn't feel right. What was it Grandpa wanted him to discover?

"Well, I hope you get that new boat," Jelly said. "You might need this when you do." She unzipped her backpack and pulled out the hand-carved *Boy's Bomb* nameplate that had been screwed to the helm.

"Jelly!" Parker stared at the sign for a long moment before reaching for it. It was like she held a bag of treasure from the deep. "How did you . . . ? Where?"

Jelly seemed more than pleased with his reaction. "The Headlands. Ella told me she'd seen it floating when they were looking for you two. Came in with this morning's tide—along with what was left of a very battered helm."

Parker traced the letters on the wood nameplate. "This is why you were searching the shoreline?"

Jelly beamed. "I was just hoping—and praying—we'd find it."

"Praying, too, eh?"

Jelly raised both hands. "Okay—true confession. I had a good talk with God. I had to admit, He was actually doing a pretty good job of handling things—even when I thought He wasn't."

"Are you saying," Ella said, "you're going to stop playing God yourself when it comes to trying to protect these boys?"

Jelly got that teasing look Parker hadn't seen for a while. "That's between me and God. But with the way these boys keep their guardian angels busy?" She raised her chin slightly and gave Ella a nod. "I still say it doesn't hurt for us girls to lend a hand once in a while."

Parker laughed right along with the others. Of *course* she wasn't going to admit much more than she did. But she'd said enough. He held up the wooden *Boy's Bomb* plaque. "Thanks for this, Jelly. It means a lot." For now? It would go on his bookcase. Next to the alligator skull—and the giant glow stick they'd picked up from the bottom of the quarry. Reminders of how God had been there for him and Wilson in the Everglades. Reminders of how God had rescued him—and now Harley again—here in Rockport.

"I talked to Wilson yesterday," Parker said. "He was totally wishing he'd been here."

Jelly shook her head. "It was hard enough keeping the two of you safe. With Wilson in the mix? We would've had to deputize another girl somewhere."

Harley just grinned and shook his head.

"Harley. Parker. There you are." Officer Greenwood called to them from his car on the circle at the end of Bearskin Neck. He motioned them over.

Parker tucked the *Boy's Bomb* nameplate under his arm and ran alongside Harley to meet him. Jelly and Ella were right behind them.

Officer Greenwood stepped out of his car. "Harley, I'm really sorry we never got your bike. But I got a piece of it. At least I think I did. I just need you to positively ID it." He held up a plastic evidence bag. Harley's lanyard with Kemosabe's key sat inside.

Harley lunged for the bag. "That's it!" He clutched the thing like he had no intention of letting it go. "Where?"

"Let's just say I found a Silverado at the Cape Ann Marina—with a bicycle in the bed. This was wrapped around the adjustable seat post."

"Scorza!" Ella practically spit the name out.

"I will neither deny nor confirm." Greenwood smiled. "But this key will make a nice exhibit in court."

"I hope he gets life," Ella said.

Jelly nodded. "Without parole."

Officer Greenwood shook his head. "Not likely. He's a minor—and if the rumors about the lawyer his dad hired are true? All he'll get is a little of this"—Greenwood slapped his own wrist. "But even if he gets off easy, he'll get a different kind of life sentence."

Parker definitely wanted to hear this. Harley took a step closer, still gripping the evidence bag.

"He'll have to live with himself," Greenwood said. "That's a life sentence I wouldn't wish on anybody."

"He's a narcissist," Jelly said. "He loves being with himself."

"Well, just make sure you never marry a guy like that," Greenwood said, "or you'll be doing time with him too."

"Ew, ew, ew," Jelly said. "Thanks for putting that ugly picture in my head. You can go now, Officer Greenwood."

Greenwood laughed like he got exactly the reaction he'd been hoping for. He swung back into the driver's seat and reached for the evidence bag.

Harley hesitated, then handed it over.

"I'll get this key back to you, Harley." Greenwood set it on the seat next to him. "As soon as I can."

Harley nodded and looked like he was swallowing down a lump in his throat.

"You going to be okay without that bike?"

Deep down, Parker wondered if this was why Officer Greenwood had really come. To make sure Harley would be okay.

"It starts today," Harley said. "Your world will change."

Immediately Parker pictured the mystery sign posted on the Dive Company door. The one, they now learned, posted by Uncle Ray to pressure Harley into selling Kemosabe.

Harley shrugged. "The prediction was true . . . but I think my world changed mostly for the better."

"That was a huge statement you just made," Greenwood said. "Tell me more."

"On the ride back from the Salvages, I realized what I had in my friends was more than a guy could ask for." Harley stared at the ground. "I wanted Kemosabe back. Bad. But until then, I don't think I really knew the value of friends who were there for me."

Harley glanced at Parker. "Friends who wouldn't give up on me. So, yeah. I'm going to be okay. I was so busy chasing the dream of getting my bike back, I didn't even notice I already had something better."

Grandpa's words flashed in Parker's mind.

"I love it," Officer Greenwood said, shifting the car into gear. "We'll be seeing you four around."

Ella waved at Greenwood. Mouthed the word *thanks*. To Parker, it was amazing to see the change in her . . . the girl who was once so leery of all police.

"Wouldn't it be great," Jelly said, "if the *Boy's Bomb* came together somehow? Now *that* would be the ultimate dream, right?"

And suddenly Parker knew what Grandpa wanted him to know. There was a time that the *Boy's Bomb* meant everything to him. It had been a good dream, and it was great while it lasted. And hey, God used the *Bomb* to jam *Deep Trouble*'s rudder, right? Yeah, Parker lost the boat, but he found something so much better when God saved him and Harley. A confidence had been forged deep inside him. A rock-solid belief that he could trust God—no matter what. That God would be with him one way or another. And the absolute confidence that God had a plan—that couldn't be thwarted. If sacrificing the *Bomb*—to help his friend—was what was needed to gain all that . . . the loss was worth it.

And as if Parker's new strength in God wasn't enough, God gave him more. He got his friend Harley back—who was going to be okay. The importance of these alone were miles beyond any dream he'd have of getting the *Boy's Bomb* back again.

Parker threw his arms around all three of them. "Sometimes God gives us our dreams." He pulled them close into a group hug. "And sometimes . . . he gives us new ones."

"I'm all for that," Jelly said. "And here's hoping those new dreams won't include the need for the Coast Guard."

The four of them burst out laughing, and somehow Parker imagined God laughing right along with them. Whatever God had planned for the four of them, He was keeping it a secret. Their story wasn't over, though—and for that, Parker was beyond grateful. Would there be more hard times? More danger? Dark chapters? Maybe.

Probably.

In fact, he was pretty sure there'd *always* be some bad chapters. But stories weren't defined just by what happened in the bad chapters—but by how the entire book turned out. And Parker knew that no matter what happened, God's story for them would be really, really good.

Special Thanks To . . .

Blackwood BBQ, Chic-fil-A, Culvers, Five Guys, Burrito Parrilla Mexicana, and Portillo's: Thanks for the fries—and the fun atmosphere every time I came to put in a few hours of writing. And Burrito Parrilla . . . that horchata is fantastic!

Tina at Dunkin: Extra-large, half-caf, extra cream, extra sugar—to go. You always sent me off with a friendly smile and great coffee—which fueled plenty of chapters of writing!

Dave and Cyndi Darsch: For providing me with the "off-grid" writing retreat when I really needed it. A place on the water where Cheryl and I could stay. Talk about an inspiring place to write! As you read the book, if a particular part moves you, know that it was probably polished while I worked on your pier!

Nancy Rue: Mentor, friend, and encourager—thank you.

Larry Weeden and Danny Huerta: For your dedication to reaching this audience . . . and for increasing this to a five-book series.

Vance Fry: For such a balanced style of editing, and for your encouragement. I appreciate you!

Cyle Young: It's nice having an agent who is in your corner, cheering you on! Thanks for the help and advice, Cyle!

My brother Matt: For always encouraging me on the latest story, and for suggesting that I visit Sea Level Diving. That started something big.

My brother-in-law Jimmy: For the nudge to get recertified as a diver so my scenes would be more real.

Fran Linnehan of Down Under Diving Ventures: For letting me tag along on a dive excursion out to the Dry Salvages—and for answering dozens of questions on the way. You'll see bits of your input in the pages of this book.

Scott Story and Rosemary Lesch: Another big thanks to the Rockport harbormasters who took my emails, phone calls, and visits without ever making me feel that my questions were an inconvenience. And by the way, I want a ride on the new *Alert 1*. What a gorgeous boat!

Dave Greenwood: For insights on how a good cop would react in clutch situations.

Cheryl: The woman who encourages my writing in so many ways. *Hair of silver, heart of gold.* And sometimes your role goes beyond being a great wife. In a way, you've been my guardian angel. Only God knows how many times He's used you to keep me from going off the deep end in some way.

My Lord and God: Sometimes You give us our dreams, and sometimes You give us new ones. You've done that for me, and I'm forever grateful. Everything I am that is good, everything I've done that is good—all of it is a testament to Your mercy and grace.

> *"You, LORD, keep my lamp burning;*
> *my God turns my darkness into light."*
> PSALM 18:28

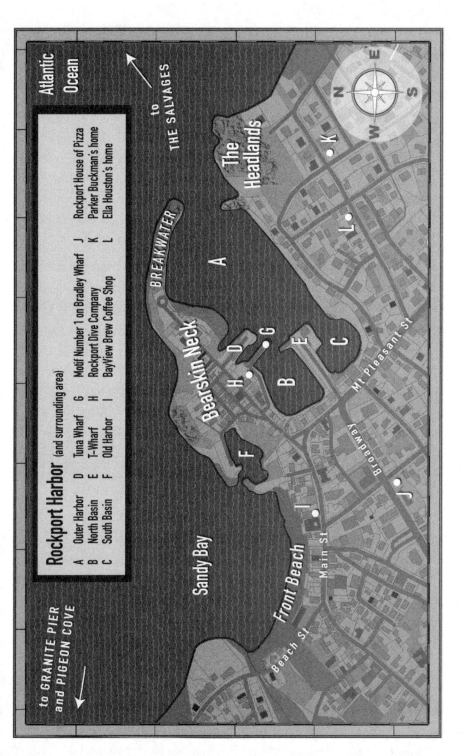